LITERATURE
Uses of the Imagination

Portions of this program were tested by the following teachers and their classes. The suggestions made by these teachers and their students have greatly affected the final form this book has taken:

Sheila Bennett
Hamilton Senior High School
Milwaukee, Wisconsin

Eugene H. Cramer
Cedarburg High School
Cedarburg, Wisconsin

Betty Crawford
Whitman Junior High School
Wauwatosa, Wisconsin

James Creevey
Tillicum Junior High School
Bellevue, Washington

Diane H. Davis
Tift County High School
Tifton, Georgia

Anne D. Fuchs
Mount Hebron High School
Ellicott City, Maryland

Faye Jacobs
G.P. Babb Junior High School
Forest Park, Georgia

Suzanne Kroupa
John Marshall Senior High School
Milwaukee, Wisconsin

Michele La Rue
Montgomery Junior High School
San Diego, California

Joyce Ousley
Hamden High School
Hamden, Connecticut

Florence Pritchard
Mount Hebron High School
Ellicott City, Maryland

Pat Stokes
G.P. Babb Junior High School
Forest Park, Georgia

Suzanne Thomas
Clairemont High School
San Diego, California

Ruth C. Wright
Swarthmore High School
Swarthmore, Pennsylvania

Marguerite Yutz
Rancocas Valley Regional High School
Mt. Holly, New Jersey

A final review and evaluation of this entire book was made by the following teachers. We gratefully acknowledge the critical assistance of:

Betty Crawford
Whitman Junior High School
Wauwatosa, Wisconsin

Faye Jacobs
G.P. Babb Junior High School
Forest Park, Georgia

Suzanne Kroupa
John Marshall Senior High School
Milwaukee, Wisconsin

Joyce Ousley
Hamden High School
Hamden, Connecticut

Florence Pritchard
Mount Hebron High School
Ellicott City, Maryland

Ruth C. Wright
Swarthmore High School
Swarthmore, Pennsylvania

W.T. JEWKES

Director of the Center for
Programs in the Humanities
Virginia Polytechnic Institute
and State University

Supervisory Editor

NORTHROP FRYE

University Professor
University of Toronto

Man the Myth-Maker

SECOND EDITION

HBJ

HARCOURT BRACE JOVANOVICH

Orlando   New York   Chicago   San Diego   Atlanta   Dallas

ISBN 0-15-333468-1

ACKNOWLEDGMENTS: *For permission to reprint copyrighted material, grateful acknowledgment is made to the following:*

Chappell & Co., Inc.: The lyrics to "Summertime" by Ira Gershwin and Dubose Heyward. Copyright © 1935 by Gershwin Publishing Corp. Copyright renewed, assigned to Chappell & Co., Inc. International Copyright secured. All rights reserved.

Christ's College: Chapters One and Two (retitled: "The Beginning of Things") and excerpt from Chapter Eleven "The Flood" from *Gods, Heroes, and Men of Ancient Greece* by W.H.D. Rouse, © 1957 by arrangement with Christ's College and the New American Library, Inc., New York.

Arthur C. Clarke and Scott Meredith Literary Agency, Inc., 845 Third Avenue, New York, New York 10022: "The Nine Billion Names of God" from *The Nine Billion Names of God* by Arthur C. Clarke. Copyright, 1953, by Ballantine Books, Inc.

Curtis Brown Ltd.: "The Palace of Olympus" from *Greek Gods and Heroes* by Robert Graves. Copyright © 1960 by Robert Graves.

E.P. Dutton & Co., Inc. and The Bodley Head: "Deirdre and the Sons of Usna" from *The Hound of Ulster,* retold by Rosemary Sutcliff, copyright © 1963 by Rosemary Sutcliff, published by E.P. Dutton & Co., Inc. and The Bodley Head.

Granada Publishing Limited: "Atalanta's Race" from *Men and Gods* by Rex Warner.

Emmet M. Greene, Executor for the Estate of Padraic Colum: "Dionysos" and "Orpheus" from *Orpheus: Myths of the World* retold by Padraic Colum. Copyright 1930 by Macmillan Publishing Co., Inc.

Grosset & Dunlap, Inc.: Chapter 16 from *A Death in the Family* by James Agee, copyright © 1967 by the James Agee Trust.

Harcourt Brace Jovanovich, Inc.: "in Just-" and "when god lets my body be" by E.E. Cummings, copyright, 1923, 1951, by E.E. Cummings from his volume *Poems 1923–1954:* "Years-End" by Richard Wilbur, copyright, 1949, by Richard Wilbur from his volume *Ceremony and Other Poems.* First published in *The New Yorker.* "Intervention of the Gods" by C.P. Cavafy from *The Complete Poems of Cavafy,* translated by Rae Dalven, © 1961, by Rae Dalven.

Harper & Row, Publishers, Inc.: "The Chronicle of Young Satan" (retitled: "The Mysterious Stranger") from *The Mysterious Stranger and Other Stories* by Mark Twain, copyright, 1922 by Mark Twain Company; renewed, 1950 by Clara Clemens Samossoud.

Holt, Rinehart and Winston, Inc.: "After Apple-Picking" from *The Poetry of Robert Frost* edited by Edward Connery Lathem, copyright 1930, 1939 by Holt, Rinehart and Winston, Inc.; copyright © 1958 by Robert Frost; copyright © 1967 by Lesley Frost Ballantine. "Once by the Pacific" and "It Is Almost the Year Two Thousand" from *The Poetry of Robert Frost* edited by Edward Connery Lathem, copyright 1928, © 1969 by Holt, Rinehart and Winston, Inc.; copyright 1942, © 1956 by Robert Frost; copyright © 1970 by Lesley Frost Ballantine.

The illustrations on pages xvi–1, 30–31, 72–73, 144–145, 176–177, 230–231 are by Alan E. Cober.

Contents

3 The End of Childhood

4 The Cataracts of Heaven

5 Changes

6 A Human Year

INTRODUCTION

Without a sense of pattern in life, we would always feel like lonely children, lost in a vast forest with night coming on. But our powers of observation do enable us to perceive patterns in the world around us: day and night; spring, summer, autumn, winter; birth, maturity, death, and rebirth.

In addition to these outer, physical patterns, we are conscious of patterns in our inner world. Our emotional life also works in patterns. We fear the harshness of winter, disease, and death. We remember with longing the warmth of summer, health, and life. With our imagination we relate our inner world to the outer world. We construct a pattern for our life that will help us to live in harmony with the world around us, to turn our wishes into reality.

How the imagination transforms the materials of outer reality into an image of desire can be seen in the way our dreams work. But dreams are too fragmentary and fleeting. We long for some more permanent and extensive vision of human life made over into the image of desire. It is this longing that has produced literature. It is this vision that has formed the backbone of every mythology.

Just as patterns recur in the physical world and in our own inner worlds, they also recur in our imaginative expressions, that is, in our literature. In fact, the recurring imaginative patterns of the whole human race are reflected in literature. As we read more and more, we find that there is a "larger" pattern into which all our reading experiences can fit. This larger story pattern takes the shape of a quest. This quest story tells of how we once possessed the secret of life; somehow we lost that secret, and we try to regain it by our own efforts.

The story of our quest for our lost inheritance can be seen as the story of human civilization. The human race itself has embarked from the dawn of time on a quest for a truly civilized society. This vision, expressed in literature, has carried civilization forward against the dehumanizing powers that have always tried to hold it back. Today, just as throughout history, these powers are still trying to capture our imagination and force it to serve their ends. Whenever such powers try to imprison the creative imagination, they are trying to steal our inheritance from us. But poets and storytellers have no ulterior motives. Their only aim is to free our imagination, as we share with them the creative experience of building a truly human society.

W. T. J.

Man the Myth-Maker

1

THE EARTH BELONGED
TO THEM ALL

Alan E. Cober -72

The Beginning
of Things

A Greek myth
Retold by W.H.D. ROUSE

In the beginning there was Chaos, a great hollow Void, in which
the seeds or beginnings of all things were mixed up together in a
shapeless mass, all moving about in all directions. By degrees these
beginnings slowly sorted themselves out; the heavier parts gathered
together and became Earth; the lighter parts flew up and became the
sky, with air between; and under the earth was a dark place called
Tartarus. In the heavens, the sun, moon, and stars appeared one by
one; on earth, the land separated from the sea; rain fell, and the rivers
ran down from the hills; trees grew up, and the world became something like what we know, and it had the shape of a great round ball,
or a disk, like a large plate.

From Chaos, the great Void, came forth many and strange children;
but first and most wonderful of all was Eros, or Love, who came no
one knows how, and was quite different from all the others; he out-
lived them all, and still lives, the most mighty of all divine powers.
From Chaos came forth also Erebus and black Night; and their child
was the Day.

From Chaos, lastly, came into being Father Uranus, or Heaven;
and Pontus, the Sea; and Mother Earth. Heaven and Earth were parents
of a great brood of children. These were called, in general, the Titans.
The brood began with monsters, but they improved as they went on.
Among the monsters were three, with fifty heads apiece and a hundred hands; their names were Cottus, Gyges, and Briareus. Three

others were named the Cyclopes; Cyclops means "goggle-eyed," and each Cyclops had one huge eye in the middle of his forehead, with one huge and bushy eyebrow above it. There were others, some of whom we shall meet later; and then came a superior brood of children. I will not tell you the names of all these now, but one was Oceanus, the ocean stream, which runs like a great river all round the earth; and one was Hyperion, who took charge of the light by night and day. He was the father of Eos, the Dawn, and Helios, the Sun, and Selene, the Moon. And the youngest of the children of Heaven and Earth was named Cronus: the youngest but the most terrible of them all.

Now Uranus hated his children and feared them; and as they were born, he hid them in secret places of the earth and kept them prisoners in darkness. But Mother Earth was angry to see her children so badly treated; so she persuaded them to rebel, and they did so, and cast down Uranus from the sky. They cast him down into Tartarus, the dark region below the earth. In the fight he was wounded by Cronus; drops of his blood fell on the sea, and from these drops sprang up Aphrodite, who became the goddess of beauty and love. Her name means "daughter of the foam," because she came up out of the foam of the sea. Other drops of his blood fell on the earth; and from these sprang up the Giants and the Furies. We shall hear of these later, for the Giants made war on the gods long afterward; and the Furies used to range about the world, when men were created, chasing and punishing those men who shed blood.

Cronus was leader of this rebellion, and he became King of Heaven in his father's place. When he became king, he cast down his brothers and sisters into Tartarus, except one, Rhea, whom he married. But he was not so careful about their children. Some of them were useful, like Dawn, and Sun, and Moon, so he left them alone. Another of the Titans had five sons. Atlas was one of those sons, and he was made to stand by the gate of Tartarus and to hold up the sky on his shoulders. Two others of this family were very famous afterward. Their names were Prometheus and Epimetheus, that is to say, Forethought and Afterthought. Prometheus was the cleverest of all the Titans, and he went to live on the earth. There he used to wander about making models out of mud to amuse himself.

Now at that time things were not quite sorted out from Chaos, and there were bits of life still in the mud or clay of the earth. So when Prometheus made this clay into all sorts of odd shapes, the shapes came alive as he made them, and became worms, and snakes, and crocodiles, and all kinds of strange creatures, which you can see in museums. As he grew more skillful, he made also birds and animals, and at last he thought he could make something in the shape of the immortals. His first attempt went on four legs, like the other animals, and had a tail like them; it was a monkey in fact. He tried all sorts of monkeys, big and small, until he found out how to make his model stand upright. Then he cut off the tail and lengthened the thumbs of the hands and twisted them inward. That may seem a very little thing, but it makes all the difference between a monkey's hands and a man's; just try and see how many things you cannot do if you tie your thumb fast to your first finger. And if you look at the skeleton of a man in the museum, you will see that you have a tiny tail in the right place, or at least the bones of it, all that is left after Prometheus cut it off.

Thousands of years afterward, the Greeks used to show in one of their temples lumps of clay, which they said were left over after Prometheus had made the first man. This clay was the color of mud and smelled a little like human flesh.

Prometheus was very much pleased with his new pet. He used to watch men hunting for food and living in caves and holes, like ants or badgers. He determined to educate men as well as he could, and he was always their friend. Cronus did not take notice of what he was doing; and now we must turn to Cronus and see what he was doing himself.

Cronus had married one of the Titans, named Rhea; and he was determined that his children should not rebel against him, as he had rebelled against his father, so as soon as one was born, he swallowed it whole. Five he swallowed up in this way; but then Rhea grew tired of this, as she wanted babies to play with, so when the sixth was born, she determined to save him. She took a big stone of the same size as a baby and wrapped it in swaddling clothes and presented it to Cronus as the last baby. Cronus promptly swallowed the stone, and was quite contented. This was really a thing easy to manage, because no doubt the gods used to do with their babies just as the Greek mothers used to do: they wrapped them round and round with a long narrow cloth, until they looked like a chrysalis, or a long plum, with the baby's head sticking out of the end. Then Rhea took the real baby, whose name was Zeus, and hid him in the island of Crete, in a cave which you can still see at this day. He was put in the charge of two nymphs, who fed him on goat's milk, and the cave was watched by armed guards; whenever the baby cried, the guards made such a din by clashing their spears on their shields that Cronus heard nothing of its cries.

Rhea bided her time; and when Zeus grew up, she told him how Cronus had swallowed his brothers and sisters, and how she had saved Zeus himself; and they made a plot against Cronus, as Cronus had done against his father. Together they managed to give Cronus a strong dose of medicine. This made Cronus very sick, and he disgorged all the children, one after another. First came the stone which Rhea had made him swallow; and Cronus was very much surprised to see that. You may see the stone, if you wish, for it was placed in the sacred place of Delphi, and it is still there, in the museum. Then came the five others in order. I must tell you their names now, because they all come into the story; they were Hestia, Demeter, Hera, Hades, and Poseidon. Strange to say, they had all grown up quite well inside their father, and now they were as big as Zeus, and ready to join in the plot. Then they all made war upon Cronus, and the war went on for ten years, but neither party could win.

Cronus got friends to help him, as far as he could, and one of them was the wise Prometheus. As the war went on, Prometheus said, "Sir, I advise you to bring up your brothers from Tartarus." But Cronus was afraid of his brothers; he said, "No, thank you, no brothers for me." When Prometheus found that Cronus was too stupid to take good advice, he went over to the side of Zeus. To Zeus he gave the same advice; and although Zeus was not very wise, he was wise enough to take this advice. So he set free the three Cyclopes named Thunderer, Lightener, and Shiner; and they were so grateful that they gave Zeus a gift each—the thunder and the lightning and the thunderbolt. They also gave Hades a cap which made him invisible when he put it on; and they gave Poseidon a trident, or three-pronged spear. Next Zeus set free the three monsters with fifty heads and a hundred hands. You see what an advantage that gave to Zeus. Each of them was like a quick-firing gun, and could throw a hundred stones for Cronus's one.

Now Zeus made a feast for his friends. He gave them nectar, the drink of the gods, and ambrosia, the food of the gods, which was the food of immortality; and he said, "Now let us fight, and make an end of this long war."

Then there was a terrible battle. The three monsters caught up a rock in each of their three hundred hands, and cast them in volleys at Cronus. Zeus thundered and lightened and launched his thunderbolts. The earth shook, the sea boiled, the forests caught fire and burned, blustering winds made confusion all round. In the end, they conquered Cronus and bound him in chains and shut him up in dark Tartarus.

As far as heaven is high above the earth, so deep is Tartarus below the earth. Nine days and nine nights a stone would fall from heaven to earth; nine days and nine nights it would fall from earth to deep Tartarus. A brazen wall runs round it, and brazen gates close it in; there Cronus was in prison, guarded by the Cyclopes and the three hundred-handed monsters. In front of the gate stands Atlas, immovable, bearing the heavens upon his shoulders. A fearful watchdog guards the gates, Cerberus, with three heads and three gaping mouths. When anyone goes in, Cerberus fawns upon him and licks his hands with his three tongues; but if anyone tries to go out, Cerberus devours him up. There Night and Day meet together and greet one another, as one passes in and the other passes out. Within dwell Sleep and Death, brothers, the children of Night. Sleep can wander over the earth at will, seizing men and letting them go; but Death, once he gets hold of a man, never lets him go again, for there is no pity in his heart.

And there dwells Styx, the lady of the black river of Hate, eldest daughter of Oceanus. When quarrels arise among the immortal gods, then Zeus sends his messenger Iris with a golden jug to bring some of the waters of Styx, which falls from a high and beetling rock. The gods must swear an oath by this water. If any of them breaks the oath, for one year he lies breathless, and cannot partake of sweet nectar and ambrosia; after that year he is cut off from the meeting of the gods for nine years more, and then only may he come back and join their company.

In that dark place the banished Titans dwell, guarded by the monsters. And the Cyclopes are always busy, forging the thunderbolts of Zeus.

After the victory, Zeus and his two brothers were ready to fight each other to decide which should be king; but the wise Prometheus persuaded them to cast lots and to share the sovereignty among them. So lots were cast. Zeus became King of Heaven, and Poseidon King of the Sea, and Hades King of dark Tartarus; but the earth belonged to them all.

By telling stories of how the gods created people, how did people create the gods?

There are often two contrasting worlds in the myths. What is associated with "above" or "up" in this myth? What is associated with "below" or "down"?

Why do you think people believed that the first and most wonderful of creatures was Love? Why did they imagine that Love was "quite different" from the other children of Chaos?

Heaven and Earth
and Man

A Chinese myth
Retold by CYRIL BIRCH

Earth with its mountains, rivers, and seas, Sky with its sun, moon, and stars: in the beginning all these were one, and the one was Chaos. Nothing had taken shape, all was a dark swirling confusion, over and under, round and round. For countless ages this was the way of the universe, unformed and unillumined, until from the midst of Chaos came P'an Ku. Slowly, slowly, he grew into being, feeding on the elements, eyes closed, sleeping a sleep of eighteen thousand years. At last the moment came when he woke from his sleeping. He opened his eyes: nothing could he see, nothing but darkness, nothing but confusion. In his anger he raised his great arm and struck out blindly in the face of the murk, and with one great crashing blow he scattered the elements of Chaos.

The swirling ceased, and in its place came a new kind of movement. No longer confined, all those things which were light in weight and pure in nature rose upward; all those things which were heavy and gross sank down. With his one mighty blow P'an Ku had freed sky from earth.

Now P'an Ku stood with his feet on earth, and the sky rested on his head. So long as he stood between the two they could not come together again. And as he stood, the rising and the sinking went on. With each day that passed earth grew thicker by ten feet and the sky rose higher by ten feet, thrust ever farther from the earth by P'an Ku's body which daily grew in height by ten feet also. For eighteen thousand years more P'an Ku continued to grow until his own body was gigantic, and until earth was formed of massive thickness and the sky had risen far above. Thousands of miles tall he stood, a great pillar separating earth from sky so that the two might never again come together to dissolve once more into a single Chaos. Throughout long ages he stood, until the time when he could be sure that earth and sky were fixed and firm in their places.

When this time came P'an Ku, his task achieved, lay down on earth to rest, and resting died. And now he, who in his life had brought shape to the universe, by his death gave his body to make it rich and beautiful. He gave the breath from his body to form the winds and clouds, his voice to be the rolling thunder, his two eyes to be the sun and moon, the hairs of his head and beard to be the stars, the sweat of his brow to be the rain and dew. To the earth he gave his body for the mountains and his hands and feet for the two poles and the extremes of east and west. His blood flowed as the rivers of earth and his veins ran as the roads which cover the land. His flesh became the soil of the fields and the hairs of his body grew on as the flowers and trees. As for his bones and teeth, these sank deep below the surface of earth to enrich it as precious metals.

And so P'an Ku brought out of Chaos the heavens in all their glory and the earth with all its splendors.

But although the earth could now present its lovely landscapes, although beasts ran in its forests and fish swam in its rivers, still it seemed to lack something, something which would make it less empty and dull for the gods who came down from Heaven to roam over its surface. One day the goddess Nu-kua, whose body was that of a dragon but whose head was of human form, grew weary of the loneliness of earth. After long thought she stooped and took from the ground a lump of clay. From this she fashioned with her dragon claws a tiny creature. The head she shaped after the pattern of her own, but to the body she gave two arms and two legs. She set the little thing back on the ground: and the first human being came to life and danced and made sounds of joy to delight the eyes and ears of the goddess. Quickly she made many more of these charming humans, and felt lonely no longer as they danced together all about her.

Then, as she rested a while from her task and watched the sons and daughters of her own creation go off together across the earth, a new thought came to her. What would become of the world when all these humans she had made grew old and died? They were fine beings, well fitted to rule over the beasts of the earth; but they would not live forever. To fill the earth with humans, then when these had gone to make more to take their place, this would mean an endless task for the goddess. And so to solve this problem Nu-kua brought together man and woman and taught them the ways of marriage. Now they could create for themselves their own sons and daughters, and these in turn could continue to people the earth throughout time.

After this gift of marriage from Nu-kua, further blessings came to man from her husband, the great god Fu-hsi. He again had a human head but the body of a dragon. He taught men how to weave ropes to make nets for fishing, and he made the lute from which men first drew music. His also was the priceless gift of fire. Men had seen and feared the fire which was struck from the forest trees by the passing of the Lord of the Thunderstorm. But Fu-hsi, who was the son of this same lord, taught men to drill wood against wood and make fire for their own use, for warmth and for cooking.

Already the creatures of Nu-kua's making could speak their thoughts to one another, but Fu-hsi now drew for them the eight precious symbols with which they could begin to make records for those who were to come after. He drew three strokes ☰ to represent Heaven; the three strokes broken ☷ represented earth. That symbol whose middle stroke was solid ☵ represented water, that whose middle stroke was broken ☲ represented fire. A solid stroke above ☶ gave the sign for mountains, a solid stroke beneath ☳ the sign for storm; a broken line below ☴ showed wind; a broken line on top ☱ showed marshland. With these eight powerful symbols man could begin to record all he observed of the world about him.

For long years men lived their lives in a world at peace. Then, suddenly, there spread from Heaven to earth a conflict which threatened to put an end to all creation. This was the battle between the Spirit of Water, Kung-kung, and the Spirit of Fire, Chu-jung. Down to earth came the turbulent, willful Kung-kung to whip up huge waves on river and lake and lead his scaly hordes against his arch-enemy, Fire. Chu-jung fought back with tongues of flame and scorching breath and halted the rebel Water in his path. Kung-kung's armies dispersed and he, their leader, turned and fled. But his flight brought with it a peril greater yet. For, dashing blindly off to the west, Kung-kung struck his head against the mountain Pu-chou-shan, which was none other than the pillar that in the western corner held up the sky.

Kung-kung made good his escape, but he left the world in a disastrous state. Great holes appeared in the sky, while the earth tilted up in the west. In that region deep cracks and fissures appeared which are still to be seen to this day. All the rivers and lakes spilled out their waters, which ran off and still run eastward: off to the southeast, where the earth had slipped down low, ran the waters together to form a vast ocean there. Meanwhile, out of the shaken mountain forests fire still raged forth, and wild beasts of every kind left their lairs to maraud through the world of helpless, terrified men.

It was left to the goddess Nu-kua to bring back order to the world, to quell the fire and flood and tame the wandering beasts. She it was also who selected from the beds of rivers stones of the most perfect coloring. These she heated until they could be moulded, then with these stones, block by block, she patched the holes in the sky. Lastly, she killed a giant turtle, and cut off its powerful legs to make pillars between which the sky is firmly held over the earth, never again to fall.

So the peace of the world was restored. But the mountains still rise in the west, and it is to there that the sun, moon, and stars still run down the tilted sky; whilst to the east, the waters of the earth still gather into the restless ocean.

What aspects of creation in this myth are the same as in the previous Greek myth?

What aspects of creation are different?

How does this myth humanize the world of nature?

Knowing all the different things that different people can do with their imaginations, are you surprised that these myths, from two different cultures, are so alike? What might account for their similarity?

The Creation
of the World

A myth of Uganda
Retold by CHARLOTTE *and* WOLF LESLAU

Kabezya-Mpungu, the highest god, had created the sky and the earth and two human beings, a man and a woman, endowed with Reason. However, these two human beings did not, as yet, possess Mutima, or Heart.

Kabezya-Mpungu had four children, the Sun, the Moon, Darkness, and Rain. He called them all together and said to them, "I want to withdraw now, so that Man can no longer see me. I will send down Mutima in my place, but before I take leave I want to know what you, Rain, are going to do." "Oh," replied Rain, "I think I'll pour down without cease and put everything under water." "No," answered the god, "don't do that! Look at these two," and he pointed to the man and the woman; "do you think they can live under water? You'd better take turns with the Sun. After you have sufficiently watered the earth, let the Sun go to work and dry it.

"And how are you going to conduct yourself?" the god asked the Sun. "I intend to shine hotly and burn everything under me," said his second child.

"No," replied Kabezya-Mpungu. "That cannot be. How do you expect the people whom I created to get food? When you have warmed the earth for a while, give Rain a chance to refresh it and make the fruit grow.

"And you, Darkness, what are your plans?"

"I intend to rule forever!" was the answer.

"Have pity," cried the god. "Do you want to condemn my creatures, the lions, the tigers, and the serpents, to see nothing of the world I made? Listen to me: give the Moon time to shine on the earth, and when you see the Moon in its last quarter, then you may again rule. But I have lingered too long; now I must go." And he disappeared.

Somewhat later, Mutima, Heart, came along, in a small container no bigger than a hand.

Heart was crying, and asked Sun, Moon, Darkness, and Rain, "Where is Kabezya-Mpungu, our father?"

"Father is gone," they said, "and we do not know where."

"Oh, how great is my desire," replied Heart, "to commune with him. But since I cannot find him I will enter into Man, and through him I will seek God from generation to generation."

And that is what happened. Ever since, all children born of Man contain Mutima, a longing for God.

How have the three myths you have read described the past as a series of conflicts and separations?

How does this myth define the future as a search for reunion?

Do you think the last statement in the myth is true?

The Four Ages

A Greek myth

The Golden Age was first, a time that cherished,
Of its own will, justice and right; no law,
No punishment, was called for; fearfulness
Was quite unknown, and the bronze tablets held
No legal threatening; no suppliant throng
Studied a judge's face; there were no judges,
There did not need to be. Trees had not yet
Been cut and hollowed, to visit other shores.
Men were content at home, and had no towns
With moats and walls around them; and no trumpets
Blared out alarms; things like swords and helmets
Had not been heard of. No one needed soldiers.
People were unaggressive, and unanxious;
The years went by in peace. And Earth, untroubled,
Unharried by hoe or plowshare, brought forth all
That men had need for, and those men were happy,
Gathering berries from the mountainsides,
Cherries, or blackcaps, and the edible acorns.
Spring was forever, with a west wind blowing
Softly across the flowers no man had planted,
And Earth, unplowed, brought forth rich grain; the field,
Unfallowed, whitened with wheat, and there were rivers
Of milk, and rivers of honey, and golden nectar
Dripped from the dark-green oak trees.

After Saturn
Was driven to the shadowy land of death,
And the world was under Jove, the Age of Silver
Came in, lower than gold, better than bronze.
Jove made the springtime shorter, added winter,
Summer, and autumn, the seasons as we know them.
That was the first time when the burnt air glowed
White-hot, or icicles hung down in winter.
And men built houses for themselves; the caverns,
The woodland thickets, and the bark-bound shelters
No longer served; and the seeds of grain were planted
In the long furrows, and the oxen struggled
Groaning and laboring under the heavy yoke.

Then came the Age of Bronze, and dispositions
Took on aggressive instincts, quick to arm,
Yet not entirely evil. And last of all
The Iron Age succeeded, whose base vein
Let loose all evil: modesty and truth
And righteousness fled Earth, and in their place
Came trickery and slyness, plotting, swindling,
Violence and the damned desire of having.
Men spread their sails to winds unknown to sailors,
The pines came down their mountainsides, to revel
And leap in the deep waters, and the ground,
Free, once, to everyone, like air and sunshine,
Was stepped off by surveyors. The rich Earth,
Good giver of all the bounty of the harvest,
Was asked for more; they dug into her vitals,
Pried out the wealth a kinder lord had hidden
In Stygian shadow, all that precious metal,
The root of evil. They found the guilt of iron,
And gold, more guilty still. And War came forth
That uses both to fight with; bloody hands
Brandished the clashing weapons. Men lived on plunder.
Guest was not safe from host, nor brother from brother,
A man would kill his wife, a wife her husband,
Stepmothers, dire and dreadful, stirred their brews
With poisonous aconite, and sons would hustle
Fathers to death, and Piety lay vanquished,

The Earth Belonged to Them All **15**

And the maiden Justice, last of all immortals,
Fled from the bloody earth.

                    Heaven was no safer.
Giants attacked the very throne of Heaven,
Piled Pelion on Ossa, mountain on mountain
Up to the very stars. Jove struck them down
With thunderbolts, and the bulk of those huge bodies
Lay on the earth, and bled, and Mother Earth,
Made pregnant by that blood, brought forth new bodies,
And gave them, to recall her older offspring,
The forms of men. And this new stock was also
Contemptuous of gods, and murder-hungry
And violent. You would know they were sons of blood.

                                        OVID
                    Translated by ROLFE HUMPHRIES

Why did the Golden Age turn to Silver, to Bronze, to Iron? Who or what
was responsible?

Do you think people need to believe in "the good old days"? Why?

What power do you think myth-making gave people?

Look at the images in the drawing that opens this unit. Which images
suggest the Age of Iron? Do any suggest a Golden Age?

Collect pairs of images of your own to show, first, how something is, and,
second, how you would like it to be. Where will you place the human
figure?

The World Is
Too Much with Us

The world is too much with us; late and soon,
Getting and spending, we lay waste our powers:
Little we see in Nature that is ours;
We have given our hearts away, a sordid boon!
This sea that bares her bosom to the moon;
The winds that will be howling at all hours,
And are up-gathered now like sleeping flowers;
For this, for everything, we are out of tune;
It moves us not. — Great God! I'd rather be
A pagan suckled in a creed outworn;
So might I, standing on this pleasant lea,
Have glimpses that would make me less forlorn;
Have sight of Proteus rising from the sea;
Or hear old Triton blow his wreathèd horn.

WILLIAM WORDSWORTH

Would you say this poet is searching for a lost Golden Age (page 14)?
Does he seem to see the present as an Iron Age?

What does he say he has lost?

The Lake Isle of Innisfree

I will arise and go now, and go to Innisfree,
And a small cabin build there, of clay and wattles made:
Nine bean-rows will I have there, a hive for the honeybee,
And live alone in the bee-loud glade.

And I shall have some peace there, for peace comes dropping slow,
Dropping from the veils of the morning to where the cricket sings;
There midnight's all a glimmer, and noon a purple glow,
And evening full of the linnet's wings.

I will arise and go now, for always night and day
I hear lake water lapping with low sounds by the shore;
While I stand on the roadway, or on the pavements gray,
I hear it in the deep heart's core.

WILLIAM BUTLER YEATS

Why will there be peace at Innisfree? How is Innisfree like the Golden Age (page 14)?

Do you think it is natural for people to search for places like "Innisfree"? How is this speaker's desire like Wordsworth's?

The Palace of Olympus

A Greek myth
Retold by ROBERT GRAVES

All the Olympians lived together in an enormous palace, set well above the usual level of clouds at the top of Mount Olympus, the highest mountain in Greece. Great walls, too steep for climbing, protected the Palace. The Olympians' masons, gigantic one-eyed Cyclopes, had built them on much the same plan as royal palaces on earth. . . .

King Zeus had an enormous throne of polished black Egyptian marble, decorated in gold. Seven steps led up to it, each of them enamelled with one of the seven colors of the rainbow. A bright blue covering above showed that the whole sky belonged to Zeus alone; and on the right arm of his throne perched a ruby-eyed golden eagle clutching jagged strips of pure tin, which meant that Zeus could kill whatever enemies he pleased by throwing a thunderbolt of forked lightning at them. A purple ram's fleece covered the cold seat. Zeus used it for magical rain-making in times of drought. He was a strong, brave, stupid, noisy, violent, conceited god, and always on the watch lest his family should try to get rid of him, having once himself got rid of his wicked, idle, cannibalistic father Cronus, King of the Titans and Titanesses. . . . One of Zeus's emblems was the eagle, another was the woodpecker.

Queen Hera had an ivory throne, with three crystal steps leading up to it. Golden cuckoos and willow leaves decorated the back, and a full moon hung above it. Hera sat on a white cowskin, which she sometimes used for rain-making magic if Zeus could not be bothered to stop a drought. She disliked being Zeus's wife, because he was frequently marrying mortal women and saying, with a sneer, that these marriages did not count—his brides would soon grow ugly and die; but she was his Queen, and perpetually young and beautiful.

When first asked to marry him, Hera had refused; and had gone on refusing every year for three hundred years. But one springtime Zeus disguised himself as a poor cuckoo caught in a thunderstorm, and tapped at her window. Hera, not seeing through his disguise, let the cuckoo in, stroked his wet feathers, and whispered: "Poor bird, I love you." At once, Zeus changed back again into his true shape, and said: "Now you must marry me!" After this, however badly Zeus behaved, Hera felt obliged to set a good example to gods and goddesses and mortals, as the Mother of Heaven. Her emblem was the cow, the most motherly of animals; but, not wishing to be thought as plain-looking and placid as a cow, she also used the peacock and the lion. . . .

Poseidon, god of the seas and rivers, had the second-largest throne. It was of gray-green white-streaked marble, ornamented with coral, gold, and mother-of-pearl. The arms were carved in the shape of sea beasts, and Poseidon sat on sealskin. For his help in banishing Cronus and the Titans, Zeus had married him to Amphitrite, the former sea goddess, and allowed him to take over all her titles. Though Poseidon hated to be less important than his younger brother, and always went about scowling, he feared Zeus's thunderbolt. His only weapon was a trident, with which he could stir up the sea and so wreck ships; but Zeus never travelled by ship. When Poseidon felt even crosser than usual, he would drive away in his chariot to a palace under the waves, near the island of Euboea, and there let his rage cool. As his emblem Poseidon chose the horse, an animal which he pretended to have created. Large waves are still called "white horses" because of this.

Opposite Poseidon sat his sister Demeter, goddess of all useful fruits, grasses, and grains. Her throne of bright green malachite was ornamented with ears of barley in gold, and little golden pigs for luck. Demeter seldom smiled, except when her daughter Persephone — unhappily married to the hateful Hades, God of the Dead — came to visit her once a year. Demeter had been rather wild as a girl, and nobody could remember the name of Persephone's father: probably some country god married for a drunken joke at a harvest festival. Demeter's emblem was the poppy, which grows red as blood among the barley.

Next to Poseidon sat Hephaestus, a son of Zeus and Hera. Being the god of goldsmiths, jewellers, blacksmiths, masons, and carpenters, he had built all these thrones himself, and made his own a masterpiece of every different metal and precious stone to be found. The seat could swivel about, the arms could move up and down, and the whole throne rolled along automatically wherever he wished, like the three-legged golden tables in his workshop. Hephaestus had hobbled ever since birth, when Zeus roared at Hera: "A brat as weak as this is unworthy of me!" — and threw him far out over the walls of Olympus. In his fall

Hephaestus broke a leg so badly that he had to wear a golden leg iron. He kept a country house on Lemnos, the island where he had struck earth; and his emblem was the quail, a bird that does a hobbling dance in springtime.

Opposite Hephaestus sat Athene, Goddess of Wisdom, who first taught him how to handle tools, and knew more than anyone else about pottery, weaving, and all useful arts. Her silver throne had golden basketwork at the back and sides, and a crown of violets, made from blue lapis lazuli, set above it. Its arms ended in grinning Gorgons' heads. Athene, wise though she was, did not know the names of her parents. Poseidon claimed her as his daughter by a marriage with an African goddess called Libya. It is true that, as a child, she had been found wandering in a goatskin by the shores of a Libyan lake; but rather than admit herself the daughter of Poseidon, whom she thought very stupid, she allowed Zeus to pretend she was his. Zeus announced that one day, overcome by a fearful headache, he had howled aloud like a thousand wolves hunting in a pack. Hephaestus, he said, then ran up with an axe and kindly split open his skull, and out sprang Athene, dressed in full armor. Athene was also a battle goddess, yet never went to war unless forced—being too sensible to pick quarrels—and when she fought, always won. She chose the wise owl as her emblem and had a town house at Athens.

Next to Athene sat Aphrodite, Goddess of Love and Beauty. Nobody knew who her parents were, either. The South Wind said that he had once seen her floating in a scallop shell off the island of Cythera, and steered her gently ashore. She may have been a daughter of Amphitrite by a smaller god named Triton, who used to blow roaring blasts on a conch, or perhaps by old Cronus. Amphitrite refused to say a word on the subject. Aphrodite's throne was silver, inlaid with beryls and aquamarines, the back shaped like a scallop shell, the seat made of swan's down, and under her feet lay a golden mat—an embroidery of golden bees, apples, and sparrows. Aphrodite had a magic girdle, which she would wear whenever she wanted to make anyone love her madly. To keep Aphrodite out of mischief, Zeus decided that she needed a hard-working, decent husband, and naturally chose his son Hephaestus. Hephaestus exclaimed: "Now I am the happiest god alive!" But she thought it disgraceful to be the wife of a sooty-faced, horny-handed, crippled smith and insisted on having a bedroom of her own. Aphrodite's emblem was the dove, and she would visit Paphos, in Cyprus, once a year to swim in the sea, for good luck.

Opposite Aphrodite sat Ares, Hephaestus's tall, handsome, boastful cruel brother, who loved fighting for its own sake. Ares and Aphrodite were continually holding hands and giggling in corners, which made Hephaestus jealous. Yet if he ever complained to the Council, Zeus would laugh at him, saying: "Fool, why did you give your wife that magic girdle? Can you blame your brother if he falls in love with her when she wears it?" Ares's throne was built of brass, strong and ugly—those huge brass knobs in the shape of skulls, and that cushion cover of human skin! Ares had no manners, no learning, and the worst of taste; yet Aphrodite thought him wonderful. His emblems were a wild boar and a bloodstained spear. He kept a country house among the rough woods of Thrace.

Next to Ares sat Apollo, the god of music, poetry, medicine, archery, and young unmarried men—Zeus's son by Leto, one of the smaller goddesses, whom he married to annoy Hera. Apollo rebelled against his father once or twice, but got well punished each time, and learned to behave more sensibly. His highly polished golden throne had magical inscriptions carved all over it, a back shaped like a lyre, and a python skin to sit on. Above hung a golden sundisk with twenty-one rays shaped like arrows, because he pretended to manage the sun. Apollo's emblem was a mouse; mice were supposed to know the secrets of earth, and tell them to him. (He preferred white mice to ordinary ones. . . .) Apollo owned a splendid house at Delphi on the top of Mount Parnassus, built around the famous oracle which he stole from Mother Earth, Zeus's grandmother.

Opposite Apollo sat his twin sister Artemis, goddess of hunting and of unmarried girls, from whom he had learned medicine and archery. Her throne was of pure silver, with a wolfskin to sit on, and the back shaped like two date palms, one on each side of a new-moon boat. Apollo married several mortal wives at different times. . . . Artemis, however, hated the idea of marriage, although she kindly took care of mothers when their babies were born. She much preferred hunting, fishing, and swimming in moonlit mountain pools. If any mortal happened to see her without clothes, she used to change him into a stag and hunt him to death. She chose as her emblem the she-bear, the most dangerous of all wild animals in Greece.

Last in the row of gods sat Hermes, Zeus's son by a smaller goddess named Maia, after whom the month of May is called: Hermes, the god of merchants, bankers, thieves, fortune tellers, and heralds, born in Arcadia. His throne was cut out of a single piece of solid gray rock, the arms shaped like rams' heads, and a goatskin for the seat. On its back he had carved a swastika, this being the shape of a fire-making machine invented by him—the fire drill. Until then, housewives used to borrow glowing pieces of charcoal from their neighbors. Hermes also invented the alphabet; and one of his emblems was the crane, because cranes fly in a V—the first letter he wrote. Another of Hermes's emblems was a peeled hazel stick, which he carried as the Messenger of the Olympians: white ribbons dangled from it, which foolish people often mistook for snakes.

Last in the row of goddesses sat Zeus's eldest sister, Hestia, Goddess of the Home, on a plain, uncarved, wooden throne, and a plain cushion woven of undyed wool. Hestia, the kindest and most peaceable of all the Olympians, hated the continual family quarrels, and never troubled to choose any particular emblem of her own. She used to tend the charcoal hearth in the middle of the Council Hall.

That made six gods and six goddesses. But one day Zeus announced that Dionysus, his son by a mortal woman named Semele, had invented wine, and must be given a seat in the Council. Thirteen Olympians would have been an unlucky number; so Hestia offered him her seat, just to keep the peace. Now there were seven gods and five goddesses, an unjust state of affairs because, when questions about women had to be discussed, the gods outvoted the goddesses. Dionysus's throne was gold-plated fir wood, ornamented with bunches of grapes carved in amethyst (a violet-colored stone), snakes carved in serpentine (a stone with many markings), and various horned animals besides, carved in onyx (a black and white stone), sard (a dark red stone), jade (a dark green stone), and carnelian (a pink stone). He took the tiger for his emblem, having once visited India at the head of a drunken army and brought tigers back as souvenirs. . . .

In a room behind the kitchen sat the Three Fates, named Clotho, Lachesis, and Atropos. They were the oldest goddesses in existence, too old for anybody to remember where they came from. The Fates decided how long each mortal should live: spinning a linen thread, to measure exactly so many inches and feet for months and years, and then snipping it off with a pair of shears. They also knew, but seldom revealed, what would be the fate of each Olympian god. Even Zeus feared them for that reason. . . .

How are some of the symbols associated with the Olympians still used today? (Consider the eagle, lion, peacock, trident, owl, dove, and tiger.)

People are storytellers. Fighting to survive in a threatening world, they have used their imagination to try to make sense out of life on the sometimes cruel, sometimes generous earth. They have told themselves stories that give human meaning to the changes and cycles they are subject to. Why does the sun come up, go down, and then come up again? Why is there summer, then winter, then summer again? Will we, like the sun and like the summer, be reborn again after death? The meaning-giving stories people have created are called *myths*.

Passed on at first by word of mouth, myths eventually stick together to form a society's storehouse of stories—or mythology. Their mythology tells a society everything it is most concerned about: Who are they? Where did they come from? What are their laws? What is their destiny?

Myths are usually stories about the gods. Though these gods are identified with the immense powers of the universe, they are often given the forms and feelings of human beings, and like humans, they form families. After all, it was much easier to make sense out of life if the gods acted the way humans do. Myths, then, created a human universe. They made it possible for people to understand and communicate with things that they could neither see nor control.

In their myths, people often imagined that they originated in a time of peace, when the seasons did not change and threaten them with cold and hunger, when they were not lonely, when they were loved by the gods. As people have advanced, they have continued to use their imagination to try to recover that sense of belonging to the earth that they had once possessed. Though the gods eventually disappeared from our stories, our literature continues to be a search for our lost human identity, a quest to rebuild or rediscover our lost perfect world.

Literature, then, is the continuous journal of

the imagination. It still expresses our desire to know, to pierce the mysteries the old myths tried to pierce, to see the universe as a human home. We still tell myths—we only call them by different names.

This book focuses on some of the patterns or "tools" the imagination uses in storytelling. It revolves around some of the myths told by the Greeks, whose mythology has been a major influence in Western literature. Some of the characters, events, stories, and images used in these Greek myths also recur in the imaginative life of many other people. These recurring characters, events, stories, and images are called archetypes. Archetype is a Greek word meaning "original pattern, or model." It is these archetypes, or very old patterns, hidden away in our stories that unify our imaginative expressions.

An archetype found in this chapter is the image of the Golden Age. The term Golden Age originated with the Greeks, but, like any archetype, the image of an original perfect world is a basic imaginative pattern. In the Chinese myth in this chapter, it is called a time of "peace." It can also be a garden of Eden, or an island called Innisfree.

By looking at certain recurring characters, events, stories, and images we can begin to see the oneness of "the journal of the imagination" we call literature. As you go through this book, make connections among the stories and poems of different cultures. Find what links these works of literature together and you will also find what links people everywhere together.

The connections are there. They have always been there. Literature has always been the one connected story of the human race, trying to find out who it is.

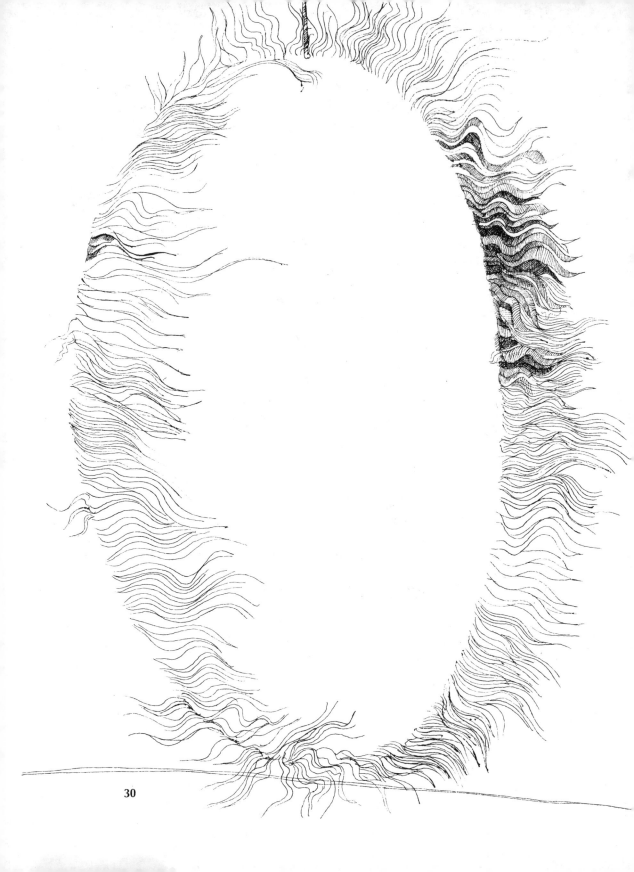

2
THE GOD-TEACHER

alan E. Cohen 1-72

Prometheus

A Greek myth
Retold by W.T. JEWKES

You will remember how Prometheus the Titan made man out of clay and helped his cousin Zeus to win the war of rebellion against Cronus. One would think that he might have won Zeus's undying thanks, but unfortunately for Prometheus, he presumed too much on Zeus's gratitude. As a result he made Zeus angry and had to suffer severe punishment.

Prometheus was very pleased with man but felt that there was a great deal left to be desired in his creation. His brother, Epimetheus, whose name means "he who thinks afterward," had had a hand in helping him make man; but true to his name, he had used up all his raw materials in giving man just a body more versatile than that of the animals. Prometheus realized that in this state man would not know how to take advantage of his upright posture. What man needed, he saw, was to have the chance to develop his mind. Athene, the goddess of wisdom, had already given Prometheus the knowledge of how to build houses, to add and subtract, to chart a course by the stars, to heal illness, and these, and many other useful arts, he soon passed on to mankind. But still man did not have enough to satisfy Prometheus. So he decided to give man the divine gift of fire.

At first Zeus did not seem to object to this idea. But trouble came when Prometheus played a joke on Zeus. It began one day when the gods were gathered together to decide which portions of the sacrificial bull should be offered to them as a gift. Since he was the most clever god, Prometheus was asked to make the decision.

"Well," he said, thinking to show them how silly they were to argue over such a matter, "give me an hour or two and I will have an answer for you."

So while the gods went off for a noontime nap, Prometheus took a bull, killed it, dismembered it, and flayed its hide. Then he made two bags from the hide. Into one he stuffed all the flesh of the bull; and on top of the flesh, at the mouth of the bag, he stuffed the bull's stomach, the least tempting part of the animal. Into the other bag, he put first the bones and then on top, at the mouth of the bag, he placed the animal's juicy fat.

When the gods returned in the early afternoon, they saw the two bags placed on a large flat stone.

"Now," said Prometheus craftily, "I've decided that the best way to resolve the argument is to let Zeus be guided by what he sees. Let the father of the gods and men choose which of these two bags he most would like. Whatever the bag contains shall hereafter be the portion of sacrifice given to the gods."

Zeus was pleased at the idea and quickly stepped up to inspect the bags. Of course, he let his greedy eyes be his guide and chose the bag whose mouth was stuffed with the fragrant fat. When the rest of the contents of the bag had been dumped on the ground, however, and he saw only a pile of dry bones, Zeus knew he had been tricked. He was furious.

"Very well, Prometheus," he raged, "so you want to make me look a fool before the other gods, do you? Well, you'll be sorry you did! You want to give mankind the gift of fire, but now you can't. I won't allow it. Let men eat their flesh raw, just as they always have!"

But Prometheus was a very persistent god. A few days later, when he thought that perhaps Zeus would not be looking, he got Athene to let him steal at night into the fire-chamber of Olympus by the back door. There, in the center of the chamber stood the flaming chariot of the sun, where Apollo had left it after its day's journey. He took a rush torch that was lying in a corner of the hall, lit it from the fiery chariot, and soon had a bright, live piece of charcoal. This he put into the hollow stalk of a giant fennel that he had brought with him, to keep it glowing, but also to hide its light. Then he quickly stole out of the chamber and came down to earth where men were sleeping. Quietly he gathered together some dry leaves and twigs, and putting his live coal in amongst them, he soon had a blazing bonfire going. At last he stepped behind a large oak tree to watch what would happen.

As it grew light, the men who dwelt near the grove got up from their beds of fern to begin the tasks of the day. Soon the news of the strange new spirit, bright as the sun, hot like the sun, so hot that it devoured logs and branches with noisy greed, spread throughout the region. Men came and gathered around the place, gazing in wonder and awe. Soon the bolder ones moved near to the fire, but it was so hot that they quickly retreated. Prometheus watched for a while, delighted with his exploit, but soon it became clear to him that he would have to instruct men in how to treat this new plaything, so that they remained in control. It would not do for fire to become their master instead of their servant. So he stepped out from behind the oak tree and called the men to him.

"This is a gift that I bring to you from Olympus, mortals. It is called 'fire,' and is stolen from the sun. But it's a dangerous gift and you must learn to treat it well. It is greedy for wood and needs to be fed constantly, but if you feed it too much, it will rage out of control and kill you. If ever it does get out of control, you can subdue it with only one thing—water. Treat it with respect and it will be the key to much happiness."

At first the men were afraid at what Prometheus told them. Stolen from the sun? Brought down from Olympus? Surely it was death to meddle with such a thing. But Prometheus meanwhile had taken up the raw haunches of a deer that lay close by. Spitting them on a sharp stick, he held them over the fire, and soon the tempting smell of roast venison brought the men hungrily to the fire's edge. In no time at all they were gulping down the delicious, hot morsels greedily. Then Prometheus showed them how to make torches by dipping branches in pitch and igniting them at the fire. He showed them also how to smelt metal from the ore in rocks. All in all, he thought, surveying men as they happily and busily went about practicing their new skills, a good day's work.

But that night Zeus happened to look down from Olympus onto the face of the earth, and there he saw something that his eyes could hardly believe. All over the landscape he spotted the glow of fires, and by the firelight he saw men cooking their food, warming their cold hands. The fires were driving back the darkness. Some men had made crude forges on which they were already beating out rough weapons, and plowshares, and nails, and iron bands to bind planks together to make ships. Others were fashioning iron rims for the wheels of chariots. Others were refining gold from the earth and making ornaments and coins. It was not hard for Zeus to guess who had been responsible for this. Only one god would have had the gall to defy his command.

In his rage, he let out a roar of thunder that split the heavens in two and sent mortals scurrying into their caves and huts.

"Prometheus!" he shouted. "Where's Prometheus? Let him come here at once. If he won't come, bring him by force!"

But Prometheus was already nearby. He knew there would be trouble, but he approached the cloud-gatherer's throne boldly. Zeus frowned blackly on him.

"What have you done, you fool?" he demanded hotly. "You knew my command. Man was not to have the gift of fire. No god can defy my power and get away with it!"

"Father of the gods and men," replied Prometheus quietly, "I won't say I did obey your command. But surely, it seemed to me, you would take pity on the race of men. See how much happier they are, now that they have fire."

"Maybe they are and maybe they aren't," Zeus stormed. "Now that they have that gift, there's no telling what they'll do. Soon they will be so proud of their accomplishments that they will think they are as great as the gods. Who knows, they might even try to storm Olympus itself!"

"Whatever they do, they can never be as powerful as you," declared Prometheus reassuringly. "You can always destroy them if they do."

"I'm not going to wait that long," raged the thunderer. "I'm going to consume them all now, once and for all, in the hugest fire you ever saw!"

But Zeus had second thoughts.

"On the other hand," he said, "I think I'll have myself some sport. What you say is true—I can always destroy them if they storm heaven. In the meantime, I think I'll watch them with their new plaything. I'm not so sure it will bring them only happiness. Soon, mark my words, they'll be at war in those chariots, killing one another with those swords and spears. Maybe they'll do the job for me.

"But you," he went on, turning to Prometheus with his eyes flashing, "you will have to be punished for your disobedience!"

So the king of Olympus called two gods, Power and Violence, to serve as guards of Prometheus. Then he turned to Hephaestus, the lame blacksmith of heaven.

"Hephaestus," he ordered, "you go along with Prometheus and his guards. They are taking him to the rocky slope of the Caucasus.

When you get there, I want you to forge the strongest iron fetters you can fashion and chain this criminal to the rocks with them. There he will stay forever, to bear the scorching heat of the sun by day and the bitter cold at night. And I will send an eagle to nest nearby. Each day it will swoop down and tear the prisoner's liver out, piece by piece. And each night the liver will repair itself, ready to make a meal for the bird the next day."

And so it was done. There Prometheus remained in torture for many and many a year. He would have been there still, except that Zeus finally relented and allowed one of the heroes to rescue him. The hero's name was Heracles. But that is another story.

What human qualities does Prometheus have?

Prometheus suffered for helping people. What effect would this story of divine sacrifice have on the people who told it?

The gift of fire drove back the darkness, and Prometheus told the people it would be the key to much happiness. But Zeus prophesied that it would bring an even greater darkness. Which prophecy do you think has been fulfilled?

Old Man

A Crow Indian myth
Retold by ELLA E. CLARK

Long before there was any land and before there was any living thing except four little ducks, the Creator, whom we call Old Man, came and said to the ducks, "Which one of you is brave?"

"I am the bravest," replied one duck.

"Dive into the water," Old Man said to the duck, "and get some dirt from the bottom. I will see what I can do with it."

The brave duck went down and was gone a long time. It came up again carrying on its beak some dirt that it gave to Old Man. He held it in his hand until it became dry. Then he blew the dirt in all directions and thus made the land and the mountains and the rivers.

Old Man, who was all-powerful, was asked by the ducks to make other living things. So he took more dirt in his hand and, after it had dried, he blew it off. And there stood a man and a woman, the first Crow Indians. Old Man explained to them how to increase their number. At first they were blind; when their eyes were opened and they saw their nakedness, they asked for something with which to clothe themselves.

So that they might have food and clothing, Old Man took the rest of the dirt brought up by Duck and made animals and plants. Then he killed one of the buffalo he had made, broke a rock, and with one of the pieces cut up the animal. Then he explained its parts and told the man and woman how to use them.

"To carry water," he said, "take the pouch from the inside of the buffalo and make a bucket. Make drinking cups from its horns and also from the horns of the mountain sheep. Use the best pieces of buffalo for food. When you have had enough to eat, make a robe from the hide."

Then he showed the woman how to dress the skin. He showed the man how to make arrowheads, axes, knives, and cooking vessels from hard stone. "To make a fire," said Old Man, "take two sticks and place a little sand on one of them and also some of the driest buffalo chips. Then take the other stick and roll it between your hands until fire comes."

Old Man told them to take a large stone and fasten to it a handle made from hide. "With it you can break animal bones to get the marrow for making soup," he said to the woman. He also showed her how to scrape skins with a bone from the foreleg of an animal, to remove the hair.

At first, Old Man gave the man and woman no horses; they had only dogs for carrying their things. Later he told them how to get horses. "When you go over that hill there, do not look back, no matter what you hear." For three days they walked without looking back, but on the third day they heard animals coming behind them. They turned around and saw horses, but the horses vanished.

Old Man told them how to build a sweat lodge and also explained its purpose. And he told the man how to get dreams and visions. "Go up in the mountains," he said, "cut a piece of flesh from yourself, and give it to me. Do not eat while you are there. Then you will have visions that will tell you what to do.

"This land is the best of the lands I have made," Old Man said to them. "Upon it you will find everything you need—pure water, vegetation, timber, game animals. I have put you in the center of it, and I have put people around you as your enemies. If I had made you in large numbers, you would be too powerful and would kill the other people I have created. You are few in number, but you are brave."

How is Old Man like Prometheus?

Why would people want to create a myth about a loving god-teacher?

The Mysterious Stranger

From the book by
MARK TWAIN

Three of us boys were always together, and had been so from the cradle, being fond of each other from the beginning, and this affection deepening as the years went on—Nikolaus Baumann, son of the principal judge of the local court; Seppi Wohlmeyer, son of the keeper of the principal inn, The Golden Stag, which had a nice garden, with shade trees, reaching down to the riverside, and pleasure boats for hire; and I was the third—Theodor Fischer, son of the church organist, who was also leader of the village band, teacher of the violin, composer, tax collector of the commune, sexton, and in other ways a useful citizen and respected by all. We knew the hills and the woods as well as the birds knew them; for we were always roaming them when we had leisure—at least when we were not swimming or boating or fishing, or playing on the ice or sliding down hill.

And we had the run of the castle park, and very few had that. It was because we were pets of the oldest serving man in the castle— Felix Brandt; and often we went there, nights, to hear him talk about old times and strange things, and smoke with him (he taught us that), and drink coffee; for he had served in the wars, and was at the siege of Vienna; and there, when the Turks were defeated and driven away, among the captured things were bags of coffee, and the Turkish prisoners explained the character of it and how to make a pleasant drink out of it, and now he always kept coffee by him, to drink himself, and also to astonish the ignorant with. When it stormed he kept us all night; and while it thundered and lightened outside he told about ghosts and horrors of every kind, and of battles and murders and mutilations, and such things, and made it pleasant and cosy inside; and he told these things from his own experience largely. He had seen many ghosts in his time, and witches and enchanters, and once he was lost in a fierce storm at midnight in the mountains, and by the glare of the lightning had seen the Wild Huntsman rage by on the blast with his specter dogs chasing after him through the driving cloud-rack. Also he had seen an incubus once, and several times he had seen the great bat that sucks the blood from the necks of people while they are asleep, fanning them softly with its wings and so keeping them drowsy till they die. He encouraged us not to fear supernatural things, such as ghosts, and said they did no harm, but only wandered about because they were lonely and distressed and wanted kindly notice and compassion; and in time we learned to not be afraid, and even went down with him in the night to the haunted chamber in the dungeons of the castle. The ghost appeared only once, and it went by very dim to the sight and floating noiseless through the air, and then disappeared; and we scarcely trembled, he had taught us so well. He said it came up sometimes in the night and woke him up by passing its clammy hand over his face, but it did him no hurt, it only wanted sympathy and notice. But the strangest thing was that he had seen angels; actual angels out of heaven, and had talked with them. They had no wings, and wore clothes, and talked and looked and acted just like any natural person, and you would never know them for angels, except for the wonderful things they did which a mortal could not do, and the way they suddenly disappeared while you were talking with them, which was also a thing which no mortal could do. And he said they were pleasant and cheerful, not gloomy and melancholy, like ghosts.

It was after that kind of a talk, one May night, that we got up next morning and had a good breakfast with him and then went down and crossed the bridge and went away up into the hills on the left to a woody hilltop which was a favorite place of ours, and there we stretched out on the grass in the shade to rest and smoke and talk over those strange things, for they were in our minds yet, and impressing us. But we couldn't smoke, because we had been heedless and left our flint and steel behind.

Soon there came a youth strolling toward us through the trees, and he sat down and began to talk in a friendly way, just as if he knew us. But we did not answer him, for he was a stranger and we were not used to strangers and were shy of them. He had new and good clothes on, and was handsome and had a winning face and a pleasant voice, and was easy and graceful and unembarrassed, not slouchy and awkward and diffident like other boys. We wanted to be friendly with him, but didn't know how to begin. Then I thought of the pipe, and wondered if it would be taken as kindly meant if I offered it to him. But I remembered that we had no fire; so I was sorry and disappointed. But he looked up bright and pleased, and said —

"Fire? Oh, that is easy — I will furnish it."

I was so astonished I couldn't speak, for I had not said anything. He took the pipe and blew his breath on it, and the tobacco glowed red and spirals of blue smoke rose up. We jumped up and were going to run, for that was natural; and we did run a few steps, although he was yearningly pleading for us to stay, and giving us his word that he would not do us any harm, but only wanted to be friends with us and have company. So we stopped and stood, and wanted to go back, being full of curiosity and wonder, but afraid to venture. He went on coaxing, in his soft persuasive way; and when we saw that the pipe did not blow up and nothing happened, our confidence returned by little and little, and presently our curiosity got to be stronger than our fear, and we ventured back — but slowly, and ready to fly, at any alarm.

He was bent on putting us at ease, and he had the right art; one could not remain timorous and doubtful where a person was so earnest and simple and gentle and talked so alluringly as he did; no, he won us over, and it was not long before we were content and comfortable and chatty, and glad we had found this new friend. When the feeling of constraint was all gone, we asked him how he had learned to do that strange thing, and he said he hadn't learned it at all, it came natural to him — like other things — other curious things.

"What ones?"

"Oh, a number; I don't know how many."

"Will you let us see you do them?"

"Do — please!" the others said.

"You won't run away again?"

"No — indeed we won't. Please do, won't you?"

"Yes, with pleasure; but you mustn't forget your promise, you know."

We said we wouldn't, and he went to a puddle and came back with water in a cup which he had made out of a leaf, and blew upon it and threw it out, and it was a lump of ice, the shape of the cup. We were astonished and charmed, but not afraid any more; we were very glad to be there, and asked him to go on and do some more things. And he did. He said he would give us any kind of fruit we liked, whether it was in season or not. We all spoke at once—

"Orange!"

"Apple!"

"Grapes!"

"They are in your pockets," he said, and it was true. And they were of the best, too, and we ate them and wished we had more, though none of us said so.

"You will find them where those came from," he said, "and everything else your appetites call for; and you need not name the thing you wish; as long as I am with you, you have only to wish and find."

And he said true. There was never anything so wonderful and so interesting. Bread, cakes, sweets, nuts—whatever one wanted, it was there. He ate nothing himself, but sat and chatted, and did one curious thing after another to amuse us. He made a toy squirrel out of clay, and it ran up a tree and sat on a limb overhead and barked down at us. Then he made a dog that was not much larger than a mouse, and it treed the squirrel and danced about the tree, excited and barking, and was as alive as any dog could be. It frightened the squirrel from tree to tree and followed it up until both were out of sight in the forest. He made birds out of clay and set them free and they flew away singing.

At last I made bold to ask him to tell us who he was.

"An angel," he said, quite simply, and set another clay bird free and clapped his hands and made it fly away.

A kind of awe fell upon us when we heard him say that, and we were afraid again; but he said we need not be troubled, there was no occasion for us to be afraid of an angel, and he liked us anyway. He went on chatting as simply and unaffectedly as ever; and while he talked he made a crowd of little men and women the size of your finger, and they went diligently to work and cleared and leveled off a space a couple of yards square in the grass and began to build a cunning little castle in it, the women mixing the mortar and carrying it up the scaffoldings in pails on their heads, just as our workwomen have always done, and the men laying the courses of masonry—five hundred of those toy people swarming briskly about and working diligently and wiping the sweat off their faces as natural as life. In the absorbing interest of watching those five hundred little people make the castle grow step by step and course by course and take shape and symmetry, that feeling of awe soon passed away, and we were quite comfortable and at home again. We asked if we might make some people, and he said yes, and told Seppi to make some cannon for the walls, and told Nikolaus to make some halberdiers with breastplates and greaves and helmets, and I was to make some cavalry, with horses; and in allotting these tasks he called us by our names, but did not say how he knew them. Then Seppi asked him what his own name was, and he said tranquilly—

"*Satan*," and held out a chip and caught a little woman on it who was falling from the scaffolding and put her back where she belonged, and said, "she is an idiot to step backward like that and not notice what she is about."

It caught us suddenly, that name did, and our work dropped out of our hands and broke to pieces—a cannon, a halberdier, and a horse. Satan laughed, and asked what was the matter. It was a natural laugh, and pleasant and sociable, not boisterous, and had a reassuring influence upon us; so I said there was nothing much the matter, only it seemed a strange name for an angel. He asked why.

"Because it's—it's—well, it's *his* name, you know."

"Yes—he is my uncle."

He said it placidly, but it took our breath, for a moment, and made our hearts beat hard. He did not seem to notice that, but partly mended our halberdiers and things with a touch, handed them to us to finish, and said—

"Don't you remember?—he was an angel himself once."

"Yes—it's true," said Seppi, "I didn't think of that."

"Before the Fall he was blameless."

"Yes," said Nikolaus, "he was without sin."

"It is a good family—ours," said Satan; "there is not a better. He is the only member of it that has ever sinned."

I should not be able to make any one understand how exciting it all was. You know that kind of quiver that trembles around through you when you are seeing something that is so strange and enchanting and wonderful that it is just a fearful joy to be alive and look at it; and you know how you gaze, and your lips turn dry and your breath comes short, but you wouldn't be anywhere but there, not for the world. I was bursting to ask one question—I had it on my tongue's end and could hardly hold it back—but I was ashamed to ask it, it might be a rudeness. Satan set an ox down that he had been making, and smiled up at me and said—

"It wouldn't be a rudeness; and I should forgive it if it was. Have

I *seen* him? Millions of times. From the time that I was a little child a thousand years old I was his second-best favorite among the nursery-angels of our blood and lineage—to use a human phrase—yes, from that time till the Fall; eight thousand years, measured as you count time."

"Eight—*thousand?*"

"Yes." He turned to Seppi, and went on as if answering something that was in Seppi's mind, "Why, naturally I look like a boy, for that is what I am. With us, what you call time is a spacious thing; it takes a long stretch of it to grow an angel to full age." There was a question in my mind, and he turned to me and answered it: "I am sixteen thousand years old—counting as you count." Then he turned to Nikolaus and said, "No, the Fall did not affect me nor the rest of the relationship. It was only he that I was named for who ate of the fruit of the tree and then beguiled the man and the woman with it. We others are still ignorant of sin; we are not able to commit it; we are without blemish, and shall abide in that estate always. We—" Two of the little workmen were quarreling, and in buzzing little bumble-bee voices they were cursing and swearing at each other; now came blows and blood, then they locked themselves together in a life-and-death struggle. Satan reached out his hand and crushed the life out of them with his fingers, threw them away, wiped the red from his fingers on his handkerchief and went on talking where he had left off: "We cannot do wrong; neither have we any disposition to do it, for we do not know what it is."

It seemed a strange speech, in the circumstances, but we barely noticed that, we were so shocked and grieved at the wanton murder he had committed—for murder it was, it was its true name, and it was without palliation or excuse, for the men had not wronged him in any way. It made us miserable; for we loved him, and had thought him so noble and beautiful and gracious, and had honestly *believed* he was an angel; and to have him do this cruel thing—ah, it lowered him so, and we had had such pride in him. He went right on talking, just as if nothing had happened: telling about his travels, and the interesting things he had seen in the big worlds of our solar system and of other solar systems far away in the remotenesses of space, and about the customs of the immortals that inhabit them, somehow fascinating us, enchanting us, charming us in spite of the pitiful scene that was now under our eyes: for the wives of the little dead men had found the crushed and shapeless bodies and were crying over them and sobbing and lamenting, and a priest was kneeling there with his hands crossed

upon his breast praying, and crowds and crowds of pitying friends were massed about them, reverently uncovered, with their bare heads bowed, and many with the tears running down—a scene which Satan paid no attention to until the small noise of the weeping and praying began to annoy him, then he reached out and took the heavy board seat out of our swing and brought it down and mashed all those people into the earth just as if they had been flies, and went on talking just the same.

An angel, and kill a priest! An angel who did not know how to do wrong, and yet destroys in cold blood a hundred helpless poor men and women who had never done him any harm! It made us sick to see that awful deed, and to think that none of those poor creatures was prepared except the priest, for none of them had ever heard a mass or seen a church. And we were witnesses; we could not get away from that thought; we had seen these murders done and it was our duty to tell, and let the law take its course.

But he went talking right along, and worked his enchantments upon us again with that fatal music of his voice. He *made* us forget everything; we could only listen to him, and love him and be his slaves, to do with as he would. He made us drunk with the joy of being with him, and of looking into the heaven of his eyes, and of feeling the ecstasy that thrilled along our veins from the touch of his hand.

He had seen everything, he had been everywhere, he knew everything, and he forgot nothing. What another must study, he learned at a glance; there were no difficulties for him. And he made things live before you when he told about them. He saw the world made; he saw Adam created; he saw Samson surge against the pillars and bring the temple down in ruins about him; he saw Caesar's death; he told of the daily life in heaven, he had seen the damned writhing in the red waves of hell; and he made us see all these things, and it was as if we were on the spot and looking at them with our own eyes. And we *felt* them, too, but there was no sign that they were anything to him, beyond being mere entertainments. Those visions of hell, those poor babes and women and girls and lads and men shrieking and supplicating in anguish—why, we could hardly bear it, but he was as bland about it as if it had been so many imitation rats in an artificial fire.

And always when he was talking about men and women here in the earth and their doings—even their grandest and sublimest—we were secretly ashamed, for his manner showed that to him they and their doings were of paltry poor consequence; often you would think he was talking about flies, if you didn't know. Once he even said, in so many words, that our people down here were quite interesting to him, notwithstanding they were so dull and ignorant and trivial and conceited, and so diseased and rickety, and such a shabby poor worthless lot all around. He said it in a quite matter-of-course way and without any bitterness, just as a person might talk about bricks or manure or any other thing that was of no consequence and hadn't feelings. I could see he meant no offence, but in my thoughts I set it down as not very good manners.

"Manners!" he said, "why it is merely the truth, and truth is good manners; manners are a fiction. The castle is done! Do you like it?"

Anyone would have been obliged to like it. It was lovely to look at, it was so shapely and fine, and so cunningly perfect in all its particulars, even to the little flags waving from the turrets. Satan said we must put the artillery in place, now, and station the halberdiers and deploy the cavalry. Our men and horses were a spectacle to see, they were so little like what they were intended for; for of course we had no art in making such things. Satan said they were the worst he had seen; and when he touched them and made them alive, it was just ridiculous the way they acted, on account of their legs not being of uniform lengths. They reeled and sprawled around as if they were drunk, and endangered everybody's lives around them, and finally fell over and lay helpless and kicking. It made us all laugh, though it was a shameful thing to see. The guns were charged with dirt, to fire a salute; but they were so crooked and so badly made that they all burst when they went off, and killed some of the gunners and crippled the others. Satan said we would have a storm, now, and an earthquake, if we liked, but we must stand off a piece, out of danger. We wanted to call the people away, too, but he said never mind them, they were of no consequence and we could make more, some time or other if we needed them.

A small storm cloud began to settle down black over the castle, and the miniature lightning and thunder began to play and the ground to quiver and the wind to pipe and wheeze and the rain to fall, and all the people flocked into the castle for shelter. The cloud settled down blacker and blacker and one could see the castle only dimly through it; the lightnings blazed out flash upon flash and they pierced the castle and set it on fire and the flames shone out red and fierce through the cloud, and the people came flying out, shrieking, but Satan brushed them back, paying no attention to our begging and crying and imploring; and in the midst of the howling of the wind and volleying of the thunder the magazine blew up, the earthquake rent the ground wide and the castle's wreck and ruin tumbled into the chasm, which swallowed it from sight and closed upon it, with all that innocent life, not one of the five hundred poor creatures escaping.

Our hearts were broken, we could not keep from crying.

"Don't cry," Satan said, "they were of no value."

"But they are gone to hell!"

"Oh, it is no matter, we can make more."

It was of no use to try to move him; evidently he was wholly without feeling, and could not understand. He was full of bubbling spirits, and as gay as if this were a wedding instead of a fiendish massacre. And he was bent on making us feel as he did, and of course his magic accomplished his desire. It was no trouble to him, he did whatever he pleased with us. In a little while we were dancing on that grave, and he was playing to us on a strange sweet instrument which he took out of his pocket; and the music—there is no music like that, unless perhaps in heaven, and that was where he brought it from, he said. It made one mad, for pleasure; and we could not take our eyes from him, and the looks that went out of our eyes came from our hearts, and their dumb speech was worship. He brought the dance from heaven, too, and the bliss of paradise was in it.

How is the Mysterious Stranger like Prometheus, yet unlike him?

How does Mark Twain feel about the gods who control the universe? What experiences might make someone feel this way?

Dionysos

A Greek myth
Retold by PADRAIC COLUM

A ship lay in a harbor; on a headland that overlooked the harbor a youth appeared. He wore a purple cloak; his hair was rich, dark, and flowing; his face was beautiful. The sailors on the ship thought that he must be a king's son, or a young king's brother. They were Tyrrhenian sea rovers, and they knew that they could never be called to account for anything that they did in that place. So they made a plan to seize the youth and hold him for ransom, or else sell him into slavery in some far land.

They seized him and they brought him on board the ship in bonds. He did not cry out; he sat upon the deck with a smile on his lips and a gleam in his dark eyes. And when the helmsman looked upon him he cried out to his companions, "Madmen, why have ye done this? I tell you that the one whom you have bound is one of the Olympians! Come! Let us set him free at once! Do not have him turn his rage against us, or the winds and the sea may be stirred up against our ship. I tell you that not even our well-built ship can carry such a one as he!"

But the master of the ship laughed at the words of the helmsman. "Madman yourself," he said, "with your talk of Olympians!" He gave command to have the ship taken out of that harbor. Then to the helmsman he said, "Leave the business of dealing with our prize to us. Mark the wind, you, and help to hoist the sail. As for the youth we have taken, I know what kind of a fellow he is. He will say nothing; he will keep smiling there. But soon he will talk, I warrant you! He will tell us where his friends and his brothers are, and how much we are likely to get by way of ransom for him. Or else he will stand in the market place until we find out what price he will fetch."

So the master of the sea rovers spoke, and the mast went up; the sail was hoisted; the wind filled it, and the ship went over the sparkling sea. The sea rovers sang, well content with all they had accomplished. Then, as they went here and there, making taut the sheets, they saw things that made them marvel. What was this that poured upon the deck, giving such fragrance? Could it be wine? Wine it was, and of a marvelous taste! Could that be fresh ivy that was spreading around the mast—ivy with dark-green leaves and berries? Could that be a vine that was growing along the sail—a vine with bunches of grapes growing from it? And what was this greenery that was garlanding the thole pins? The sea rovers marveled. Then, suddenly, their marveling was turned to fright. There was a lion on the ship—it was filled with his roarings. The sailors fled to where the helmsman was and they crowded about him. "Turn back—turn back the ship!" They cried. And then the lion sprang upon the master of the ship and seized him; the lion shook him and then flung him into the sea. The sailors waited for no more; they sprang into the sea, every man of them. The helmsman was about to spring into the sea after them. He looked around him; there was no lion there. He saw the youth they had taken aboard; the bonds were no longer upon him; there was a smile on his lips and in his dark eyes, and on his brow was a wreath of ivy rich with berries. The helmsman threw himself on the deck before him. "Take courage, man," said the youth, now known, indeed, for one of the Olympians. "The others have been changed to dolphins in the sea. You have found favor with me. And I am Dionysos whom Semele bore to Zeus."

He was that god who was so marvelously born. Zeus, lord of the thunder, had loved Semele, the daughter of King Kadmos. She had begged her lover to show himself to her in all the splendor of his godhead. Zeus came to her in his radiance; then Semele was smitten and consumed and the life went from her.

Zeus took her unborn child; opening his thigh he laid the unborn thing within and had the flesh sewn over it. The child was born from the thigh of Zeus upon Mount Nysa, in a secret place, remote from the presence of Hera, the spouse of Zeus. The nymphs of the mountain received the child from Zeus; they took him to their bosoms and reared him in the dells of Nysa. He was fed on ambrosia and nectar, the food of the Immortals. He grew up in an ivy-covered cave that was filled with the scent of flowers and of grapes.

He grew into a stripling; then he wandered through the wooded valleys of Mount Nysa, a wreath of ivy always upon his brow. The nymphs followed him, and the woods and valleys were filled with their outcries. A king who heard these outcries, who saw the ivy-crowned stripling and the nymphs following him with wands in their hands, became enraged at the sight. Lykourgos was that king's name. He had his men chase them, striking at the nymphs and at Dionysos with their heavy ox goads. The nymphs flung their wands upon the ground and flew to the mountaintop. Dionysos went down to the seashore. As for Lykourgos, he was smitten with blindness; he did not stay long amongst men afterwards, for he was hated by the immortal gods.

Now the ship with the faithful helmsman in charge of it brought Dionysos to the island of Naxos. There the daughter of King Minos, Ariadne, became his bride. He went to Egypt and was received with honor by the King of Egypt; he went to India and had his dwelling place by the River Ganges. And everywhere he went he showed men how to grow the vine and how to make wine that gladdens hearts and liberates minds from their close-pressing cares.

And everywhere he went women followed him; they had a frenzied joy from being near him; they danced; they clashed cymbals; they kept up revels that were hidden from men. With trains of women attending him, Dionysos turned back to the land he was born in. He went riding in a car that was drawn by leopards that the King of India had given him, and on his brow was a wreath of ivies and of vine leaves.

So he came back to Thebes—to Thebes that had been ruled over by Kadmos, the father of Semele. Kadmos was an old man now, and he had given the rule of the country to Pentheus, his daughter's son. Dionysos came, saying that he was the son of Semele, and Pentheus denounced him as an impostor. Then the women of Thebes, neglecting their households, joined the band that followed Dionysos and had their revels in the mountains—revels which no man was allowed to look upon. Pentheus became more and more angered at what his subjects, under the influence of this rover from India, were being brought to think and do.

He forbade the growing of the vine in Thebes; he would not allow the Thebans to make or to drink wine. And this he did, although his father, a wine cup in his hand, came before him, and warned him against persecuting the followers of Dionysos.

He shut Dionysos in his prison house, and he followed the women of Thebes to their secret meeting place on the top of the mountain. He climbed a pine tree so that he might overlook their revels. And he was there when the women saw him. In a frenzy they dashed to the tree; they tore the man out of its branches. Pentheus saw the women threatening him; he saw his own mother Agave there—the foremost amongst them. She did not know him, but kept crying, "A boar, a boar has come amongst us; destroy this boar." They tore at him; they tore the body of Pentheus to pieces, his own mother, Agave, in her frenzy, leading the others on. So Pentheus perished, and so Dionysos triumphed in the land where Semele saw her divine lover in his splendor and was crushed by his radiance and his might.

Dionysos, the last god to be admitted as an Olympian, was not entirely divine. How did his birth set him apart from mortals, as well as from the other gods? What miraculous powers does the god have?

What gifts does Dionysos give to the human race? What happened to the mortals who refused to accept the god's gifts?

The fire brought by Prometheus to earth was a two-edged gift. It could bring happiness, but it could also cause destruction. How is the gift brought by Dionysos associated with joy and freedom, as well as with grief and brutality? Is Twain's Mysterious Stranger in any way like Dionysos? How is he different from the god?

The drawing that opens this unit shows an artist's conception of a modern god-teacher. This computer seems to be balancing precariously on a tight rope and heading toward a dangerous ring of fire. Describe an imaginary god-teacher of your own. What powers set this god-teacher apart from those he or she teaches? Can the god-teacher's gift bring joy as well as grief?

Snake

A snake came to my water trough
On a hot, hot day, and I in pajamas for the heat,
To drink there.

In the deep, strange-scented shade of the great dark carobtree
I came down the steps with my pitcher
And must wait, must stand and wait, for there he was at the trough
    before me.

He reached down from a fissure in the earth-wall in the gloom
And trailed his yellow-brown slackness soft-bellied down, over the
    edge of the stone trough
And rested his throat upon the stone bottom,
And where the water had dripped from the tap, in a small clearness,
He sipped with his straight mouth,
Softly drank through his straight gums, into his slack long body,
Silently.

Someone was before me at my water trough,
And I, like a second comer, waiting.

He lifted his head from his drinking, as cattle do,
And looked at me vaguely, as drinking cattle do,
And flickered his two-forked tongue from his lips, and mused a
    moment,
And stooped and drank a little more,
Being earth-brown, earth-golden from the burning bowels of the
    earth
On the day of Sicilian July, with Etna smoking.
The voice of my education said to me
He must be killed,

For in Sicily the black, black snakes are innocent, the gold are veno-
mous.

And voices in me said, If you were a man
You would take a stick and break him now, and finish him off.

But must I confess how I liked him,
How glad I was he had come like a guest in quiet, to drink at my water
trough
And depart peaceful, pacified, and thankless,
Into the burning bowels of this earth?

Was it cowardice, that I dared not kill him?
Was it perversity, that I longed to talk to him?
Was it humility, to feel so honored?
I felt so honored.

And yet those voices:
If you were not afraid, you would kill him!

And truly I was afraid, I was most afraid,
But even so, honored still more
That he should seek my hospitality
From out the dark door of the secret earth.

He drank enough
And lifted his head, dreamily, as one who has drunken,
And flickered his tongue like a forked night on the air, so black,
Seeming to lick his lips,
And looked around like a god, unseeing, into the air,
And slowly turned his head,
And slowly, very slowly, as if thrice adream,
Proceeded to draw his slow length curving round
And climb again the broken bank of my wall-face.

And as he put his head into that dreadful hole,
And as he slowly drew up, snake-easing his shoulders, and entered
farther,
A sort of horror, a sort of protest against his withdrawing into that
horrid black hole,

Deliberately going into the blackness, and slowly drawing himself
    after,
Overcame me now his back was turned.

I looked round, I put down my pitcher,
I picked up a clumsy log
And threw it at the water trough with a clatter.

I think it did not hit him,
But suddenly that part of him that was left behind convulsed in undig-
    nified haste,
Writhed like lightning, and was gone
Into the black hole, the earth-lipped fissure in the wall-front,
At which, in the intense still noon, I stared with fascination.

And immediately I regretted it.
I thought how paltry, how vulgar, what a mean act!
I despised myself and the voices of my accursed human education.

And I thought of the albatross,
And I wished he would come back, my snake.

For he seemed to me again like a king,
Like a king in exile, uncrowned in the underworld,
Now due to be crowned again.

And so, I missed my chance with one of the lords
Of life.
And I have something to expiate;
A pettiness.

D.H. LAWRENCE

The first myth in this book tells of gods who were cast into the underworld.
Where does this poet suggest his snake is like an exiled god?

How is the snake a teacher? What does the poet learn?

Why do you think Old Man (in the myth on page 37) told the Crow people
they could have visions in the *mountains,* and, as a punishment, this snake
is exiled to the *underworld?*

The Program

From 2001: A Space Odyssey
ARTHUR C. CLARKE

The drought had lasted now for ten million years, and the reign of the terrible lizards had long since ended. Here on the Equator, in the continent which would one day be known as Africa, the battle for existence had reached a new climax of ferocity, and the victor was not yet in sight. In this barren and desiccated land, only the small or the swift or the fierce could flourish, or even hope to survive.

The man-apes of the veldt were none of these things, and they were not flourishing; indeed, they were already far down the road to racial extinction. About fifty of them occupied a group of caves overlooking a small, parched valley, which was divided by a sluggish stream fed from snows in the mountains two hundred miles to the north. In bad times the stream vanished completely, and the tribe lived in the shadow of thirst.

It was always hungry, and now it was starving. When the first faint glow of dawn crept into the cave, Moon-Watcher saw that his father had died in the night. He did not know that the Old One was his father, for such a relation was utterly beyond his understanding, but as he looked at the emaciated body he felt a dim disquiet that was the ancestor of sadness.

The two babies were already whimpering for food, but became silent when Moon-Watcher snarled at them. One of the mothers, defending the infant she could not properly feed, gave him an angry growl in return; he lacked the energy even to cuff her for her presumption.

Now it was light enough to leave. Moon-Watcher picked up the shriveled corpse and dragged it after him as he bent under the low overhang of the cave. Once outside, he threw the body over his shoulder and stood upright—the only animal in all this world able to do so.

Among his kind, Moon-Watcher was almost a giant. He was nearly five feet high, and though badly undernourished weighed over a hundred pounds. His hairy muscular body was halfway between ape and man, but his head was already much nearer to man than ape. The forehead was low, and there were ridges over the eye sockets, yet he unmistakably held in his genes the promise of humanity. As he looked out upon the hostile world of the Pleistocene, there was already something in his gaze beyond the capacity of any ape. In those dark, deep-set eyes was a dawning awareness—the first intimations of an intelligence that could not possibly fulfill itself for ages yet, and might soon be extinguished forever.

There was no sign of danger, so Moon-Watcher began to scramble down the almost vertical slope outside the cave, only slightly hindered by his burden. As if they had been waiting for his signal, the rest of the tribe emerged from their own homes farther down the rock face, and began to hasten toward the muddy waters of the stream for their morning drink.

Moon-Watcher looked across the valley to see if the Others were in sight, but there was no trace of them. Perhaps they had not yet left their caves, or were already foraging farther along the hillside. Since they were nowhere to be seen, Moon-Watcher forgot them; he was incapable of worrying about more than one thing at a time.

First he must get rid of the Old One, but this was a problem that demanded little thought. There had been many deaths this season, one of them in his own cave; he had only to put the corpse where he had left the new baby at the last quarter of the moon, and the hyenas would do the rest.

They were already waiting, where the little valley fanned out into the savanna, almost as if they had known that he was coming. Moon-Watcher left the body under a small bush—all the earlier bones were already gone—and hurried back to rejoin the tribe. He never thought of his father again.

His two mates, the adults from the other caves, and most of the youngsters were foraging among the drought-stunted trees farther up the valley, looking for berries, succulent roots and leaves, and occasional windfalls like small lizards or rodents. Only the babies and the feeblest of the old folk were left in the caves; if there was any surplus food at the end of the day's searching, they might be fed. If not, the hyenas would soon be in luck once more.

But this day was a good one—though as Moon-Watcher had no real remembrance of the past, he could not compare one time with another. He had found a hive of bees in the stump of a dead tree, and so had enjoyed the finest delicacy that his people could ever know; he still licked his fingers from time to time as he led the group homeward in the late afternoon. Of course, he had also collected a fair number of stings, but he had scarcely noticed them. He was now as near to contentment as he was ever likely to be; for though he was still hungry, he was not actually weak with hunger. That was the most to which any man-ape could ever aspire.

His contentment vanished when he reached the stream. The Others were there. They were there every day, but that did not make it any the less annoying.

There were about thirty of them, and they could not have been distinguished from the members of Moon-Watcher's own tribe. As they saw him coming, they began to dance, shake their arms, and shriek on their side of the stream, and his own people replied in kind.

And that was all that happened. Though the man-apes often fought and wrestled one another, their disputes very seldom resulted in serious injuries. Having no claws or fighting canine teeth, and being well protected by hair, they could not inflict much harm on one another. In any event, they had little surplus energy for such unproductive behavior; snarling and threatening was a much more efficient way of asserting their points of view.

The confrontation lasted about five minutes; then the display died out as quickly as it had begun, and everyone drank his fill of the muddy water. Honor had been satisfied; each group had staked its claim to its own territory. This important business having been settled, the tribe moved off along its side of the river. The nearest worthwhile grazing was now more than a mile from the caves, and they had to share it with a herd of large, antelopelike beasts who barely tolerated their presence. They could not be driven away, for they were armed with ferocious daggers on their foreheads—the natural weapons which the man-apes did not possess.

So Moon-Watcher and his companions chewed berries and fruit and leaves and fought off the pangs of hunger—while all around them, competing for the same fodder, was a potential source of more food than they could ever hope to eat. Yet the thousands of tons of succulent meat roaming over the savanna and through the bush was not only beyond their reach; it was beyond their imagination. In the midst of plenty, they were slowly starving to death.

The tribe returned to its cave without incident, in the last light of the day. The injured female who had remained behind cooed with pleasure as Moon-Watcher gave her the berry-covered branch he had brought back, and began to attack it ravenously. There was little enough nourishment here, but it would help her to survive until the wound the leopard had given her had healed, and she could forage for herself again.

Over the valley, a full moon was rising, and a chill wind was blowing down from the distant mountains. It would be very cold tonight—but cold, like hunger, was not a matter for any real concern; it was merely part of the background of life.

Moon-Watcher barely stirred when the shrieks and screams echoed up the slope from one of the lower caves, and he did not need to hear the occasional growl of the leopard to know exactly what was happening. Down there in the darkness old White Hair and his family were fighting and dying, and the thought that he might help in some way never crossed Moon-Watcher's mind. The harsh logic of survival ruled out such fancies, and not a voice was raised in protest from the listening hillside. Every cave was silent, lest it also attract disaster.

The tumult died away, and presently Moon-Watcher could hear the sound of a body being dragged over rocks. That lasted only a few seconds; then the leopard got a good hold on its kill. It made no further noise as it padded silently away, carrying its victim effortlessly in its jaws.

For a day or two, there would be no further danger here, but there might be other enemies abroad, taking advantage of this cold Little Sun that shone only by night. If there was sufficient warning, the smaller predators could sometimes be scared away by shouts and screams. Moon-Watcher crawled out of the cave, clambered onto a large boulder beside the entrance, and squatted there to survey the valley.

Of all the creatures who had yet walked on Earth, the man-apes were the first to look steadfastly at the Moon. And though he could not remember it, when he was very young Moon-Watcher would sometimes reach out and try to touch that ghostly face rising above the hills.

He had never succeeded, and now he was old enough to understand why. For first, of course, he must find a high enough tree to climb.

Sometimes he watched the valley, and sometimes he watched the Moon, but always he listened. Once or twice he dozed off, but he slept with a hair-trigger alertness, and the slightest sound would have disturbed him. At the great age of twenty-five, he was still in full possession of all his faculties; if his luck continued, and he avoided accidents, disease, predators, and starvation, he might survive for as much as another ten years.

The night wore on, cold and clear, without further alarms, and the Moon rose slowly amid equatorial constellations that no human eye would ever see. In the caves, between spells of fitful dozing and fearful waiting, were being born the nightmares of generations yet to be.

And twice there passed slowly across the sky, rising up to the zenith and descending into the east, a dazzling point of light more brilliant than any star.

Late that night, Moon-Watcher suddenly awoke. Tired out by the day's exertions and disasters, he had been sleeping more soundly than usual, yet he was instantly alert at the first faint scrabbling down in the valley.

He sat up in the fetid darkness of the cave, straining his senses out into the night, and fear crept slowly into his soul. Never in his life— already twice as long as most members of his species could expect— had he heard a sound like this. The great cats approached in silence, and the only thing that betrayed them was a rare slide of earth, or the occasional cracking of a twig. Yet this was a continuous crunching noise, that grew steadily louder. It seemed that some enormous beast was moving through the night, making no attempt at concealment, and ignoring all obstacles. Once Moon-Watcher heard the unmistakable sound of a bush being uprooted; the elephants and dinotheria did this often enough, but otherwise they moved as silently as the cats.

And then there came a sound which Moon-Watcher could not possibly have identified, for it had never been heard before in the history of the world. It was the clank of metal upon stone.

Moon-Watcher came face to face with the New Rock when he led the tribe down to the river in the first light of morning. He had almost forgotten the terrors of the night, because nothing had happened after that initial noise, so he did not even associate this strange thing with danger or with fear. There was, after all, nothing in the least alarming about it.

It was a rectangular slab, three times his height but narrow enough to span with his arms, and it was made of some completely transparent material; indeed, it was not easy to see except when the rising sun glinted on its edges. As Moon-Watcher had never encountered ice, or even crystal-clear water, there were no natural objects to which he could compare this apparition. It was certainly rather attractive, and though he was wisely cautious of most new things, he did not hesitate for long before sidling up to it. As nothing happened, he put out his hand, and felt a cold, hard surface.

After several minutes of intense thought, he arrived at a brilliant explanation. It was a rock, of course, and it must have grown during the night. There were many plants that did this — white, pulpy things shaped like pebbles, that seemed to shoot up during the hours of darkness. It was true that they were small and round, whereas this was large and sharp-edged; but greater and later philosophers than Moon-Watcher would be prepared to overlook equally striking exceptions to their theories.

This really superb piece of abstract thinking led Moon-Watcher, after only three or four minutes, to a deduction which he immediately put to the test. The white, round pebble-plants were very tasty (though there were a few that produced violent illness); perhaps this tall one . . . ?

A few licks and attempted nibbles quickly disillusioned him. There was no nourishment here; so like a sensible man-ape, he continued on his way to the river and forgot all about the crystalline monolith, during the daily routine of shrieking at the Others.

The foraging today was very bad, and the tribe had to travel several miles from the caves to find any food at all. During the merciless heat of noon one of the frailer females collapsed, far from any possible shelter. Her companions gathered round her, twittering and meeping sympathetically, but there was nothing that anyone could do. If they had been less exhausted they might have carried her with them, but there was no surplus energy for such acts of kindness. She had to be left behind, to recover or not with her own resources.

They passed the spot on the homeward trek that evening; there was not a bone to be seen.

In the last light of day, looking round anxiously for early hunters, they drank hastily at the stream and started the climb up to their caves. They were still a hundred yards from the New Rock when the sound began.

It was barely audible, yet it stopped them dead, so that they stood paralyzed on the trail with their jaws hanging slackly. A simple, maddeningly repetitive vibration, it pulsed out from the crystal, and hypnotized all who came within its spell. For the first time—and the last, for three million years—the sound of drumming was heard in Africa.

The throbbing grew louder, more insistent. Presently the man-apes began to move forward, like sleepwalkers, toward the source of that compulsive sound. Sometimes they took little dancing steps, as their blood responded to rhythms that their descendants would not create for ages yet. Totally entranced, they gathered round the monolith, forgetting the hardships of the day, the perils of the approaching dusk, and the hunger in their bellies.

The drumming became louder, the night darker. And as the shadows lengthened and the light drained from the sky, the crystal began to glow.

First it lost its transparency, and became suffused with a pale, milky luminescence. Tantalizing, ill-defined phantoms moved across its surface and in its depths. They coalesced into bars of light and shadow, then formed intermeshing, spoked patterns that began slowly to rotate.

Faster and faster spun the wheels of light, and the throbbing of the drums accelerated with them. Now utterly hypnotized, the man-apes could only stare slack-jawed into this astonishing display of pyrotechnics. They had already forgotten the instincts of their forefathers and the lessons of a lifetime; not one of them, ordinarily, would have been so far from his cave, so late in the evening. For the surrounding brush was full of frozen shapes and staring eyes, as the creatures of the night suspended their business to see what would happen next.

Now the spinning wheels of light began to merge, and the spokes fused into luminous bars that slowly receded into the distance, rotating on their axes as they did so. They split into pairs, and the resulting sets of lines started to oscillate across one another, slowly changing their angles of intersection. Fantastic, fleeting geometrical patterns flickered in and out of existence as the glowing grids meshed and unmeshed; and the man-apes watched, mesmerized captives of the shining crystal.

They could never guess that their minds were being probed, their bodies mapped, their reactions studied, their potentials evaluated. At first, the whole tribe remained half crouching in a motionless tableau, as if frozen into stone. Then the man-ape nearest to the slab suddenly came to life.

He did not move from his position, but his body lost its trancelike rigidity and became animated as if it were a puppet controlled by invisible strings. The head turned this way and that; the mouth silently opened and closed; the hands clenched and unclenched. Then he bent down, snapped off a long stalk of grass, and attempted to tie it into a knot with clumsy fingers.

He seemed to be a thing possessed, struggling against some spirit or demon who had taken over control of his body. He was panting for breath, and his eyes were full of terror as he tried to force his fingers to make movements more complex than any that they had ever attempted before.

Despite all his efforts, he succeeded only in breaking the stalk into pieces. As the fragments fell to the ground, the controlling influence left him, and he froze once more into immobility.

Another man-ape came to life, and went through the same routine. This was a younger, more adaptable specimen; it succeeded where the older one had failed. On the planet Earth, the first crude knot had been tied. . . .

Others did stranger and still more pointless things. Some held their hands out at arm's length, and tried to touch their fingertips together—first with both eyes open, then with one closed. Some were made to stare at ruled patterns in the crystal, which became more and more finely divided until the lines had merged into a gray blur. And all heard single pure sounds, of varying pitch, that swiftly sank below the level of hearing.

When Moon-Watcher's turn came, he felt very little fear. His main sensation was a dull resentment, as his muscles twitched and his limbs moved at commands that were not wholly his own.

Without knowing why, he bent down and picked up a small stone. When he straightened up, he saw that there was a new image in the crystal slab.

The grids and the moving, dancing patterns had gone. Instead, there was a series of concentric circles, surrounding a small black disk.

Obeying the silent orders in his brain, he pitched the stone with a clumsy, overarm throw. It missed the target by several feet.

Try again, said the command. He searched around until he had found another pebble. This time it hit the slab with a ringing, bell-like tone. He was still a long way off, but his aim was improving.

At the fourth attempt, he was only inches from the central bull's-eye. A feeling of indescribable pleasure, almost sexual in its intensity, flooded his mind. Then the control relaxed; he felt no impulse to do anything, except to stand and wait.

One by one, every member of the tribe was briefly possessed. Some succeeded, but most failed at the tasks they had been set, and all were appropriately rewarded by spasms of pleasure or of pain.

Now there was only a uniform, featureless glow in the great slab, so that it stood like a block of light superimposed on the surrounding darkness. As if waking from a sleep, the man-apes shook their heads, and presently began to move along the trail to their place of shelter. They did not look back, or wonder at the strange light that was guiding them to their homes — and to a future unknown, as yet, even to the stars.

Moon-Watcher and his companions had no recollection of what they had seen, after the crystal had ceased to cast its hypnotic spell over their minds and to experiment with their bodies. The next day, as they went out to forage, they passed it with scarcely a second thought; it was now part of the disregarded background of their lives. They could not eat it, and it could not eat them; therefore it was not important.

Down at the river, the Others made their usual ineffectual threats. Their leader, a one-eared man-ape of Moon-Watcher's size and age, but in poorer condition, even made a brief foray toward the tribe's territory, screaming loudly and waving his arms in an attempt to scare the opposition and to bolster his own courage. The water of the stream was nowhere more than a foot deep, but the farther One-Ear moved out into it, the more uncertain and unhappy he became. Very soon he slowed to a halt, and then moved back, with exaggerated dignity, to joint his companions.

Otherwise, there was no change in the normal routine. The tribe gathered just enough nourishment to survive for another day, and no one died.

And that night, the crystal slab was still waiting, surrounded by its pulsing aura of light and sound. The program it had contrived, however, was now subtly different.

Some of the man-apes it ignored completely, as if it was concentrating on the most promising subjects. One of them was Moon-Watcher; once again he felt inquisitive tendrils creeping down the unused byways of his brain. And presently, he began to see visions.

They might have been within the crystal block; they might have been wholly inside his mind. In any event, to Moon-Watcher they were completely real. Yet somehow the usual automatic impulse to drive off invaders of his territory had been lulled into quiescence.

He was looking at a peaceful family group, differing in only one respect from the scenes he knew. The male, female, and two infants that had mysteriously appeared before him were gorged and replete, with sleek and glossy pelts—and this was a condition of life that Moon-Watcher had never imagined. Unconsciously, he felt his own protruding ribs; the ribs of *these* creatures were hidden in rolls of fat. From time to time they stirred lazily, as they lolled at ease near the entrance of a cave, apparently at peace with the world. Occasionally, the big male emitted a monumental burp of contentment.

There was no other activity, and after five minutes the scene suddenly faded out. The crystal was no more than a glimmering outline in the darkness; Moon-Watcher shook himself as if awaking from a dream, abruptly realized where he was, and let the tribe back to the caves.

He had no conscious memory of what he had seen; but that night, as he sat brooding at the entrance of his lair, his ears attuned to the noises of the world around him, Moon-Watcher felt the first faint twinges of a new and potent emotion. It was a vague and diffuse sense of envy—of dissatisfaction with his life. He had no idea of its cause, still less of its cure; but discontent had come into his soul, and he had taken one small step toward humanity.

Night after night, the spectacle of those four plump man-apes was repeated, until it had become a source of fascinated exasperation, serving to increase Moon-Watcher's eternal, gnawing hunger. The evidence of his eyes could not have produced this effect; it needed psychological reinforcement. There were gaps in Moon-Watcher's life now that he would never remember, when the very atoms of his simple brain were being twisted into new patterns. If he survived, those patterns would become eternal, for his genes would pass them on to future generations.

It was a slow, tedious business, but the crystal monolith was patient. Neither it, nor its replicas scattered across half the globe, expected to succeed with all the scores of groups involved in the experiment. A hundred failures would not matter, when a single success could change the destiny of the world.

By the time of the next new moon, the tribe had seen one birth and two deaths. One of these had been due to starvation; the other had occurred during the nightly ritual, when a man-ape had suddenly collapsed while attempting to tap two pieces of stone delicately together. At once, the crystal had darkened, and the tribe had been released from the spell. But the fallen man-ape had not moved; and by the morning, of course, the body was gone.

There had been no performance the next night; the crystal was still analyzing its mistake. The tribe streamed past it through the gathering dusk, ignoring its presence completely. The night after, it was ready for them again.

The four plump man-apes were still there, and now they were doing extraordinary things. Moon-Watcher began to tremble uncontrollably; he felt as if his brain would burst, and wanted to turn away his eyes. But that remorseless mental control would not relax its grip; he was compelled to follow the lesson to the end, though all his instincts revolted against it.

Those instincts had served his ancestors well, in the days of warm rains and lush fertility, when food was to be had everywhere for the plucking. Now times had changed, and the inherited wisdom of the past had become folly. The man-apes must adapt, or they must die — like the greater beasts who had gone before them, and whose bones now lay sealed within the limestone hills.

So Moon-Watcher stared at the crystal monolith with unblinking eyes, while his brain lay open to its still uncertain manipulations. Often he felt nausea, but always he felt hunger; and from time to time his hands clenched unconsciously in the patterns that would determine his new way of life.

As the line of warthogs moved snuffling and grunting across the trail, Moon-Watcher came to a sudden halt. Pigs and man-apes had always ignored each other, for there was no conflict of interest between them. Like most animals that did not compete for the same food, they merely kept out of each other's way.

Yet now Moon-Watcher stood looking at them, wavering back and forth uncertainly as he was buffeted by impulses which he could not understand. Then, as if in a dream, he started searching the ground — though for what, he could not have explained even if he had had the power of speech. He would recognize it when he saw it.

It was a heavy, pointed stone about six inches long, and though it did not fit his hand perfectly, it would do. As he swung his hand around, puzzled by its suddenly increased weight, he felt a pleasing sense of power and authority. He started to move toward the nearest pig.

It was a young and foolish animal, even by the undemanding

standards of warthog intelligence. Though it observed him out of the corner of its eye, it did not take him seriously until much too late. Why should it suspect these harmless creatures of any evil intent? It went on rooting up the grass until Moon-Watcher's stone hammer obliterated its dim consciousness. The remainder of the herd continued grazing unalarmed, for the murder had been swift and silent.

All the other man-apes in the group had stopped to watch, and now they crowded round Moon-Watcher and his victim with admiring wonder. Presently one of them picked up the blood-stained weapon, and began to pound the dead pig. Others joined in with any sticks and stones that they could gather, until their target began a messy disintegration.

Then they became bored; some wandered off, while others stood hesitantly around the unrecognizable corpse—the future of a world waiting upon their decision. It was a surprisingly long time before one of the nursing females began to lick the gory stone she was holding in her paws.

And it was longer still before Moon-Watcher, despite all that he had been shown, really understood that he need never be hungry again.

Is the crystal rock like Prometheus in the Greek myth (page 32), or like Twain's Mysterious Stranger (page 39)? Or does it share their qualities?

In desiring to save people from extinction, what "gift" does the crystal rock give to them? Could this "gift," like the gift of fire, bring both good and evil?

Do you think we have god-teachers today? Who or what would they be?

If a society believed that this story was a true account of their origins, what do you imagine they would think of themselves and of their destiny? How would their sense of human identity differ from the sense of identity had by the Crow people who told the myth about Old Man (page 37)?

The first myth in this book takes place "in the beginning." When in time do you think this science fiction story takes place? Write an imaginative beginning story about the origin of the crystal slabs. Who are they? Who made them? What are their laws? What is their destiny? Who is their god-teacher?

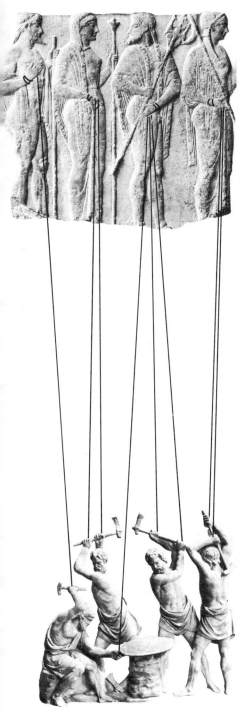

The myths describe gods who were to be worshipped but also feared. These gods created life, but they also seemed to destroy without warning or reason. People, alone in a world full of terrors, felt that all their activities, customs, and discoveries had to be approved by the gods. They were afraid to risk punishment by doing something that was taboo, forbidden by the gods.

Yet it was unthinkable that the remote all-high gods would ever come into direct contact with lowly mortals to teach them what was right or wrong, approved or forbidden. The imagination had to build a bridge to connect the human world with the unapproachable divine world. An intermediary was needed, a link between heaven and earth, a channel for divine sympathy. Myths about the god-teacher provided this divine sanction for the rituals and traditions people lived by. Such myths assured people that all their human activities stemmed from divine instruction.

Fire, one of our most important discoveries, has always been associated with the divine. Some people thought that fire was a god visiting earth, or that it was a property the gods had stored away in wood. Some felt that in making fire people could rekindle the power of the sun-god himself. Fire, then, like the gods, was both feared and desired. It could be both comforting and terrifying. It could help people create the world they wished for, but it could also create a nightmare of pain and destruction.

In myths, one of the god-teacher's gifts to people is almost always fire. It was a gift that reduced the power which fate and chance had over human life. Fire, the gods' secret, gave people godlike power to determine their own destiny. But in Greek mythology, the god who shared the divine secret of fire is also a tragic victim. Prometheus dared to cross the highest god and he was punished. He dared to have sympathy for people and he was tortured and humiliated for it. He tried to help people achieve the

70

world of wish, and he was punished by being chained to the world of nightmare.

The Prometheus figure, then, is the character who takes pity on ignorant people, who teaches them arts and skills. But he is also the god who dares to lead people out of an ignorant, innocent state and give them godlike knowledge and awareness and the responsibilities of civilization.

The major archetype in this unit is the figure of Prometheus, the far-seeing, wise god who saved the human race with the gift of fire. (An archetype, remember, is an imaginative pattern used in telling stories.) The modern writers in this unit are working with the archetype of the god-teacher to present a character very different from the one presented by the ancient storytellers. Twain's Satan is like a demon, a distortion of god-teacher that implies an ironic view of human nature and the universe. Lawrence combines the god-teacher with the tempter-snake who offered Eve the fruit of knowledge and brought down the punishment of God. However, he feels that this "gift" of knowledge lost for us the impulses of instinct, drowning them out with the cold voices of "human" education. Clarke has taken humanity away from the god-teacher and has made him a computer-like machine, performing an experiment on a pathetic race of nearly extinct "man-apes."

We create our personal and social identities through the stories we tell and through the ways in which we use the old archetypes to tell these stories. Thales, the Greek philosopher, said "All things are full of gods." Today we don't describe things in that way. We define fire as combustion and put it in the dictionary instead of in a mythology. Yet we still ask ourselves "What's it all about?" and the way we use archetypal characters like Prometheus tells us something about what our answer may be.

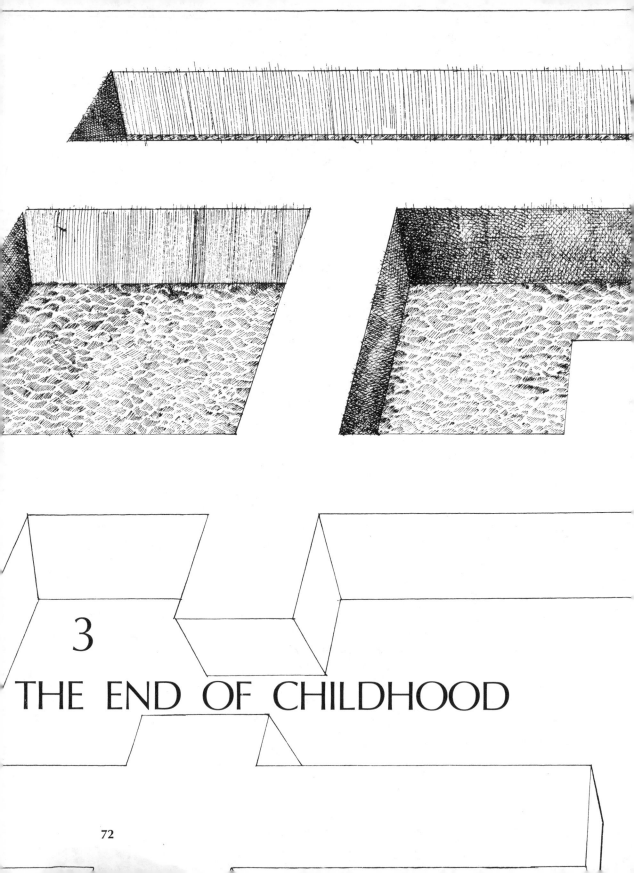

3

THE END OF CHILDHOOD

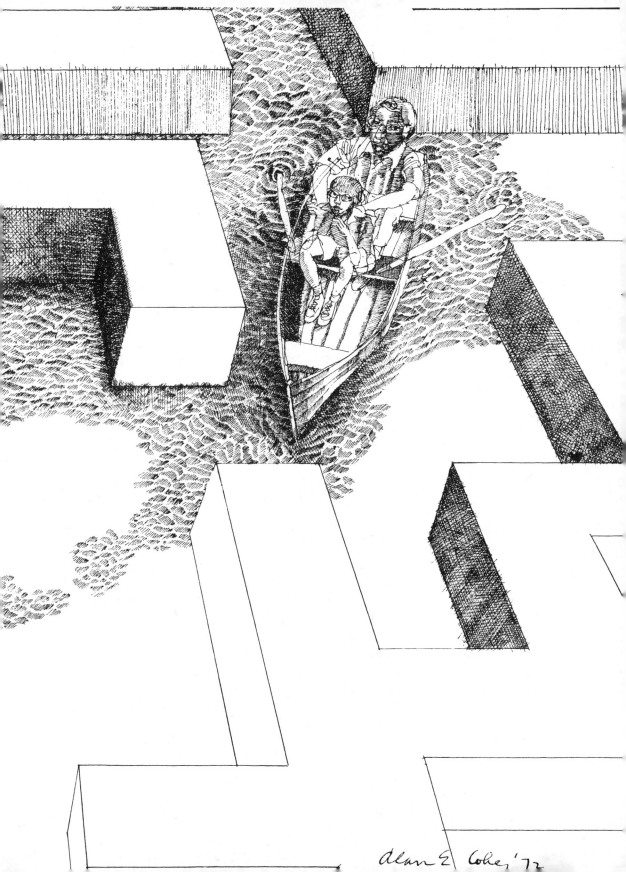

Alan E Cohen '72

Pandora

A Greek myth
Retold by W.T. JEWKES

It was not enough for Zeus that Prometheus be punished; the father of gods knew that man also bore some responsibility for the act of defiance. So the cloud-gatherer sent for Hephaestus, the blacksmith of Olympus.

"Hephaestus," he thundered, "as the price of the fire which men have received from Prometheus, I am resolved to give them an evil thing, something that they will cherish and take delight in, but that will bring upon them unending grief. Go back to your workshop and set to work. Take earth and plaster it with water, infuse into it a human voice, breathe into it the breath of life. Make limbs that move, beautiful limbs like those of a supple young girl, and a face like that of an immortal goddess. Let Athene help you; tell her I want her to teach this woman her household arts, and especially how to do intricate weaving. And then put Aphrodite to work, filling her heart with desire and longing and words of golden endearment. And see that you leave her head empty, ready for my gift."

So, while the lame smith hobbled away to his workshop, Zeus himself set to work on a project of his own. He found a large jar with a lid, and in it he imprisoned all the Spites that might plague mankind—Old Age, Labor, Madness, Sickness, Hunger, Treachery—all the troubles that could come upon man, day or night. This he set to one side, and waited for Hephaestus.

Meanwhile, back in his workshop, the lame smith took a large tub of clay, and began to work and model it in the likeness of a graceful young girl. When he had finished, he called Athene to come and dress her, and the Graces to array her with necklaces and dazzling gold ornaments. The Seasons combed out her beautiful black tresses and put on her head a coronal of spring flowers. Then the four Winds came from the corners of the earth and breathed life into her. Last of all,

Hermes came to view the work. The herald of the gods put a soft, persuasive voice in her and gave her the name Pandora, which signified that the Olympian gods had each given her a gift. And Zeus laughed long and loud when he saw how well his fellow gods had carried out his wishes. It was some satisfaction to think that this bewitching, enticing creature would bring misery on disobedient man.

"Hermes," he roared, "she is superb! She will suit my plan to perfection. Now she is ready for my gift."

And the cloud-gatherer took his gift, fatal curiosity, placed it on his hand, and blew thunderously. Off flew the treacherous gift and entered into Pandora's head. Zeus laughed again and turned to Hermes.

"Now, slayer of Argus, it is fitting that you get the honor of taking her to that slow-witted brother of Prometheus. You mustn't let him know what a deceptive-looking bargain she is. Tell him that I am sending her to him to show my good will. And take this jar along with you as a personal gift from me."

So off Hermes sped, propelled by his winged sandals across the heavens, with Pandora in his arms, and the jar strapped to his side. In no time at all he had met up with Epimetheus, who was sitting with his head in his hands, sadly meditating on his poor brother's fate.

"Epimetheus," said the messenger of the gods as he alighted beside him, "why so gloomy? You look as though you'd lost your best friend."

"I have," replied Epimetheus. "Prometheus is more than a friend to me; he is a brother. I don't know how I'll get along without him. It is just too terrible. To think that Zeus could be so vengeful."

"Well, there is an end to his anger, anyway," declared Hermes. "Look, I have brought this woman for you, at his request. It is his way of trying to ease the pain he has caused you by punishing Prometheus."

Epimetheus had already found that he was unable to take his eyes off the dazzlingly beautiful young woman who stood beside Hermes, smiling in a very friendly and enticing way at him. He wasn't sure he was even hearing Hermes aright.

"Did you say she has been sent for me?" he asked, in a daze. "For me?"

"That's what I said. Zeus wants her to be your wife."

Somewhere in the very back of his mind, among misty memories, there stirred the echo of something Prometheus had once said to his brother: "Remember, Epimetheus, never accept anything that Zeus may send as a gift to you. The father of gods often intends evil to mankind, and there is no telling how he might try to disguise his purpose." But it was only an echo, a far-back faint voice, and poor Epimetheus's head was still swimming from the vision of dark hair and flashing eyes that stood before him.

Surely even Prometheus would have admitted that a woman as beautiful as Pandora could not be part of an evil plot. Now the jar— that was something different. Who knew what it contained, closed tightly by that lid. That indeed might be a trick.

"What is her name?" he finally managed to ask.

"Pandora," replied Hermes.

"Does she want to be my wife?"

"Yes she does. Can't you see how much she likes you?"

"Well," Epimetheus declared, "I never thought I'd have such luck!"

So it was settled. They were married, and Epimetheus took her to live with him. And he found that besides being beautiful, it was very pleasant to have her around, even if she was inclined to chatter a good deal, and needed a firm hand at times when she was minded to be willful.

One day, as she was restlessly wandering around the courtyard, Pandora noticed the beautiful urn standing on a low wall.

"Oh, husband," she cried, stroking its smooth, curved sides, "what a beautiful jar! Where did it come from?

"Oh, that? Hermes brought it when he brought you. It's a personal gift from Zeus."

"But why do you keep it covered?" she went on, trying to remove the tight-fitting lid from the jar.

"Don't take off that lid!" shouted Epimetheus, jumping up and snatching back her hand.

"But why not?" she pouted.

"Because I suspect something is wrong with that jar. Zeus sent it as a personal gift, and my brother Prometheus warned me about the danger of gifts from Zeus. And Prometheus always was smarter than I. So it's best that we do what he asked."

But Pandora was not to be put off by her husband's cautions.

"Sometimes I think he is just plain stupid!" she mused that evening as she looked once again at the intriguing jar. "Or maybe he does it just to spite me. I simply can't go on not knowing what the inside of that jar is like."

She looked around the shadowy courtyard, and seeing that no one was near, she took the jar firmly in one hand, while with the other she worked at the lid. It was stiff, but it began to give. Then, suddenly, it came loose on one edge. At once there issued a fearsome noise, wild groans and shrieks, and a terrible smell like burning sulfur. There followed a dank, rushing wind from the jar, and black shapes sprang forth and began to bite and pinch at the poor girl. In terror she dropped back the lid and began to scream. Almost at once Epimetheus came at a run to see what was the matter, and he too was attacked before he could reach her. Smarting with the pain of the nips and pinches, he grabbed Pandora by the arm, dragged her into the nearest room, and slammed and barred the door.

"Oh, husband," sobbed the terrified young woman, "you came just in time!"

"No," replied Epimetheus, shaking his head. "Too late, Pandora, too late. You've ruined everything now."

But though neither of them knew it at the time, Pandora had not quite ruined everything. When Zeus had been imprisoning all those Spites in the jar, something else had sneaked in unknown to him, and had settled right to the bottom.

And though she had let the Spites loose from the jar, Pandora had also released the one thing that would comfort men through ages of anxiety. This was Hope.

How is the story of Pandora like the biblical story of Adam and Eve?

Why do you think people would make a myth like this one about Pandora?

Prometheus had warned that fire was a dangerous gift. It had two faces, the helper and the devourer. How is the curse of the Spites the "other face" of the gift of fire?

What does this myth say about the price of progress? Do you think it is appropriate to our own age? In what way?

Try writing a myth-like story about the "price of progress." You could set the story in a future time. Tell what happens to people as a result of a "gift" received that helps them make material progress. Who gives the gift? Does the gift have two faces? Is there a "price" placed on the gift? Does a flaw in someone's character cause the other face of the gift to show itself?

It Is Better
To Die Forever

A Blackfoot Indian myth
Retold by CHEWING BLACKBONES

Long, long ago, there were only two persons in the world: Old Man and Old Woman. One time when they were traveling about the earth, Old Woman said to Old Man, "Now let us come to an agreement of some kind. Let us decide how the people shall live when they shall be on the earth."

"Well," replied Old Man, "I am to have the first say in everything."

"I agree with you," said Old Woman. "That is—if I may have the second say."

Then Old Man began his plans. "The women will have the duty of tanning the hides. They will rub animals' brains on the hides to make them soft and scrape them with scraping tools. All this they will do very quickly, for it will not be hard work."

"No," said Old Woman, "I will not agree to this. They must tan hides in the way you say; but it must be very hard work, so that the good workers may be found out."

"Well," said Old Man, "we will let the people have eyes and mouths, straight up and down in their faces."

"No," replied Old Woman, "let us not have them that way. We will have the eyes and mouths in the faces, as you say, but they shall be set crosswise."

"Well," said Old Man, "the people shall have ten fingers on each hand."

"Oh, no!" replied Old Woman. "That will be too many. They will be in the way. There will be four fingers and one thumb on each hand."

So the two went on until they had provided for everything in the lives of the people who were to be.

"What shall we do about life and death?" asked Old Woman. "Should the people live forever, or should they die?"

Old Woman and Old Man had difficulty agreeing about this. Finally Old Man said, "I will tell you what we will do. I will throw a buffalo chip into the water. If it floats, the people will die for four days and then come to life again; if it sinks, they will die forever."

So he threw a buffalo chip into the water, and it floated.

"No," said Old Woman, "we will not decide in that way. I will throw this rock into the water. If it floats, the people will die for four days; if it sinks, they will die forever."

Then Old Woman threw the rock into the water, and it sank to the bottom.

"There," said she. "It is better for the people to die forever. If they did not, they would not feel sorry for each other, and there would be no sympathy in the world."

"Well," said Old Man, "let it be that way."

After a time, Old Woman had a daughter, who soon became sick and died. The mother was very sorry then that they had agreed that people should die forever. "Let us have our say over again," she said.

"No," replied Old Man. "Let us not change what we have agreed upon."

And so people have died ever since.

Do you think this myth was comforting to the people who told it? Why?

The Origin
of Death

A Hottentot myth
Retold by PAUL RADIN

The Moon, it is said, once sent an insect to men, saying, "Go to men and tell them, 'As I die, and dying live; so you shall also die, and dying live.'"

The insect started with the message, but, while on his way, was overtaken by the hare, who asked, "On what errand are you bound?"

The insect answered, "I am sent by the Moon to men, to tell them that as she dies and dying lives, so shall they also die and dying live."

The hare said, "As you are an awkward runner, let me go." With these words he ran off, and when he reached men, he said, "I am sent by the Moon to tell you, 'As I die and dying perish, in the same manner you also shall die and come wholly to an end.'"

The hare then returned to the Moon and told her what he had said to men. The Moon reproached him angrily, saying, "Do you dare tell the people a thing which I have not said?"

With these words the Moon took up a piece of wood and struck the hare on the nose. Since that day the hare's nose has been slit, but men believe what Hare had told them.

Do you think this myth was comforting to the people who told it? Why?

What does this myth suggest to you about the power of words?

Each of the first three myths in this unit offers an explanation of why suffering and death are part of human life. How are the explanations alike? How are they different?

Phaethon

A Greek myth
Retold by EDITH HAMILTON

The palace of the Sun was a radiant place. It shone with gold and gleamed with ivory and sparkled with jewels. Everything without and within flashed and glowed and glittered. It was always high noon there. Shadowy twilight never dimmed the brightness. Darkness and night were unknown. Few among mortals could have long endured that unchanging brilliancy of light, but few had ever found their way thither.

Nevertheless, one day a youth, mortal on his mother's side, dared to approach. Often he had to pause and clear his dazzled eyes, but the errand which had brought him was so urgent that his purpose held fast and he pressed on, up to the palace, through the burnished doors, and into the throne room where surrounded by a blinding, blazing splendor the Sun-god sat. There the lad was forced to halt. He could bear no more.

Nothing escapes the eyes of the Sun. He saw the boy instantly and he looked at him very kindly. "What brought you here?" he asked. "I have come," the other answered boldly, "to find out if you are my father or not. My mother said you were, but the boys at school laugh when I tell them I am your son. They will not believe me. I told my mother and she said I had better go and ask you." Smiling, the Sun took off his crown of burning light so that the lad could look at him without distress. "Come here, Phaethon," he said. "You are my son. Clymene told you the truth. I expect you will not doubt my word too? But I will give you a proof. Ask anything you want of me and you shall have it. I call the Styx to be witness to my promise, the river of the oath of the gods."

No doubt Phaethon had often watched the Sun riding through the heavens and had told himself with a feeling, half awe, half excitement,

"It is my father up there." And then he would wonder what it would be like to be in that chariot, guiding the steeds along that dizzy course, giving light to the world. Now at his father's words this wild dream had become possible. Instantly he cried, "I choose to take your place, Father. That is the only thing I want. Just for a day, a single day, let me have your car to drive."

The Sun realized his own folly. Why had he taken that fatal oath and bound himself to give in to anything that happened to enter a boy's rash young head? "Dear lad," he said, "this is the only thing I would have refused you. I know I cannot refuse. I have sworn by the Styx. I must yield if you persist. But I do not believe you will. Listen while I tell you what this is you want. You are Clymene's son as well as mine. You are mortal and no mortal could drive my chariot. Indeed, no god except myself can do that. The ruler of the gods cannot. Consider the road. It rises up from the sea so steeply that the horses can hardly climb it, fresh though they are in the early morning. In mid-heaven it is so high that even I do not like to look down. Worst of all is the descent, so precipitous that the Sea-gods waiting to receive me wonder how I can avoid falling headlong. To guide the horses, too, is a perpetual struggle. Their fiery spirits grow hotter as they climb and they scarcely suffer my control. What would they do with you?

"Are you fancying that there are all sorts of wonders up there, cities of the gods full of beautiful things? Nothing of the kind. You will have to pass beasts, fierce beasts of prey, and they are all that you will see. The Bull, the Lion, the Scorpion, the great Crab, each will try to harm you. Be persuaded. Look around you. See all the goods the rich world holds. Choose from them your heart's desire and it shall be yours. If what you want is to be proved my son, my fears for you are proof enough that I am your father."

But none of all this wise talk meant anything to the boy. A glorious prospect opened before him. He saw himself proudly standing in that wondrous car, his hands triumphantly guiding those steeds which Jove himself could not master. He did not give a thought to the dangers his father detailed. He felt not a quiver of fear, not a doubt of his own powers. At last the Sun gave up trying to dissuade him. It was hopeless, as he saw. Besides, there was no time. The moment for starting was at hand. Already the gates of the east glowed purple, and Dawn had opened her courts full of rosy light. The stars were leaving the sky; even the lingering morning star was dim.

There was need for haste, but all was ready. The seasons, the gatekeepers of Olympus, stood waiting to fling the doors wide. The horses had been bridled and yoked to the car. Proudly and joyously Phaethon mounted it and they were off. He had made his choice. Whatever came of it he could not change now. Not that he wanted to in that first exhilarating rush through the air, so swift that the East Wind was outstripped and left far behind. The horses' flying feet went through the low-banked clouds near the ocean as through a thin sea mist and then up and up in the clear air, climbing the height of heaven. For a few ecstatic moments Phaethon felt himself the Lord of the Sky. But suddenly there was a change. The chariot was swinging wildly to and fro; the pace was faster; he had lost control. Not he, but the horses were directing the course. That light weight in the car, those feeble hands clutching the reins, had told them their own driver was not there. They were the masters then. No one else could command them. They left the road and rushed where they chose, up, down, to the right, to the left. They nearly wrecked the chariot against the Scorpion; they brought up short and almost ran into the Crab. By this time the poor charioteer was half fainting with terror, and he let the reins fall.

That was the signal for still more mad and reckless running. The horses soared up to the very top of the sky and then, plunging head-long down, they set the world on fire. The highest mountains were the first to burn, Ida and Helicon, where the Muses dwell, Parnassus, and heaven-piercing Olympus. Down their slopes the flames ran to the low-lying valleys and the dark forest lands, until all things everywhere were ablaze. The springs turned into steam; the rivers shrank. It is said that it was then the Nile fled and hid his head, which still is hidden.

In the car Phaethon, hardly keeping his place there, was wrapped in thick smoke and heat as if from a fiery furnace. He wanted nothing except to have this torment and terror ended. He would have wel-comed death. Mother Earth, too, could bear no more. She uttered a great cry which reached up to the gods. Looking down from Olympus they saw that they must act quickly if the world was to be saved. Jove seized his thunderbolt and hurled it at the rash, repentant driver. It struck him dead, shattered the chariot, and made the maddened horses rush down into the sea.

Phaethon all on fire fell from the car through the air to the earth. The mysterious river Eridanus, which no mortal eyes have ever seen, received him and put out the flames and cooled the body. The naiads, in pity for him, so bold and so young to die, buried him and carved upon the tomb:

Here Phaethon lies who drove the Sun-god's car.
Greatly he failed, but he had greatly dared.

His sisters, the Heliades, the daughters of Helios, the Sun, came to his grave to mourn for him. There they were turned into poplar trees, on the bank of the Eridanus,

Where sorrowing they weep into the stream forever.
And each tear as it falls shines in the water
A glistening drop of amber.

Many myths are narratives that reflect a society's important rituals. On one level, the story of Phaethon may reflect a sacrifice ritual in ancient Greece. One day a year, at sunset, a king would pretend to die. A young boy, chosen as a temporary king or *interrex*, would marry the queen, reign for one day, and then be killed, often dragged behind a sun-chariot drawn by wild horses. How is the Phaethon story related to the ritual of the *interrex*?

On another level, how do you think Phaethon's quest may be a search to find out who he is?

What does he discover?

Phaethon

Apollo through the heavens rode
   In glinting gold attire;
His car was bright with chrysolite,
   His horses snorted fire.
He held them to their frantic course
   Across the blazing sky.
His darling son was Phaethon,
   Who begged to have a try.

"The chargers are ambrosia-fed
   They barely brook control;
On high beware the Crab, the Bear,
   The Serpent round the Pole;
Against the Archer and the Bull
   Thy form is all unsteeled!"
But Phaethon could lay it on;
   Apollo had to yield.

Out of the purple doors of dawn
   Phaethon drove the horses;
They felt his hand could not command.
   They left their wonted courses.
And from the chariot Phaethon
   Plunged like a falling star—
And so, my boy, no, no, my boy,
   You cannot take the car.

MORRIS BISHOP

This excerpt from a novel is told from the point of view of a six-year-old boy, whose father has just died in a car accident.

A Death in the Family

From the novel by
JAMES AGEE

When breakfast was over he wandered listlessly into the sitting room and looked all around, but he did not see any place where he would like to sit down. He felt deeply idle and empty and at the same time gravely exhilarated, as if this were the morning of his birthday, except that this day seemed even more particularly his own day. There was nothing in the way it looked which was not ordinary, but it was filled with a noiseless and invisible kind of energy. He could see his mother's face while she told them about it and hear her voice, over and over, and silently, over and over, while he looked around the sitting room and through the window into the street, words repeated themselves, He's dead. He died last night while I was asleep and now it was already morning. He has already been dead since way last night and I didn't even know until I woke up. He has been dead all night while I was asleep and now it is morning and I am awake but he is still dead and he will stay right on being dead all afternoon and all night and all tomorrow while I am asleep again and wake up again and go to sleep again and he can't come back home again ever any more but I will see him once more before he is taken away. Dead now. He died last night while I was asleep and now it is already morning.

A boy went by with his books in a strap.

Two girls went by with their satchels.

He went to the hat rack and took his satchel and his hat and started back down the hall to the kitchen to get his lunch; then he remembered his new cap. But it was upstairs. It would be in Mama's and Daddy's room, he could remember when she took it off his head. He did not want to go in for it where she was lying down and now he realized, too, that he did not want to wear it. He would like to tell her good-by before he went to school, but he did not want to go in and see her lying down and looking like that. He kept on toward the kitchen. He would tell Aunt Hannah good-by instead.

She was at the sink washing dishes and Catherine sat on a kitchen chair watching her. He looked all around but he could not see any lunch. I guess she doesn't know about lunch, he reflected. She did not seem to realize that he was there so, after a moment, he said, "Good-by."

"What-*is*-it?" she said and turned her lowered head, peering. "Why, Rufus!" she exclaimed, in such a tone that he wondered what he had done. "You're not going to *school*," she said, and now he realized that she was not mad at him.

"I can stay out of school?"

"Of course you can. You must. Today and tomorrow as well and— for a sufficient time. A few days. Now put up your things, and stay right in this house, child."

He looked at her and said to himself: but then they can't see me; but he knew there was no use begging her; already she was busy with the dishes again.

He went back along the hall toward the hat rack. In the first moment he had been only surprised and exhilarated not to have to go to school, and something of this sense of privilege remained, but almost immediately he was also disappointed. He could now see vividly how they would all look up when he came into the schoolroom and how the teacher would say something nice about his father and about him, and he knew that on this day everybody would treat him well, and even look up to him, for something had happened to him today which had not happened to any other boy in school, any other boy in town. They might even give him part of their lunches.

He felt even more profoundly empty and idle than before.

He laid down his satchel on the seat of the hat rack, but he kept his hat on. She'll spank me, he thought. Even worse, he could foresee her particular, crackling kind of anger. I won't let her find out, he told himself. Taking great care to be silent, he let himself out the front door.

The air was cool and gray and here and there along the street, shapeless and watery sunlight strayed and vanished. Now that he was in this outdoor air he felt even more listless and powerful; he was alone, and the silent, invisible energy was everywhere. He stood on the porch and supposed that everyone he saw passing knew of an event so famous. A man was walking quickly up the street and as Rufus watched him, and waited for the man to meet his eyes, he felt a great quiet lifting within him of pride and of shyness, and he felt his face break into a smile, and then an uncontrollable grin, which he knew he must try to make sober again; but the man walked past without looking at him, and so did the next man who walked past in the other direction. Two schoolboys passed whose faces he knew, so he knew that they must know his, but they did not even seem to see him. Arthur and Alvin Tripp came down their front steps and along the far sidewalk and now he was sure, and came down his own front steps and halfway out to the sidewalk, but then he stopped, for now, although both of them looked across into his eyes, and he into theirs, they did not cross the street to him or even say hello, but kept on their way, still looking into his eyes with a kind of shy curiosity, even when their heads were turned almost backward on their necks, and he turned his own head slowly, watching them go by, but when he saw that they were not going to speak he took care not to speak either.

What's the matter with them, he wondered, and still watched them; and even now, far down the street, Arthur kept turning his head, and for several steps Alvin walked backward.

What are they mad about?

Now they no longer looked around, and now he watched them vanish under the hill.

Maybe they don't know, he thought. Maybe the others don't know, either.

He came out to the sidewalk.

Maybe everybody knew. Or maybe he knew something of great importance which nobody else knew. The alternatives were not at all distinct in his mind; he was puzzled, but no less proud and expectant than before. My daddy's dead, he said to himself slowly, and then, shyly, he said it aloud: "My daddy's dead." Nobody in sight seemed to have heard; he had said it to nobody in particular. "My daddy's dead," he said again, chiefly for his own benefit. It sounded powerful, solid, and entirely creditable, and he knew that if need be he would tell people. He watched a large, slow man come toward him and waited for the man to look at him and acknowledge the fact first, but when the man was just ahead of him, and still did not appear even to have seen him, he told him, "My daddy's dead," but the man did not seem to hear him, he just swung on by. He took care to tell the next man sooner and the man's face looked almost as if he were dodging a blow but he went on by, looking back a few steps later with a worried face; and after a few steps more he turned and came slowly back.

"What was that you said, sonny?" he asked; he was frowning slightly.

"My daddy's dead," Rufus said, expectantly.

"You mean that sure enough?" the man asked.

"He died last night when I was asleep and now he can't come home ever any more."

The man looked at him as if something hurt him.

"Where do you live, sonny?"

"Right here"; he showed with his eyes.

"Do your folks know you out here wandern round?"

He felt his stomach go empty. He looked frankly into his eyes and nodded quickly.

The man just looked at him and Rufus realized: He doesn't believe me. How do they always know?

"You better just go on back in the house, son," he said. "They won't like you being out here on the street." He kept looking at him, hard.

Rufus looked into his eyes with reproach and apprehension, and turned in at his walk. The man still stood there. Rufus went on slowly up his steps, and looked around. The man was on his way again but at the moment Rufus looked around, he did too, and now he stopped again.

He shook his head and said, in a friendly voice which made Rufus feel ashamed, "How would your daddy like it, you out here telling strangers how he's dead?"

Rufus opened the door, taking care not to make a sound, and stepped in and silently closed it, and hurried into the sitting room. Through the curtains he watched the man. He still stood there, lighting a cigarette, but now he started walking again. He looked back once and Rufus felt, with a quailing of shame and fear, he sees me; but the man immediately looked away again and Rufus watched him until he was out of sight.

How would your daddy like it?

He thought of the way they teased him and did things to him, and how mad his father got when he just came home. He thought how different it would be today if he only didn't have to stay home from school.

He let himself out again and stole back between the houses to the alley, and walked along the alley, listening to the cinders cracking under each step, until he came near the sidewalk. He was not in front of his own home now, or even on Highland Avenue; he was coming into the side street down from his home, and he felt that here nobody would identify him with his home and send him back to it. What he could see from the mouth of the alley was much less familiar to him, and he took the last few steps which brought him out onto the sidewalk with deliberation and shyness. He was doing something he had been told not to do.

He looked up the street and he could see the corner he knew so well, where he always met the others so unhappily, and, farther away, the corner around which his father always disappeared on the way to work, and first appeared on his way home from work. He felt it would be good luck that he would not be meeting them at that corner. Slowly, uneasily, he turned his head, and looked down the side street in the other direction; and there they were; three together, and two along the far side of the street, and one alone, farther off, and another alone, farther off, and, without importance to him, some girls here and there, as well. He knew the faces of all of these boys well, though he was not sure of any of their names. The moment he saw them all he was sure they saw him, and sure that they knew. He stood still and waited for them, looking from one to another of them, into their eyes, and step by step at their several distances, each of them at all times looking into his eyes and knowing, they came silently nearer. Waiting, in silence, during those many seconds before the first of them came really near him, he felt that it was so long to wait, and be watched so closely and silently, and to watch back, that he wanted to go back into the alley and not be seen by them or by anybody else, and yet at the same time he knew that they were all approaching him with the realization that something had happened to him that had not happened to any other boy in town, and that now at last they were bound to think well of him; and the nearer they came but were yet at a distance, the more the gray, sober air was charged with the great energy and with a sense of glory and of danger, and the deeper and more exciting the silence became, and the more tall, proud, shy, and exposed he felt; so that as they came still nearer he once again felt his face break into a wide smile, with which he had nothing to do, and, feeling that there was something deeply wrong in such a smile, tried his best to quieten his face and told them, shyly and proudly, "My daddy's dead."

Of the first three who came up, two merely looked at him and the third said, "Huh! Betcha he ain't"; and Rufus, astounded that they did not know and that they should disbelieve him, said, "Why he is so!"

"Where's your satchel at?" said the boy who had spoken. "You're just making up a lie so you can lay out of school."

"I am not laying out," Rufus replied. "I was going to school and my Aunt Hannah told me I didn't have to go to school today or tomorrow or not till—not for a few days. She said I mustn't. So I am not laying out. I'm just staying out."

And another of the boys said, "That's right. If his daddy is dead he don't have to go back to school till after the funerl."

While Rufus had been speaking two other boys had crossed over to join them and now one of them said, "He don't have to. He can lay out cause his daddy got killed," and Rufus looked at the boy gratefully and the boy looked back at him, it seemed to Rufus, with deference.

But the first boy who had spoken said, resentfully, "How do *you* know?"

And the second boy, while his companion nodded, said, "Cause my daddy seen it in the paper. Can't your daddy read the paper?"

The paper, Rufus thought; it's even in the paper! And he looked wisely at the first boy. And the first boy, interested enough to ignore the remark against his father, said, "Well how did he get killed, then?" and Rufus, realizing with respect that it was even more creditable to get killed than just to die, took a deep breath and said, "Why, he was . . ."; but the boy whose father had seen it in the paper was already talking, so he listened, instead, feeling as if all this were being spoken for him, and on his behalf, and in his praise, and feeling it all the more as he looked from one silent boy to the next and saw that their eyes were constantly on him. And Rufus listened, too, with as much interest as they did, while the boy said with relish, "In his ole Tin Lizzie, that's how. He was driving along in his ole Tin Lizzie and it hit a rock and throwed him out in the ditch and run up a eight-foot bank and then fell back and turned over and over and landed right on top of him *whomph* and mashed every bone in his body, that's all. And somebody come and found him and he was dead already time they got there, that's how."

"He was instantly killed," Rufus began, and expected to go ahead and correct some of the details of the account, but nobody seemed to hear him, for two other boys had come up and just as he began to speak one of them said, "Your daddy got his name in the paper didn he, and you too," and he saw that now all the boys looked at him with new respect.

"He's dead," he told them. "He got killed."

"That's what my daddy says," one of them said, and the other said, "What you get for driving a auto when you're drunk, that's what my dad says," and the two of them looked gravely at the other boys, nodding, and at Rufus.

"What's drunk?" Rufus asked.

"What's drunk?" one of the boys mocked incredulously: "Drunk is fulla good ole whisky"; and he began to stagger about in circles with his knees weak and his head lolling. "At's what drunk is."

"Then he wasn't," Rufus said.

"How do *you* know?"

"He wasn't drunk because that wasn't how he died. The wheel hit a rock and the other wheel, the one you steer with, just hit him on the chin, but it hit him so hard it killed him. He was instantly killed."

"What's instantly killed?' one of them asked.

"What do *you* care?" another said.

"Right off like that," an older boy explained, snapping his fingers. Another boy joined the group. Thinking of what instantly meant, and how his father's name was in the paper and his own too, and how he had got killed, not just died, he was not listening to them very clearly for a few moments, and then, all of a sudden, he began to realize that he was the center of everything and that they all knew it and that they waited to hear him tell the true account of it.

"I don't know nothing about no chin," the boy whose father saw it in the paper was saying. "Way I heard it he was a-drivin along in his ole Tin Lizzie and he hit a rock and ole Tin Lizzie run off the road and throwed him out and run up a eight-foot bank and turned over and over and fell back down on top of him *whomp.*"

"How do *you* know?" an older boy was saying. "*You* wasn't there. Anybody here knows it's *him.*" And he pointed at Rufus and Rufus was startled from his revery.

"Why?" asked the boy who had just come up.

"Cause it's his daddy," one of them explained.

"It's my daddy," Rufus said.

"What happened?" asked still another boy, at the fringe of the group.

"My daddy got killed," Rufus said.

"His daddy got killed," several of the others explained.

"My daddy says he bets he was drunk."

"Good ole whisky!"

"Shut up, what's *your* daddy know about it."

"Was he drunk?"

"No," Rufus said.

"No," two others said.

"Let *him* tell it."

"Yeah, *you* tell it."

"Anybody here ought to know, it's him."

"Come on and tell us."

"Good ole whisky."

"Shut your mouth."

"Well come on and tell us, then."

They became silent and all of them looked at him. Rufus looked back into their eyes in the sudden deep stillness. A man walked by, stepping into the gutter to skirt them.

Rufus said, quietly, "He was coming home from Grampa's last night, Grampa Follet. He's very sick and Daddy had to go up way in the middle of the night to see him, and he was hurrying as fast as he could to get back home because he was so late. And there was a cotter pin worked loose."

"What's a cotter pin?"

"Shut up."

"A cotter pin is what holds things together underneath, that you steer with. It worked loose and fell out so that when one of the front wheels hit a loose rock it wrenched the wheel and he couldn't steer and the auto ran down off the road with an awful bump and they saw where the wheel you steer with hit him right on the chin and he was instantly killed. He was thrown all the way out of the auto and it ran up an eight-foot emb—embackment and then it rolled back down and it was upside down beside him when they found him. There was not a mark on his body. Only a little tiny blue mark right on the end of the chin and another on his lip."

In the silence he could see the auto upside down with its wheels in the air and his father lying beside it with the little blue marks on his chin and on his lip.

"Heck," one of them said, "how can *that* kill anybody?"

He felt a kind of sullen stirring among the others, and he felt that he was not believed, or that they did not think very well of his father for being killed so easily.

"It was just exactly the way it just happened to hit him, Uncle Andrew says. He says it was just a chance in a million. It gave him a concush, con, concush—it did something to his brain that killed him."

"Just a chance in a million," one of the older boys said gravely, and another gravely nodded.

"A million trillion," another said.

"Knocked him crazy as a loon," another cried, and with a waggling forefinger he made a rapid blubbery noise against his loose lower lip.

"Shut yer mouth," an older boy said coldly. "Ain't you got no sense at all?"

"Way I heard it, ole Tin Lizzie just rolled right back on top of him *whomp*."

This account of it was false, Rufus was sure, but it seemed to him more exciting than his own, and more creditable to his father and to him, and nobody could question, scornfully, whether that could kill, as they could of just a blow on the chin; so he didn't try to contradict. He felt that he was lying, and in some way being disloyal as well, but he said only, "He was instantly killed. He didn't have to feel any pain."

"Never even knowed what hit him," a boy said quietly. "That's what my dad says."

"No," Rufus said. It had not occurred to him that way. "I guess he didn't." Never even knowed what hit him. Knew.

"Reckon that ole Tin Lizzie is done for now. Huh?"

He wondered if there was some meanness behind calling it an old Tin Lizzie. "I guess so," he said.

"Good ole waggin, but she done broke down."

His father sang that.

"No more joy rides in that ole Tin Lizzie, huh Rufus?"

"I guess not," Rufus replied shyly.

He began to realize that for some moments now a bell, the school bell, had been weltering on the dark gray air; he realized it because at this moment the last of its reverberations were fading.

"Last bell," one of the boys said in sudden alarm.

"Come on, we're goana git hell," another said; and within another second Rufus was watching them all run dwindling away up the street, and around the corner into Highland Avenue, as fast as they could go, and all round him the morning was empty and still. He stood still and watched the corner for almost half a minute after the fattest of them, and then the smallest, had disappeared; then he walked slowly back along the alley, hearing once more the sober crumbling of the cinders under each step, and up through the narrow side yard between the houses, and up the steps of the front porch.

In the paper! He looked for it beside the door, but it was not there. He listened carefully, but he could not hear anything. He let himself quietly through the front door, at the moment his Aunt Hannah came from the sitting room into the front hall. She wore a cloth over her hair and in her hands she was carrying the smoking stand. She did not see him at first and he saw how fierce and lonely her face looked. He tried to make himself small but just then she wheeled on him, her lenses flashing, and exclaimed, "Rufus Follet, where on earth have you been!" His stomach quailed, for her voice was so angry it was as if it were crackling with sparks.

"Outdoors."

"Where, outdoors! I've been looking for you all over the place."

"Just out. Back in the alley."

"Didn't you hear me calling you?"

He shook his head.

"I shouted until my voice was hoarse."

He kept shaking his head. "Honest," he said.

"Now listen to me carefully. You mustn't go outdoors today. Stay right here inside this house, do you understand?"

He nodded. He felt suddenly that he had done an awful thing.

"I know it's hard to," she said more gently, "but you've got to. Help Catherine with her coloring. Read a book. You promise?"

"Yes'm."

"And don't do anything to disturb your mother."

"No'm."

She went on down the hall and he watched her. What was she doing with the pipes and the ash trays, he wondered. He considered sneaking behind her, for he knew that she could not see at all well, yet he would be sure to get caught, for her hearing was very sharp. All the same, he sneaked along to the back of the hall and watched her empty the ashes into the garbage pail and rap out the pipes against its rim. Then she stood with the pipes in her hand, looking around uncertainly; finally she put the pipes and the ash tray on the cupboard shelf, and set the smoking stand in the corner of the kitchen behind the stove. He went back along the hall on tiptoe and into the sitting room.

Catherine sat in the little chair by the side window with a picture book on her knees. Her crayons were all over the window sill and she was working intently with an orange crayon. She looked up when he came in and looked down again and kept on working.

He did not want to help her, he wanted to be by himself and see if he could find the paper with the names in it, but he felt that he ought to try to be good, for by now he felt a dark uneasiness about something, he was not quite sure what, that he had done. He walked over to her. "I'll help you," he said.

"No," Catherine said, without even looking up. It was the Mother Goose book and with her orange crayon she was scrawling all over the cow which jumped over the moon, inside and outside the lines of the cow.

"Aunt Hannah says to," he said, disgusted to see what she was doing to the cow.

"No," Catherine said, and again she did not look up or stop scrawling for a second.

"That ain't no color for a cow," he said. "Whoever saw an orange cow?" She made no reply, but he could see that her face was getting red. "Besides, you're not even coloring inside the cow," he said. "Just look at that. You're just running that crayon around all over the place and it isn't even the right color." She bore down even harder and harder with the crayon and pushed it in a wider and wider tangle of lines and all of a sudden it snapped and the long part rolled to the floor. "See now, you busted it," Rufus said.

"Leave me alone!" She tried to draw with the stub of the crayon but it was too short, and the paper got in the way. She looked along the window sill and selected a brown crayon.

"What you goana do with that brown one?" Rufus said. "You already got all that orange all over everything, what you goana do with that brown one?" Catherine took the brown crayon and made a brutal tangle of dark lines all over the orange lines. "Now all you did is just spoil it," Rufus said. "You don't know how to draw!"

"*Quit* it!" Catherine yelled, and all of a sudden she was crying. He heard his Aunt Hannah's sharp voice from the kitchen: "Rufus?"

He was furious with Catherine. "Crybaby," he whispered with cold hatred: "Tattletale!"

And there was Aunt Hannah at the door, just as mad as a hornet. "Now, what's the matter? What have you done to her!" She walked straight at him.

It wasn't fair. How did she know he was doing anything? With a feeling of real righteousness he talked back: "I didn't do one single thing to her. She was just messing everything up on her picture and I tried to help her like you told me to and all of a sudden she started to cry."

"What did he do, Catherine?"

"He wouldn't let me alone."

"Why good night, I never even touched you and you're a liar if you say I did!"

All of a sudden he felt himself gripped by the shoulders and shaken and he turned his rattling head from his sister to look into his Aunt Hannah's freezing glare.

"Now you just listen to me," she said. "Are you listening?" she sputtered. *"Are you listening?"* she said still more intensely.

"Yes," he managed to get out, though the word was all shaken up.

"I don't want to spank you on this day of all days, but if I hear you say one more rough thing like that to your sister I'll give you a spanking you'll remember to your dying day, do you hear me? *Do you hear me?"*

"Yes."

"And if you tease her or make her cry just one more time I'll—I'll turn the whole matter over to your Uncle Andrew and we'll see what *he'll* do about it. Do you want me to call him? He's upstairs this minute! Shall I call him?" She stopped shaking him and looked at him. "Shall I?" He shook his head; he was terrified. "All right, but this is my last warning. Do you understand?"

"Yes'm."

"Now if you can't play with Catherine in peace like a decent boy just—stay by yourself. Look at some pictures. Read a book. But you be quiet. And good. Do you hear me?"

"Yes'm."

"Very well." She stood up and her joints snapped. "Come with me, Catherine," she said. "Let's bring your crayons." And she helped Catherine gather up the crayons and the stubs from the window sill and from the carpet. Catherine's face was still red but she was not crying any more. As she passed Rufus she gave him a glance filled with satisfaction, and he answered it with a glance of helpless malevolence.

He listened toward upstairs. If his Uncle Andrew had overheard this, there would really be trouble. But there was no evidence that he had. Rufus felt weak in the knees and in the stomach. He went over to the chair beside the fireplace and sat down.

It was mean to pester Catherine like that but he hadn't wanted to do anything for her anyway. And why did she have to holler like that and bring Aunt Hannah running? He remembered the way her face got red and he knew that he had really been mean to her and he was sorry. But what did she holler for, like a regular crybaby? He would be very careful today, but sooner or later he sure would get back on her. Darn crybaby. Tattletale.

The others really did pay him some attention, though. Anybody here ought to know, it's him. His daddy got killed. Yeah *you* tell it. Come on and tell us. Just a chance in a million. A million trillion. Never even knowed, knew, what hit him. Shut yer mouth. Ain't you got no sense at all?

Instantly killed.

Concussion, that was it. Concussion of the brain.

Knocked him crazy as a loon, bibblibblebble.

Shut yer mouth.

But there was something that made him feel wrong.

Ole Tin Lizzie.

What you get for driving a auto when you're drunk, that's what my dad says.

Good ole whisky.

Something he did.

Ole Tin Lizzie just rolled back down on top of him *whomp.*

Didn't either.

He didn't say it didn't. Not clear enough.

Heck, how can that kill anybody?

Did, though. Just a chance in a million. Million trillion.

Instantly killed.

Worse than that, he did.

What.

How would your daddy like it?

He would like me to be with them without them teasing; looking up to me.

How would your daddy like it?

Like what?

Going out in the street like that when he is dead.

Out in the street like what?

Showing off to people because he is dead.

He wants me to get along with them.

So I tell them he is dead and they look up to me, they don't tease me.

Showing off because he's dead, that's all you can show off about. Any other thing they'd tease me and I wouldn't fight back.

How would your daddy like it?

But he likes me to get along with them. That's why I — went out — showed off.

He felt so uneasy, deep inside his stomach, that he could not think about it any more. He wished he hadn't done it. He wished he could go back and not do anything of the kind. He wished his father could know about it and tell him that yes he was bad but it was all right he didn't mean to be bad. He was glad his father didn't know because if his father knew he would think even worse of him than ever. But if his father's soul was around, always, watching over them, then he knew. And that was worst of anything because there was no way to hide from a soul, and no way to talk to it, either. He just knows, and it couldn't say anything to him, and he couldn't say anything to it. It couldn't whip him either, but it could sit and look at him and be ashamed of him.

"I didn't mean it," he said aloud. "I didn't mean to do bad."

I wanted to show you my cap, he added, silently.

He looked at his father's morsechair.

Not a mark on his body.

He still looked at the chair. With a sense of deep stealth and secrecy he finally went over and stood beside it. After a few moments, and after listening most intently, to be sure that nobody was near, he smelled of the chair, its deeply hollowed seat, the arms, the back. There was only a cold smell of tobacco and, high along the back, a faint smell of hair. He thought of the ash tray on its weighted strap on the arm; it was empty. He ran his finger inside it; there was only a dim smudge of ash. There was nothing like enough to keep in his pocket or wrap up in a paper. He looked at his finger for a moment and licked it; his tongue tasted of darkness.

In the Phaethon myth, the Sun in a sense "dies" to allow his son a chance to prove himself. How is Rufus's father like Phaethon's father, in this and in other ways?

How is Rufus like Phaethon? What does he discover?

Atalanta's Race

A Greek myth
Retold by REX WARNER

The huntress Atalanta, whom Meleager, before he died, had loved, could run faster even than the fastest runners among men. Nor was her beauty inferior to her swiftness of foot; both were beyond praise.

When Atalanta asked the oracle about whom she ought to marry, the god replied: "Do not take a husband, Atalanta. If you do, it will bring disaster on you. Yet you will not escape, and though you will continue to live, you will not be yourself."

Terrified by these words, Atalanta lived in the dark woods unmarried. There were many men who wished to marry her, but to them, in their eagerness, she said: "No one can have me for his wife unless first he beats me in a race. If you will, you may run with me. If any of you wins, he shall have me as a prize. But those who are defeated will have death for their reward. These are the conditions for the race."

Cruel indeed she was, but her beauty had such power that numbers of young men were impatient to race with her on these terms.

There was a young man called Hippomenes, who had come to watch the contest. At first he had said to himself: "What man in his senses would run such a risk to get a wife?" and he had condemned the young men for being too madly in love. But when he saw her face and her body all stripped for the race—a face and a body like Venus's own—he was lost in astonishment and, stretching out his hands, he said: "I had no right to blame the young men. I did not know what the prize was for which they were running."

As he spoke his own heart caught on fire with love for her and, in jealous fear, he hoped that none of the young men would be able to beat her in the race. Then he said to himself: "But why should not I try my fortune? When one takes a risk, the gods help one."

By now the race had started, and the girl sped past him on feet that seemed to have wings. Though she went fast as an arrow, he admired her beauty still more. Indeed, she looked particularly beautiful when running. In the breeze her hair streamed back over her ivory shoulders; the ribbons with their bright borders fluttered at her knees; the white of her young body flushed rose red, as when a purple awning is drawn over white marble and makes the stone glow with its own color. While Hippomenes fixed his eyes on her, she reached the winning post and was crowned with the victor's garland. The young men, with groans, suffered the penalty of death according to the agreement which they had made.

Their fate, however, had no effect on Hippomenes. He came forward and, fixing his eyes on Atalanta, said: "Why do you win an easy glory by conquering these slow movers? Now run with me. If I win, it will be no disgrace to you. I am a king's son and Neptune is my great-grandfather. And, if you defeat me, it will be an honor to be able to say that you defeated Hippomenes."

As he spoke, Atalanta looked at him with a softer expression in her eyes. She wondered whether she really wanted to conquer or to be conquered. She thought to herself: "What god, envious of beautiful young men, wants to destroy this one and makes him seek marriage with me at the risk of his dear life? In my opinion, I am not worth it. It is not his beauty that touches me (though I might easily be touched by that); it is because he is still only a boy. And then there is his courage, and the fact that he is willing to risk so much for me. Why should he die, simply because he wants to live with me? I wish he would go, while he still may, and realize that it is fatal to want to marry me. Indeed he deserves to live. If only I were happier, if only the fates had not forbidden me to marry, he would be the man that I would choose."

Meanwhile, Atalanta's father and the whole people demanded that the race should take place. Hippomenes prayed to Venus and said: "O goddess, you put this love into my heart. Now be near me in my trial and aid me!"

A gentle breeze carried his prayer to the goddess and she was moved by it. Little time, however, remained in which she could help him. But it happened that she had just returned from her sacred island of Cyprus, where in one of her temple gardens grows a golden apple tree. The leaves are gold; the branches and the fruit rattle with metal as the wind stirs them. Venus had in her hand three golden apples which she had just picked from this tree. Now she came down to earth, making herself visible only to Hippomenes, and showed him how to use the apples.

Then the trumpets sounded and the two runners darted forward from the starting post, skimming over the sandy course with feet so light that it would seem they might have run over the sea or over the waving heads of standing corn. The crowd shouted their applause. "Now, Hippomenes," they cried, "run as you have never run before! You are winning." It would be difficult to say whether Hippomenes or Atalanta herself was most pleased with this encouragement. For some time, Atalanta, though she might have passed the young man, did not do so. She ran by his side, looking into his face. Then, half unwillingly, she left him behind. He, with parched throat and straining lungs, followed after; still the winning post was far in the distance; and now he took one of the golden apples which Venus had given him and threw it in her way. The girl looked with wonder at the shining fruit and, longing to have it, stopped running so that she could pick it up. Hippomenes passed her and again the spectators shouted out their applause. Soon, however, Atalanta made up the ground that she had lost and again left Hippomenes behind. He threw the second apple, once more took the lead and once more was overtaken. Now they were in sight of the winning post, and Hippomenes, with a prayer to Venus, threw the last apple rather sideways, so that it went some distance from the course. Atalanta seemed to hesitate whether she should go after it or not, but Venus made her go, and, when she had picked up the apple, she made it heavier, handicapping the girl not only by the time she had lost but by the weight of what she was carrying. This time she could not catch up Hippomenes. He passed the winning post first and claimed her as his bride.

Then, indeed, Hippomenes should have offered thanks to Venus, but he forgot entirely the goddess who had helped him, neither giving thanks nor making sacrifice.

Venus was angry and determined to make an example of them both. On their way to the home of Hippomenes they came to a holy temple, sacred to the mother of the gods, great Cybele. No mortal was allowed to pass the night in this temple, so hallowed was the spot; but Venus put it into the hearts of Hippomenes and Atalanta, who were tired from their journey, to rest there all night and treat the temple of the goddess as though it were a common inn. So in the most holy of the temple's shrines, where wooden images of the ancient gods turned away their eyes in horror at the profanation, they rested together. But the terrible goddess, her head crowned with a crown of towers, appeared to them. She covered their necks, which had been so smooth, with tawny manes of hair; their fingers became sharp claws, and their arms turned to legs. Most of their weight went to their chests, and behind them they swept the sandy ground with long tails. Instead of the palace they had hoped for, they lived in the savage woods, a lion and a lioness, terrible to others but, when Cybele needed them, tame enough to draw her chariot, champing the iron bits between their gnashing jaws.

How are Atalanta and Hippomenes like Phaethon (page 81) in their attitude toward the gods? Are they entirely innocent victims of the gods, or do they also help to bring about their own tragedy?

How does this myth show that people will test their limits, despite the possibility of tragedy? How did this couple, by daring to love each other, only succeed in becoming less than human?

Why do you think the myth-makers would imagine that love could persuade people to forget that they do not have the power of the gods?

The mythical Greek hero Theseus narrates this story, which tells of an episode that occurred when he was seven years old. The story is set in Troizen, an ancient town south of Athens, where the Olympian gods were worshipped, particularly the god Poseidon.

The Horse-God

From The King Must Die
MARY RENAULT

The Citadel of Troizen, where the Palace stands, was built by giants before anyone remembers. But the Palace was built by my great-grandfather. At sunrise, if you look at it from Kalauria across the strait, the columns glow fire-red and the walls are golden. It shines bright against the dark woods on the mountainside.

Our house is Hellene, sprung from the seed of Ever-Living Zeus. We worship the Sky Gods before Mother Dia and the gods of earth. And we have never mixed our blood with the blood of the Shore People, who had the land before us.

My grandfather had about fifteen children in his household when I was born. But his queen and her sons were dead, leaving only my mother born in wedlock. As for my father, it was said in the Palace that I had been fathered by a god. By the time I was five, I had perceived that some people doubted this. But my mother never spoke of it; and I cannot remember a time when I should have cared to ask her.

When I was seven, the Horse Sacrifice came due, a great day in Troizen.

It is held four-yearly, so I remembered nothing of the last one. I knew it concerned the King Horse, but thought it was some act of homage to him. To my mind, nothing could have been more fitting. I knew him well.

He lived in the great horse field, down on the plain. From the Palace roof I had often watched him, snuffing the wind with his white mane flying, or leaping on his mares. And only last year I had seen him do battle for his kingdom. One of the House Barons, seeing from afar the duel begin, rode down to the olive slopes for a nearer sight, and took me on his crupper. I watched the great stallions rake the earth with their forefeet, arch their necks, and shout their war cries; then charge in with streaming manes and teeth laid bare. At last the loser foundered; the King Horse snorted over him, threw up his head neighing, and trotted off toward his wives. He had never been haltered and was as wild as the sea. Not the King himself would ever throw a leg across him. He belonged to the god.

His valor alone would have made me love him. But I had another cause as well. I thought he was my brother.

Poseidon, as I knew, can look like a man or like a horse, whichever he chooses. In his man shape, it was said, he had begotten me. But there were songs in which he had horse sons too, swift as the north wind, and immortal. The King Horse, who was his own, must surely be one of these. It seemed clear to me, therefore, that we ought to meet. I had heard he was only five years old. "So," I thought, "though he is the bigger, I am the elder. It is for me to speak first."

Next time the Master of the Horse went down to choose colts for the chariots, I got him to take me. While he did his work, he left me with a groom, who presently drew in the dust a gambling board and fell to play with a friend. Soon they forgot me. I climbed the palisade and went seeking the King Horse.

The horses of Troizen are pure-bred Hellene. We have never crossed them with the little strain of the Shore People, whom we took the land from. When I was in with them, they looked very tall. As I reached up to pat one, I heard the Horse Master shout behind me; but I closed my ears. "Everyone gives me orders," I thought. "It comes of having no father. I wish I were the King Horse; no one gives them to him." Then I saw him, standing by himself on a little knoll, watching the end of the pasture where they were choosing colts. I went nearer, thinking, as every child thinks once for the first time, "Here is beauty."

He had heard me and turned to look. I held out my hand, as I did in the stables, and called, "Son of Poseidon!" On this he came trotting up to me, just as the stable horses did. I had brought a lump of salt, and held it out to him.

There was some commotion behind me. The groom bawled out, and looking round I saw the Horse Master beating him. My turn would be next, I thought; men were waving at me from the railings, and cursing each other. I felt safer where I was. The King Horse was so near that I could see the lashes of his dark eyes. His forelock fell between them like a white waterfall between shining stones. His teeth were as big as the ivory plates upon a war helm; but his lip, when he licked the salt out of my palm, felt softer than my mother's breast. When the salt was finished, he brushed my cheek with his, and snuffed at my hair. Then he trotted back to his hillock, whisking his long tail. His feet, with which as I learned later he had killed a mountain lion, sounded neat on the meadow, like a dancer's.

Now I found myself snatched from all sides and hustled from the pasture. It surprised me to see the Horse Master as pale as a sick man. He heaved me on his mount in silence, and hardly spoke all the way home. After so much to-do, I feared my grandfather himself would beat me. He gave me a long look as I came near; but all he said was, "Theseus, you went to the horse field as Peiros' guest. It was unmannerly to give him trouble. A nursing mare might have bitten your arm off. I forbid you to go again."

This happened when I was six years old; and the Horse Feast fell next year.

It was the chief of all feasts at Troizen. The Palace was a week getting ready. First my mother took the women down to the river Hyllikos to wash the clothes. They were loaded on mules and brought down to the clearest water, the basin under the fall. Even in drought the Hyllikos never fails or muddies; but now in summer it was low. The old women rubbed light things at the water's edge, and beat them on the stones; the girls picked up their petticoats and trod the heavy mantles and blankets in midstream. One played a pipe, which they kept time to, splashing and laughing. When the wash was drying on the sunny boulders, they stripped and bathed, taking me in with them. That was the last time I was allowed there; my mother saw that I understood the jokes.

On the feast day I woke at dawn. My old nurse dressed me in my best: my new doeskin drawers with braided borders, my red belt rolled upon rope and clasped with crystal, and my necklace of gold beads. When she had combed my hair, I went to see my mother dressing. She was just out of her bath, and they were dropping her petticoat over her head. The seven-tiered flounces, sewn with gold drops and pendants, clinked and glittered as she shook them out. When they clipped together her gold-worked girdle and her bodice waist, she held her breath in hard and let it out laughing. Her breasts were as smooth as milk, and the tips so rosy that she never painted them, though she was still wearing them bare, not being, at that time, much above three and twenty.

They took her hair out of the crimping-plaits (it was darker than mine, about the color of polished bronze) and began to comb it. I ran outside on the terrace, which runs all round the royal rooms, for they stand on the roof of the Great Hall. Morning was red, and the crimson-painted columns burned in it. I could hear, down in the courtyard, the House Barons assembling in their war dress. This was what I had waited for.

They came in by twos and threes, the bearded warriors talking, the young men laughing and scuffling, shouting to friends, or feinting at each other with the butts of their spears. They had on their tall-plumed leather helmets, circled with bronze or strengthened with rolls of hide. Their broad breasts and shoulders, sleekly oiled, shone russet in the rosy light; their wide leather drawers stood stiffly out from the thigh, making their lean waists, pulled in with the thick rolled sword belts, look slenderer still. They waited, exchanging news and chaff, and striking poses for the women, the young men lounging with the tops of their tall shields propping their left armpits, their right arms stretched out grasping their spears. Their upper lips were all fresh shaved, to make their new beards show clearer. I scanned the shield devices, birds or fish or serpents worked upon the hide, picking out friends to hail, who raised their spears in greeting. Seven or eight of them were uncles of mine. My grandfather had got them in the Palace on various women of good blood, prizes of his old wars, or gifts of compliment from neighbor kings.

The land barons were coming in from their horses or their chariots; they too bare to the waist, for the day was warm, but wearing all their jewels; even their boot tops had golden tassels. The sound of men's voices grew louder and deeper and filled the air above the courtyard. I squared back my shoulders and nipped my belt in; gazed at a youth whose beard was starting and counted years on my fingers.

Talaos came in, the War Leader, a son of my grandfather's youth, got upon a chief's wife taken in battle. He had on his finest things: his prize helmet from the High King of Mycenae's funeral games, all plated, head and cheeks, with the carved teeth of boars, and both his swords, the long one with the crystal pommel which he sometimes let me draw, the short one with a leopard hunt inlaid in gold. The men touched their spear shafts to the brows; he numbered them off with his eye, and went in to tell my grandfather they were ready. Soon he came out, and standing on the great steps before the king-column that carried the lintel, his beard jutting like a warship's prow, shouted, "The god goes forth!"

They all trooped out of the courtyard. As I craned to see, my grand-father's body servant came and asked my mother's maid if the Lord Theseus was ready to go with the King.

I had supposed I should be going with my mother. So I think had she. But she sent word that I was ready whenever her father wished.

She was Chief Priestess of Mother Dia in Troizen. In the time of the Shore People before us, that would have made her sovereign queen; and if we ourselves had been sacrificing at the Navel Stone, no one would have walked before her. But Poseidon is husband and lord of the Mother, and on his feast day the men go first. So, when I heard I was going with my grandfather, I saw myself a man already.

I ran to the battlements, and looked out between their teeth. Now I saw what god it was that the men were following. They had let loose the King Horse, and he was running free across the plain.

The village too, it seemed, had turned out to welcome him. He went through standing corn in the common fields, and no one raised a hand to stop him. He crossed the beans and the barley and would have gone up to the olive slopes; but some of the men were there and he turned away. While I was watching, down in the empty court a chariot rattled. It was my grandfather's; and I remembered I was to ride in it. By myself on the terrace I danced for joy.

They fetched me down. Eurytos the charioteer was up already, standing still as an image in his short white tunic and leather greaves, his long hair bound in a club; only his arm muscles moved, from hold-ing in the horses. He lifted me in, to await my grandfather. I was eager to see him in his war things, for in those days he was tall. Last time I was in Troizen, when he was turned eighty, he had grown light and dry as an old grasshopper, piping by the hearth. I could have lifted him in my hands. He died a month after my son, having I suppose nothing to hold him longer. But he was a big man then.

He came out, after all, in his priestly robe and fillet, with a scepter instead of a spear. He heaved himself in by the chariot rail, set his feet in the bracers, and gave the word to go. As we clattered down the cobbled road, you could not have taken him for anything but a warrior, fillet or no. He rode with the broad rolling war straddle a man learns driving cross-country with weapons in his hands. Whenever I rode with him, I had to stand on his left; it would have set his teeth on edge to have anything in front of his spear arm. Always I seemed to feel thrown over me the shelter of his absent shield.

Seeing the road deserted, I was surprised, and asked him where the people were. "At Sphairia," he said, grasping my shoulder to steady me over a pothole. "I am taking you to see the rite, because soon you will be waiting on the god there, as one of his servants."

The news startled me. I wondered what service a horse god wanted, and pictured myself combing his forelock or putting ambrosia before him in golden bowls. But he was also Poseidon Bluehair, who raises storms; and the great black Earth Bull whom, as I had heard, the Cretans fed with youths and girls. After some time I asked my grandfather, "How long shall I stay?"

He looked at my face and laughed, and ruffled my hair with his big hand. "A month at a time," he said. "You will only serve the shrine and the holy spring. It is time you did your duties to Poseidon, who is your birth-god. So today I shall dedicate you, after the sacrifice. Behave respectfully, and stand still till you are told; remember, you are with me."

We had reached the shore of the strait, where the ford was. I had looked forward to splashing through it in the chariot; but a boat was waiting, to save our best clothes. On the other side we mounted again and skirted for a while the Kalaurian shore, looking across at Troizen. Then we turned inward, through pines. The horses' feet drummed on a wooden bridge and stopped. We had come to the little holy island at the big one's toe; and kings must walk in the presence of the gods.

The people were waiting. Their clothes and garlands, the warriors' plumes, looked bright in the clearing beyond the trees. My grandfather took my hand and led me up the rocky path. On either side a row of youths was standing, the tallest lads of Troizen and Kalauria, their long hair tied up to crest their heads like manes. They were singing, stamping the beat with their right feet all together, a hymn to Poseidon Hippios. It said how the Horse Father is like the fruitful earth; like the seaway whose broad back bears the ships safe home; his plumed head and bright eye are like daybreak over the mountains, his back and loins like the ripple in the barley field; his mane is like the surf when it blows streaming off the wave crests; and when he stamps the ground, men and cities tremble, and kings' houses fall.

I knew this was true, for the roof of the sanctuary had been rebuilt in my own lifetime; Poseidon had overthrown its wooden columns and several houses and made a crack in the Palace walls. I had not felt myself that morning; they had asked me if I was sick, at which I only cried. But after the shock I was better. I had been four years old then, and had almost forgotten.

Our part of the world had always been sacred to Earth-Shaker; the youths had many of his deeds to sing about. Even the ford, their hymn said, was of his making; he had stamped in the strait, and the sea had sunk to a trickle, then risen to flood the plain. Up till that time, ships had passed through it; there was a prophecy that one day he would strike it with his fish spear, and it would sink again.

As we walked between the boys, my grandfather ran his eyes along them, for likely warriors. But I had seen ahead, in the midst of the sacred clearing, the King Horse himself, browsing quietly from a tripod.

He had been hand-broken this last year, not for work but for this occasion, and today he had had the drugged feed at dawn. But without knowing this, I was not surprised he should put up with the people round him; I had been taught it was the mark of a king to receive homage with grace.

The shrine was garlanded with pine boughs. The summer air bore scents of resin and flowers and incense, of sweat from the horse and the young men's bodies, of salt from the sea. The priests came forward, crowned with pine, to salute my grandfather as chief priest of the god. Old Kannadis, whose beard was as white as the King Horse's forelock, laid his hand on my head nodding and smiling. My grandfather beckoned to Diokles, my favorite uncle, a big young man eighteen years old, with the skin of a leopard, which he had killed himself, hanging on his shoulder. "Look after the boy," said my grandfather, "till we are ready for him."

Diokles said, "Yes, sir," and led me to the steps before the shrine, away from where he had been standing with his friends. He had on his gold snake arm ring with crystal eyes, and his hair was bound with a purple ribbon. My grandfather had won his mother at Pylos, second prize in the chariot race, and had always valued her highly; she was the best embroidress in the Palace. He was a bold gay youth, who used to let me ride on his wolfhound. But today he looked at me solemnly, and I feared I was a burden to him.

Old Kannadis brought my grandfather a pine wreath bound with wool, which would have been ready, but had been found after some delay. There is always some small hitch at Troizen; we do not do these things with the smoothness of Athens. The King Horse munched from the tripod, and flicked off flies with his tail.

There were two more tripods; one bowl held water, the other water and wine. In the first my grandfather washed his hands, and a young server dried them. The King Horse lifted his head from the feed, and it seemed they looked at one another. My grandfather set his hand on the white muzzle and stroked down hard; the head dipped and rose with a gentle toss. Diokles leaned down to me and said, "Look, he consents."

I looked up at him. This year his beard showed clearly against the light. He said, "It means a good omen. A lucky year." I nodded, thinking the purpose of the rite accomplished; now we would go home. But my grandfather sprinkled meal on the horse's back from a golden dish; then took up a little knife bright with grinding and cut a lock from his mane. He gave a small piece to Talaos, who was standing near, and some to the first of the barons. Then he turned my way and beckoned. Diokles' hand on my shoulder pushed me forward. "Go up," he whispered. "Go and take it."

I stepped out, hearing men whisper and women coo like mating pigeons. I knew already that the son of the Queen's own daughter ranked before the sons of the Palace women; but I had never had it noticed publicly. I thought I was being honored like this because the King Horse was my brother.

Five or six strong white hairs were put in my hand. I had meant to thank my grandfather; but now I felt come out of him the presence of the King, solemn as a sacred oak wood. So, like the others, I touched the lock to my brow in silence. Then I went back, and Diokles said, "Well done."

My grandfather raised his hands and invoked the god. He hailed him as Earth-Shaker, Wave-Gatherer, brother of King Zeus and husband of the Mother, Shepherd of Ships, Horse-Lover. I heard a whinny from beyond the pine woods, where the chariot teams were tethered, ready to race in honor of the god. The King Horse raised his noble head and softly answered.

The prayer was long, and my mind wandered, till I heard by the note that the end was coming. "Be it so, Lord Poseidon, according to our prayer; and do you accept the offering." He held out his hand, and someone put in it a great cleaver with a bright-ground edge. There were tall men standing with ropes of oxhide in their hands. My grandfather felt the cleaver's edge and, as in his chariot, braced his feet apart.

It was a good clean killing. I myself, with all Athens watching, am content to do no worse. Yet, even now, I still remember. How he reared up like a tower, feeling his death, dragging the men like children; the scarlet cleft in the white throat, the rank hot smell; the ruin of beauty, the fall of strength, the ebb of valor; and the grief, the burning pity as he sank upon his knees and laid his bright head in the dust. That blood seemed to tear the soul out of my breast, as if my own heart had shed it.

As the newborn babe, who has been rocked day and night in his soft cave knowing no other, is thrust forth where the harsh air pierces him and the fierce light stabs his eyes, so it was with me. But between me and my mother, where she stood among the women, was the felled carcass twitching in blood and my grandfather with the crimson cleaver. I looked up; but Diokles was watching the death throe, leaning easily on his spear. I met only the empty eye-slits of the leopard skin, and the arm-snake's jewelled stare.

My grandfather dipped a cup into the offering bowl and poured the wine upon the ground. I seemed to see blood stream from his hand. The smell of dressed hide from Diokles' shield, and the man's smell of his body, came to me mixed with the smell of death. My grandfather gave the server the cup and beckoned. Diokles shifted his spear to his shield arm and took my hand. "Come," he said. "Father wants you. You have to be dedicated now."

I thought, "So was the King Horse." The bright day rippled before my eyes which tears of grief and terror blinded. Diokles swung round his shield on its shoulder sling to cover me like a house of hide and wiped his hard young hand across my eyelids. "Behave," he said. "The people are watching. Come, where's the warrior? It's only blood."

He took the shield away; and I saw the people staring.

At the sight of all their eyes, memories came back to me. "Gods' sons fear nothing," I thought. "Now they will know, one way or the other." And though within me was all dark and crying, yet my foot stepped forward.

Then it was that I heard a sea sound in my ears; a pulse and a surging, going with me, bearing me on. I heard it then for the first time.

I moved with the wave, as if it broke down a wall before me; and Diokles led me forward. At least, I know that I was led; by him, or one who took his shape as the Immortals may. And I know that having been alone, I was alone no longer.

My grandfather dipped his finger in the blood of the sacrifice and made the sign of the trident on my brow. Then he and old Kannadis took me under the cool thatch that roofed the holy spring and dropped in a votive for me, a bronze bull with gilded horns. When we came out, the priests had cut off the god's portion from the carcass, and the smell of burned fat filled the air. But it was not till I got home, and my mother asked, "What is it?" that at last I wept.

Between her breasts, entangled in her shining hair, I wept as if to purge away my soul in water. She put me to bed and sang to me and said when I was quiet, "Don't grieve for the King Horse; he has gone to the Earth Mother, who made us all. She has a thousand thousand children and knows each one of them. He was too good for anyone here to ride; but she will find him some great hero, a child of the sun or the north wind, to be his friend and master; they will gallop all day and never be tired. Tomorrow you shall take her a present for him, and I will tell her it comes from you."

Next day we went down together to the Navel Stone. It had fallen from heaven long ago, before anyone remembers. The walls of its sunken court were mossy, and the Palace noises fell quiet around. The sacred House Snake had his hole between the stones; but he only showed himself to my mother, when she brought him his milk. She laid my honey cake on the altar and told the Goddess whom it was for. As we went, I looked back and saw it lying on the cold stone and remembered the horse's living breath upon my hand, his soft lip warm and moving.

I was sitting among the house dogs, at the doorway end of the Great Hall, when my grandfather passed through and spoke to me in greeting.

I got up and answered; for one did not forget he was the King. But I stood looking down and stroking my toe along a crack in the flagstones. Because of the dogs, I had not heard him coming, or I would have been gone. "If he could do this," I had been thinking, "how can one trust the gods?"

He spoke again, but I only said "Yes," and would not look at him. I could feel him high above me, standing in thought. Presently he said, "Come with me."

I followed him up the corner stairs to his own room above. He had been born there and got my mother and his sons, and it was the room he died in. Then I had been there seldom; in his old age he lived all day in it, for it faced south, and the chimney of the Great Hall went through to warm it. The royal bed at the far end was seven feet long by six feet wide, made of polished cypress, inlaid and carved. The blue wool cover with its border of flying cranes had taken my grandmother half a year on the great loom. There was a bronze-bound chest by it, for his clothes; and for his jewels an ivory coffer on a painted stand. His arms hung on the wall: shield, bow, longsword and dagger, his hunting knife, and his tall-plumed helmet of quilted hide, lined with crimson leather the worse for wear. There was not much else, except the skins on the floor and a chair. He sat and motioned me to the footstool.

Muffled up the stairway came the noises of the Hall: women scrubbing the long trestles with sand and scolding men out of their way; a scuffle and a laugh. My grandfather's head cocked, like an old dog's at a footstep. Then he rested his hands on the chair arms carved with lions and said, "Well, Theseus? Why are you angry?"

I looked up as far as his hand. His fingers curved into a lion's open mouth; on his forefinger was the royal ring of Troizen, with the Mother being worshiped on a pillar. I pulled at the bearskin on the floor, and was silent.

"When you are a king," he said, "you will do better than we do here. Only the ugly and the base shall die; what is brave and beautiful shall live forever. That is how you will rule your kingdom?"

To see if he was mocking me, I looked at his face. Then it was as if I had only dreamed the priest with the cleaver. He reached out and drew me in against his knees and dug his fingers in my hair as he did with his dogs when they came up to be noticed.

"You knew the King Horse; he was your friend. So you know if it was his own choice to be King, or not." I sat silent, remembering the great horse fight and the war calls. "You know he lived like a king, with first pick of the feed, and any mare he wanted; and no one asked him to work for it."

I opened my mouth and said, "He had to fight for it."

"Yes, that is true. Later, when he was past his best, a younger stallion would have come and won the fight and taken his kingdom. He would have died hard or been driven from his people and his wives to grow old without honor. You saw that he was proud."

I asked, "Was he so old?"

"No." His big wrinkled hand lay quietly on the lion mask. "No older for a horse than Talaos for a man. He died for another cause. But if I tell you why, then you must listen, even if you do not understand. When you are older, if I am here, I will tell it you again; if not, you will have heard it once, and some of it you will remember."

While he spoke, a bee flew in and buzzed among the painted

rafters. To this day, that sound will bring it back to me.

"When I was a boy," he said, "I knew an old man, as you know me. But he was older; the father of my grandfather. His strength was gone, and he sat in the sun or by the hearthside. He told me this tale, which I shall tell you now, and you, perhaps, will tell one day to your son." I remember I looked up then, to see if he was smiling.

"Long ago, so he said, our people lived in the northland, beyond Olympus. He said, and he was angry when I doubted it, that they never saw the sea. Instead of water they had a sea of grass, which stretched as far as the swallow flies, from the rising to the setting sun. They lived by the increase of their herds and built no cities; when the grass was eaten, they moved where there was more. They did not grieve for the sea, as we should, or for the good things earth brings forth with tilling; they had never known them; and they had few skills, because they were wandering men. But they saw a wide sky, which draws men's mind to the gods; and they gave their firstfruits to Ever-Living Zeus, who sends the rain.

"When they journeyed, the barons in their chariots rode round about, guarding the flocks and the women. They bore the burden of danger, then as now; it is the price men pay for honor. And to this very day, though we live in the Isle of Pelops and build walls, planting olives and barley, still for the theft of cattle there is always blood. But the horse is more. With horses we took these lands from the Shore People who were here before us. The horse will be the victor's sign, as long as our blood remembers.

"The folk came south by little and little, leaving their first lands. Perhaps Zeus sent no rain, or the people grew too many, or they were pressed by enemies. But my great-grandfather said to me that they came by the will of All-Knowing Zeus, because this was the place of their moira."

He paused in thought. I said to him, "What is that?"

"Moira?" he said. "The finished shape of our fate, the line drawn round it. It is the task the gods allot us, and the share of glory they allow; the limits we must not pass; and our appointed end. Moira is all these."

I thought about this, but it was too big for me. I asked, "Who told them where to come?"

"The Lord Poseidon, who rules everything that stretches under the sky, the land and the sea. He told the King Horse; and the King Horse led them."

I sat up; this I could understand.

"When they needed new pastures, they let him loose; and he, taking care of his people as the god advised him, would smell the air seeking food and water. Here in Troizen, when he goes out for the god, they guide him round the fields and over the ford. We do it in memory. But in those days he ran free. The barons followed him, to give battle if his passage was disputed; but only the god told him where to go.

"And so, before he was loosed, he was always dedicated. The god only inspires his own. Can you understand this, Theseus? You know that when Diokles hunts, Argo will drive the game to him; but he would not do it for you, and by himself he would only hunt small game. But because he is Diokles' dog, he knows his mind.

"The King Horse showed the way; the barons cleared it; and the King led the people. When the work of the King Horse was done, he was given to the god, as you saw yesterday. And in those days, said my great-grandfather, as with the King Horse, so with the King."

I looked up in wonder; and yet, not in astonishment. Something within me did not find it strange. He nodded at me and ran down his fingers through my hair, so that my neck shivered.

"Horses go blindly to the sacrifice; but the gods give knowledge to men. When the King was dedicated, he knew his moira. In three years, or seven, or nine, or whenever the custom was, his term would end and the god would call him. And he went consenting, or else he was no king, and power would not fall on him to lead the people. When they came to choose among the Royal Kin, this was his sign: that he chose short life with glory, and to walk with the god, rather than live long, unknown like the stall-fed ox. And the custom changes, Theseus, but this token never. Remember, even if you do not understand."

I wanted to say I understood him. But I was silent, as in the sacred oak wood.

"Later the custom altered. Perhaps they had a King they could not spare, when war or plague had thinned the Kindred. Or perhaps Apollo showed them a hidden thing. But they ceased to offer the King at a set time. They kept him for the extreme sacrifice, to appease the gods in their great angers, when they had sent no rain, or the cattle died, or in a hard war. And it was no one's place to say to him, 'It is time to make the offering.' He was the nearest to the god, because he consented to his moira; and he himself received the god's commandment."

He paused; and I said, "How?"

"In different ways. By an oracle, or an omen, or some prophecy

Hansel & Grethel

But the Old Woman only shook her head, and
said : " Ah, dear children, who brought you here ?
Come in and stay with me ; you will come to no
harm."

117

118

© 1971 Walt Disney Productions

DON'T
TRUST
ANYONE
OVER
30

THERE'S A LESSON TO BE
LEARNED HERE SOMEWHERE, BUT
I DON'T KNOW WHAT IT IS...

I WANT YOU
FOR U.S. ARMY
NEAREST RECRUITING STATION

being fulfilled; or, if the god came close to him, by some sign between them, something seen, or a sound. And so it is still, Theseus. We know our time."

I neither spoke nor wept, but laid my head against his knee. He saw that I understood him.

"Listen, and do not forget, and I will show you a mystery. It is not the sacrifice, whether it comes in youth or age, or the god remits it; it is not the bloodletting that calls down power. It is the consenting, Theseus. The readiness is all. It washes heart and mind from things of no account and leaves them open to the god. But one washing does not last a lifetime; we must renew it, or the dust returns to cover us. And so with this. Twenty years I have ruled in Troizen, and four times sent the King Horse to Poseidon. When I lay my hand on his head to make him nod, it is not only to bless the people with the omen. I greet him as my brother before the god and renew my moira."

He ceased. Looking up, I saw him staring out between the red pillars of the window, at the dark-blue line of the sea. We sat some while, he playing with my hair as a man will scratch his dog to quiet it, lest its importunities disturb his thoughts. But I had no word to say to him. The seed is still when first it falls into the furrow.

At last he sat up with a start and looked at me. "Well, well, child, the omens said I should reign long. But sometimes they talk double; and too early's better than too late. All this is heavy for you. But the man in you challenged it, and the man will bear it." He got up rather stiffly from his chair and stretched and strode to the doorway; his shout echoed down the twisted stair. Presently Diokles running up from below said, "Here I am, sir."

"Look at this great lad here," my grandfather said, "growing out of his clothes, and nothing to do but sit with the house dogs, scratching. Take him away and teach him to ride."

What mysteries are revealed to Theseus in this story?

Phaethon (page 81) wants to "find out" if the Sun-god is his father and to fulfill his "wild dream." Rufus (page 86) wants to find out why he feels "deeply empty" and why he "tastes darkness." Theseus wants to understand "moira." How do all of these desires reveal an effort to understand something about personal identity?

"If he could do this," Theseus thinks angrily of his grandfather, "how can one trust the gods?" Why does Theseus at this point fear the power of adults and of the gods? What do Phaethon (page 81) and Atalanta (page 100) learn about their own moira, and about the power of the gods?

How does each story—Phaethon's (page 81), Rufus's (page 86), Atalanta's (page 100), and Theseus's—dramatize the "end of childhood"?

Athene and Arachne

A Greek myth
Retold by W.T. JEWKES

There was one thing that the goddess Athene was particularly jealous of, and that was her skill in the household arts, especially in spinning and weaving. One poor mortal, who did not realize the extent of Athene's jealousy, brought down the goddess's wrath upon her head in no uncertain fashion.

She was a Maeonian girl named Arachne, really a nobody as far as birth and breeding go. Her father was a humble wool-dyer, and her mother too was a common sort of person. But their daughter proved to have a remarkable talent as a spinner and weaver; and so famous did her skill become that word traveled through all the Lydian towns; and even the nymphs themselves used to gather to watch her as she wound the yarn into balls, pressing it with skillful fingers as she pulled it off the distaff all soft and cloudlike, drawing it into long threads, or as she twisted the spindle with deft thumb, or sent her needle flashing like a firefly. They were ready to swear she had been taught by Athene herself, and the girl, her head turned giddy by all this admiration, boasted openly that she was indeed a better weaver than the goddess herself. "In fact," she rashly challenged one day, "I really believe that if Athene and I were to have a contest, I would carry off the prize."

This was too much for Athene, and she came to visit the vain girl, disguised as an old woman with gray hair, half-crippled, her hobbling steps assisted by a crooked cane.

"My dear," she quavered, "old age has some advantages, and the best of these is experience. Let me give you some advice. I hear you have challenged Athene to a weaving contest. There is still time to back down, you know. Be wise and defer to the goddess; confine your contests to other mortals. Ask pardon for your arrogance; the goddess is gracious and will forgive you."

But the reckless girl was only angered by these kindly words.

"Who wants your advice?" she cried scornfully. "The trouble with you old folks is that you've lived too long, and you can't bear the thought of no one paying attention to you any more. Go and meddle in the affairs of your own sons and daughters, and leave me to my own. Anyway, the goddess hasn't answered my challenge. That proves she is really afraid to compete with me."

"There's where you are wrong!" cried Athene, changing in a flash into her divine shape. "If you really insist on a contest, then we'll have one—right now."

The nymphs and the native women fell on their knees in awe at the shining figure, but Arachne, although she turned a little paler and trembled, still maintained an attitude of defiance, rushing to her doom in blind passion.

"Very well," she declared, "I'm ready."

So two looms were set up, the warp was stretched, and the web was made fast to the beam. The threads were kept apart by reeds as their busy fingers began to speed the shuttle through the woof. Deftly their hands shifted back and forth; and the darker purple threads began to shade off into lighter colors, soft like those of a rainbow after a thunderstorm, a myriad of colors all subtly blending so that the eye could not detect where one left off and another began. Then, as threads of gold were woven in, each loom began to tell a story in design.

Athene's tapestry depicted the hill of Ares in Athens, the scene of the quarrel she once had with Poseidon about the name of the land. There she set the twelve gods of the heavens on their high thrones, with Zeus presiding. There also stood Poseidon, striking the cleft in the rock from which sprang the salt water that asserted his claim to the city. On herself Athene depicted the helmet, and the aegis breastplate; and growing out of the place where her spear touched the earth was her gift to the land, the gray-green olive thickly hung with ripe fruit. It was a scene of the goddess in victory; but just in case her rival did not recognize the hidden warning of what her reward might be for her rashness, Athene wove four more smaller pictures, one in each corner, colored bright, but each one telling of danger. One corner showed Haemus and Rhodope, daring mortals who had assumed the name of the most high gods, now turned to cold mountains. The second corner displayed the fate of the Pygmy queen, turned into a crane by Hera and forced to attack the very people she had ruled over. The third portrayed Antigone, who had dared to compete with Hera, and for her pride was transformed into a white-winged stork. And in the last corner she wove the picture of Cinyras, vainly hugging the temple steps that had once been his daughters; poor man, his tears could be seen falling on the hard stones. And last of all, the goddess bordered the whole work with olive leaves, her own signature.

Meanwhile, Arachne was busy with her design, but her subjects were different—mostly stories of how the gods deceived poor mortals. There was Europa, led astray by the bull's disguise; and so clever was the work one would think it a real bull, and a real girl looking back as she rides the waves, lifting her small feet to keep them above the swell of the water. There too was Leda, lying under the swan's wing, and Antiope with her twins, whose father she believed to be a satyr, though he was, in fact, Zeus himself. The father of gods took Alcmena in the shape of her husband while he was away fighting; he visited Danae in a shower of gold, appeared to Aegina as a flame, and took the shape of a mottled snake for Deo's daughter. And Zeus was not the only dissembler she pictured on her tapestry. His brother Poseidon's tricks were also there for all to see, looking like a bull to one Aeolian girl, like a river to another, and once even like a ram. He appeared as a stallion to Demeter, the goddess of the fields, and as a dolphin to Melantho. To all these scenes Arachne gave the proper background, and to each figure vivid, lifelike features. Apollo was there, disguised like a shepherd to deceive Isse; at another place he appeared like a hawk, and once like a brindled lion. And she did not leave out Dionysus, whose bunch of purple grapes deceived Erigone. Finally, round the border she wove gay flowers twined with sinewy ivy.

When she was done, no one could find a flaw in the work, not even Athene herself. Now indeed the fair-haired goddess was furious. In a rage she tore at the tapestry that showed the crimes of the gods, and then, snatching up her shuttle, she began to rain blows on Arachne's head until the wretched girl could no longer bear it. Off she ran sobbing to an orchard and tried to hang herself with a stout vine drooping from a tree. At the pitiful sight, Athene was partly moved to compassion, and lifted her up to keep her from strangling.

"Well, you need not kill yourself, you foolish girl," she declared. "You may go on living, but just to keep you mindful of what it is to defy the gods, you shall hang all the rest of your days, you and the rest of your offspring."

With that, she sprinkled hell-bane on Arachne's head. When the poison touched her, her long tresses fell off, her nose and ears disappeared, her head became shrunken and the rest of her body withered and tiny. Only a large belly remained; from it sprang long fingers that seemed to cling to the sides like legs. And from her belly she still kept on spinning and spinning. Since that day the spider has not forgotten the skill she used to have.

In the previous four stories, "childhood" disappears when a young, innocent person comes face-to-face with a harsher world than he or she has ever experienced before. In this story, a girl's "childhood" is also destroyed. Do you think Arachne is less innocent than the young people in the other stories?

On another level this myth is an imaginative explanation of the origin of the spider. Write a story about the origin of some other animal who was once a human being. Choose a creature that seems very peculiar to you, or one that performs a task that seems mysterious. (Perhaps a cockroach, which must live in damp dark places; a fly which must flit from place to place; or an earthworm, which must eat dirt.) What kind of person was the creature at first? Why was he or she transformed? Did powerful gods have anything to do with it?

This legend is set in ancient Ireland.
Cuchulain (coo hoo'lĭn) is Champion
of the Red Branch, a warrior
band who serve King Conor of Ulster.

Deirdre and
the Sons of Usna

An Irish legend
Retold by ROSEMARY SUTCLIFF

Now when Cuchulain and Emer had been together a few years in the sunny house that he had built at Dun Dealgan, a great sorrow and the shadow of a great threat fell upon Ulster. But the beginning of that wild story was long before, in the year that Cuchulain first went to the Boys' House.

In that year a certain Ulster chieftain called Felim made a great feast for the King and the Red Branch Warriors. And when the feasting was at its height, and the Greek wine was going round and the harp song shimmering through the hall, word was brought to Felim from the women's quarters that his wife had borne him a daughter.

The warriors sprang to their feet to drink health and happiness upon the bairn, and then the King, half-laughing, bade Cathbad, who was with him, to foretell the babe's fortune and make it a bright one. Cathbad went to the door of the hall and stood for a long while gazing up at the summer stars that were big and pollen-soft in the sky, and when he came back into the torchlight there was shadow in his face, and for a while he would not answer when they asked him the meaning of it. But at last he said, "Call her Deirdre, for that name has the sound of sorrow, and sorrow will come by her to all Ulster. Bright-haired she will be, a flame of beauty; warriors will go into exile for her sake, and many shall fight and die because of her, yet in the end she shall lie in a little grave apart by herself, and better it would be that she had never been born."

Then the warriors would have had the babe killed there and then, and even Felim, standing gray-faced among them, had nothing to say against it; but Conor Mac Nessa, his own Queen having died a while since in bearing Follaman their youngest son, had another thought and he said, "Ach now, there shall be no slaying, for clearly this fate that Cathbad reads in the stars can only mean that some chieftain of another province or even maybe of the Islands or the Pict Lands over the water will take her for his wife and for some cause that has to do with her, will make war on us. Therefore, she shall grow up in some place where no man may set eyes on her, and when she is of age to marry, then I myself will take her for Queen. In that way the doom will be averted, for no harm can come to Ulster through her marriage to me."

So Conor Mac Nessa took charge of the child, and gave her to Levarcham his old nurse who was one of the wisest women in all Emain Macha. And in a hidden glen of Slieve Gallion he had a little house built, with a roof of green sods so that above ground it would look no more than one of the little green hillocks of the Sidhe, and a turf wall ringing it round, and a garden with apple trees for shade and fruit and pleasure. And there he set the two of them, to have no more sight of men, save that once a year his own most trusted warriors should bring them supplies of food and clothing, until the child was fifteen and ready to become his Queen.

So in the little secret homestead with her foster mother, Deirdre grew from a baby into a child and from a child into a maiden, knowing no world beyond the glen, and seeing no man in all that time, for every year when the warriors came, Levarcham would shut her within doors until they were gone again. Every year the King would send her some gift, a silver rattle hung with tiny bells of green glass, a coral-footed dove in a wicker cage, a length of wonderfully patterned silk that had come in a ship from half the world away. "What *is* a ship?" said Deirdre to her foster mother, "and how far is half the world away? Could I get there if I set out very early in the morning and walked all day until the first stars came out?" And at that, Levarcham grew anxious, knowing that her charge was beginning to wonder about the world beyond the glen.

In the year that she was fourteen, her gift was a string of yellow amber that smelled fragrant as a flower when she warmed it between her hands, and that year the King brought it himself, and came with it into the house under the sheltering turf. And so for the first time, he saw Deirdre, and he with the first gray hairs already in his beard. And sorrow upon it, from that moment he gave her his heart's love, and she could never be free of it again.

That was in the summer, and before the cuckoo was gone, and before the last scarlet leaves fell from the wild cherry trees, and before the first snow came, the King returned to the glen for another sight of Deirdre. She knew that she was to be his Queen, but 'twas little enough that meant to her for good or ill, for it was a thing that belonged to the outside world, and the outside world as yet seemed very far away.

And then one winter night the outside world came to her threshold.

A wild night it was, with the wind roaring up through the woods and the sleety rain of it hushing across the turf roof, and Deirdre was sitting at old Levarcham's feet, spinning saffron wool by the light of the burning peats, when she thought she heard a strange cry, mingled with the voices of the storm, and lifted her head to listen. "What was that, my Mother?"

"Only a bird calling to its mate through the storm. Nothing that need concern you," said Levarcham.

But the cry came again, nearer now, and Deirdre said, "It sounded like a human voice—and the voice of one in sore trouble."

"It is only the wild geese flying over. Bide by the fire and go on spinning."

And then between gust and gust of the wind there came a fumbling and a thumping against the timbers of the small strong door, and the voice cried, "Let me in! In the name of the sun and the moon let me in!"

And heedless of the old woman crying out to stop her, Deirdre leaped up and ran to unbar and lift the rowan-wood pin; and the door swung open and the wind and rain leaped in upon her, and with the wind and the rain, a man stumbled into the house place, and his sodden cloak like spread wings about him, as though he were indeed some great storm-driven bird.

He aided Deirdre to force shut the door. And as he came into the firelight that shone on his rain-drenched hair that was black as a crow's wing and on his face, and on the great height of him, Levarcham took one look at him and said, "Naisi, Son of Usna, it is not the time to be bringing up the year's supplies. You have no right in this place."

"Myself not being the King," Naisi said, and let his sodden cloak fall from his shoulders, though indeed he was as wet within it as without. "A storm-driven man has a right to any shelter that opens to him."

"And shall we have your brothers at the door next? Seldom it is that you three are apart!"

"We have been hunting together, but Ardan and Ainle turned homeward before I did," said the tall man, and swayed. "Give me leave to sit by your fire until the storm sinks, for I have been lost and wandering a long while until I saw your light and—it is weary I am."

"Ach well, if you tell no man that you have been here, there'll be no harm done, maybe," said Levarcham. "Sit, then, and eat and drink while you're here, for by the looks of you, if I turn you away now, the Red Branch will be one fewer by morning."

So Naisi sank down with a sigh upon the piled sheepskins, almost into the warm peat ash, and sat there with hanging head, the sodden hunting-leathers steaming upon him. Deirdre brought barley bread, and curd from their little black cow, and a cup of pale Greek wine, and set all beside him. He had been careful until then not to look at her, but when she gave the cup into his hands, he looked up to thank her; and having looked, could not look away again. And Deirdre could not look away either.

And Levarcham, watching both of them out of her small bright eyes, while she went on with Deirdre's abandoned spinning, saw how it was with them, and how the blood came back into Naisi's face that had been gray as a skull, and how the girl's face answered his, and thought to herself, "Trouble! Grief upon me! I see such trouble coming, for there's no gray in *his* beard, and she with all the candles lit behind her eyes for him! I should have turned him away to die in the storm." But there was a little smile on her, all the same, for despite her loyalty to Conor Mac Nessa who had been her nursling, she had felt it always a sad thing that Deirdre should be wed to the King who was old enough to have fathered her.

After that, King Conor was not the only one to come visiting Deirdre, for again and again Naisi would come to speak with her, and Levarcham knew that she should tell this to the King, but the time went by and the time went by and she listened to Deirdre's pleading and did not tell him.

Then one evening when the wind blew over the shoulder of Slieve Gallion from the south and the first cold smell of spring was in the air, Deirdre said to Naisi when it was time for him to go, "Let you take me with you, and not leave me to be Queen beside a King that has gray hairs in his beard."

And Naisi groaned. "How can I do as you ask? I that am one of the King's own bodyguard, his hearth companion?"

And he went away, vowing in his heart that he would come no

more to the turf house in the hidden glen. But always he came again, and always Deirdre would plead, "Naisi, Naisi, take me away with you, it is you that I love. I have given no troth to the King for none has ever been asked of me, and it is yours that I am."

For a long while he held out against her, and against his own heart. But at last, when the apple trees behind the house were white with blossom, and Deirdre's wedding to the King no more than a few weeks away, the time came when he could hold out no longer. And he said, "So be it then, bird-of-my-heart, there are other lands across the sea and other kings to serve. For your sake I will live disgraced and die dishonored, and not think the price high to pay, if you love me, Deirdre."

In the darkness of the next night he came with horses, and with Ardan and Ainle his brothers; and they carried off both Deirdre and Levarcham, for the old woman said, "Grief upon me! I have done ill for your sakes, and let you not leave me now to the King's wrath!"

They fled to the coast and took ship for Scotland, and there Naisi and his brothers took service with the Pictish King. But after a while the King cast his looks too eagerly in Deirdre's direction, and they knew that the time had come to be moving on again.

After that they wandered for a long while, until they came at last to Glen Etive, and there they built a little huddle of turf bothies on the loch shore, and the men hunted and Deirdre and the old nurse cooked for them and spun and wove the wool of their few mountain sheep; and so the years went by.

And in all those years, three, maybe, or four, Conor Mac Nessa made no sign, but sat in his palace at Emain Macha, and did not forget. And from time to time some ragged herdsman or wandering harper would pass through Glen Etive and beg shelter for the night, and afterward return to Conor the King and tell him all that there was to tell of Deirdre and the sons of Usna—and they thinking themselves safe hidden all the while.

At last it seemed to the King, from the things told him by his spies, that the sons of Usna were growing restless in their solitudes; their thoughts turning back, maybe, to the life in a king's hall, and the feasting and the fighting to which they had been bred. Then he sent for Conall of the Victories, and Cuchulain, and old Fergus Mac Roy, and said to them, "It is in my mind that the sons of Usna have served long enough in exile, and the time comes to call them home."

"In friendship?" said Cuchulain, for he had never judged his kinsman one who would easily forgive a wrong, even after so long a time.

"In friendship," said the King. "I had a fool's fondness for the girl, but that is over long since. More it means to me to have the young men of my bodyguard about me. Therefore, one of you three shall go to Glen Etive, and tell them that the past is past, and bring them again to Emain Macha."

"And which of us three?" said Conall.

And the King considered, turning his frowning gaze from one to the other. "Conall, what would you do if I were to choose you, and harm came to them through me, after all?"

And Conall returned his gaze as frowningly. "I should know how to avenge them, and my own honor that would lie dead with them."

"That sounds like a threat," said the King, "but it makes no matter, since the question is but an empty one." And he turned to Cuchulain.

"I can answer only as Conall has answered," Cuchulain said, "but I think that after the revenge was over, men would no longer call me the Hound of Ulster but the Wolf of Ulster." And he looked long and hard into the King's eyes. "Therefore, it is as well, I think, that it is not myself that you will be sending to bring home the sons of Usna."

"No, it is not yourself, but Fergus Mac Roy that I shall send," said Conor the King. And Fergus, who was no fool in the general way of things, was so filled with gladness—for he loved Naisi and his brothers almost as much as did Cuchulain, as much as he loved his own sons, and his heart had wearied for them in their exile—that he lost his judgment and he did not see the look that Cuchulain had turned upon the King.

So Fergus went down to the coast and took ship for Scotland and at last and at last he came on a quiet evening to the cluster of green bothies on the shore of Glen Etive; and when Naisi and his brothers, who were but just returned from their hunting, saw him drawing near along the shore, they came racing to meet him and fling their arms about his shoulders, greeting him and marveling at his coming, and demanding what would be the latest news out of Ireland.

"The news out of Ireland is this," said Fergus, as they turned back toward the bothies together. "That Conor the King has put from his mind the thing that happened four springs ago between you and Deirdre and himself, and can no longer get the full pleasure of his mead-horn nor the full sweetness of harp song unless you return in friendship to enjoy them with him as you used to do."

Now at this the three brothers set up a shout, for they were as joyful to hear his news as he was to tell it. But Deirdre, who had come from the bothies to join them, said, "The sons of Usna do well enough here in Scotland. Let you be welcome here at our hearth, and then go back and tell King Conor that."

"We do well enough here," said Naisi, "but each man does best in the land that bred him, for it is there that the roots of his heart are struck."

"Ah, Naisi, Naisi, I have seen you and Ardan and Ainle growing weary of this happy Glen Etive; I know how you have longed for the King's Hall, and to be driving again like the wind behind the swift horses of Ulster. Yet I have had evil dreams of late and there is a shadow on my heart."

"Deirdre, what is it that you are afraid of?"

"I scarcely know," said Deirdre. "I find it hard to believe in the King's forgiveness. What safeguard have we if we give ourselves back into his power?"

And Fergus Mac Roy said, "Mine. And I think that no king in all Ireland would dare to violate that."

Then while they ate the evening meal about the peat fire in the house place, Naisi laughed at her for her fears, swaggering a little with his thumbs in his belt, because the King had sent for him to come back to his old place again. And next day they gathered up all that they had of goods and gear, and went down to the coast, to where the ship that had brought Fergus from Ireland lay waiting on the tide line. And the bothies by the loch shore were left empty and forsaken.

The rowers bent to their oars and the long corach slipped seaward; and sitting in the stern with old Levarcham against her knee, Deirdre looked back past the man at the steering oar toward the shores of Scotland, and a lament rose in her, and would not be held back.

"My love to you, oh land of Alban; pleasant are your harbors and your clear green-sided hills. Glen Archan, my grief! High its hart's tongue and bright its flowers; never were young men lighter hearted than the three sons of Usna in Glen Archan. Glen-da-Rua, my grief! Glen-da-Rua! Sweet is the voice of the cuckoo in the woods of Glen-da-Rua. Glen Etive, my grief! Ochone! Glen Etive; it was there I built my first house, and slept under soft coverings with Naisi's hand beneath my head. And never would I have left you, Glen Etive, but that I go with Naisi my love."

Scarcely had they set foot in Ulster once more, when Baruch, a veteran of the Red Branch, came to meet them, and bade Fergus, as an old friend, to feast with him that night in his Dun close by. And with him were Fergus's two sons, Illan the Fair and Buinne the Red, come to greet him on his return. Now Fergus did not know that the King had ordered that feast, but he knew that his oath to Conor Mac Nessa bound him to bring Deirdre and the sons of Usna straight from their landing place to Emain Macha, and he tried to win clear of the thing, saying that he could not turn aside from his way until he had brought Deirdre and the three brothers under safe conduct to the King's presence. But Baruch would not be denied, and bade him remember that his geise forbade him ever to refuse when bidden to a feast, and so at last despite Deirdre's pleading (for no warrior might go against his geise) he bade his sons to take charge of the party, and himself went with Baruch.

When the six of them drew near to Emain Macha, Deirdre said, "See now, how it will be. If Conor the King bids us to his own hall and his own hearth-side, then he means us no ill; but if we are lodged apart in the Red Branch Hostel, then grief upon us! For all that I fear will come to pass."

And when they came into the Royal Dun they were lodged in the Red Branch Hostel, to wait until the King should send for them. And Deirdre said, without hope of being heeded, "Did I not tell you how it would be?"

But Naisi only laughed and held her warm in his arms, saying, "Soon the King will send for us in friendship, and all things will be as they used to be."

But first the King sent for old Levarcham, and she went and made her peace with him where he sat moodily in his sleeping-chamber with his favorite hound at his feet. And he asked her how it was with Deirdre, and if her beauty was on her yet, after so many years in the wilderness.

"Ach now, what would you be expecting? Life in the wilderness deals hardly with a woman," said Levarcham. "The skin that was so white is brown now, and the wind has chapped her lips and the sun has faded her hair. Her beauty is all gone from her and if you were to see her now you would think her any farmer's woman."

"Then I will not send for her when I send for the sons of Usna," said the King, and he sighed. "Since Naisi has had her beauty, let him keep her. I will not see her again."

But when Levarcham had been gone a while he began to doubt in his heart whether she had told him the truth, and he called to him his shield-bearer, and said, "Go you and find some means to look secretly at the woman that is in the Red Branch Guest House, and come back and tell me whether she is yet fair to look upon."

So it was that when those within the Guest House were taking their ease after the evening meal, Deirdre and Naisi playing chess together while the others lay about the fire, Ardan cried out suddenly and sprang to his feet, pointing to the high window in the gable wall. And looking where he pointed, Naisi saw the face of the King's shield-bearer peering in; and he caught up a golden chessman from the board and flung it at him, and it caught him in the face and struck out his left eye.

The man loosed his hold on the window ledge with a sobbing cry and dropped to the ground, and ran and stumbled back to King Conor with his bloody face in his hands.

"The woman in the Red Branch Guest House is the fairest that ever I have seen. And if Naisi Son of Usna had not seen me and put out my eye with the fling of a golden chess piece, it is in my heart that I would have been clinging to the window ledge and gazing at her still."

Then Conor Mac Nessa in a black fury came out into his great hall and shouted to his warriors that were feasting there to be out and bring the three sons of Usna before him, he cared not whether alive or dead, or if they must pull down the Red Branch Hostel timber by timber and turf by turf to do it; for they were traitors that had done him foul wrong in the matter of the woman Deirdre.

The warriors sprang from the benches and snatched up their weapons and ran out, shouting, tossing the war cry to and fro among them, and some, in passing the fires, pulled out flaming branches and whirled them above their heads as they ran, and so Naisi and the rest within the Hostel saw the red flicker of the firebrands through the high windows, and heard the shouting. And Deirdre cried out, wild as a storm-driven bird, "Treachery! Naisi, Naisi, I told you that I feared evil, but you would not listen to me!"

And in the same moment Naisi himself had leaped to drop the mighty bar across the door.

"Look to the windows! The windows, my brothers, and you sons of Fergus who came here with us in his stead!"

And each catching up his weapons, they ran to their places, and for a breath of time there was stillness in the hall. Then the great voice of Celthair Son of Uthica cried to them from before the door. "Out with you, thieves and rievers! Come out to us now, and bring with you the woman you stole from the King!"

And standing within the door Naisi shouted back, "Neither thieves nor rievers are we, for the woman came to me for love and of her own wish; and with me and with my brothers she shall remain, though every champion of the Red Branch comes against us!"

But it was not long that they could hold the Hostel, for someone shouted, "Burn them out, then, we have the firebrands!" And the shouting rose to a roar, and the warriors thrust their blazing branches under the thatch. And Deirdre cried out at the sight of the red flame running among the rafters, and the hall began to fill with smoke.

Then Naisi said, "It is time to unbar the door, for it is better to die by the cold blade than the choking reek of fire!"

So they heaved up the bar and flung wide the door, and leaped to meet the King's warriors who were ready for them like terriers at the mouth of a rat hole. A great fight there was, about the threshold of the Red Branch Guest House, and many of the warriors of Ulster fell before the blades of the sons of Usna and the sons of Fergus Mac Roy. And in the fighting Illan the Fair got his death, but to Buinne the Red a worse thing befell, for the King contrived to have him surrounded and brought living out of the fight, and bought him with the promise of much land.

Then with the Red Branch Hostel roaring up in flames behind them, Naisi and his brothers linked their three shields together and set Deirdre in the midst of them, and so made a great charge to break through the press of Conor's warriors. And spent and wounded as they were they might yet have won clear, but that Conor Mac Nessa, seeing how it was, bade certain of his Druids to make a strong magic against them, and the Druids made the seeming of a dark wild sea that rose and rose around the island of linked shields, so that the sons of Usna were fighting against the waves of it more than the warriors of the King's Guard. And Naisi, feeling the cold buffeting of the sea rise higher about him and seeing the white hissing break of the waves against their linked shields, caught Deirdre up onto his shoulder to save her from the sea. And they were choking and half drowned, while all the while, to all men save themselves, the King's forecourt was dry as summer drought in the red glare of the burning Hostel.

So at last their strength failed them and the Red Branch Warriors closed about them and struck the swords from their hands, and took and bound them and dragged them before King Conor where he stood looking on.

Then Conor Mac Nessa called for man after man to come forward and slay him the three, but it seemed that none of them heard him, neither Conall of the Victories nor Cethern Son of Findtan, nor Dubthach the Beetle of Ulster, nor Cuchulain himself, who was but that moment come upon the scene, until at last Owen Prince of Ferney stepped forward and took up Naisi's own sword from the ground where it lay.

"Let you strike the heads from all three of us at one blow," said Naisi then. "The blade has skill enough for that; and so we shall all be away on the same breath." And as they stood there side by side, and their arms bound behind them, the Prince of Ferney shored off their three proud heads at the one stroke. And all the Red Branch Warriors let out three heavy shouts above them. And Deirdre broke free of the men who held her, and she tore her bright hair and cast herself upon the three headless bodies and cried out to them as though they could still hear her. "Long will be the days without you, O sons of Usna, the days that were never wearisome in your company. The High King of Ulster, my first betrothed, I forsook for the love of Naisi, and sorrow is to me and those that loved me. Make keening for the heroes that were killed by treachery at their coming back to Ulster. The sons of Usna fell in the fight like three branches that were growing straight and strong; their birth was beautiful and their blossoming, and now they are cut down.

"Oh young men digging the new grave, do not make it narrow, leave space there for me that follows after, for I am Deirdre without gladness, and my life at its end!"

And as they would have dragged her away from Naisi's body, she snatched a little sharp knife from the belt of one of the men who held her, and with a last desolate cry, drove the blade home into her breast, and the life of her was gone from between their hands like a bird from its cage.

They buried Deirdre and Naisi not far apart, at the spot where in later times rose the great church of Armagh, and out of her grave and out of Naisi's there grew two tall yew trees, whose tops, when they were full grown, met above the church roof, mingling their dark branches so that no man might part them more. And when the sea wind hushed through the boughs, the people said, "Listen, Deirdre and Naisi are singing together." And when in summer the small red berries burned like jewels among the furred darkness of the boughs, they said, "See, Deirdre and Naisi are decked for their wedding."

How is Deirdre like Pandora and Eve? Do you think her secret homestead in Slieve Gallion and her dwelling in Glen Etive are like the Garden of Eden? Why?

How is Conor, like Zeus in the myth on page 74, a destroyer of innocence?

Arachne and Atalanta were destroyed because they challenged a higher power. Was Deirdre destroyed for the same reason?

Do you think the gap of generations was partly responsible for Deirdre's tragedy? How did the conflict of generations affect even the gods in the first myth in this book?

How does the myth of the Four Ages (page 14) also tell about the death of "childhood"?

In the drawing that opens this unit, we see a man and a boy "in the same boat"—entering a maze. Create a game using a maze or labyrinth as the path which all players must travel in order to reach a goal and win the game (or escape the maze). What determines the number of steps a player may take—a toss of dice (chance), an answer to a question (knowledge), performance of a task (achievement)? What are the obstacles to be overcome along the path? Is your game like a journey? Or is it more like a puzzle to be solved? How is it like life? Can a player retrace his or her steps? What reward does the winner receive? What do the losers suffer?

Arms and the Boy

Let the boy try along this bayonet blade
How cold steel is, and keen with hunger of blood;
Blue with all malice, like a madman's flash;
And thinly drawn with famishing for flesh.

Lend him to stroke these blind, blunt bullet heads
Which long to nuzzle in the heart of lads,
Or give him cartridges of fine zinc teeth,
Sharp with the sharpness of grief and death.

For his teeth seem for laughing round an apple.
There lurk no claws behind his fingers supple;
And god will grow no talons at his heels,
Nor antlers through the thickness of his curls.

WILFRED OWEN

Why is "childhood" destroyed in this poem? Who destroys it?

Pegasus, the famous winged horse of Greek mythology, has been used through the ages as a symbol of freedom.

Pegasus

My soul was an old horse
Offered for sale in twenty fairs.
I offered him to the Church—the buyers
Were little men who feared his unusual airs.
One said: "Let him remain unbid
In the wind and rain and hunger
Of sin and we will get him—
With the winkers thrown in—for nothing."

Then the men of State looked at
What I'd brought for sale.
One minister, wondering if
Another horse body would fit the tail
That he'd kept for sentiment— ·
The relic of his own soul—
Said, "I will graze him in lieu of his labor."
I lent him for a week or more
And he came back a hurdle of bones,
Starved, overworked, in despair.
I nursed him on the roadside grass
To shape him for another fair.

I lowered my price. I stood him where
The broken-winded, spavined stand
And crooked shopkeepers said that he
Might do for a season on the land—
But not for high-paid work in towns.
He'd do a tinker, possibly.
I begged, "O make some offer now,
A soul is a poor man's tragedy.

He'll draw your dungiest cart," I said,
"Show you short cuts to Mass,
Teach weather lore, at night collect
Bad debts from poor men's grass."
                              And they would not.

              Where the
Tinkers quarrel I went down
With my horse, my soul.
I cried, "Who will bid me half a crown?"
From their rowdy bargaining
Not one turned. "Soul," I prayed,
"I have hawked you through the world
Of Church and State and meanest trade.
But this evening, halter off,
Never again will it go on.
On the south side of ditches
There is grazing of the sun.
No more haggling with the world. . . ."

As I said these words he grew
Wings upon his back. Now I may ride him
Every land my imagination knew.

                              PATRICK KAVANAGH

This speaker uses a metaphor and identifies his soul as an "old horse."
What does he learn from his bitter experience in trying to sell his soul?
When is his soul transformed into Pegasus?

Is this a poem about the "end of childhood" or is it about the beginning
of something else?

Do you think the "end" of childhood is inevitable? Why? Do you think that
any aspects of childhood can be recaptured or recovered?

Ring around the rosie,
A pocket full of posies—
Ashes, ashes,
We all fall down.

Children play a circle game with this jingle. But, surprisingly, they sing and dance to what is really a tragedy. They sing: We are playing in a garden of roses now, but there will come a time when our flowers will turn to ashes, when perhaps we ourselves will turn to ashes. That will be the time of our falling down.

The surprising combination of wish and nightmare in the jingle tells us something about ourselves. Even as children, we look out onto the world with a double vision: we see a world we want to keep and a world we want to reject. The imagination puts this split in our vision into perspective. It helps us stand back from the terrible things in life, and control them and shape them and share them by talking and singing and writing about them.

What is the meaning of "lost childhood" or of "falling down"? In life, it is called "growing up," that time when innocence somehow fades away and is replaced by experience or knowledge of the world. But in the imagination, it is the opening of a forbidden jar, the eating of forbidden fruit, the death of a loved one, the destruction of something beautiful. In other words, it is a story or an event that is a symbol of a universal human experience. When such imaginative stories or events are so common as to be used over and over by many cultures, they are called archetypes.

The fall from innocence is an archetypal event. It signifies the realization that we cannot hide from time. It is the discovery that all the potential for happiness that we feel in childhood is often not realized in adulthood. It is the discovery that playing

142

house is not the same as running a home, that playing war is not the same as putting a bullet through a person's head. The fall is facing the fact of death and the facts of life, seeing the reality behind the mystery, and the mystery behind the reality.

What causes the fall from innocence? Myths and stories give us many answers: discontent, chance, fate, time, a god's whim or human pride. It is often a challenge made by one human to another (Pandora to Epimetheus, Eve to Adam, Athene in the form of an old woman to Arachne), as though human beings are fated to draw each other into the web of experience, as though we feel that a person must "fall" before he or she can know what it is to be a part of the human family.

At one time, people marked the passage from childhood to adulthood with rituals. These initiation customs may now have become tokens, but many of them still survive and still convey a sense of mystery. Why does a bride wear a color that symbolizes innocence? Why is she carried over a threshold? Why must an initiate go through an ordeal before being accepted as a member of a club or fraternity?

Literature, which organizes all human experience, offers some ways of recovering aspects of childhood, some ways of regaining innocence. We have stories about evil being overcome by the power of innocence; we have heroes who defeat evil with honor or courage or suffering; we have images of the golden world that we still believe in and are trying to rebuild. Literature, like all art, as it conquers time, recovers for us certain aspects of childhood and innocence.

If some innocence is regained, what kind of innocence is it? How has it changed? Perhaps it is "mature innocence," or integrity, or nobility, or identity. Perhaps this regaining of innocence is what it means to be fully human — it is the imaginative return to the golden garden, the one place where we can truly be ourselves.

4

THE CATARACTS OF HEAVEN

Once by the Pacific

The shattered water made a misty din.
Great waves looked over others coming in,
And thought of doing something to the shore
That water never did to land before.
The clouds were low and hairy in the skies,
Like locks blown forward in the gleam of eyes.
You could not tell, and yet it looked as if
The shore was lucky in being backed by cliff,
The cliff in being backed by continent;
It looked as if a night of dark intent
Was coming, and not only a night, an age.
Someone had better be prepared for rage.
There would be more than ocean-water broken
Before God's last *Put out the Light* was spoken.

ROBERT FROST

The Flood

A Greek myth
Retold by W.H.D. ROUSE

Now in this Iron Age, Zeus visited the earth, to see whether men were as bad as they were said to be; and he came to the realm of one Lycaon, who was King in Arcadia. Lycaon laughed, on hearing that Zeus had come, and said, "Now then, let us see if he is really a god!" So he killed an innocent man, a hostage in fact, whom he was bound to protect, and cooked his flesh, and set it before Zeus his guest, to see if he would eat it. But Zeus struck the King's house with a thunderbolt, and Lycaon fled terrified to the hills. His rough coat changed into bristling hairs all over his body. He tried to shout, and out came a snarl, for he had turned into a wolf, destined to delight in blood all the rest of his days.

Zeus called a council of the gods, and told them what had been done; and then he declared that he thought it best to destroy mankind. The others said, "But what shall we do? There will be no one to offer sacrifices to the gods." "Never mind for that," said Zeus. "I will provide." The question then came, whether he should launch his thunderbolts on the world and set it afire; but Zeus was afraid that so great a conflagration might rise to the upper air, and set that also on fire, so that the Olympians themselves would be burned up.

It seemed best therefore to use water. The winds were bidden to gather the clouds; the rains descended; and the floods came and overwhelmed the whole country of Greece, so that all who dwelt there were drowned. Men and beasts, wolves and sheep, lions and tigers were carried down to the sea, and seals and dolphins swam about in the forests.

But one solitary pair remained: Deucalion, a son of Prometheus, and his wife, Pyrrha, the daughter of Epimetheus. They were good people both, no one more just and no one more strict in worshiping the gods. They had got into a little chest or ark, which was in the house, and the waters carried them to the slopes of Mount Parnassus, close to the cleft where Mother Earth had an oracle. The shrine at that time was in charge of Themis, goddess of Justice, for Apollo had not yet come that way. They gave thanks to Themis, and prayed to the nymphs of that place. When Zeus saw that this innocent pair had been saved, he told Poseidon to recall his floods, and Poseidon bade his trumpeter Triton sound the recall. Triton blew a blast into his hollow shell, and the waves were stayed. Then Zeus made a great hole in the earth, and the waters all ran down, and the land began to appear. For thousands of years, this hole used to be shown in the sacred place of Olympia.

Deucalion looked around on the world, all shining with mud, and said to Pyrrha, "My wife, see, we are the whole population of the world! And the clouds are still dark above us. What should I do, if I were alone? or you, without me? Let us ask what is the will of God."

So they entered the shrine of Themis, and said, "Themis, if the anger of Zeus is satisfied, tell us how to recover the human race." And Themis said, "Go down to the plain, and cover your heads with a veil, and throw behind you your mother's bones."

They went out, and Pyrrha said to her husband, "I am afraid, my dear husband. How can we find our mother's bones? And if we could find them, would it not be wicked to disturb them?"

But Deucalion was not his father's son for nothing; he had some of this father's wisdom, and he replied, "Wife, the gods often speak in riddles. I think Themis means the bones of Mother Earth, that is, stones. Let us try them, it can do no harm to try."

Then they veiled their heads, and each of them picked up stones, and threw them behind their backs. Perhaps you will hardly believe it, but the stones as they fell took on human shapes. Deucalion's became men, and Pyrrha's became women. Even now we show traces of this origin, for we have veins in our bodies, like the veins in a piece of marble, both called by the same name; and men are called peoples, because they grew out of pebbles.

Whether or not human sacrifices actually took place historically, they did take place in the imagination. What is the myth-maker using human sacrifice to symbolize in this story?

Like fire, water has both good and bad qualities. It suggests both divine and demonic images to the imagination. Name some ways you associate water with death, destruction, winter, and darkness. Name some ways you associate water with birth, life, spring, and light.

*The hero Odysseus has just set sail
for adventure. On board ship, he
encourages a young piper to tell the
crew a tale appropriate to the
beginning of a new voyage. The piper,
addressing himself, sings out this story.*

The Piper's Tale

From The Odyssey: A Modern Sequel

"Go to it, piper, snatch your tune, kick it about,"
he sang, "strike sparks on the hard ground till rocks fling fire,
shut your poor squint-eyes tight and sing all that you see!
Empty are land and sea and crystal clear the air
that neither smoke of chimney dulls nor man's breath sways;
nor has the mind appeared as yet to send it tempest tossed.
Like two twin, groping moles, my eyes dug deep in earth
and to their sockets in the dead of night returned:
'Master, the world is waste, not a soul or worm's abroad.'
But from my heart I heard a murmuring in the grass
and two small palpitating hearts dared answer me,
ah, two green worms poked through the crust of the upper world!
My heart cried out and fluttered, then sank low to earth
and joined the crawling friends that we might trudge together.
In waste, in desolate waste, even a worm's shade is good.
I walked the river bank in stealth, crept in the weeds,
my eyes and ears perked up with awe, my nostrils flared:
these were not worms, dear friends! I knelt and bowed down low,
much-suffering Lord and Mother, forebears of all mankind!

When day appeared, the worms stood in the sun for warmth,
but God discerned them from on high and his eyes flashed:
'I see two worms! Who cast them in my fruitful vineyards?
Rise out of snow, O frigid Frost, freeze them to ice!'

Then Frost fell silently on earth in soft snowfalls,
unwound a thick white shroud and pallid dead man's sheet,
then grasped and smothered the high peaks and swept the fields.
The poor worms shook with fear and crawled in a deep cave,
and when he saw his small wife weep, the male worm said:
'I will not let the snow take you from me, beloved.
Lean on me, dear, and press your body to my warm chest;
a murderer rules the sky, jealous of Mother Earth,
and from his white lips drip nine kinds of deadly poison;
but I shall rear my head against him, Lady, for love of you.'
The words hung on his lips still when the twisted brain
of God Almighty flung in the cave his lightning flash;
but the worm rushed to the holy fire and lit his torch,
piled heap on heap of dry leaves till the bonfire rose
to highest heaven and singed the grisly beard of God.
Then the child-eating Father stormed and yelled for the hag
with hanging dugs and face of plague to come before him:
'O Hunger, thin lean daughter with your slender scythe,
fall on the earth and thresh it well, fall in their guts,
tear up each overweening root, body and all!
I won't allow a soul on earth to rear its head!'
Then bony Hunger crawled to earth, mowed down the grass,
mowed down the pregnant bowels, and like a lean hyena
licked with her scabrous tongue both bones and meager meat.
The two souls were drained hollow, their eyes dulled and glazed,
and the male worm crawled slowly to his fainting mate;
'Dear wife, don't let the fire go out, crawl near the hearth,
blow with your breath upon it, feed and tend it well,
for I have carved myself a bow to hunt the stag.'
The livelong day and night the female fed the fire
and in her husband kept her faith and mocked at God:
'Keep thundering on, you slayer, and do whatever you dare!
My husband's a stout hunter and he'll fetch me game!'

Her lips were twitching still when she heard manly strides
and saw the male worm gladly burdened with wild game;
the fire blazed till the whole cavern leapt and laughed;
the female carved a lean long stick, and singing shrilly
her stubborn, scornful tune, she twirled the spitted meat.
When they had eaten and revived, they sat by the hearth

and the male worm turned round and spoke to his brave spouse:
'Dear wife, if only God would let us rest a while
to fix the heart firm in its breast and to stop trembling!
How good to sit in the cool evening after meals
and spend the night, beloved, in sweet and gentle talk.'
But the meat's odor rose and stuck in God's wild nostrils
so that he grabbed with rage the rain's black hanging dugs:
'Burst open, you cataracts of heaven, deluge the world!
I scorn to share the earth with others, it's all mine!'
The unceasing waters fell and flooded the upper world,
the land was drowned, the mountains' snowy peaks sank under,
and God rolled choked in laughter above the deluged earth.
'The world's all mine to flood or fire as I well please!
I'm not a fool to let the dust rear up its head!'
He roared until a whirlwind whipped the waves to froth.
But in a high ship then, at the world's edge, there loomed
the great worm scudding swiftly by with swelling sails.
The oldest Murderer shook and crawled in his blue cave
then roared and called his first-born son and greatest heir:
'Help me, dear faithful Death, help me, my life's imperiled!
Two small worms rear their heads on earth and threat to eat me!'

Death took his sharpest knives, crawled down into the cave,
crept close beside the two small worms and spread his feet
to warm himself by the hearthstones and spy with greed
on the pair's simple and calm gossip around the fire.
And when the male worm saw him there, his small heart froze,
but he said nothing, for fear his wife might faint with fright,
and when night fell at length and they lay down to sleep
the worm crawled slowly, careful not to waken Death,
and in the darkness hugged his mate in tight embrace.
Death's dry bones glowed with light in the erotic dark
but he woke not nor felt the two warm bodies merge;
the male worm then took heart and in his wife's ear whispered:
'With one sweet kiss, dear wife, we've conquered conquering
    Death!' "

NIKOS KAZANTZAKIS
Translated by KIMON FRIAR

In this poem, God is called the oldest Murderer. Do any other stories you have read show a divine character with a demonic side?

What forces of nature are personified as menacing and demonic in this poem?

How are the two worms in this poem like Deucalion and Pyrrha in the Greek myth? How are they like Noah and his family in the Bible?

The authors of the myth, the Bible, and the poem are using the same archetypes (the flood story, the good man and woman) to say something about what it means to be a human being. What do you think they are trying to say?

A Hard Rain's
A Gonna Fall

A/ Oh, where have you been, my blue-eyed son?
Oh, where have you been, my darling young one?

B/ I've stumbled on the side of twelve misty mountains,
I've walked and I've crawled on six crooked highways,
I've stepped in the middle of seven sad forests,
I've been out in front of a dozen dead oceans,

C/ I've been ten thousand miles in the mouth of a graveyard,
And it's a hard, and it's a hard, it's a hard, and it's a hard,
And it's a hard rain's a gonna fall.

A/ Oh, what did you see, my blue-eyed son?
Oh, what did you see, my darling young one?

B/ I saw a new-born baby with wild wolves all around it,
I saw a highway of diamonds with nobody on it,
I saw a black branch with blood that kept drippin',
I saw a room full of men with their hammers a-bleedin',
I saw a white ladder all covered with water,
I saw ten thousand talkers whose tongues were all broken,

C/ I saw guns and sharp swords in the hands of young children,
And it's a hard, and it's a hard, it's a hard, it's a hard,
And it's a hard rain's a gonna fall.

A/ And what did you hear, my blue-eyed son?
And what did you hear, my darling young one?

B/ I heard the sound of a thunder, it roared out a warnin',
Heard the roar of a wave that could drown the whole world,
Heard one hundred drummers whose hands were a blazin',
Heard ten thousand whisperin' and nobody listenin',
Heard one person starve, I heard many people laughin',
Heard the song of a poet who died in the gutter,

C/ Heard the sound of a clown who cried in the alley,
And it's a hard, and it's a hard, it's a hard, it's a hard,
And it's a hard rain's a gonna fall.

A/ Oh, who did you meet, my blue-eyed son?
Who did you meet, my darling young one?

B/ I met a young child beside a dead pony,
I met a white man who walked a black dog,
I met a young woman whose body was burning,
I met a young girl, she gave me a rainbow,
I met one man who was wounded in love,

C/ I met another man who was wounded with hatred,
And it's a hard, it's a hard, it's a hard, it's a hard,
It's a hard rain's a gonna fall.

A/ Oh, what'll you do now, my blue-eyed son?
Oh, what'll you do now, my darling young one?

B/ I'm a goin' back out 'fore the rain starts a fallin',
I'll walk to the depth of the deepest black forest,
Where the people are many and their hands are all empty,
Where the pellets of poison are flooding their waters,
Where the home in the valley meets the damp dirty prison,
Where the executioner's face is always well hidden,
Where hunger is ugly, where souls are forgotten,
Where black is the color, where none is the number,
And I'll tell it and think it and speak it and breathe it,

And reflect it from the mountain so all souls can see it,
Then I'll stand on the ocean until I start sinkin',

C/ But I'll know my song well before I start singin',
    And it's a hard, it's a hard, it's a hard, it's a hard
    It's a hard rain's a gonna fall.

BOB DYLAN

Like Zeus in the Greek flood myth, the blue-eyed son goes on a journey.
How are his experiences like those of Zeus?

Zeus, king of the gods, comes up with one solution to what he has seen.
The blue-eyed son, only a human being, arrives at his own personal solution. What does he decide to do?

Gilgamesh's closest friend has died.
Grieved to think that death puts an
end to friendship, he endures a long
and difficult quest to find Utnapishtim,
the one person who has been granted
immortality by the gods. Gilgamesh
finally finds the old man on the shore
of the sea of death. As they walk,
Utnapishtim tells the story of why he
was chosen to live forever.

"Unanswerable questions . . ."

From Gilgamesh, *a Babylonian epic*

There was a city called Shurrupak
On the bank of the Euphrates.
It was very old and so many were the gods
Within it. They converged in their complex hearts
On the idea of creating a great flood.
There was Anu, their aging and weak-minded father,
The military Enlil, his adviser,
Ishtar, the sensation craving one,
And all the rest. Ea, who was present
At their council, came to my house
And, frightened by the violent winds that filled the air,
Echoed all that they were planning and had said.
Man of Shurrupak, he said, tear down your house
And build a ship. Abandon your possessions
And the works that you find beautiful and crave
And save your life instead. Into the ship
Bring the seed of all the living creatures.

I was overawed, perplexed,
And finally downcast. I agreed to do
As Ea said but I protested: What shall I say
To the city, the people, the leaders?

Tell them, Ea said, you have learned that Enlil
The war god despises you and will not
Give you access to the city any more.
Tell them for this Ea will bring the rains.

That is the way gods think, he laughed. His tone
Of savage irony frightened Gilgamesh
Yet gave him pleasure, being his friend.
They only know how to compete or echo.

But who am I to talk? He sighed as if
Disgusted with himself; I did as he
Commanded me to do. I spoke to them
And some came out to help me build the ship
Of seven stories each with nine chambers.
The boat was cube in shape, and sound; it held
The food and wine and precious minerals
And seed of living animals we put
In it. My family then moved inside
And all who wanted to be with us there:
The game of the field, the goats of the Steppe,
The craftsmen of the city came, a navigator
Came. And then Ea ordered me to close
The door. The time of the great rains had come.
O there was ample warning, yes, my friend,
But it was terrifying still. Buildings
Blown by the winds for miles like desert brush.
People clung to branches of trees until
Roots gave way. New possessions, now debris,
Floated on the water with their special
Sterile vacancy. The riverbanks failed
To hold the water back. Even the gods
Cowered like dogs at what they had done.
Ishtar cried out like a woman at the height
Of labor: O how could I have wanted
To do this to my people! They were *hers*,
Notice. Even her sorrow was possessive.
Her spawn that she had killed too soon.
Old gods are terrible to look at when
They weep, all bloated like spoiled fish.

One wonders if they ever understand
That they have caused their grief. When the seventh day
Came, the flood subsided from its slaughter
Like hair drawn slowly back
From a tormented face.
I looked at the earth and all was silence.
Bodies lay like alewives dead
And in the clay. I fell down
On the ship's deck and wept. Why? Why did they
Have to die! I couldn't understand. I asked
Unanswerable questions a child asks
When a parent dies—for nothing. Only slowly
Did I make myself believe—or hope—they
Might all be swept up in their fragments
Together
And made whole again
By some compassionate hand.
But my hand was too small
To do the gathering.
I have only known this feeling since
When I look out across the sea of death,
This pull inside against a littleness—myself—
Waiting for an upward gesture.

O the dove, the swallow, and the raven
Found their land. The people left the ship.
But I for a long time could only stay inside.
I could not face the deaths I knew were there.
Then I received Enlil, for Ea had *chosen* me;
The war god touched my forehead; he blessed
My family and said:
Before this you were just a man, but now
You and your wife shall be like gods. You
Shall live in the distance at the rivers' mouth,
At the source. I allowed myself to be
Taken far away from all that I had seen.
Sometimes even in love we yearn to leave mankind.
Only the loneliness of the Only One
Who never acts like gods
Is bearable.

I am downcast because of what I've seen,
Not what I still have hope to yearn for.
Lost youths restored to life,
Lost children to their crying mothers,
Lost wives, lost friends, lost hopes, lost homes,
I want to bring these back to them.
But now there is you.
We must find something for you.
How will you find eternal life
To bring back to your friend?
He pondered busily, as if
It were just a matter of getting down to work
Or making plans for an excursion.
Then he relaxed, as if there were no use
In this reflection. I would grieve
At all that may befall you still
If I did not know you must return
And bury your own loss and build
Your world anew with your own hands.
I envy you your freedom.

As he listened, Gilgamesh felt tiredness again
Come over him, the words now so discouraging,
The promise so remote, so unlike what he sought.
He looked into the old man's face, and it seemed changed,
As if this one had fought within himself a battle
He would never know, that still went on.

Retold by HERBERT MASON

What features do this Babylonian flood story, the Greek flood story, and the story of Noah's flood have in common?

In earlier units, we have seen huge gods, who were as immense as the universe. On the other hand, we have seen people characterized as pets, or as tiny playthings. In "Snake" (page 54), a man felt a "pettiness" and in this story a man feels a "littleness." How does the imagination use images of size to say something about what it means to be a human being?

It Is Almost the Year Two Thousand

To start the world of old
We had one age of gold
Not labored out of mines,
And some say there are signs
The second such has come,
The true Millennium,
The final golden glow
To end it. And if so
(And science ought to know)
We well may raise our heads
From weeding garden beds
And annotating books
To watch this end de luxe.

ROBERT FROST

How is gold used as a divine image and a demonic image in this poem?

In what important respect is the "flood" described in this poem different from the others in this unit?

The Nine Billion
Names of God

ARTHUR C. CLARKE

"This is a slightly unusual request," said Dr. Wagner, with what he hoped was commendable restraint. "As far as I know, it's the first time anyone's been asked to supply a Tibetan monastery with an Automatic Sequence Computer. I don't wish to be inquisitive, but I should hardly have thought that your—ah—establishment had much use for such a machine. Could you explain just what you intend to do with it?"

"Gladly," replied the lama, readjusting his silk robes and carefully putting away the slide rule he had been using for currency conversions. "Your Mark V Computer can carry out any routine mathematical operation involving up to ten digits. However, for our work we are interested in *letters,* not numbers. As we wish you to modify the output circuits, the machine will be printing words, not columns of figures."

"I don't quite understand. . . ."

"This is a project on which we have been working for the last three centuries—since the lamasery was founded, in fact. It is somewhat alien to your way of thought, so I hope you will listen with an open mind while I explain it."

"Naturally."

"It is really quite simple. We have been compiling a list which shall contain all the possible names of God."

"I beg your pardon?"

"We have reason to believe," continued the lama imperturbably, "that all such names can be written with not more than nine letters in an alphabet we have devised."

"And you have been doing this for three centuries?"

"Yes: we expected it would take us about fifteen thousand years to complete the task."

"Oh," Dr. Wagner looked a little dazed. "Now I see why you wanted to hire one of our machines. But exactly what is the *purpose* of this project?"

The lama hesitated for a fraction of a second, and Wagner wondered if he had offended him. If so, there was no trace of annoyance in the reply.

"Call it ritual, if you like, but it's a fundamental part of our belief. All the many names of the Supreme Being—God, Jehovah, Allah, and so on—they are only man-made labels. There is a philosophical problem of some difficulty here, which I do not propose to discuss, but somewhere among all the possible combinations of letters that can occur are what one may call the *real* names of God. By systematic permutation of letters, we have been trying to list them all."

"I see. You've been starting at AAAAAAA . . . and working up to ZZZZZZZZ. . . . "

"Exactly—though we use a special alphabet of our own. Modifying the electromatic typewriters to deal with this is, of course, trivial. A rather more interesting problem is that of devising suitable circuits to eliminate ridiculous combinations. For example, no letter must occur more than three times in succession."

"Three? Surely you mean two."

"Three is correct: I am afraid it would take too long to explain why, even if you understood our language."

"I'm sure it would," said Wagner hastily. "Go on."

"Luckily, it will be a simple matter to adapt your Automatic Sequence Computer for this work, since once it has been programed properly it will permute each letter in turn and print the result. What would have taken us fifteen thousand years it will be able to do in a hundred days."

Dr. Wagner was scarcely conscious of the faint sounds from the Manhattan streets far below. He was in a different world, a world of natural, not man-made, mountains. High up in their remote aeries these monks had been patiently at work, generation after generation, compiling their lists of meaningless words. Was there any limit to the follies of mankind? Still, he must give no hint of his inner thoughts. The customer was always right. . . .

"There's no doubt," replied the doctor, "that we can modify the Mark V to print lists of this nature. I'm much more worried about the problem of installation and maintenance. Getting out to Tibet, in these days, is not going to be easy."

"We can arrange that. The components are small enough to travel by air—that is one reason why we chose your machine. If you can get them to India, we will provide transport from there."

"And you want to hire two of our engineers?"

"Yes, for the three months that the project should occupy."

"I've no doubt that Personnel can manage that." Dr. Wagner scribbled a note on his desk pad. "There are just two other points—"

Before he could finish the sentence the lama had produced a small slip of paper.

"This is my certified credit balance at the Asiatic Bank."

"Thank you. It appears to be—ah—adequate. The second matter is so trivial that I hesitate to mention it—but it's surprising how often the obvious gets overlooked. What source of electrical energy have you?"

"A diesel generator providing fifty kilowatts at a hundred and ten volts. It was installed about five years ago and is quite reliable. It's made life at the lamasery much more comfortable, but of course it was really installed to provide power for the motors driving the prayer wheels."

"Of course," echoed Dr. Wagner. "I should have thought of that."

The view from the parapet was vertiginous, but in time one gets used to anything. After three months, George Hanley was not impressed by the two-thousand-foot swoop into the abyss or the remote checkerboard of fields in the valley below. He was leaning against the wind-smoothed stones and staring morosely at the distant mountains whose names he had never bothered to discover.

This, thought George, was the craziest thing that had ever happened to him. "Project Shangri-La," some wit back at the labs had christened it. For weeks now the Mark V had been churning out acres of sheets covered with gibberish. Patiently, inexorably, the computer had been rearranging letters in all their possible combinations, exhausting each class before going on to the next. As the sheets had emerged from the electromatic typewriters, the monks had carefully cut them up and pasted them into enormous books. In another week, heaven be praised, they would have finished. Just what obscure calculations had convinced the monks that they needn't bother to go on to words of ten, twenty, or a hundred letters, George didn't know. One of his recurring nightmares was that there would be some change of plan, and that the high lama (whom they'd naturally called Sam Jaffe, though he didn't look a bit like him) would suddenly announce that the project would be extended to approximately A.D. 2060. They were quite capable of it.

George heard the heavy wooden door slam in the wind as Chuck came out onto the parapet beside him. As usual, Chuck was smoking one of the cigars that made him so popular with the monks—who, it seemed, were quite willing to embrace all the minor and most of the major pleasures of life. That was one thing in their favor: they might be crazy, but they weren't bluenoses. Those frequent trips they took down to the village, for instance . . .

"Listen, George," said Chuck urgently. "I've learned something that means trouble."

"What's wrong? Isn't the machine behaving?" That was the worst contingency George could imagine. It might delay his return, and nothing could be more horrible. The way he felt now, even the sight of a TV commercial would seem like manna from heaven. At least it would be some link with home.

"No—it's nothing like that." Chuck settled himself on the parapet, which was unusual because normally he was scared of the drop. "I've just found what all this is about."

"What d'ya mean? I thought we knew."

"Sure—we know what the monks are trying to do. But we didn't know *why*. It's the craziest thing—"

"Tell me something new," growled George.

"—but old Sam's just come clean with me. You know the way he drops in every afternoon to watch the sheets roll out. Well, this time he seemed rather excited, or at least as near as he'll ever get to it. When I told him that we were on the last cycle he asked me, in that cute English accent of his, if I'd ever wondered what they were trying to do. I said, 'Sure'—and he told me."

"Go on: I'll buy it."

"Well, they believe that when they have listed all His names—and they reckon that there are about nine billion of them—God's purpose will be achieved. The human race will have finished what it was created to do, and there won't be any point in carrying on. Indeed, the very idea is something like blasphemy."

"Then what do they expect us to do? Commit suicide?"

"There's no need for that. When the list's completed, God steps in and simply winds things up . . . bingo!"

"Oh, I get it. When we finish our job, it will be the end of the world."

Chuck gave a nervous little laugh.

"That's just what I said to Sam. And do you know what happened? He looked at me in a very queer way, like I'd been stupid in class, and said, 'It's nothing as trivial as *that*.'"

George thought this over for a moment.

"That's what I call taking the Wide View," he said presently. "But what d'you suppose we should do about it? I don't see that it makes the slightest difference to us. After all, we already knew that they were crazy."

"Yes—but don't you see what may happen? When the list's complete and the Last Trump doesn't blow—or whatever it is they expect—*we* may get the blame. It's our machine they've been using. I don't like the situation one little bit."

"I see," said George slowly. "You've got a point there. But this sort of thing's happened before, you know. When I was a kid down in Louisiana we had a crackpot preacher who once said the world was going to end next Sunday. Hundreds of people believed him—even sold their homes. Yet when nothing happened, they didn't turn nasty, as you'd expect. They just decided that he'd made a mistake in his calculations and went right on believing. I guess some of them still do."

"Well, this isn't Louisiana, in case you hadn't noticed. There are just two of us and hundreds of these monks. I like them, and I'll be sorry for old Sam when his lifework backfires on him. But all the same, I wish I was somewhere else."

"I've been wishing that for weeks. But there's nothing we can do until the contract's finished and the transport arrives to fly us out."

"Of course," said Chuck thoughtfully, "we could always try a bit of sabotage."

"Like hell we could! That would make things worse."

"Not the way I meant. Look at it like this. The machine will finish its run four days from now, on the present twenty-hours-a-day basis. The transport calls in a week. OK—then all we need to do is to find something that needs replacing during one of the overhaul periods—something that will hold up the works for a couple of days. We'll fix it, of course, but not too quickly. If we time matters properly, we can be down at the airfield when the last name pops out of the register. They won't be able to catch us then."

"I don't like it," said George. "It will be the first time I ever walked out on a job. Besides, it would make them suspicious. No, I'll sit tight and take what comes."

"I *still* don't like it," he said, seven days later, as the tough little mountain ponies carried them down the winding road. "And don't you think I'm running away because I'm afraid. I'm just sorry for those poor old guys up there, and I don't want to be around when they find what suckers they've been. Wonder how Sam will take it?"

"It's funny," replied Chuck, "but when I said good-by I got the idea he knew we were walking out on him — and that he didn't care because he knew the machine was running smoothly and that the job would soon be finished. After that — well, of course, for him there just isn't any After That. . . . "

George turned in his saddle and stared back up the mountain road. This was the last place from which one could get a clear view of the lamasery. The squat, angular buildings were silhouetted against the afterglow of the sunset: here and there, lights gleamed like portholes in the side of an ocean liner. Electric lights, of course, sharing the same circuit as the Mark V. How much longer would they share it? wondered George. Would the monks smash up the computer in their rage and disappointment? Or would they just sit down quietly and begin their calculations all over again?

He knew exactly what was happening up on the mountain at this very moment. The high lama and his assistants would be sitting in their silk robes, inspecting the sheets as the junior monks carried them away from the typewriters and pasted them into the great volumes. No one would be saying anything. The only sound would be the incessant patter, the never-ending rainstorm of the keys hitting the paper, for the Mark V itself was utterly silent as it flashed through its thousands of calculations a second. Three months of this, thought George, was enough to start anyone climbing up the wall.

"There she is!" called Chuck, pointing down into the valley. "Ain't she beautiful!"

She certainly was, thought George. The battered old DC-3 lay at the end of the runway like a tiny silver cross. In two hours she would be bearing them away to freedom and sanity. It was a thought worth savoring like a fine liqueur. George let it roll round his mind as the pony trudged patiently down the slope.

The swift night of the high Himalayas was now almost upon them. Fortunately, the road was very good, as roads went in that region, and they were both carrying torches. There was not the slightest danger, only a certain discomfort from the bitter cold. The sky overhead was perfectly clear, and ablaze with the familiar, friendly stars. At least there would be no risk, thought George, of the pilot being unable to take off because of weather conditions. That had been his only remaining worry.

He began to sing, but gave it up after a while. This vast arena of mountains, gleaming like whitely hooded ghosts on every side, did not encourage such ebullience. Presently George glanced at his watch.

"Should be there in an hour," he called back over his shoulder to Chuck. Then he added, in an afterthought: "Wonder if the computer's finished its run. It was due about now."

Chuck didn't reply, so George swung round in his saddle. He could just see Chuck's face, a white oval turned toward the sky.

"Look," whispered Chuck, and George lifted his eyes to heaven. (There is always a last time for everything.)

Overhead, without any fuss, the stars were going out.

How is the end of the world in this story different from the end of the world in the other stories in this unit?

The flood stories we have seen all end by beginning a new story of survival and rebirth. Does this story do the same thing? Do you think there is a "Deucalion" or a "Noah" in this story?

Suppose that the earth were going to be completely destroyed. Only one man, one woman, and one box of things will survive. There is no way to tell which one man and woman will survive, but it is up to you to decide what things will be sealed in the box. What would you choose?

Intervention of the Gods

Now this will be done and then that;
and later on, in a year or two — as I reckon —
actions will be thus and so, manners will be thus and so.
We will not try for a far-off hereafter.
We will try for the best.
And the more we try, the more we will spoil,
we will complicate matters till we find ourselves
in utter confusion. And then we will stop.
It will be the hour for the gods to work.
The gods always come. They will come down
from their machines, and some they will save,
others they will lift forcibly, abruptly
by the middle; and when they bring some order
they will retire. And then this one will do one thing,
that one another; and in time the others
will do their things. And we will start over again.

C. P. CAVAFY
Translated by RAE DALVEN

What Thomas an Buile
Said in a Pub

I saw God. Do you doubt it?
  Do you dare to doubt it?
I saw the Almighty Man. His hand
Was resting on a mountain, and
He looked upon the World and all about it:
I saw Him plainer than you see me now,
  You mustn't doubt it.

He was not satisfied;
  His look was all dissatisfied.
His beard swung on a wind far out of sight
Behind the world's curve, and there was light
Most fearful from His forehead, and He sighed,
"That star went always wrong, and from the start
  I was dissatisfied."

He lifted up His hand—
  I say He heaved a dreadful hand
Over the spinning Earth. Then I said, "Stay,
You must not strike it, God; I'm in the way;
And I will never move from where I stand."
He said, "Dear child, I feared that you were dead,"
  And stayed His hand.

JAMES STEPHENS

Literature often tells about our relationship to the divine order. What kinds of relationships do Deucalion (page 147) and Gilgamesh (page 157) and the blue-eyed son (page 154) have with their gods? What kind of a relationship does Thomas have with his?

Put yourself into a poem about the end of the world. What has caused it? Where are you? How do you feel? What do you do? Are you a Deucalion or a Thomas or someone else?

Our myths tell of the past, present, and future of the human race. We have already seen stories of our creation, our education by the gods, and our fall from innocence. However, there is one story pattern, or archetype, which tells in miniature the entire imaginative story of the human race. It is the story of the "flood"—a cycle of birth, death, and rebirth.

It is peculiarly human that we never imagine that people will be completely annihilated by the gods. Death is something we know we must face individually, but the pull of life is strong. So we create a vision that enables us to cope with the day of doom by imagining another birth and another chance.

The myth-makers often imagine that the destruction of the world will be carried out by water, and that new life will arise from a cleansed earth. People, always symbol-makers, were quick to associate the natural world with the human and divine worlds, and so droughts and floods became signs of divine action. Why would the gods execute their power against people in these ways? Why would they want to destroy the creatures they had made? The imagination came up with several answers: to punish people for their corruption, to clean up the earth, to start a fresh new race, to remind us of a final day of doom.

The flood in literature, then, has been imagined as a destruction that enables a new creation to take place. It kills in order to cleanse. It washes away the order of earth so that a new order can be established. Perhaps people have used the image of water in this dual way because water is an element that not only is life-giving and life-threatening, but also is one that can take on different forms: it knows the dark depths of the ocean as well as the light ethereal spaces of the heavens.

Because water is a vehicle of destruction and fertility, of light and darkness, it is a common symbol

Detail of "Guernica"
by Pablo Picasso

in initiation rites. An initiation is a ritual which symbolizes a crossing over into a new stage of life. A person symbolically "dies" to one form of life in order to be "reborn" into another. This image of water as an agent of both chaos and rebirth is also found in many quest stories. Every hero — Greek sailor, Babylonian king, medieval knight, space explorer — undertakes a journey during which he or she must undergo a struggle against a great chaotic natural force. Such a journey is a kind of initiation. The image of water is often used in these stories as a symbol of the internal chaos that must be conquered before the hero can give birth to his or her own best qualities.

But rebirth or the successful completion of the quest does not take place without a struggle. The stories of floods and perilous journeys over seas and rivers emphasize the qualities that we need in order to triumph over the forces of chaos and death: honor, integrity, love, courage, perseverance through the storm. Through these struggles we gain power — the power to pass through death, and turn survival into triumph.

Just as we no longer think of fire as a god, we do not think of water in that way either. Science has told us that a flood is due to excessive precipitation, or to meteorologic conditions. Yet we still use the image of a "hard rain" to suggest the kind of wholesale destruction we fear today, an atomic one. And perhaps the question that people used to ask — "Why are the gods doing this to us?" — has been changed to "Why are we doing this to ourselves?" Whose "dark intent" is it that causes the atomic flood — is it human or divine? Will we put out our own light? Will we be reborn? These seem to be today's "unanswerable questions."

5
CHANGES

Apollo and Daphne

A Greek myth

Now the first girl Apollo loved was Daphne,
Whose father was the river-god Peneus,
And this was no blind chance, but Cupid's malice.
Apollo, with pride and glory still upon him
Over the Python slain, saw Cupid bending
His tight-strung little bow. "O silly youngster,"
He said, "What are you doing with such weapons?
Those are for grown-ups! The bow is for my shoulders;
I never fail in wounding beast or mortal,
And not so long ago I slew the Python
With countless darts; his bloated body covered
Acre on endless acre, and I slew him!
The torch, my boy, is enough for you to play with,
To get the love fires burning. Do not meddle
With honors that are mine!" And Cupid answered:
"Your bow shoots everything, Apollo—maybe—
But mine will fix you! You are far above
All creatures living, and by just that distance
Your glory less than mine." He shook his wings,
Soared high, came down to the shadows of Parnassus,
Drew from his quiver different kinds of arrows,
One causing love, golden and sharp and gleaming,
The other blunt, and tipped with lead, and serving
To drive all love away, and this blunt arrow
He used on Daphne, but he fired the other,
The sharp and golden shaft, piercing Apollo
Through bones, through marrow, and at once he loved
And she at once fled from the name of lover,

Rejoicing in the woodland hiding places
And spoils of beasts which she had taken captive,
A rival of Diana, virgin goddess.
She had many suitors, but she scorned them all;
Wanting no part of any man, she traveled
The pathless groves, and had no care whatever
For husband, love, or marriage. Her father often
Said, "Daughter, give me a son-in-law!" and "Daughter,
Give me some grandsons!" But the marriage torches
Were something hateful, criminal, to Daphne,
So she would blush, and put her arms around him,
And coax him: "Let me be a virgin always;
Diana's father said she might. Dear father!
Dear father—please!" He yielded, but her beauty
Kept arguing against her prayer. Apollo
Loves at first sight; he wants to marry Daphne,
He hopes for what he wants—all wishful thinking!—
Is fooled by his own oracles. As stubble
Burns when the grain is harvested, as hedges
Catch fire from torches that a passer-by
Has brought too near, or left behind in the morning,
So the god burned, with all his heart, and burning
Nourished that futile love of his by hoping.
He sees the long hair hanging down her neck
Uncared for, says, "But what if it were combed?"
He gazes at her eyes—they shine like stars!
He gazes at her lips, and knows that gazing
Is not enough. He marvels at her fingers,
Her hands, her wrists, her arms, bare to the shoulder,
And what he does not see he thinks is better.
But still she flees him, swifter than the wind,
And when he calls she does not even listen:
"Don't run away, dear nymph! Daughter of Peneus,
Don't run away! I am no enemy,
Only your follower: don't run away!
The lamb flees from the wolf, the deer the lion,
The dove, on trembling wing, flees from the eagle.
All creatures flee their foes. But I, who follow,
Am not a foe at all. Love makes me follow,
Unhappy fellow that I am, and fearful

You may fall down, perhaps, or have the briars
Make scratches on those lovely legs, unworthy
To be hurt so, and I would be the reason.
The ground is rough here. Run a little slower,
And I will run, I promise, a little slower.
Or wait a minute: be a little curious
Just who it is you charm. I am no shepherd,
No mountain dweller, I am not a plowboy,
Uncouth and stinking of cattle. You foolish girl,
You don't know who it is you run away from,
That must be why you run. I am lord of Delphi
And Tenedos and Claros and Patara.
Jove is my father. I am the revealer
Of present, past, and future; through my power
The lyre and song make harmony; my arrow
Is sure in aim— there is only one arrow surer,
The one that wounds my heart. The power of healing
Is my discovery; I am called the Healer
Through all the world: all herbs are subject to me.
Alas for me, love is incurable
With any herb; the arts which cure the others
Do me, their lord, no good!"
                              He would have said
Much more than this, but Daphne, frightened, left him
With many words unsaid, and she was lovely
Even in flight, her limbs bare in the wind,
Her garments fluttering, and her soft hair streaming,
More beautiful than ever. But Apollo,
Too young a god to waste his time in coaxing,
Came following fast. When a hound starts a rabbit
In an open field, one runs for game, one safety,
He has her, or thinks he has, and she is doubtful
Whether she's caught or not, so close the margin,
So ran the god and girl, one swift in hope,
The other in terror, but he ran more swiftly,
Borne on the wings of love, gave her no rest,
Shadowed her shoulder, breathed on her streaming hair.
Her strength was gone, worn out by the long effort
Of the long flight; she was deathly pale, and seeing
The river of her father, cried "O help me,

If there is any power in the rivers,
Change and destroy the body which has given
Too much delight!" And hardly had she finished,
When her limbs grew numb and heavy, her soft breasts
Were closed with delicate bark, her hair was leaves,
Her arms were branches, and her speedy feet
Rooted and held, and her head became a tree top,
Everything gone except her grace, her shining.
Apollo loved her still. He placed his hand
Where he had hoped and felt the heart still beating
Under the bark; and he embraced the branches
As if they still were limbs, and kissed the wood,
And the wood shrank from his kisses, and the god
Exclaimed: "Since you can never be my bride,
My tree at least you shall be! Let the laurel
Adorn, henceforth, my hair, my lyre, my quiver:
Let Roman victors, in the long procession,
Wear laurel wreaths for triumph and ovation.
Beside Augustus's portals let the laurel
Guard and watch over the oak, and as my head
Is always youthful, let the laurel always
Be green and shining!" He said no more. The laurel,
Stirring, seemed to consent, to be saying *Yes*.

OVID
Translated by ROLFE HUMPHRIES

How does this myth show that anything is possible in the imagination?

When people use a metaphor, they are saying that one thing is another, different thing. Why do you think people would need or want to create metaphors?

Try listing some metaphors you use in everyday conversation. (For example, "This car is a lemon.") Write a story about how one of these metaphors came to be used.

Baucis and Philemon

A Greek myth
Retold by EDITH HAMILTON

In the Phrygian hill country there were once two trees which all the peasants near and far pointed out as a great marvel, and no wonder, for one was an oak and the other a linden, yet they grew from a single trunk. The story of how this came about is a proof of the immeasurable power of the gods, and also of the way they reward the humble and the pious.

Sometimes when Jupiter was tired of eating ambrosia and drinking nectar up in Olympus and even a little weary of listening to Apollo's lyre and watching the Graces dance, he would come down to the earth, disguise himself as a mortal and go looking for adventures. His favorite companion on these tours was Mercury, the most entertaining of all the gods, the shrewdest and the most resourceful. On this particular trip Jupiter had determined to find out how hospitable the people of Phrygia were. Hospitality was, of course, very important to him, since all guests, all who seek shelter in a strange land, were under his especial protection.

The two gods, accordingly, took on the appearance of poor wayfarers and wandered through the land, knocking at each lowly hut or great house they came to and asking for food and a place to rest in. Not one would admit them; every time they were dismissed insolently and the door barred against them. They made trial of hundreds; all treated them in the same way. At last they came upon a little hovel of the humblest sort, poorer than any they had yet found, with a roof made only of reeds. But here, when they knocked, the door was opened wide and a cheerful voice bade them enter. They had to stoop to pass through the low entrance, but once inside they found themselves in a snug and very clean room, where a kindly-faced old man and woman welcomed them in the friendliest fashion and bustled about to make them comfortable.

The old man set a bench near the fire and told them to stretch out on it and rest their tired limbs, and the old woman threw a soft covering over it. Her name was Baucis, she told the strangers, and her husband was called Philemon. They had lived in that cottage all their married life and had always been happy. "We are poor folk," she said, "but poverty isn't so bad when you're willing to own up to it, and a contented spirit is a great help, too." All the while she was talking, she was busy doing things for them. The coals under the ashes on the dark hearth she fanned to life until a cheerful fire was burning. Over this she hung a little kettle full of water and just as it began to boil her husband came in with a fine cabbage he had got from the garden. Into the kettle it went, with a piece of the pork which was hanging from one of the beams. While this cooked, Baucis set the table with her trembling old hands. One table leg was too short, but she propped it up with a bit of broken dish. On the board she placed olives and radishes and several eggs which she had roasted in the ashes. By this time the cabbage and bacon were done, and the old man pushed two rickety couches up to the table and bade his guests recline and eat.

Presently he brought them cups of beechwood and an earthenware mixing bowl which held some wine very like vinegar, plentifully diluted with water. Philemon, however, was clearly proud and happy at being able to add such cheer to the supper and he kept on the watch to refill each cup as soon as it was emptied. The two old folks were so pleased and excited by the success of their hospitality that only very slowly a strange thing dawned upon them. The mixing bowl kept full. No matter how many cups were poured out from it, the level of the wine stayed the same, up to the brim. As they saw this wonder each looked in terror at the other, and dropping their eyes they prayed silently. Then in quavering voices and trembling all over they begged their guests to pardon the poor refreshments they had offered. "We have a goose," the old man said, "which we ought to have given your lordships. But if you will only wait, it shall be done at once." To catch the goose, however, proved beyond their powers. They tried in vain until they were worn out, while Jupiter and Mercury watched them greatly entertained.

But when both Philemon and Baucis had had to give up the chase panting and exhausted, the gods felt that the time had come for them to take action. They were really very kind. "You have been hosts to gods," they said, "and you shall have your reward. This wicked country which despises the poor stranger will be bitterly punished, but not you." They then escorted the two out of the hut and told them to look around them. To their amazement all they saw was water. The whole countryside had disappeared. A great lake surrounded them. Their neighbors had not been good to the old couple; nevertheless, standing there they wept for them. But of a sudden their tears were dried by an overwhelming wonder. Before their eyes the tiny, lowly hut which had been their home for so long was turned into a stately pillared temple of whitest marble with a golden roof.

"Good people," Jupiter said, "ask whatever you want and you shall have your wish." The old people exchanged a hurried whisper, then Philemon spoke. "Let us be your priests, guarding this temple for you—and oh, since we have lived so long together, let neither of us ever have to live alone. Grant that we may die together."

The gods assented, well pleased with the two. A long time they served in that grand building, and the story does not say whether they ever missed their little cozy room with its cheerful hearth. But one day standing before the marble and golden magnificence they fell to talking about the former life, which had been so hard and yet so happy. By now both were in extreme old age. Suddenly as they exchanged memories each saw the other putting forth leaves. Then bark was growing around them. They had time only to cry, "Farewell, dear companion." As the words passed their lips they became trees, but still they were together. The linden and the oak grew from one trunk.

From far and wide people came to admire the wonder, and always wreaths of flowers hung on the branches in honor of the pious and faithful pair.

The myth-makers could imagine people becoming trees or flowers or animals. The Chinese myth in the first unit shows that people could also imagine a god transforming himself into the earth itself. How do you think the idea of metamorphosis affected people's relationship to heaven and to nature? Do you think it drew them closer to these other worlds?

when god lets
my body be

when god lets my body be

From each brave eye shall sprout a tree
fruit that dangles therefrom

the purpled world will dance upon
Between my lips which did sing

a rose shall beget the spring
that maidens whom passion wastes

will lay between their little breasts
My strong fingers beneath the snow

Into strenuous birds shall go
my love walking in the grass

their wings will touch with her face
and all the while shall my heart be

With the bulge and nuzzle of the sea

E. E. CUMMINGS

How is this poet doing exactly the same thing the ancient myth-makers did?

We have seen the sea used as an image of chaos. How is it used here?

Midas

A Greek myth
Retold by OLIVIA COOLIDGE

Midas was king in Phrygia, which is a land in Asia Minor, and he was both powerful and rich. Nevertheless, he was foolish, obstinate, and hasty, without the sense to appreciate good advice.

It happened one time that Dionysus with his dancing nymphs and satyrs passed through Phrygia. As they went, the old, fat Silenus, nodding on an ass, strayed from the others, who danced on without missing him. The ass took his half-conscious master wherever he wanted, until some hours later, as they came to a great rose garden, the old man tumbled off. The King's gardeners found him there and roused him, still sleepy and staggering, not quite sure who or where he was. Since, however, the revels of Dionysus had spread throughout the land, they recognized him as the god's companion and made much of him. They wreathed his neck with roses and, one on each side and one behind, they supported him to the palace and up the steps, while another went to fetch Midas.

The King came out to meet Silenus, overjoyed at the honor done him. He clapped his hands for his servants and demanded such a feast as never was. There was much running to and fro, setting up of tables, fetching of wine, and bringing up of sweet-scented oil. While slaves festooned the hall with roses and made garlands for the feasters, Midas conducted his guest to the bath with all honor, that he might refresh himself and put on clean garments for the feast.

A magnificent celebration followed. For ten days, by daylight and by torchlight, the palace of the King stood open, and all the notables of Phrygia came up and down its steps. There were sounds of lyre and pipe and singing. There was dancing. Everywhere the scent of roses and of wine mingled with the costly perfumes of King Midas in the hot summer air. In ten days' time, as the revels were dying down from sheer exhaustion, Dionysus came in person to seek his friend. When he found how Silenus had been entertained and honored, he was greatly pleased and promised Midas any gift he cared to name, no matter what it was.

The King thought a little, glancing back through his doors at the chaos in his hall of scattered rose petals, overturned tables, bowls for the wine mixing, and drinking cups. It had been a good feast, the sort of feast a king should give, only he was very weary now and could not think. A king should entertain thus and give kingly presents to his guests, cups of beaten gold, such as he had seen once, with lifelike pictures of a hunt running round them, or the golden honeycomb which Daedalus made exactly as though it were the work of bees. Gods, like these guests, should have golden statues. Even a king never had enough.

"Give me," he said to Dionysus suddenly, "the power to turn all I touch to gold."

"That is a rash thing to ask," said Dionysus solemnly. "Think again." But Eastern kings are never contradicted, and Midas only felt annoyed.

"It is my wish," he answered coldly.

Dionysus nodded. "You shall have it," he said. "As you part from me here in the garden, it shall be yours."

Midas was so excited when he came back through the garden that he could not make up his mind what to touch first. Presently he decided on the branch of an oak tree which overhung his path. He took a look at it first, counting the leaves, noticing the little veins in them, the jagged edges, the fact that one of them had been eaten half away. He put out his hand to break it off. He never saw it change. One moment it was brown and green; the next it wasn't. There it was, stiff and shining, nibbled leaf and all. It was hard and satisfyingly heavy and far more natural than anything Daedalus ever made.

Now he was the greatest king in the world. Midas looked down at the grass he was walking over. It was still green; the touch was evidently in his hands. He picked up a stone to see; it became a lump of gold. He tried a clod of earth and found himself with another lump. Midas was beside himself with joy; he went into his palace to see what he could do. In the doorway he stopped at a sudden thought. He went outside again and walked down all the long row of pillars, laying his hands on each one. No king in the world had pillars of solid gold. He considered having a gold house but rejected the idea; the gold pillars looked better against the stone. Midas picked a gold apple and went inside again to eat.

His servants set his table for him, and he amused himself by turning the cups and dishes into gold. He touched the table too by mistake — not that it really mattered, but he would have to be careful. Absently he·picked up a piece of bread and bit it and nearly broke his teeth. Midas sat with the golden bread in his hand and looked at it a long time. He was horribly frightened. "I shall have to eat it without touching it with my hands," he said to himself after a while, and he put his head down on the table and tried that way. It was no good. The moment his lips touched the bread, he felt it turn hard and cold. In his shock he groped wildly for his winecup and took a big gulp. The stuff flowed into his mouth all right, but it wasn't wine any more. He spat it out hastily before he choked himself. This time he was more than frightened; he was desperate. "Great Dionysus," he prayed earnestly with uplifted hands, "forgive my foolishness, and take away your gift."

"Go to the mountain of Tmolus," said the voice of the god into his ear, "and bathe in the stream that springs there so that the golden touch may be washed away. The next time think more carefully before you set your judgment against that of the gods."

Midas thanked the god with his whole heart, but he paid more attention to his promise than to his advice. He lost no time in journeying to the mountain and dipping himself in the stream. There the golden touch was washed away from Midas, but the sand of the river bottom shone bright gold as the power passed into the water, so that the stream flowed over golden sand from that time on.

Midas had learned his lesson in a way but was still conceited. He had realized at least that gold was not the most important thing. Indeed, having had too much gold at one time, he took a violent dislike to it and to luxury in general. He spent his time in the open country now, listening to the music of the streams and the woodlands, while his kingdom ran itself as best it might. He wanted neither his elaborate palace, his embroidered robes, his splendid feasts, nor his trained dancers and musicians. Instead he wished to be at home in the woodlands with simple things that were natural and unspoiled.

It happened at the time that in the woods of Tmolus, the goat-god Pan had made himself a pipe. It was a simple hollow reed with holes for stops cut in it, and the god played simple tunes on it like birdcalls and the various noises of the animals he had heard. Only he was very skillful and could play them fast and slow, mixed together or repeated, until the listener felt that the woods themselves were alive with little creatures. The birds and beasts made answer to the pipe so that it seemed the whole wood was an orchestra of music. Midas himself was charmed to ecstasy with the beauty of it and begged the shaggy god to play hour by hour till the very birds were weary of the calls. This Pan was quite ready to do, since he was proud of his invention. He even wanted to challenge Apollo himself, sure that any judge would put his instrument above Apollo's golden lyre.

Apollo accepted the challenge, and Tmolus, the mountain, was himself to be the judge. Tmolus was naturally a woodland god and friendly to Pan, so he listened with solemn pleasure as the pipe trilled airs more varied and more natural than it had ever played before. The woods echoed, and the happy Midas, who had followed Pan to the contest, was almost beside himself with delight at the gaiety and abandon of it all. When, however, Tmolus heard Apollo play the music of gods and heroes, of love, longing, heroism, and the mighty dead, he forgot his own woods around him and the animals listening in their tiny nests and holes. He seemed to see into the hearts of men and understand the pity of their lives and the beauty that they longed for.

Even after the song had died away, Tmolus sat there in forgetful silence with his thoughts on the loves and struggles of the ages and the half-dried tears on his cheeks. There was a great quiet around him too, he realized, as he came to his senses. Even Pan had put down his pipe thoughtfully on the grass.

Tmolus gave the prize to Apollo, and in the whole woodland there was no one to protest but Midas. Midas had shut his ears to Apollo; he would neither listen nor care. Now he forgot where he was and in whose presence. All he remembered was that he was a great king who always gave his opinion and who, his courtiers told him, was always right. Leaping up, he protested loudly to Tmolus and was not even quiet when the mountain silently frowned on him. Getting no answer, he turned to Apollo, still objecting furiously to the unfairness of the judgment.

Apollo looked the insistent mortal up and down. "The fault is in your ears, O King. We must give them their true shape," he said. With that he turned away and was gone to Olympus, while the unfortunate Midas put his hands to his ears and found them long and furry. He could even wriggle them about. Apollo had given him asses' ears in punishment for his folly.

From that time on King Midas wore a scarlet turban and tried to make it seem as though wearing this were a privilege that only the king could enjoy. He wore it day and night—he was so fond of it. Presently, however, his hair began to grow so long and straggly that something had to be done. The royal barber had to be called.

The barber of King Midas was a royal slave, so it was easy enough to threaten him with the most horrible punishment if, whether waking or sleeping, he ever let fall the slightest hint of what was wrong with the King. The barber was thoroughly frightened. Unfortunately he was too frightened, and the King's threats preyed on his mind. He began to dream he had told his secret to somebody, and what was worse, his fellow servants began to complain that he was making noises in his sleep, so that he was desperately afraid he would talk. At last it seemed that if he could only tell somebody once and get it over, his mind would be at rest. Yet tell somebody was just what he dared not do. Finally, he went down to a meadow which was seldom crossed because it was waterlogged, and there, where he could see there was no one around to hear him, he dug a hole in the ground, put his face close down, and whispered into the wet mud, "King Midas has asses' ears." Then he threw some earth on top and went away, feeling somehow much relieved.

Nothing happened for a while except that the hole filled up with water. Presently, though, some reeds began to grow in it. They grew taller and rustled as the wind went through them. After a while someone happened to go down that way and came racing back, half-amused and half-terrified. Everyone crowded around to listen to him. It was certainly queer, but it was a bit amusing too.

Everybody streamed down the path to investigate. Sure enough, as they came close to it, they could hear the whole thing distinctly. The reeds were not rustling in the wind; they were whispering to one another, "King Midas has asses' ears . . . asses' ears . . . asses' ears."

How does this myth humanize nature? How does it give a divine shape to nature? What does the myth-maker seem to say about human nature?

Requiem for a Modern Croesus

To him the moon was a silver dollar, spun
Into the sky by some mysterious hand; the sun
  Was a gleaming golden coin—
    His to purloin;
The freshly minted stars were dimes of delight
  Flung out upon the counter of the night.

  In yonder room he lies,
  With pennies on his eyes.

LEW SARETT

Croesus was an extremely rich king whose name has come to be associated with great wealth. What metaphors did this dead man believe in? How was he another Midas?

What metamorphoses does every human being experience?

Pygmalion

A Greek myth

OVID, *translated by* MARY M. INNES

When Pygmalion saw these women, living such wicked lives, he was revolted by the many faults which nature has implanted in the female sex, and long lived a bachelor existence, without any wife to share his home. But meanwhile, with marvelous artistry, he skillfully carved a snowy ivory statue. He made it lovelier than any woman born, and fell in love with his own creation. The statue had all the appearance of a real girl, so that it seemed to be alive, to want to move, did not modesty forbid, so cleverly did his art conceal its art. Pygmalion gazed in wonder, and in his heart there rose a passionate love for this image of a human form. Often he ran his hands over the work, feeling it to see whether it was flesh or ivory, and would not yet admit that ivory was all it was. He kissed the statue, and imagined that it kissed him back, spoke to it and embraced it, and thought he felt his fingers sink into the limbs he touched, so that he was afraid lest a bruise appear where he had pressed the flesh. Sometimes he addressed it in flattering speeches, sometimes brought the kind of presents that girls enjoy: shells and polished pebbles, little birds and flowers of a thousand hues, lilies and painted balls, and drops of amber which fall from the trees that were once Phaethon's sisters. He dressed the limbs of his statue in woman's robes, and put rings on its fingers, long necklaces round its neck. Pearls hung from its ears, and chains were looped upon its breast. All this finery became the image well, but it was no less lovely unadorned. Pygmalion then placed the statue on a couch that was covered with cloths of Tyrian purple, laid its head to rest on soft down pillows, as if it could appreciate them, and called it his bedfellow.

The festival of Venus, which is celebrated with the greatest pomp all through Cyprus, was now in progress, and heifers, their crooked horns gilded for the occasion, had fallen at the altar as the ax struck their snowy necks. Smoke was rising from the incense, when Pygmalion, having made his offering, stood by the altar and timidly prayed, saying: "If you gods can give all things, may I have as my wife, I pray—" he did not dare to say: "the ivory maiden," but finished: "one like the ivory maid." However, golden Venus, present at her festival in person, understood what his prayers meant, and as a sign that the gods were kindly disposed, the flames burned up three times, shooting a tongue of fire into the air. When Pygmalion returned home, he made straight for the statue of the girl he loved, leaned over the couch, and kissed her. She seemed warm: he laid his lips on hers again, and touched her breast with his hands—at his touch the ivory lost its hardness, and grew soft: his fingers made an imprint on the yielding surface, just as wax melts in the sun and, worked by men's fingers, is fashioned into many different shapes, and made fit for use by being used. The lover stood, amazed, afraid of being mistaken, his joy tempered with doubt, and again and again stroked the object of his prayers. It was indeed a human body! The veins throbbed as he pressed them with his thumb. Then Pygmalion of Paphos was eloquent in his thanks to Venus. At long last, he pressed his lips upon living lips, and the girl felt the kisses he gave her, and blushed. Timidly raising her eyes, she saw her lover and the light of day together. The goddess Venus was present at the marriage she had arranged and, when the moon's horns had nine times been rounded into a full circle, Pygmalion's bride bore a child, Paphos, from whom the island takes its name.

How is this a story of wish fulfillment? Why do you think the idea of metamorphosis would have such a powerful appeal to the imagination?

As illustrated in the drawing that opens this unit, we are aware of two kinds of metamorphosis—that which we can control and that which we cannot control. We cannot stop a girl from growing into a woman, or a caterpillar from becoming a butterfly. But—if we want to—we can *use our imagination* to change a wolf into a bird or a bird into a wolf. List five things that you would shape-change if you could. List five things that shape-change whether you want them to or not.

Flowers for Algernon

DANIEL KEYES

progris riport 1 — martch 5 1965

Dr Strauss says I shud rite down what I think and evrey thing that happins to me from now on. I dont know why but he says its importint so they will see if they will use me. I hope they use me. Miss Kinnian says maybe they can make me smart. I want to be smart. My name is Charlie Gordon. I am 37 years old and 2 weeks ago was my birthday. I have nuthing more to write now so I will close for today.

progris riport 2 — martch 6

I had a test today. I think I faled it. and I think that maybe now they wont use me. What happind is a nice young man was in the room and he had some white cards with ink spilled all over them. He sed Charlie what do you see on this card. I was very skared even tho I had my rabits foot in my pockit because when I was a kid I always faled tests in scool and I spilled ink to.

I told him I saw a inkblot. He said yes and it made me feel good. I thot that was all but when I got up to go he stopped me. He said now sit down Charlie we are not thru yet. Then I don't remember so good but he wantid me to say what was in the ink. I dint see nuthing in the ink but he said there was picturs there other pepul saw some picturs. I cudnt see any picturs. I reely tryed to see. I held the card close up and then far away. Then I said if I had my glases I could see better I usally only ware my glases in the movies or TV but I said they are in the closit in the hall. I got them. Then I said let me see that card agen I bet Ill find it now.

I tryed hard but I still coudnt find the picturs I only saw the ink. I told him maybe I need new glases. He rote something down on a paper and I got skared of faling the test. I told him it was a very nice inkblot with littel points all around the eges. He looked very sad so that wasnt it. I said please let me try agen. Ill get it in a few minits becaus Im not so fast sometimes. Im a slow reeder too in Miss Kinnians class for slow adults but Im trying very hard.

He gave me a chance with another card that had 2 kinds of ink spilled on it red and blue.

He was very nice and talked slow like Miss Kinnian does and he explaned it to me that it was a *raw shok*.[1] He said pepul see things in the ink. I said show me where. He said think. I told him I think a ink-blot but that wasnt rite eather. He said what does it remind you— pretend something. I closd my eyes for a long time to pretend. I told him I pretend a fowntan pen with ink leeking all over a table cloth. The he got up and went out.

I dont think I passd the *raw shok* test.

progris riport 3 — martch 7

Dr Strauss and Dr Nemur say it dont matter about the inkblots. I told them I dint spill the ink on the cards and I couldn't see anything in the ink. They said that maybe they will still use me. I said Miss Kinnian never gave me tests like that one only spelling and reading. They said Miss Kinnian told that I was her bestist pupil in the adult nite scool becaus I tryed the hardist and reely wantid to lern. They said how come you went to the adult nite scool all by yourself Charlie. How did you find it. I said I askd pepul and sumbody tole me where I shud go to lern to read and spell good. They said why did you want to. I told them becaus all my life I wantid to be smart and not dumb. But its very hard to be smart. They said you know it will probly be tempirery. I said yes. Miss Kinnian told me. I dont care if it herts.

Later I had more crazy tests today. The nice lady who gave it me told me the name and I asked her how do you spell it so I can rite it in my progris riport. THEMATIC APPERCEPTION TEST. I dont know the first 2 words but I know what *test* means. You got to pass it or you get bad marks. This test looked easy becaus I coud see the pictures. Only this time she dint want me to tell her the pictures. That mixd me up. I said the man yesterday said I shoud tell him what I saw in the ink she said that dont make no difrence. She said make up storys about the pepul in the pictures.

---

1 **raw shok:** Rorschach test, a psychological test in which the subject interprets a series of inkblots.

I told her how can you tell storys about pepul you never met. I said why shud I make up lies. I never tell lies any more becaus I always get caut.

She told me this test and the other one the raw shok was for getting personalty. I laffed so hard. I said how can you get that thing from inkblots and fotos. She got sore and put her picturs away. I dont care. It was sily. I gess I faled that test too.

Later some men in white coats took me to a difernt part of the hospitil and gave me a game to play. It was like a race with a white mouse. They called the mouse Algernon. Algernon was in a box with a lot of twists and turns like all kinds of walls and they gave me a pencil and a paper with lines and lots of boxes. On one side it said START and on the other end it said FINISH. They said it was *amazed* and that Algernon and me had the same *amazed* to do. I dint see how we coud have the same *amazed* if Algernon had a box and I had a paper but I dint say nothing. Anyway there wasnt time becaus the race started.

One of the men had a watch he was trying to hide so I woudnt see it so I tryed not to look and that made me nervus.

Anyway that test made me feel worser than all the others because they did it over 10 times with difernt *amazeds* and Algernon won every time. I dint know that mice were so smart. Maybe thats because Algernon is a white mouse. Maybe white mice are smarter than other mice.

progris riport 4 — Mar 8

Their going to use me! Im so excited I can hardly write. Dr Nemur and Dr Strauss had a argament about it first. Dr Nemur was in the office when Dr Strauss brot me in. Dr Nemur was worryed about using me but Dr Strauss told him Miss Kinnian rekemmended me the best from all the people who she was teaching. I like Miss Kinnian becaus shes a very smart teacher. And she said Charlie your going to have a second chance. If you volenteer for this experament you mite get smart. They dont know if it will be perminint but theirs a chance. Thats why I said ok even when I was scared because she said it was an operashun. She said dont be scared Charlie you done so much with so little I think you deserv it most of all.

So I got scaird when Dr Nemur and Dr Strauss argud about it. Dr Strauss said I had something that was very good. He said I had a good *motor-vation.* I never even knew I had that. I felt proud when he said that not every body with an eye-q of 68 had that thing. I dont know what it is or where I got it but he said Algernon had it too. Algernons *motor-vation* is the cheese they put in his box. But it cant be that because I didnt eat any cheese this week.

Then he told Dr Nemur something I dint understand so while they were talking I wrote down some of the words.

He said Dr Nemur I know Charlie is not what you had in mind as the first of your new brede of intelek** (coudnt get the word) superman. But most people of his low ment** are host** and uncoop** they are usualy dull apath** and hard to reach. He has a good natcher hes intristed and eager to please.

Dr Nemur said remember he will be the first human beeng ever to have his inteligence trippled by surgicle meens.

Dr Strauss said exakly. Look at how well hes lerned to read and write for his low mentel age its as grate an acheve** as you and I lerning einstines therey of **vity without help. That shows the intenss motorvation. Its comparat** a tremen** achev** I say we use Charlie.

I dint get all the words and they were talking to fast but it sounded like Dr Strauss was on my side and like the other one wasnt.

Then Dr Nemur nodded he said all right maybe your right. We will use Charlie. When he said that I got so exited I jumped up and shook his hand for being so good to me. I told him thank you doc you wont be sorry for giving me a second chance. And I mean it like I told him. After the operashun Im gonna try to be smart. Im gonna try awful hard.

progris ript 5 — Mar 10

Im skared. Lots of people who work here and the nurses and the people who gave me the tests came to bring me candy and wish me luck. I hope I have luck. I got my rabits foot and my lucky penny and my horse shoe. Only a black cat crossed me when I was comming to the hospitil. Dr Strauss says dont be supersitis Charlie this is sience. Anyway Im keeping my rabits foot with me.

I asked Dr Strauss if Ill beat Algernon in the race after the operashun and he said maybe. If the operashun works Ill show that mouse I can be as smart as he is. Maybe smarter. Then Ill be abel to read better and spell the words good and know lots of things and be like other people. I want to be smart like other people. If it works perminint they will make everybody smart all over the world.

They dint give me anything to eat this morning. I dont know what that eating has to do with getting smart. Im very hungry and Dr Nemur took away my box of candy. That Dr Nemur is a grouch. Dr Strauss says I can have it back after the operashun. You cant eat befor a operashun. . . .

Progress Report 6 — Mar 15

The operashun dint hurt. He did it while I was sleeping. They took off the bandijis from my eyes and my head today so I can make a PROGRESS REPORT. Dr Nemur who looked at some of my other ones says I spell PROGRESS wrong and he told me how to spell it and REPORT too. I got to try and remember that.

I have a very bad memary for spelling. Dr Strauss says its ok to tell about all the things that happin to me but he says I shoud tell more about what I feel and what I think. When I told him I dont know how to think he said try. All the time when the bandijis were on my eyes I tryed to think. Nothing happened. I dont know what to think about. Maybe if I ask him he will tell me how I can think now that Im suppose to get smart. What do smart people think about. Fancy things I suppose. I wish I knew some fancy things alredy.

Progress Report 7 — Mar 19

Nothing is happining. I had lots of tests and different kinds of races with Algernon. I hate that mouse. He always beats me. Dr Strauss said I got to play those games. And he said some time I got to take those tests over again. Those inkblots are stupid. And those pictures are stupid too. I like to draw a picture of a man and a woman but I wont make up lies about people.

I got a headache from trying to think so much. I thot Dr Strauss was my frend but he dont help me. He dont tell me what to think or when Ill get smart. Miss Kinnian dint come to see me. I think writing these progress reports are stupid too.

Progress Report 8 — Mar 23

I'm going back to work at the factery. They said it was better I shud go back to work but I cant tell anyone what the operashun was for and I have to come to the hospitil for an hour every night after work. They are gonna pay me money every month for lerning to be smart.

Im glad Im going back to work because I miss my job and all my frends and all the fun we have there.

Dr Strauss says I shud keep writing things down but I dont have to do it every day just when I think of something or something speshul happins. He says dont get discoridged because it takes time and it happins slow. He says it took a long time with Algernon before he got 3 times smarter than he was before. Thats why Algernon beats me all the time because he had that operashun too. That makes me feel better. I coud probly do that *amazed* faster than a reglar mouse. Maybe some day Ill beat Algernon. Boy that would be something. So far Algernon looks like he mite be smart perminent.

Mar 25 (I dont have to write PROGRESS REPORT on top any more just when I hand it in once a week for Dr Nemur to read. I just have to put the date on. That saves time.)

We had a lot of fun at the factery today. Joe Carp said hey look where Charlie had his operashun what did they do Charlie put some brains in. I was going to tell him but I remembered Dr Strauss said no. Then Frank Reilly said what did you do Charlie forget your key and open your door the hard way. That made me laff. Their really my friends and they like me.

Sometimes somebody will say hey look at Joe or Frank or George he really pulled a Charlie Gordon. I dont know why they say that but they always laff. This morning Amos Borg who is the 4 man at Donne-gans used my name when he shouted at Ernie the office boy. Ernie lost a packige. He said Ernie for godsake what are you trying to be a Charlie Gordon. I dont understand why he said that. I never lost any packiges.

Mar 28 Dr Strauss came to my room tonight to see why I dint come in like I was suppose to. I told him I dont like to race with Algernon any more. He said I dont have to for a while but I shud come in. He had a present for me only it wasnt a present but just for lend. I thot it was a little television but it wasnt. He said I got to turn it on when I go to sleep. I said your kidding why shud I turn it on when Im going to sleep. Who ever herd of a thing like that. But he said if I want to get smart I got to do what he says. I told him I dint think I was going to get smart and he put his hand on my sholder and said Charlie you dont know it yet but your getting smarter all the time. You wont notice for a while. I think he was just being nice to make me feel good because I dont look any smarter.

Oh yes I almost forgot. I asked him when I can go back to the class at Miss Kinnians school. He said I wont go their. He said that soon Miss Kinnian will come to the hospital to start and teach me speshul. I was mad at her for not comming to see me when I got the operashun but I like her so maybe we will be frends again.

Mar 29 That crazy TV kept me up all night. How can I sleep with something yelling crazy things all night in my ears. And the nutty pictures. Wow. I dont know what it says when Im up so how am I going to know when Im sleeping.

Dr Strauss says its ok. He says my brains are lerning when I sleep and that will help me when Miss Kinnian starts my lessons in the hospitil (only I found out it isnt a hospitil its a labatory). I think its all crazy. If you can get smart when your sleeping why do people go to school. That thing I dont think will work. I use to watch the late show and the later late show on TV all the time and it never made me smart. Maybe you have to sleep while you watch it.

PROGRESS REPORT 9—*April* 3

Dr Strauss showed me how to keep the TV turned low so now I can sleep. I dont hear a thing. And I still dont understand what it says. A few times I play it over in the morning to find out what I lerned when I was sleeping and I dont think so. Miss Kinnian says maybe its another langwidge or something. But most times it sounds american. It talks so fast faster than even Miss Gold who was my teacher in 6 grade and I remember she talked so fast I couldnt understand her.

I told Dr Strauss what good is it to get smart in my sleep. I want to be smart when Im awake. He says its the same thing and I have two minds. Theres the *subconscious* and the *conscious* (thats how you spell it.) And one dont tell the other one what its doing. They dont even talk to each other. Thats why I dream. And boy have I been having crazy dreams. Wow. Ever since that night TV. The late late late late late show.

I forgot to ask him if it was only me or if everybody had those two minds.

(I just looked up the word in the dictionary Dr Strauss gave me. The word is *subconscious. adj. Of the nature of mental operations yet not present in consciousness; as, subconscious conflict of desires.*) There's more but I still dont know what it means. This isnt a very good dictionary for dumb people like me.

Anyway the headache is from the party. My friends from the factery Joe Carp and Frank Reilly invited me to go with them to Muggsys Saloon for some drinks. I dont like to drink but they said we will have lots of fun. I had a good time.

Joe Carp said I shoud show the girls how I mop out the toilet in the factery and he got me a mop. I showed them and everyone laffed when I told that Mr Donnegan said I was the best janiter he ever had because I like my job and do it good and never come late or miss a day except for my operashun.

I said Miss Kinnian always said Charlie be proud of your job because you do it good.

Everybody laffed and we had a good time and they gave me lots of drinks and Joe said Charlie is a card when hes potted. I dont know what that means but everybody likes me and we have fun. I cant wait to be smart like my best friends Joe Carp and Frank Reilly.

I dont remember how the party was over but I think I went out to buy a newspaper and coffee for Joe and Frank and when I come back there was no one their. I looked for them all over till late. Then I dont remember so good but I think I got sleepy or sick. A nice cop brot me back home. Thats what my landlady Mrs Flynn says.

But I got a headache and a big lump on my head and black and blue all over. I think maybe I fell but Joe Carp says it was the cop they beat up drunks some times. I dont think so. Miss Kinnian says cops are to help people. Anyway I got a bad headache and Im sick and hurt all over. I dont think Ill drink anymore.

April 6 I beat Algernon! I dint even know I beat him until Burt the tester told me. Then the second time I lost because I got so exited I fell off the chair before I finished. But after that I beat him 8 more times. I must be getting smart to beat a smart mouse like Algernon. But I dont *feel* smarter.

I wanted to race Algernon some more but Burt said thats enough for one day. They let me hold him for a minut. Hes not so bad. Hes soft like a ball of cotton. He blinks and when he opens his eyes their black and pink on the eges.

I said can I feed him because I felt bad to beat him and I wanted to be nice and make frends. Burt said no Algernon is a very specshul mouse with an operashun like mine, and he was the first of all the animals to stay smart so long. He told me Algernon is so smart that every day he has to solve a test to get his food. Its a thing like a lock on a door that changes every time Algernon goes in to eat so he has to lern something new to get his food. That made me sad because if he couldnt lern he would be hungry.

I dont think its right to make you pass a test to eat. How woud

Dr Nemur like it to have to pass a test every time he wants to eat. I think Ill be frends with Algernon.

April 9 Tonight after work Miss Kinnian was at the laboratory. She looked like she was glad to see me but scared. I told her dont worry Miss Kinnian Im not smart yet and she laffed. She said I have confidence in you Charlie the way you struggled so hard to read and right better than all the others. At werst you will have it for a littel wile and your doing somthing for sience.

We are reading a very hard book. I never read such a hard book before. Its called *Robinson Crusoe* about a man who gets merooned on a dessert Iland. Hes smart and figers out all kinds of things so he can have a house and food and hes a good swimmer. Only I feel sorry because hes all alone and has no frends. But I think their must be somebody else on the iland because theres a picture with his funny umbrella looking at footprints. I hope he gets a frend and not be lonly.

April 10 Miss Kinnian teaches me to spell better. She says look at a word and close your eyes and say it over and over until you remember. I have lots of truble with *through* that you say *threw* and *enough* and *tough* that you don't say *enew* and *tew*. You got to say *enuff* and *tuff*. Thats how I use to write it before I started to get smart. Im confused but Miss Kinnian says theres no reason in spelling.

Apr 14 Finished *Robinson Crusoe*. I want to find out more about what happens to him but Miss Kinnian says thats all there is. *Why*.

Apr 15 Miss Kinnian says Im lerning fast. She read some of the Progress Reports and she looked at me kind of funny. She says Im a fine person and Ill show them all. I asked her why. She said never mind but I shoudnt feel bad if I find out that everybody isnt nice like I think. She said for a person who god gave so little to you done more than a lot of people with brains they never even used. I said all my frends are smart people but there good. They like me and they never did anything that wasn't nice. Then she got something in her eye and she had to run out to the ladys room.

Apr 16 Today, I learned, the *comma,* this is a comma (,) a period, with a tail, Miss Kinnian, says its importent, because, it makes writing, better, she said, somebody, coud lose, a lot of money, if a comma, isnt, in the, right place, I dont have, any money, and I dont see, how a comma, keeps you, from losing it.

But she says, everybody, uses commas, so Ill use, them too.

Apr 17 I used the comma wrong. Its punctuation. Miss Kinnian told me to look up long words in the dictionary to lern to spell them. I said whats the difference if you can read it anyway. She said its part of your education so from now on Ill look up all the words Im not sure how to spell. It takes a long time to write that way but I think Im re-membering. I only have to look up once and after that I get it right. Anyway thats how come I got the word *punctuation* right. (Its that way in the dictionary.) Miss Kinnian says a period is punctuation too, and there are lots of other marks to lern. I told her I thot all the periods had to have tails but she said no.

You got to mix them up, she showed? me" how. to mix! them) up,. and now; I can! mix up all kinds" of punctuation, in! my writing? There, are lots! of rules? to lern; but Im gettin'g them in my head.

One thing I? like about, Dear Miss Kinnian: (thats the way it goes in a business letter if I ever go into business) is she, always gives me' a reason" when — I ask. She's a gen'ius! I wish I cou'd be smart" like, her;

(Punctuation, is; fun!)

April 18 What a dope I am! I didn't even understand what she was talking about. I read the grammar book last night and it explanes the whole thing. Then I saw it was the same way as Miss Kinnian was trying to tell me, but I didn't get it. I got up in the middle of the night, and the whole thing straightened out in my mind.

Miss Kinnian said that the TV working in my sleep helped out. She said I reached a plateau. That's like the flat top of a hill.

After I figgered out how punctuation worked, I read over all my old Progress Reports from the beginning. Boy, did I have crazy spelling and punctuation! I told Miss Kinnian I ought to go over the pages and fix all the mistakes but she said, "No, Charlie, Dr. Nemur wants them just as they are. That's why he let you keep them after they were photo-stated, to see your own progress. You're coming along fast, Charlie."

That made me feel good. After the lesson I went down and played with Algernon. We don't race any more.

April 20 I feel sick inside. Not sick like for a doctor, but inside my chest it feels empty like getting punched and a heartburn at the same time.

I wasn't going to write about it, but I guess I got to, because its important. Today was the first time I ever stayed home from work.

Last night Joe Carp and Frank Reilly invited me to a party. There were lots of girls and some men from the factory. I remembered how sick I got last time I drank too much, so I told Joe I didn't want anything to drink. He gave me a plain coke instead. It tasted funny, but I thought it was just a bad taste in my mouth.

We had a lot of fun for a while. Joe said I should dance with Ellen and she would teach me the steps. I fell a few times and I couldn't understand why because no one else was dancing besides Ellen and me. And all the time I was tripping because somebody's foot was always sticking out.

Then when I got up I saw the look on Joe's face and it gave me a funny feeling in my stomack. "He's a scream," one of the girls said. Everybody was laughing.

Frank said, "I ain't laughed so much since we sent him off for the newspaper that night at Muggsy's and ditched him."

"Look at him. His face is red."

"He's blushing. Charlie is blushing."

"Hey, Ellen, what'd you do to Charlie? I never saw him act like that before."

I didn't know what to do or where to turn. Everyone was looking at me and laughing and I felt naked. I wanted to hide myself. I ran out into the street and I threw up. Then I walked home. It's a funny thing I never knew that Joe and Frank and the others liked to have me around all the time to make fun of me.

Now I know what it means when they say "to pull a Charlie Gordon."

I'm ashamed.

PROGRESS REPORT 10

April 21 Still didn't go into the factory. I told Mrs. Flynn my landlady to call and tell Mr. Donnegan I was sick. Mrs. Flynn looks at me very funny lately like she's scared of me.

I think it's a good thing about finding out how everybody laughs at me. I thought about it a lot. It's because I'm so dumb and I don't even know when I'm doing something dumb. People think it's funny when a dumb person can't do things the same way they can.

Anyway, now I know I'm getting smarter every day. I know punctuation and I can spell good. I like to look up all the hard words in the dictionary and I remember them. I'm reading a lot now, and Miss Kinnian says I read very fast. Sometimes I even understand what I'm reading about, and it stays in my mind. There are times when I can close my eyes and think of a page and it all comes back like a picture.

Besides history, geography and arithmetic, Miss Kinnian said I should start to learn a few foreign languages. Dr. Strauss gave me some more tapes to play while I sleep. I still don't understand how that conscious and unconscious mind works, but Dr. Strauss says not to worry yet. He asked me to promise that when I start learning college subjects next week I wouldn't read any books on psychology—that is, until he gives me permission.

I feel a lot better today, but I guess I'm still a little angry that all the time people were laughing and making fun of me because I wasn't so smart. When I become intelligent like Dr. Strauss says, with three times my I.Q. of 68, then maybe I'll be like everyone else and people will like me and be friendly.

I'm not sure what an I.Q. is. Dr. Nemur said it was something that measured how intelligent you were—like a scale in the drugstore weighs pounds. But Dr. Strauss had a big argument with him and said an I.Q. didn't weigh intelligence at all. He said an I.Q. showed how much intelligence you could get, like the numbers on the outside of a measuring cup. You still had to fill the cup up with stuff.

Then when I asked Burt, who gives me my intelligence tests and works with Algernon, he said that both of them were wrong (only I had to promise not to tell them he said so). Burt says that the I.Q. measures a lot of different things including some of the things you learned already, and it really isn't any good at all.

So I still don't know what I.Q. is except that mine is going to be over 200 soon. I didn't want to say anything, but I don't see how if they don't know *what* it is, or *where* it is—I don't see how they know *how much* of it you've got.

Dr. Nemur says I have to take a *Rorshach Test* tomorrow. I wonder what *that is.*

April 22 I found out what a *Rorshach* is. It's the test I took before the operation—the one with the inkblots on the pieces of cardboard. The man who gave me the test was the same one.

I was scared to death of those inkblots. I knew he was going to ask me to find the pictures and I knew I wouldn't be able to. I was thinking to myself, if only there was some way of knowing what kind of pictures were hidden there. Maybe there weren't any pictures at all. Maybe it was just a trick to see if I was dumb enough to look for something that wasn't there. Just thinking about that made me sore at him.

"All right, Charlie," he said, "you've seen these cards before, remember?"

"Of course I remember."

The way I said it, he knew I was angry, and he looked surprised. "Yes, of course. Now I want you to look at this one. What might this be? What do you see on this card? People see all sorts of things in these inkblots. Tell me what it might be for you — what it makes you think of."

I was shocked. That wasn't what I had expected him to say at all. "You mean there are no pictures hidden in those inkblots?"

He frowned and took off his glasses. "What?"

"Pictures. Hidden in the inkblots. Last time you told me that everyone could see them and you wanted me to find them too."

He explained to me that the last time he had used almost the exact same words he was using now. I didn't believe it, and I still have the suspicion that he misled me at the time just for the fun of it. Unless — I don't know any more — could I have been *that* feebleminded?

We went through the cards slowly. One of them looked like a pair of bats tugging at something. Another one looked like two men fencing with swords. I imagined all sorts of things. I guess I got carried away. But I didn't trust him any more, and I kept turning them around and even looking on the back to see if there was anything there I was supposed to catch. While he was making his notes, I peeked out of the corner of my eye to read it. But it was all in code that looked like this:

$$WF + A \quad DdF - Ad \text{ orig.} \quad WF - A \quad SF + obj$$

The test still doesn't make sense to me. It seems to me that anyone could make up lies about things that they didn't really see. How could he know I wasn't making a fool of him by mentioning things that I didn't really imagine? Maybe I'll understand it when Dr. Strauss lets me read up on psychology.

April 25 I figured out a new way to line up the machines in the factory, and Mr. Donnegan says it will save him $10,000 a year in labor and increased production. He gave me a $25 bonus.

I wanted to take Joe Carp and Frank Reilly out to lunch to celebrate, but Joe said he had to buy some things for his wife, and Frank said he was meeting his cousin for lunch. I guess it'll take a little time for them to get used to the changes in me. Everybody seems to be frightened of me. When I went over to Amos Borg and tapped him on the shoulder he jumped up in the air.

People don't talk to me much any more or kid around the way they used to. It makes the job kind of lonely.

April 27 I got up the nerve today to ask Miss Kinnian to have dinner with me tomorrow night to celebrate my bonus.

At first she wasn't sure it was right, but I asked Dr Strauss and he said it was okay. Dr. Strauss and Dr. Nemur don't seem to be getting along so well. They're arguing all the time. This evening when I came in to ask Dr. Strauss about having dinner with Miss Kinnian, I heard them shouting. Dr. Nemur was saying that it was *his* experiment and *his* research, and Dr. Strauss was shouting back that he contributed just as much, because he found me through Miss Kinnian and he performed the operation. Dr. Strauss said that someday thousands of neurosurgeons might be using his technique all over the world.

Dr. Nemur wanted to publish the results of the experiment at the end of this month. Dr. Strauss wanted to wait a while longer to be sure. Dr. Strauss said that Dr. Nemur was more interested in the Chair of Psychology at Princeton than he was in the experiment. Dr. Nemur said that Dr. Strauss was nothing but an opportunist who was trying to ride to glory on *his* coattails.

When I left afterward, I found myself trembling. I don't know why for sure, but it was as if I'd seen both men clearly for the first time. I remember hearing Burt say that Dr. Nemur had a shrew of a wife who was pushing him all the time to get things published so that he could become famous. Burt said that the dream of her life was to have a big-shot husband.

Was Dr. Strauss really trying to ride on his coattails?

April 28 I don't understand why I never noticed how beautiful Miss Kinnian really is. She has brown eyes and feathery brown hair that comes to the top of her neck. She's only thirty-four! I think from the beginning I had the feeling that she was an unreachable genius—and very, very old. Now, every time I see her she grows younger and more lovely.

We had dinner and a long talk. When she said that I was coming along so fast that soon I'd be leaving her behind, I laughed.

"It's true, Charlie. You're already a better reader than I am. You can read a whole page at a glance while I can take in only a few lines at a time. And you remember every single thing you read. I'm lucky if I can recall the main thoughts and the general meaning."

"I don't feel intelligent. There are so many things I don't understand."

She took out a cigarette and I lit it for her. "You've got to be a *little* patient. You're accomplishing in days and weeks what it takes normal people half a lifetime to do. That's what makes it so amazing. You're like a giant sponge now, soaking things in. Facts, figures, general knowledge. And soon you'll begin to connect them, too. You'll see how the different branches of learning are related. There are many levels, Charlie, like steps on a giant ladder that take you up higher and higher to see more and more of the world around you.

"I can see only a little bit of that, Charlie, and I won't go much higher than I am now, but you'll keep climbing up and up, and see more and more, and each step will open new worlds that you never even knew existed." She frowned. "I hope . . . I just hope to God ——"

"What?"

"Never mind, Charles. I just hope I wasn't wrong to advise you to go into this in the first place."

I laughed. "How could that be? It worked, didn't it? Even Algernon is still smart."

We sat there silently for awhile and I knew what she was thinking about as she watched me toying with the chain of my rabbit's foot and my keys. I didn't want to think of that possibility any more than elderly people want to think of death. I *knew* that this was only the beginning. I knew what she meant about levels because I'd seen some of them already. The thought of leaving her behind made me sad.

I'm in love with Miss Kinnian.

PROGRESS REPORT 11

April 30 I've quit my job with Donnegan's Plastic Box Company. Mr. Donnegan insisted that it would be better for all concerned if I left. What did I do to make them hate me so?

The first I knew of it was when Mr. Donnegan showed me the petition. Eight hundred and forty names, everyone connected with the factory, except Fanny Girden. Scanning the list quickly, I saw at once that hers was the only missing name. All the rest demanded that I be fired.

Joe Carp and Frank Reilly wouldn't talk to me about it. No one else would either, except Fanny. She was one of the few people I'd known who set her mind to something and believed it no matter what the rest of the world proved, said or did—and Fanny did not believe that I should have been fired. She had been against the petition on principle and despite the pressure and threats she'd held out.

"Which don't mean to say," she remarked, "that I don't think there's something mighty strange about you, Charlie. Them changes. I don't know. You used to be a good, dependable, ordinary man—not too bright maybe, but honest. Who knows what you done to yourself to get so smart all of a sudden. Like everybody around here's been saying, Charlie, it's not right."

"But how can you say that, Fanny? What's wrong with a man becoming intelligent and wanting to acquire knowledge and understanding of the world around him?"

She stared down at her work and I turned to leave. Without looking at me, she said: "It was evil when Eve listened to the snake and ate from the tree of knowledge. It was evil when she saw that she was naked. If not for that none of us would ever have to grow old and sick, and die."

Once again now I have the feeling of shame burning inside me. This intelligence has driven a wedge between me and all the people I once knew and loved. Before, they laughed at me and despised me for my ignorance and dullness; now, they hate me for my knowledge and understanding. What in God's name do they want of me?

They've driven me out of the factory. Now I'm more alone than ever before. . . .

May 15 Dr. Strauss is very angry at me for not having written any progress reports in two weeks. He's justified because the lab is now paying me a regular salary. I told him I was too busy thinking and reading. When I pointed out that writing was such a slow process that it made me impatient with my poor handwriting, he suggested that I learn to type. It's much easier to write now because I can type nearly seventy-five words a minute. Dr. Strauss continually reminds me of the need to speak and write simply so that people will be able to understand me.

I'll try to review all the things that happened to me during the last two weeks. Algernon and I were presented to the American Psychological Association sitting in convention with the World Psychological Association last Tuesday. We created quite a sensation. Dr. Nemur and Dr. Strauss were proud of us.

I suspect that Dr. Nemur, who is sixty—ten years older than Dr. Strauss—finds it necessary to see tangible results of his work. Undoubtedly the result of pressure by Mrs. Nemur.

Contrary to my earlier impressions of him, I realize that Dr. Nemur is not at all a genius. He has a very good mind, but it struggles under the specter of self-doubt. He wants people to take him for a genius. Therefore, it is important for him to feel that his work is accepted by the world. I believe that Dr. Nemur was afraid of further delay because he worried that someone else might make a discovery along these lines and take the credit from him.

Dr. Strauss, on the other hand, might be called a genius, although I feel that his areas of knowledge are too limited. He was educated in the tradition of narrow specialization; the broader aspects of background were neglected far more than necessary—even for a neurosurgeon.

I was shocked to learn that the only ancient languages he could read were Latin, Greek, and Hebrew, and that he knows almost nothing of mathematics beyond the elementary levels of the calculus of variations. When he admitted this to me, I found myself almost annoyed. It was as if he'd hidden this part of himself in order to deceive me, pretending—as do many people, I've discovered—to be what he is not. No one I've ever known is what he appears to be on the surface.

Dr. Nemur appears to be uncomfortable around me. Sometimes when I try to talk to him, he just looks at me strangely and turns away. I was angry at first when Dr. Strauss told me I was giving Dr. Nemur an inferiority complex. I thought he was mocking me and I'm oversensitive at being made fun of.

How was I to know that a highly respected psychoexperimentalist like Nemur was unacquainted with Hindustani and Chinese? It's absurd when you consider the work that is being done in India and China today in the very field of his study.

I asked Dr. Strauss how Nemur could refute Rahajamati's attack on his method and results if Nemur couldn't even read them in the first place. That strange look on Dr. Strauss's face can mean only one of two things. Either he doesn't want to tell Nemur what they're saying in

India, or else—and this worries me—Dr. Strauss doesn't know either. I must be careful to speak and write clearly and simply so that people won't laugh.

May 18 I am very disturbed. I saw Miss Kinnian last night for the first time in over a week. I tried to avoid all discussions of intellectual concepts and to keep the conversation on a simple, everyday level, but she just stared at me blankly and asked me what I meant about the mathematical variance equivalent in Dorberman's Fifth Concerto.

When I tried to explain, she stopped me and laughed. I guess I got angry, but I suspect I'm approaching her on the wrong level. No matter what I try to discuss with her, I am unable to communicate. I must review Vrostadt's equations in *Levels of Semantic Progression.* I find that I don't communicate with people much any more. Thank God for books and music and things I can think about. I am alone in my apartment at Mrs. Flynn's boarding house most of the time and seldom speak to anyone.

May 20 I would not have noticed the new dishwasher, a boy of about sixteen, at the corner diner where I take my evening meals if not for the incident of the broken dishes.

They crashed to the floor, shattering and sending bits of white china under the tables. The boy stood there, dazed and frightened, holding the empty tray in his hand. The whistles and catcalls from the customers (the cries of "hey, there go the profits!" . . . "*Mazeltov!*" . . . and "well, *he* didn't work here very long . . ." which invariably seem to follow the breaking of glass or dishware in a public restaurant) all seemed to confuse him.

When the owner came to see what the excitement was about, the boy cowered as if he expected to be struck and threw up his arms as if to ward off the blow.

"All right! All right, you dope," shouted the owner, "don't just stand there! Get the broom and sweep that mess up. A broom . . . a broom, you idiot! It's in the kitchen. Sweep up all the pieces."

The boy saw that he was not going to be punished. His frightened expression disappeared and he smiled and hummed as he came back with the broom to sweep the floor. A few of the rowdier customers kept up the remarks, amusing themselves at his expense.

"Here, sonny, over here there's a nice piece behind you . . ."

"C'mon, do it again . . ."

"He's not so dumb. It's easier to break 'em than to wash 'em . . ."

As his vacant eyes moved across the crowd of amused onlookers, he slowly mirrored their smiles and finally broke into an uncertain grin at the joke which he obviously did not understand.

I felt sick inside as I looked at his dull, vacuous smile, the wide, bright eyes of a child, uncertain but eager to please. They were laughing at him because he was mentally retarded.

And I had been laughing at him, too.

Suddenly I was furious at myself and all those who were smirking at him. I jumped up and shouted, "Shut up! Leave him alone! It's not his fault he can't understand! He can't help what he is! But for God's sake . . . he's still a human being!"

The room grew silent. I cursed myself for losing control and creating a scene. I tried not to look at the boy as I paid my bill and walked out without touching my food. I felt ashamed for both of us.

How strange it is that people of honest feelings and sensibility, who would not take advantage of a man born without arms or legs or eyes—how such people think nothing of abusing a man born with low intelligence. It infuriated me to think that not too long ago I, like this boy, had foolishly played the clown.

And I had almost forgotten.

I'd hidden the picture of the old Charlie Gordon from myself because now that I was intelligent it was something that had to be pushed out of my mind. But today in looking at that boy, for the first time I saw what I had been. *I was just like him!*

Only a short time ago, I learned that people laughed at me. Now I can see that unknowingly I joined with them in laughing at myself. That hurts most of all.

I have often reread my progress reports and seen the illiteracy, the childish naiveté, the mind of low intelligence peering from a dark room, through the keyhole, at the dazzling light outside. I see that even in my dullness I knew that I was inferior, and that other people had something I lacked—something denied me. In my mental blindness, I thought that it was somehow connected with the ability to read and write, and I was sure that if I could get those skills I would automatically have intelligence, too.

Even a feeble-minded man wants to be like other men.

A child may not know how to feed itself, or what to eat, yet it knows of hunger.

This then is what I was like. I never knew. Even with my gift of intellectual awareness, I never really knew.

This day was good for me. Seeing the past more clearly, I have decided to use my knowledge and skills to work in the field of increasing human intelligence levels. Who is better equipped for this work? Who else has lived in both worlds? These are my people. Let me use my gift to do something for them.

Tomorrow, I will discuss with Dr. Strauss the manner in which I can work in this area; I may be able to help him work out the problems of widespread use of the technique which was used on me. I have several good ideas of my own.

There is so much that might be done with this technique. If I could be made into a genius, what about thousands of others like myself? What fantastic levels might be achieved by using this technique on normal people? On *geniuses?*

There are so many doors to open. I am impatient to begin.

PROGRESS REPORT 12

May 23 It happened today. Algernon bit me. I visited the lab to see him as I do occasionally, and when I took him out of his cage, he snapped at my hand. I put him back and watched him for a while. He was unusually disturbed and vicious.

May 24 Burt, who is in charge of the experimental animals, tells me that Algernon is changing. He is less cooperative; he refuses to run the maze any more; general motivation has decreased. And he hasn't been eating. Everyone is upset about what this may mean.

May 25 They've been feeding Algernon, who now refuses to work the shifting-lock problem. Everyone identifies me with Algernon. In a way we're both the first of our kind. They're all pretending that Algernon's behavior is not necessarily significant for me. But it's hard to hide the fact that some of the other animals who were used in this experiment are showing strange behavior.

Dr. Strauss and Dr. Nemur have asked me not to come to the lab any more. I know what they're thinking but I can't accept it. I am going ahead with my plans to carry their research forward. With all due respect to both of these fine scientists, I am well aware of their limitations. If there is an answer, I'll have to find it out for myself. Suddenly, time has become very important to me.

May 29 I have been given a lab of my own and permission to go ahead with the research. I'm on to something. Working day and night. I've had a cot moved into the lab. Most of my writing time is spent on the notes which I keep in a separate folder, but from time to time I feel it necessary to put down my moods and my thoughts out of sheer habit.

I find the *calculus of intelligence* to be a fascinating study. Here is the place for the application of all the knowledge I have acquired. In a sense it's the problem I've been concerned with all my life.

May 31 Dr. Strauss thinks I'm working too hard. Dr. Nemur says I'm trying to cram a lifetime of research and thought into a few weeks. I know I should rest, but I'm driven on by something inside that won't let me stop. I've got to find the reason for the sharp regression in Algernon. I've got to know *if* and *when* it will happen to me.

June 4

LETTER TO DR. STRAUSS *(copy)*

Dear Dr. Strauss:

Under separate cover I am sending you a copy of my report entitled "The Algernon–Gordon Effect: A Study of Structure and Function of Increased Intelligence," which I would like to have you read and have published.

As you see, my experiments are completed. I have included in my report all of my formulas, as well as mathematical analysis in the appendix. Of course, these should be verified.

Because of its importance to both you and Dr. Nemur (and need I say to myself, too?) I have checked and rechecked my results a dozen times in the hope of finding an error. I am sorry to say the results must stand. Yet for the sake of science, I am grateful for the little bit that I here add to the knowledge of the function of the human mind and of the laws governing the artificial increase of human intelligence.

I recall your once saying to me that an experimental *failure* or the *disproving* of a theory was as important to the advancement of learning as a success would be. I know now that this is true. I am sorry, however, that my own contribution to the field must rest upon the ashes of the work of two men I regard so highly.

Yours truly,

CHARLES GORDON

encl.: rept.

June 5 I must not become emotional. The facts and the results of my experiments are clear, and the more sensational aspects of my own rapid climb cannot obscure the fact that the tripling of intelligence by the surgical technique developed by Drs. Strauss and Nemur must be viewed as having little or no practical applicability (at the present time) to the increase of human intelligence.

As I review the records and data on Algernon, I see that although he is still in his physical infancy, he has regressed mentally. Motor activity is impaired; there is a general reduction of glandular activity; there is an accelerated loss of coordination.

There are also strong indications of progressive amnesia.

As will be seen by my report, these and other physical and mental deterioration syndromes can be predicted with statistically significant results by the application of my formula.

The surgical stimulus to which we were both subjected has resulted in an intensification and acceleration of all mental processes. The unforeseen development, which I have taken the liberty of calling the *Algernon–Gordon Effect*, is the logical extension of the entire intelligence speedup. The hypothesis here proven may be described simply in the following terms: Artificially increased intelligence deteriorates at a rate of time directly proportional to the quantity of the increase.

I feel that this, in itself, is an important discovery.

As long as I am able to write, I will continue to record my thoughts in these progress reports. It is one of my few pleasures. However, by all indications, my own mental deterioration will be very rapid.

I have already begun to notice signs of emotional instability and forgetfulness, the first symptoms of the burnout.

June 10 Deterioration progressing, I have become absent-minded. Algernon died two days ago. Dissection shows my predictions were right. His brain had decreased in weight and there was a general smoothing out of cerebral convolutions as well as a deepening and broadening of brain fissures.

I guess the same thing is or will soon be happening to me. Now that it's definite, I don't want it to happen.

I put Algernon's body in a cheese box and buried him in the backyard. I cried.

June 15 Dr. Strauss came to see me again. I wouldn't open the door and I told him to go away. I want to be left to myself. I have become touchy and irritable. I feel the darkness closing in. It's hard to throw off thoughts of suicide. I keep telling myself how important this introspective journal will be.

It's a strange sensation to pick up a book that you've read and enjoyed just a few months ago and discover that you don't remember it. I remembered how great I thought John Milton was, but when I picked up *Paradise Lost* I couldn't understand it at all. I got so angry I threw the book across the room.

I've got to try to hold on to some of it. Some of the things I've learned. Oh, God, please don't take it all away.

June 19 Sometimes, at night, I go out for a walk. Last night I couldn't remember where I lived. A policeman took me home. I have the strange feeling that this has all happened to me before — a long time ago. I keep telling myself I'm the only person in the world who can describe what's happening to me.

June 21 Why can't I remember? I've got to fight. I lie in bed for days and I don't know who or where I am. Then it comes back to me in a flash. Fugues of amnesia. Symptoms of senility — second childhood. I can watch them coming on. It's so cruelly logical. I learned so much and so fast. Now my mind is deteriorating rapidly. I won't let it happen. I'll fight it. I can't help thinking of the boy in the restaurant, the blank expression, the silly smile, the people laughing at him. No — please — not that again . . .

June 22 I'm forgetting things that I learned recently. It seems to be following the classic pattern — the last things learned are the first things forgotten. Or is that the pattern? I'd better look it up again. . . .

I reread my paper on the *Algernon–Gordon Effect* and I get the strange feeling that it was written by someone else. There are parts I don't even understand.

Motor activity impaired. I keep tripping over things, and it becomes increasingly difficult to type.

June 23 I've given up using the typewriter completely. My coordination is bad. I feel that I'm moving slower and slower. Had a terrible shock today. I picked up a copy of an article I used in my research, Krueger's "Über Psychische Ganzheit," to see if it would help me understand what I had done. First I thought there was something wrong with my

METAMORPHOSIS

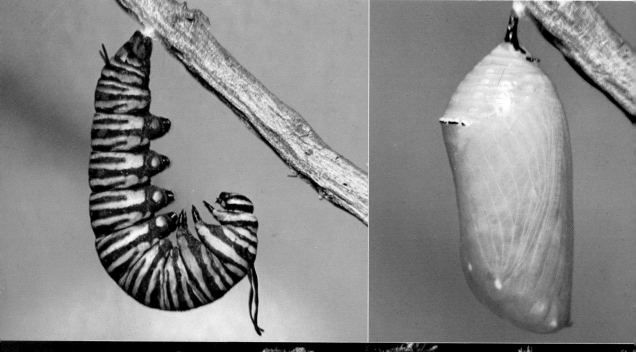

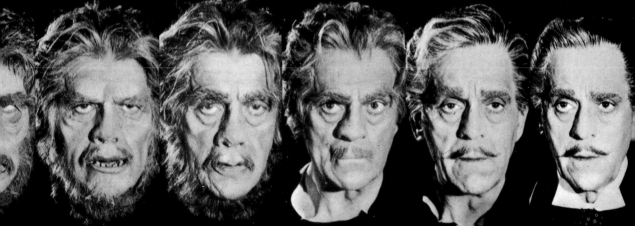

eyes. Then I realized I could no longer read German. I tested myself in other languages. All gone.

June 30 A week since I dared to write again. It's slipping away like sand through my fingers. Most of the books I have are too hard for me now. I get angry with them because I know that I read and understood them just a few weeks ago.

I keep telling myself I must keep writing these reports so that somebody will know what is happening to me. But it gets harder to form the words and remember spellings. I have to look up even simple words in the dictionary now and it makes me impatient with myself.

Dr. Strauss comes around almost every day, but I told him I wouldn't see or speak to anybody. He feels guilty. They all do. But I don't blame anyone. I knew what might happen. But how it hurts.

July 7 I don't know where the week went. Todays Sunday I know because I can see through my window people going to church. I think I stayed in bed all week but I remember Mrs. Flynn bringing food to me a few times. I keep saying over and over Ive got to do something but then I forget or maybe its just easier not to do what I say Im going to do.

I think of my mother and father a lot these days. I found a picture of them with me taken at a beach. My father has a big ball under his arm and my mother is holding me by the hand. I don't remember them the way they are in the picture. All I remember is my father drunk most of the time and arguing with mom about money.

He never shaved much and he used to scratch my face when he hugged me. My mother said he died but Cousin Miltie said he heard his mom and dad say that my father ran away with another woman. When I asked my mother she slapped my face and said my father was dead. I don't think I ever found out which was true but I dont care much. (He said he was going to take me to see cows on a farm once but he never did. He never kept his promises. . . .)

July 10 My landlady Mrs Flynn is worried about me. She says the way I lay around all day and dont do anything I remind her of her son before she threw him out of the house. She said she doesnt like loafers. If Im sick its one thing, but if Im a loafer thats another thing and she wont have it. I told her I think Im sick.

I try to read a little bit every day, mostly stories, but sometimes I have to read the same thing over and over again because I dont know what it means. And its hard to write. I know I should look up all the words in the dictionary but its so hard and Im so tired all the time.

Then I got the idea that I would only use the easy words instead of the long hard ones. That saves time. I put flowers on Algernons grave about once a week. Mrs Flynn thinks Im crazy to put flowers on a mouses grave but I told her that Algernon was special.

July 14 Its sunday again. I dont have anything to do to keep me busy now because my television set is broke and I dont have any money to get it fixed. (I think I lost this months check from the lab. I dont re-member.)

I get awful headaches and asperin doesnt help me much. Mrs Flynn knows Im really sick and she feels very sorry for me. Shes a wonderful woman whenever someone is sick.

July 22 Mrs Flynn called a strange doctor to see me. She was afraid I was going to die. I told the doctor I wasnt too sick and that I only forgot sometimes. He asked me did I have any friends or relatives and I said no I dont have any. I told him I had a friend called Algernon once but he was a mouse and we used to run races together. He looked at me kind of funny like he thought I was crazy.

He smiled when I told him I used to be a genius. He talked to me like I was a baby and he winked at Mrs Flynn. I got mad and chased him out because he was making fun of me the way they all used to.

July 24 I have no more money and Mrs Flynn says I got to go to work somewhere and pay the rent because I havent paid for over two months. I dont know any work but the job I used to have at Donnegans Plastic Box Company. I dont want to go back there because they all knew me when I was smart and maybe theyll laugh at me. But I dont know what else to do to get money.

July 25 I was looking at some of my old progress reports and its very funny but I can't read what I wrote. I can make out some of the words but they dont make sense.

Miss Kinnian came to the door but I said go away I dont want to see you. She cried and I cried too but I wouldnt let her in because I didnt want her to laugh at me. I told her I didnt like her any more. I told her I didnt want to be smart any more. Thats not true. I still love her and I still want to be smart but I had to say that so shed go away.

She gave Mrs Flynn money to pay the rent. I dont want that. I got to get a job.

Please . . . please let me not forget how to read and write . . .

July 27 Mr Donnegan was very nice when I came back and asked him for my old job as janitor. First he was very suspicious but I told him what happened to me then he looked very sad and put his hand on my shoulder and said Charlie Gordon you got guts.

Everybody looked at me when I came downstairs and started working in the toilet sweeping it out like I used to I told myself Charlie if they make fun of you dont get sore because you remember their not so smart as you once thot they were. And besides they were once your friends and if they laughed at you that doesnt mean anything because they liked you too.

One of the new men who came to work there after I went away made a nasty crack he said hey Charlie I hear your a very smart fella a real quiz kid. Say something intelligent. I felt bad but Joe Carp came over and grabbed him by the shirt and said leave him alone you lousy cracker or Ill break your neck. I didnt expect Joe to take my part so I guess hes really my friend.

Later Frank Reilly came over and said Charlie if anybody bothers you or trys to take advantage you call me or Joe and we will set em straight. I said thanks Frank and I got choked up so I had to turn around and go into the supply room so he wouldnt see me cry. Its good to have friends.

July 28 I did a dumb thing today I forgot I wasnt in Miss Kinnians class at the adult center any more like I used to be. I went in and sat down in my old seat in the back of the room and she looked at me funny and she said Charles. I dint remember she ever called me that before only Charlie so I said hello Miss Kinnian Im redy for my lesin today only I lost my reader that we was using. She startid to cry and run out of the room and everybody looked at me and I saw they wasnt the same pepul who use to be in my class.

Then all of a suddin I remembered some things about the opera-shun and me getting smart and I said holy smoke I reely pulled a Charlie Gordon that time. I went away before she come back to the room.

Thats why Im going away from New York for good. I dont want to do nothing like that agen. I dont want Miss Kinnian to feel sorry for me. Evry body feels sorry at the factery and I dont want that eather so Im going someplace where nobody knows that Charlie Gordon was once a genus and now he cant even reed a book or rite good.

Im taking a cuple of books along and even if I cant reed them Ill practise hard and maybe I wont forget every thing I lerned. If I try reel hard maybe Ill be a littel bit smarter than I was before the operashun. I got my rabits foot and my luky penny and maybe they will help me.

If you ever reed this Miss Kinnian dont be sorry for me Im glad I got a second chanse to be smart becaus I lerned a lot of things that I never even new were in this world and Im grateful that I saw it all for a littel bit. I dont know why Im dumb agen or what I did wrong maybe its becaus I dint try hard enuff. But if I try and practis very hard maybe Ill get a littel smarter and know what all the words are. I remember a littel bit how I had a nice feeling with the blue book that has the torn cover when I red it. Thats why Im gonna keep trying to get smart so I can have that feeling agen. Its a good feeling to know things and be smart. I wish I had it rite now if I did I would sit down and reed all the time. Anyway I bet Im the first dumb person in the world who ever found out something importent for sience. I remember I did something but I dont remember what. So I gess its like I did it for all the dumb pepul like me.

Good-by Miss Kinnian and Dr Strauss and everybody. And P.S. please tell Dr Nemur not be such a grouch when pepul laff at him and he would have more frends. Its easy to make frends if you let pepul laff at you. Im going to have lots of frends where I go. P.P.S. Please if you get a chanse put some flowers on Algernons grave in the bakyard. . . .

What kind of metamorphosis does this modern story describe? Who are the gods in this story? Are they like Zeus or Prometheus (page 32)? Are they like Clarke's crystal slab (page 57), or Twain's Mysterious Stranger (page 39)?

How is this a story about the death of childhood? Why does Fanny Girden remind Charlie of the story of Eve and the snake?

"No one I've ever known is what he appears to be on the surface." Could Charlie's statement suggest that life consists of many kinds of metamorphoses?

Narcissus

A Greek myth
Retold by JAY MACPHERSON

As beautiful as Adonis was the ill-fated Narcissus, who from his childhood was loved by all who saw him but whose pride would let him love no one in return. At last one of those who had hopelessly courted him turned and cursed him, exclaiming: "May he suffer as we have suffered! May he too love in vain!" The avenging goddess Nemesis heard and approved this prayer.

There was nearby a clear pool, with shining silvery waters. No shepherd had ever come there, nor beast nor bird nor falling branch marred its surface: the grass grew fresh and green around it, and the sheltering woods kept it always cool from the midday sun.

Here once came Narcissus, heated and tired from the chase, and lay down by the pool to drink. As he bent over the water, his eyes met the eyes of another young man, gazing up at him from the depths of the pool. Deluded by his reflection, Narcissus fell in love with the beauty that was his own. Without thought of food or rest he lay beside the pool addressing cries and pleas to the image, whose lips moved as he spoke but whose reply he could never catch. Echo came by, the most constant of his disdained lovers. She was a nymph who had once angered Hera, the wife of Zeus, by talking too much, and in consequence was deprived of the use of her tongue for ordinary conversation: all she could do was repeat the last words of others. Seeing Narcissus lying there, she pleaded with him in his own words. "I will die unless you pity me," cried Narcissus to his beloved. "Pity me," cried Echo as vainly to hers. Narcissus never raised his eyes to her at all, though she remained day after day beside him on the bank, pleading as well as she was able. At last she pined away, withering and wasting with unrequited love, till nothing was left of her but her voice, which the traveler still hears calling unexpectedly in woods and waste places.

As for the cruel Narcissus, he fared no better. The face that looked back at him from the water became pale, thin, and haggard, till at last poor Echo caught and repeated his last "Farewell!" But when she came with the other nymphs to lament over his body, it was nowhere to be found. Instead, over the pool bent a new flower, white with a yellow center, which they called by his name. From this flower the Furies, the avengers of guilt, twist garlands to bind their hateful brows.

Try to rewrite this myth in a recognizable modern setting. What will you do with the metamorphosis at the end?

Sonnet One

From fairest creatures we desire increase,
That thereby beauty's rose might never die,
But as the riper should by time decrease,
His tender heir might bear his memory.
But thou, contracted to thine own bright eyes,
Feed'st thy light's flame with self-substantial fuel,
Making a famine where abundance lies,
Thyself thy foe, to thy sweet self too cruel.
Thou that art now the world's fresh ornament
And only herald to the gaudy spring,
Within thine own bud buriest thy content
And, tender churl, makest waste in niggarding.
  Pity the world, or else this glutton be,
  To eat the world's due, by the grave and thee.

WILLIAM SHAKESPEARE

How is this poem a warning to another Narcissus?

When the Roman writer Ovid collected the Greek myths in order to tell the mythological story of the human race, he began by saying, "My intention is to tell of bodies changed to different forms." He called the story *Metamorphoses*, which is the Greek word for "changes of form." Today we use science to turn living trees into writing paper. We use technology to turn machines into intelligent decision-makers. And we use cosmetics to turn age into youth. Whether we call it progress or science, our fascination with "changes of form" is just as great as Ovid's.

When we look at the natural world, we notice that it is something distinct from ourselves. It cannot communicate with us. It seems to have no thoughts or feelings. Its form is very different from our own. Many aspects of the natural world are even hostile to us. From earliest times, then, people have tried to make themselves at home in a world that they feel separate from, and in which they are often lonely and frightened.

One of our earliest activities was to use words as symbols for things. We used language to classify what we saw around us. We could divide the world into an almost endless array of distinct parts. Birds were different from wolves, trees were different from grass, rain was different from sunshine. But this kind of mental activity also impressed upon us our own separation from nature. It may have increased our power and confidence, but it also increased our sense of aloneness.

Yet even as we categorized and named objects in the natural world, we also discovered that boundaries in nature did not seem to be fixed. The pale seed becomes the green plant. The water comes down as rain, rises as steam, and returns as morning dew. A worm becomes a butterfly, a tadpole becomes a frog. The scientific question "how" was accom-

228

panied, and perhaps preceded, by the imaginative question "why not?"

This idea of flux, of things flowing into one another, appeals to our imaginative desire to make the universe "one." If it is possible that the natural, human, and divine worlds can flow in and out of each other, then we need not feel alone and apart from things around us. The imagination, after all, is not practical. It turns its back on logic. It can see life as a continuous whole in which nothing need remain fixed or static.

Certain American Indian people, for example, believed that they assumed the power of an animal when they put on certain masks. This is a metamorphosis, expressed in a ritual. Poets or storytellers, in using metaphors, work from the same impulse. Saying this *is* that, they accent the likenesses in life rather than the differences. A poet can say that a woman is *like* a red rose, or that she *is* a rose. The poet might even call her Rose. The imagination wants to see beyond the distinct and separate shapes of life.

All the stories and poems in this unit use the archetype of change, or metamorphosis. These stories and poems show that in the imagination people themselves can "become" something else. In reality, of course, such a desire cannot be achieved. But the imagination is not subject to "reality." In "reality" we are subject to the changes of time, but we can imagine changes that are not.

The idea of metamorphosis is an expression of our wishes and our nightmares. It reflects our ambition to become like gods, to conquer death, while also reflecting our fear of being reduced to something less than human or to nothing. Both possibilities exist in the human imagination, and it is the peculiar changeability of people that keeps them open to either alternative.

6

A HUMAN YEAR

Alan E. Cober '72

Rock-a-by baby
On the tree top,
When the wind blows
The cradle will rock.
When the bough breaks
The cradle will fall
And down will come baby
Cradle and all.

Humpty Dumpty sat on a wall.
Humpty Dumpty had a great fall.
All the King's horses
And all the King's men
Couldn't put Humpty together again.

He loves me,
He don't,
He'll have me,
He won't,
He would
If he could,
But he can't
So he won't.

Ring around the rosie,
A pocket full of posies—
Ashes, ashes,
We all fall down.

What specific images in each of these rhymes contrast a world of wish with a world of nightmare?

Do you think these childhood songs could be placed in unit three, with stories of the origins of death and evil and of the end of childhood? Why?

A ritual, in its simplest form, is an action which people perform to imitate nature. What natural cycles do these rhymes imitate? Why do you think these cycles would be expressed in children's games?

Demeter and Persephone

A Greek myth
Retold by W.T. JEWKES

Demeter, goddess of the cornfields and the fruitful harvest, had a daughter by Zeus called Persephone. She was a beautiful girl with long golden hair, bronzed skin, and fair blue eyes. Many men looked longingly at her when she had grown up, thinking to themselves what a wonderful bride she would make. But it seemed that no one was to marry Persephone, for she was devoted to her mother and to the chaste goddess Artemis, to whose service she had vowed to devote herself.

But Aphrodite was not very pleased that such a beautiful young girl should go unmarried. And one day, when she saw Hades, who had come up from dark Tartarus to inspect the foundations of the world, she thought of a way to kill two birds with one stone. She called out to her mischievous son Eros, who was in the courtyard, rubbing his bow with resin.

"Eros, I've got something for you to do. You see Hades out there driving along the cliffs. Well, do you realize that he has never been in love? All the gods of Olympus have felt my power, as well as all the mortals that live on earth." The goddess stamped her pretty white foot and her eyes flashed. "It's about time the underworld felt it too. So string up your bow there, and shoot one of your burning arrows into the heart of that arrogant Hades. Make him fall in love with Demeter's daughter Persephone. And that will teach her to defy me and prefer Artemis's service to mine!"

So Eros, with a delighted twinkle in his eyes, wet the string of his bow with his spittle, drew an arrow from his quiver, and dipped it in the glowing brazier that stood close by. Then, drawing the string taut to his cheek, he let the shaft fly in a hissing arc across the sky until it lodged dead center in Hades's left breast. Eros's victims hardly feel the first wound of love, for the arrows are so sharp that they pierce right through without more sting than a bee. But once that fire begins to work, they soon find their hearts inflamed with passion. Hades was no exception and it was not long before he became feverish. So he stopped his chariot beside a stream to take a cooling drink.

While he lay there under the shade of a sea-pine, he looked across the fields that stretched between the cliffs and the white-walled town of Eleusis. And there in the fields he saw Persephone wandering happily in the sunshine, her golden hair streaming in the breeze. From time to time she stooped to pick a wild daisy or a cornflower, which she put in a basket that she carried on her arm. Such a gay, lively, and graceful figure did she make that Hades fell passionately in love with her. He was a man of action, and without waiting to make her acquaintance, he leaped into his chariot and drove into the meadow. Persephone did not see him until he had almost reached her, by which time it was too late to run. Pulling up beside her, Hades seized her in his strong right arm and lifted her into the chariot. Then off the horses raced at top speed, with the terrified Persephone struggling to get free and crying for help. But there was no one to see, except Helios, the sun-god, and he was minded to favor Hades in the struggle. The dark-browed goddess Hecate heard her cries from afar but didn't know what caused them. Soon, all trace of the girl had vanished from the fields and meadows of Eleusis.

When the shadows of the day began to lengthen and Persephone had not come home for her evening meal, her mother began to grow very anxious. She asked around the town if anyone had seen her daughter that day, but no one seemed to have news of the girl. At last she met a goatherd who told her that he had seen Persephone setting off that morning for a ramble in the fields. So the frantic mother took a torch and set off in search. But she could not find any trace of her girl, and soon it was too dark to see. She lay down beside a hedge and fell into a troubled sleep. As soon as Apollo hitched his horses to their flaming chariot, and the eastern sky began to grow light, she was up and off again on her search. For ten days and nights she wandered across the fields and lanes of the countryside, her hair flying in wild disorder, her face streaked with tears. At last, on the morning of the tenth day, she found Persephone's basket, which had fallen from her arm, and the withered flowers that had spilled out from it. Now she was sure that her daughter was dead, and she sat down by a pond, weeping bitterly. As she sat there, a shepherd named Eumolpus passed by and stopped to comfort her.

"What troubles you, lady?" he asked, as he stopped to offer her a drink of water from a gourd he carried on his belt. "Is there anything I can do to help?"

"Nothing you can do," sobbed Demeter, pushing away the drink. "Leave me alone to my grief. My only daughter has vanished, and no one knows where she has gone. The only trace I've found is this basket. Oh, I know she's dead, I know it!"

"That's curious," said the shepherd, shaking his head. He picked up the basket and looked at it. "Where did you find this?"

"Right over there in that field," replied Demeter sadly.

"How long ago did you miss her?"

"Ten days or more."

"Well, it may be only a coincidence," continued the shepherd, laying his hand gently on her arm, "but about ten days ago a very mysterious thing happened, right there in that field. My brother was tending his pigs there. Suddenly before he had time to run, there was an earthquake. The ground split open and swallowed the whole herd. And while he was staring at the hole in terror, he heard a galloping sound and a great chariot swept past him, going like the wind. If he hadn't jumped aside, he'd have been killed. In the chariot was a tall, dark figure, and he had his arm around a young woman who was struggling to get away and crying out piteously for help. But before my brother could catch his breath, the chariot had vanished into the hole in the ground. After that, the earth heaved again, and the hole closed up."

"Oh!" wailed the stricken mother, "that was no coincidence. It was my daughter. And now she's gone from me forever. There's no point in searching any more!"

The sympathetic shepherd took Demeter by the arm and led her back to Eleusis. There she met with the goddess Hecate and told her the sad tale of Persephone's abduction. Hecate, however, was not prepared to let things rest.

"Let's at least go to Helios," she advised. "Since it happened in the daytime, he's bound to know who it was, since he sees everything with his golden eye."

So the two goddesses went to visit Helios, shielding their eyes from the bright glow of the sun as they neared his courtyard.

"Yes," said the old sun-god when he had heard their tale. "I know what happened. It was Hades, king of the underworld, who stole away your daughter in his chariot and took her with him to Tartarus. He means to make her his queen there, I'm sure."

"Well," said Hecate, shaking her head with its black locks, "then there is nothing that can be done. I know the ways of the underworld. Once she is there, she can't come back. Come, Demeter, you must go home and learn to accept the loss of your loved one."

Back at Eleusis, however, the goddess Demeter was not to be consoled. Day after day she grieved. In her anger and sorrow, she forbade the fruit trees to bear fruit. She called for rains to flood the fields and blacken the corn. She went around the farms breaking up the plows and the mattocks. Soon the whole land was as desolate as the goddess's heart. The cries of stricken men and women and the lowing of hungry cattle grew so loud that Zeus the cloud-gatherer heard them from his seat on Olympus.

"What on earth is happening?" he demanded angrily. "I can't get any rest for all that groaning."

He soon discovered what was the matter. He was a little ashamed that his daughter had been carried off from her mother without his knowledge, and rather than face Demeter himself, he sent a group of gods and goddesses to her with gifts. But she refused to be consoled.

"Take back the gifts!" she cried resentfully. "Do you think even the richest gift on Olympus could ever take the place of my lovely daughter? Go back to Zeus, and tell him things will be this way as long as I can never set eyes on her again."

So the gods trooped apologetically back to the palace of Zeus the thunderer. And the father of the gods knew that before complete disaster befell the earth, he would have to swallow his pride and plead with Demeter himself. So he came down to Eleusis to visit her.

"Demeter," he begged, "you must stop this perpetual mourning. What good will it do to make the earth and men and even the gods suffer for what happened?"

"Cloud-gatherer Zeus," said the goddess sternly, "you ought never to have let this happen. Persephone is your own daughter. How can you let her be taken away from me, her mother? I bore her, and I've brought her up with the tenderest care a mother could give. Hecate heard her cries when Hades seized her. I know she went against her will."

"Maybe she did," replied Zeus in a coaxing tone, "but perhaps by now she is quite happy there. After all, you know, Hades has as much power in Tartarus as I have on Olympus. Persephone ought to be flattered that so powerful a god wants her for his queen. She's the first woman he ever fell in love with.''

''I don't know anything about that,'' declared Demeter impatiently. ''I do know I want her back with me. If you don't do anything about it, things will stay as they are now. There will be no more harvests on earth as long as she remains below. That I swear, and I can make it happen!''

There was silence as the father of the gods contracted his great brows. There seemed to be only one way out.

''Very well,'' he said. ''You shall have her back. I'll send a messenger down to Hades and tell him only he can solve this problem by giving back what he stole. But you know that if she has eaten any food while she has been down in Tartarus, she can't come back.''

So Zeus called Hermes to him and sent him with a message to Hades. Down in the underworld, its king had been trying every way he knew to make Persephone at home, but to no avail. Most of the time she just sat sadly on the queenly throne beside Hades, her pale face stained with tears. Sometimes she got up and wandered dejectedly around the dim courtyards and gloomy gardens of Tartarus. She never talked at all, nor did she seem to have any appetite. And though he still burned with the heat of Eros's arrow, Hades began to regret that he had snatched her so violently from her mother and her home.

''It's no pleasure to have a wife who grieves all the time,'' he brooded. ''And besides, she is growing so thin and pale, she'll soon lose all her beauty.''

So when Hermes came with Zeus's request, Hades did not feel he could refuse.

''All right, all right,'' he agreed, throwing up his hands in despair. ''She can go back to her mother. I still love her, but I can't bear to see her waste away here below. She's eaten nothing at all, as far as I can tell, since I brought her here.''

So Hades went to fetch Persephone from her bedroom. As he helped her on with her light-blue cloak, he told her the good news that he was letting her go back to Demeter.

''I can't bear to see you pine away,'' he declared. ''You've eaten nothing at all. Now at least maybe you will eat again and the color will come back to your cheeks. Here, love, take this pomegranate and eat it. It will give you strength for your journey.''

So he led her back to the hall where Hermes waited, and as they entered, the happy girl bit into the lovely red pomegranate that Hades had given her.

"Stop! Stop!" cried Hermes when he saw her bite into the fruit, and he quickly seized it and threw it away.

But it was too late to prevent Persephone from having swallowed half the pomegranate. Quickly Hermes took her in his arms, and his winged sandals whirled him up, up, up, until at last they emerged from a cave into the bright sunlight.

As soon as her eyes got used to the bright light, Persephone saw her mother and Zeus standing before her. With a glad cry, she flung herself into her mother's arms, and the two hugged each other for a long time, weeping tears of joy.

But Hermes had the sad duty of reporting to Zeus that she had eaten half the pomegranate before he could stop her.

"That poses a problem, indeed," said Zeus, striking the heels of his hands together in vexation. "Since I said she could not come back if she had eaten anything, she really must go back to Hades. But on the other hand, if she does, her mother will grieve so much that the earth will forever be barren."

"Perhaps," suggested Hermes, "Since she ate only half the pomegranate, she could live with Hades for that half of the year. Then she could come up to visit her mother, and the earth would bring forth flowers and fruits and grain once more, enough to keep men and beasts alive for the rest of the year."

And so it was decided. Every fall, when the leaves drift down from the trees, and the harvests are gathered and stored, Persephone says good-by to her mother and descends to the underworld, where she sits on the throne beside Hades as his queen. Although she is not happy there, she no longer grieves, because she knows that when the first crocuses peep from the frosty ground in spring, she will once more come from the gloomy realms of Tartarus into the sunlight of the upper world. There she spends each summer with her mother, wandering happily in the meadows full of flowers.

In an age when science was too young to satisfy the desire to know, people used their imagination to express the mysteries of the universe in human terms. What mystery did this myth express? What changes do we experience that would help us link our own life with the life of the year?

Adonis

A Greek myth

Cupid, it seems, was playing,
Quiver on shoulder, when he kissed his mother,
And one barb grazed her breast; she pushed him away,
But the wound was deeper than she knew; deceived,
Charmed by Adonis's beauty, she cared no more
For Cythera's shores nor Paphos' sea-ringed island,
Nor Cnidos, where fish teem, nor high Amathus,
Rich in its precious ores. She stays away
Even from Heaven, Adonis is better than Heaven.
She is beside him always; she has always,
Before this time, preferred the shadowy places,
Preferred her ease, preferred to improve her beauty
By careful tending, but now, across the ridges,
Through woods, through rocky places thick with brambles,
She goes, more like Diana than like Venus,
Bare-kneed and robes tucked up. She cheers the hounds,
Hunts animals, at least such timid creatures
As deer and rabbits; no wild boars for her,
No wolves, no bears, no lions. And she warns him
To fear them too, as if there might be good
In giving him warnings. "Be bold against the timid,
The running creatures, but against the bold ones
Boldness is dangerous. Do not be reckless.
I share whatever risk you take; be careful!
Do not attack those animals which Nature
Has given weapons, lest your thirst for glory

May cost me dear. Beauty and youth and love
Make no impression on bristling boars and lions,
On animal eyes and minds. The force of lightning
Is in the wild boar's tusks, and tawny lions
Are worse than thunderbolts. I hate and fear them.

                    . . . Do not hunt them,
Adonis: let all beasts alone, which offer
Breasts to the fight, not backs, or else your daring
Will be the ruin of us both."
                  Her warning
Was given, and the goddess took her way,
Drawn by her swans through air. But the young hunter
Scorned all such warnings, and one day, it happened,
His hounds, hard on the trail, roused a wild boar,
And as he rushed from the wood, Adonis struck him
A glancing blow, and the boar turned, and shaking
The spear from the side, came charging at the hunter,
Who feared, and ran, and fell, and the tusk entered
Deep in the groin, and the youth lay there dying
On the yellow sand, and Venus, borne through air
In her light swan-guided chariot, still was far
From Cyprus when she heard his groans, and, turning
The white swans from their course, came back to him,
Saw, from high air, the body lying lifeless
In its own blood, and tore her hair and garments,
Beat her fair breasts with cruel hands, came down
Reproaching Fate. "They shall not have it always
Their way," she mourned, "Adonis, for my sorrow,
Shall have a lasting monument: each year
Your death will be my sorrow, but your blood
Shall be a flower. If Persephone
Could change to fragrant mint the girl called Mentha,
Cinyras' son, my hero, surely also
Can be my flower." Over the blood she sprinkled
Sweet-smelling nectar, and as bubbles rise
In rainy weather, so it stirred, and blossomed,
Before an hour, as crimson in its color
As pomegranates are, as briefly clinging

To life as did Adonis, for the winds
Which gave a name to the flower, anemone,
The wind-flower, shake the petals off, too early,
Doomed all too swift and soon.

OVID

Translated by
ROLFE HUMPHRIES

What do Adonis and Persephone have in common?

Do their stories confront the same mystery? How?

Describe a ritual that you imagine might be performed by a society that is trying to participate in the changing of the seasons. Remember what Adonis and Persephone represented, what happened to them, and how they were "reborn."

The Many Deaths
of Winter

From the Norse myth
Retold by JAMES BALDWIN

Siegfried, when he came to Gunther's castle, thought of staying there but a few days only. But the king and his brothers made everything so pleasant for their honored guest that weeks slipped by unnoticed, and still the hero remained in Burgundy.

Spring had fairly come, and the weeping April clouds had given place to the balmy skies of May. The young men and maidens, as was their custom, made ready for the May-day games; and Siegfried and his knights were asked to take part in the sport.

On the smooth greensward, which they called Nanna's carpet, beneath the shade of ash trees and elms, he who played Old Winter's part lingered with his few attendants. These were clad in the dull gray garb which becomes the sober season of the year, and were decked with yellow straw, and dead, brown leaves. Out of the wood came the May king and his followers, clad in the gayest raiment, and decked with evergreens and flowers. With staves and willow withes they fell upon Old Winter's champions and tried to drive them from the sward. In friendly fray they fought, and many mishaps fell to both parties. But at length the May king won; and grave Winter, battered and bruised, was made prisoner, and his followers were driven from the field. Then, in merry sport, sentence was passed on the luckless fellow, for he was found guilty of killing the flowers and of covering the earth with hoar frost; and he was doomed to a long banishment from music and the sunlight. The laughing party then set up a wooden likeness of the worsted winter king, and pelted it with stones and turf; and when they were tired they threw it down and put out its eyes and cast it into the river. And then a pole, decked with wild flowers and fresh green leaves, was planted in the midst of the sward, and all joined in merry dance around it. And they chose the most beautiful of all the maidens to be the Queen of May, and they crowned her with a wreath of violets and yellow buttercups; and for a whole day all yielded fealty to her and did her bidding.

It was thus that May Day came in Burgundy.

What do Persephone (page 234), Adonis (page 241), and the May Queen have in common?

Old Winter is an example of a scapegoat, a person or animal who represents all of a community's troubles or crimes and who is driven away or killed at a certain time each year. What do you think would be the purposes of such a ritual? What season would seem most appropriate for it?

How is this story like the sacrifice of the King Horse in unit three (page 104)? How is it different?

in Just-

in Just-
spring   when the world is mud-
luscious the little
lame balloonman

whistles   far   and wee

and eddieandbill come
running from marbles and
piracies and it's
spring

when the world is puddle-wonderful

the queer
old balloonman whistles
far   and   wee
and bettyandisbel come dancing

from hop-scotch and jump-rope and

it's
spring
and
    the

       goat-footed

balloonMan   whistles
far
and
wee

E.E. CUMMINGS

What images of spring in this poem are the same as those in the previous
selections in this unit?

Summertime

A lullaby from Porgy and Bess

Summertime, and the livin' is easy,
Fish are jumpin', an' the cotton is high.
Oh, yo' daddy's rich,
An' yo' ma is good-lookin',
So hush, little baby, don' you cry.

One of these mornin's you goin' to rise up singin',
Then you'll spread yo' wings an' you'll take the sky.
But till that mornin' there's a nothin' can harm you
With Daddy an' Mammy standin' by.

IRA GERSHWIN *and* DUBOSE HEYWARD

What images in this song remind you of the Golden Age?

Why do you think summertime would be imagined as a time when the "livin' is easy"?

What metamorphosis does the singer look forward to?

*The hero Theseus narrates this story,
which continues the tale begun on page
104. Theseus, now a young man, is
journeying to Athens. Eleusis, the town
he enters here, follows a very old
religion, the worship of the Earth
Mother Demeter.*

The King Must Die

From the novel by
MARY RENAULT

I rose at daybreak, waked by the herd's bleating, and washed in the
stream; a thing my hosts beheld with wonder, having had their last
bath at the midwife's hands. From there on, the road grew easier, and
dropped seaward. Soon across a narrow water I saw the island of
Salamis, and all about me a fertile plain, with fruit and cornlands. The
road led down to a city on the shore, a seaport full of shipping. Some
merchants I met on the road told me it was Eleusis.

It was good to see a town again, and be in a land of law; and better
still that this was the last stop before Athens. I would have my horses
fed and groomed, I thought, while I ate and saw the sights. Then, as I
came to the edge of the town, I saw the road all lined with staring
people, and the rooftops thick with them.

Young men like to think themselves somebody; but even to me this
seemed surprising. Besides, I found it strange that out of so many
come to see me, no one called out or asked for news.

Before me was the market place. I pulled my pair to a walk, to save
the traders' pitches. Then I drew rein; before me the people stood in a
solid wall. No one spoke; and mothers hushed the babes they carried,
to make them still.

In the midst, straight before me, stood a stately woman, with a
slave holding a sunshade over her head. She was about seven and
twenty; her hair, which was crowned with a diadem of purple stitched
with gold, was as red as firelit copper. A score of women stood about
her, like courtiers about a king; but there was no man near her, except

the servant with the parasol. She must be both priestess and reigning queen. A Minyan kingdom, sure enough. That is what the Shore People call themselves, in their own places. Everyone knows that among them news travels faster than one can tell how.

Out of respect, I got down from my chariot and led the horses forward. Not only was she looking at me; I saw it was for me she waited. As I drew near and saluted her, all the crowd fell into a deeper silence, like people who hear the harper tune his strings.

I said, "Greeting, Lady, in the name of whatever god or goddess is honored here above the rest. For I think you serve a powerful deity, to whom the traveler ought to pay some homage or other, before he passes by. A man should respect the gods of his journey, if he wants it to end as he would wish."

She said to me, in a slow Greek with the accent of the Minyans, "Truly your journey has been blessed, and here it ends."

I stared at her surprised. She seemed to be speaking words prepared for her; behind all this another woman peeped out in secret. I said, "Lady, I am a stranger in the land, traveling to Athens. The guest you look for is someone of more mark; a chief, or maybe a king."

At this she smiled. All the people drew closer, murmuring; not in anger, but like the goatherds by the fire, all ears.

"There is only one journey," she said, "that all men make. They go forth from the Mother, and do what men are born to do, till she stretches forth her hand, and calls them home."

Plainly this land was of the old religion. Touching my brow in respect, I said, "We are all her children." What could she want of me, which the city knew already?

"But some," she said, "are called to a higher destiny. As you are, stranger, who come here fulfilling the omens, on the day when the King must die."

Now I understood. But I would not show it. My wits were stunned and I needed time.

"High Lady," I said, "if your lord's sign calls him, what has that to do with me? What god or goddess is angry? No one is in mourning; no one looks hungry; no smoke is in the sky. Well, it is for him to say. But if he needs me to serve his death, he will send for me himself."

She drew herself up frowning. "What is a man to choose? Woman bears him; he grows up and seeds like grass, and falls into the furrow. Only the Mother, who brings forth men and gods and gathers them again, sits at the hearthstone of the universe and lives for ever." She lifted her hand; the attendant women fell back around her; a man came forward to lead my horses. "Come," she said. "You must be made ready for the wrestling."

I found myself walking at her side. All round us followed the people, whispering like waves upon a shoal. Clothed in their expectation, I felt not myself but what they called me to be. One does not guess the power of these mysteries, till one is given part in them.

As I walked in silence beside the Queen, I recalled what a man had told me, about a land where the custom is the same. He said that in all those parts there is no rite in the year that moves and holds the people like the death of the King. "They see him," this man said, "at the height of fortune, sitting in glory, wearing gold; and coming on him, sometimes unknown and secret, sometimes marked by the omens before all the people, is the one who brings his fate. Sometimes the people know it before the King himself has word." So solemn is the day, he said, that if anyone who watches has grief or fear or trouble of his own, it is all purged out of him by pity and terror; he comes away calmed and falls into a sleep. "Even the children feel it," he said. "The herdboys up-country, who cannot leave their flocks to see the sight, will play out for one another on the hillsides, with songs and miming, the death day of the King."

This thought awakened me. "What am I doing?" I thought. "I have offered my forelock to Apollo; I have served Poseidon, the Mother's husband and lord, who is immortal. Where is this woman leading me? To kill the man who killed someone last year, and lie with her four seasons to bless the corn, till she gets up from my bed to fetch my killer to me? Is that my moira? *She* may have omens; but none have come to me. No, an Earthling dream is leading me, like the King Horse drunk with poppy. How shall I get free?"

All the same, I was looking aside at her, as a man will at a woman he knows is his for the taking. Her face was too broad and the mouth not fine enough; but her waist was like a palm tree, and to be unmoved by her breasts a man would need to be dead. The Minyans of Eleusis have mixed their blood with the Hellene kingdoms either side; her color and form were Hellene but not her face. She felt me look and walked straight on with her head held high. The fringe of the crimson sunshade tickled my hair.

I thought, "If I refuse, the people will tear me to pieces. I am the sower of their harvest. And this lady, who is the harvest field, will be very angry." One can tell some things from a woman's walking, even though she will not look. "She is a priestess and knows earth magic, and her curse will stick. Mother Dia must have her eye on me already. I was begotten to appease her anger. And she is not a goddess to treat lightly."

We had come to the sea road. I looked eastward and saw the hills of Attica, dry with summer and pale with noon, a morning's journey. I thought, "How could I go to my father, whose sword I carry, and say, 'A woman called me to fight, but I ran away?' No. Fate has set in my path this battle of the stallions, as it set Skiron the robber. Let me do the thing at hand, and trust in the gods."

"Lady," I said, "I was never this side of the Isthmus until now. What are you called?" She gazed before her and said softly, "Persephone. But it is forbidden for men to speak it." Coming nearer, I said, "A whispering name. A name for the dark." But she did not answer; so I asked, "And what is the King's name, whom I am to kill?"

She looked at me surprised, and answered carelessly, "His name is Kerkyon," as if I had asked it of some masterless dog. For a very little, it seemed, she would have said that he had no name.

Just inshore, the road sloped upward to a flat open place at the foot of a rocky bluff. Stairs led up it to the terrace where the Palace stood: red columns with black bases and yellow walls. The cliff below it was undercut; the hollow looked dark and gloomy and had a deep cleft in its floor that plunged into the earth. The breeze bore from it a faint stench of rotten flesh.

She pointed to the level place before it and said, "There is the wrestling ground." I saw the Palace roof and the terrace thick with people. Those who had come with us spread themselves on the slopes. I looked at the cleft and said, "What happens to the loser?"

She said, "He goes to the Mother. At the autumn sowing his flesh is brought forth and plowed into the fields and turns to corn. A man is happy who in the flower of youth wins fortune and glory, and whose thread runs out before bitter old age can fall on him." I answered, "He has been happy indeed," and looked straight at her. She did not blush, but her chin went up.

"This Kerkyon," I said; "we meet in combat, not as the priest offers the victim?" That would have been against my stomach, seeing the man had not chosen his own time. I was glad when she nodded her head. "And the weapons?" I asked. "Only those," she said, "that men are born with." I looked about and said, "Will a man of your people tell me the rules?" She looked at me puzzled; I thought it was my Hellene speech and said again, "The laws of battle?" She raised her brows and answered, "The law is that the King must die."

Then, on the broad steps that climbed up to the Citadel, I saw him coming down to meet me. I knew him at once, because he was alone.

The steps were crowded with people from the Palace; but they all hung back from him and stood wide, as if his death were a catching sickness. He was older than I. His black beard was enough to hide his jaw; I don't think he was less than twenty. As he looked down at me, I could tell I seemed a boy to him. He was not much above my height, being tall only for a Minyan; but he was lean and sinewy as mountain lions are. His strong black hair, too short and thick to hang in love-locks, covered his neck like a curling mane. As we met each other's eyes, I thought, "He has stood where I stand now, and the man he fought with is bones under the rock." And then I thought, "He has not consented to his death."

All about us was a great silence full of eyes. And it moved me as a strange and powerful thing, that these watching people did not feel even themselves as they felt us. I wondered if for him it was the same.

As we stood thus, I saw that after all he was not quite alone. A woman had come up behind him and stood there weeping. He did not turn to look. If he heard, he had other things to think of.

He came a few steps lower, looking not at the Queen but only at me. "Who are you, and where do you come from?" He spoke Greek very foreignly, but I understood him. It seemed to me we would have understood each other if he had had none at all.

"I am Theseus, from Troizen in the Isle of Pelops. I came in peace, passing through to Athens. But our life threads are crossed, it seems."

"Whose son are you?" he asked. Looking at his face, I saw he had no purpose in his questions, except to know he was still King, and a man walking in sunlight above the earth. I answered, "My mother hung up her girdle for the Goddess. I am a son of the myrtle grove."

The listeners made their soft murmur, like rustling reeds. But I felt the Queen move beside me. She was staring at me; and Kerkyon, now, at her. Then he burst out laughing. His teeth were strong and white above his young black beard. The people stirred, surprised; I was no wiser than they. All I knew, as the King laughing turned my way, was that his jest was bitter. He stood on the stairs and laughed; and the woman behind him covered her face in her two hands and crouched down and rocked herself to and fro.

He came down. Face to face, I saw he was as strong as I had thought.

"Well, Son of the Grove, let us do the appointed thing. This time the odds will be even; the Lady won't know whom to beat the gong for." I did not understand him; but I saw he was speaking for her ears, not for mine.

A sanctuary house near by had been opened while we spoke, and a tall throne brought out, painted red, with devices of serpents and sheaves. They stood it near the floor, and by it a great bronze gong upon a stand. The Queen sat down with her women round her, holding the gong stick like a scepter.

"No," I thought, "the odds will not be even. He is fighting for his kingdom, which I do not want, and his life, which I don't want either. I cannot hate him, as a warrior should his enemy; nor even be angry, except with his people, who are turning from him like rats from an empty barn. If I were an Earthling, I should feel their wishes fighting for me. But I cannot dance to their piping; I am a Hellene."

A priestess led me to a corner of the ground, where two men stripped and oiled me and gave me a wrestler's linen apron. They plaited back my hair and bound it in a club and led me forth to be seen. The people cheered me, but I was not warmed by it; I knew they would cheer whoever came to kill the King. Even now when he was stripped and I could see his strength, I could not hate him. I looked at the Queen, but could not tell if I was angry with her or not, because I desired her. "Well," I thought, "is that not quarrel enough?"

The elder of the men, who looked to have been a warrior, said, "How old are you, boy?" People were listening, so I said, "Nineteen." It made me feel stronger. He looked at my chin, which had less down than a gosling, but said no more.

We were led to the throne, where she sat under her fringed sunshade. Her gold-sewn flounces caught the light, and her jeweled shoes. Her deep breasts looked gold and rosy, bloomed like the cheeks of peaches, and her red hair glowed. She had a gold cup in her hands, and held it out to me. The warm sun brought out the scents of spiced wine, honey, and cheese. As I took it I smiled at her, "For," I thought, "she is a woman, or what are we about?" She did not toss her head as she had before, but looked into my eyes as if to read an omen; and in hers I saw fear.

A girl will scream as you chase her through the wood, who when caught is quiet enough. I saw no more than that in it; it stirred my blood, and I was glad to have said I was nineteen. I drank of the mixed drink, and the priestess gave it to the King.

He drank deep. The people gazed at him; but no one cheered. Yet he stripped well, and bore himself bravely; and for a year he had been their king. I remembered what I had heard of the old religion. "They care nothing for him," I thought, "though he is going to die for them, or so they hope, and put his life into the corn. He is the scapegoat. Looking at him, they see only the year's troubles, the crop that failed, the barren cows, the sickness. They want to kill their troubles with him, and start again." I was angry to see his death not in his own hand, but the sport of rabble who did not share the sacrifice, who offered nothing of their own; I felt that out of all these people, he was the only one I could love. But I saw from his face that none of this came strange to him; he was bitter at it, but did not question it, being Earthling as they were. "He too," I thought, "would think me mad if he knew my mind. I am a Hellene; it is I, not he, who am alone."

We faced each other on the wrestling ground; the Queen stood up, with the gong stick in her hand. After that I only looked at his eyes. Something told me he was not like the wrestlers of Troizen.

Wood tapped sharply on the gong. I waited on my toes, to see if he would come straight in, like a Hellene, and grab for a body hold. No; I had guessed right. He was edging round, trying to get the sun in my eyes. He did not fidget on his feet, but moved quite slowly and softly, like a cat before it springs. Not for nothing I had felt, while he spoke bad Greek, that we yet had a common language. Now we spoke it. He, too, was a wrestler who thought.

His eyes were golden brown, light like a wolf's. "Yes," I thought, "and he will be as fast. Let him come in first; if he is going to take a risk, he will do it then. Afterward he may know better."

He aimed a great buffet at my head. It was meant to sway me left; so I jumped right. That was well, for where my guts should have been he landed a kick like a horse's. Even glancing, it hurt, but not too much, and I grabbed his leg. As I tipped him over I jumped at him, throwing him sideways and trying to land on him with a headlock. But he was fast, fast as a cat. He got me by the foot and turned my fall and almost before I had touched ground was slipping round to get a scissors on me. I jabbed my fist at his chin and saved myself by a lizard's tail flick. Then the mill on the ground began in earnest. I soon forgot I had been slow to anger; you cease to ask what wrong a man has done you when his hands are feeling for your life.

He had the look of a gentleman. But the Queen's stare had warned me, when I asked the rules. All-in is all-in among the Shore People, and nothing barred. This slit in my ear, like a fighting dog's, I got in that fight as a dog gets it. Once he nearly gouged out my eye and only gave over to keep his thumb unbroken. Soon I got too angry rather than too cold; but I could not afford to take a risk, just for the pleasure of hurting him. He was like tanned oxhide with a core of bronze.

As we twisted and kicked and struck, I could make believe no longer I was nineteen. I was fighting a man in his flower of strength, before I had come to mine. My blood and bones began to whisper he would out-stay me. Then the gong began.

The starting stroke had come from the butt of the stick. This was the blow of the padded hammer. It gave a great singing roar; I swear one could even feel the sound in the ground underfoot. And as it quivered and hummed, the women chanted.

The voices sank and rose, sank and rose higher. It was like the north wind when it blows screaming through mountain gorges; like the keening of a thousand widows in a burning town; like the cry of she-wolves to the moon. And under it, over it, through our blood and skulls and entrails, the bellow of the gong.

The din maddened me. As it washed over me again and again, I began to be filled with the madman's single purpose. I must kill my man, and stop the noise.

As this frenzied strength built up in me, my hands and back felt him flagging. With each gong throb his strength was trickling from him. It was his death that was singing to him; wrapping him round like smoke, drawing him down into the ground. Everything was against him: the people, the Mystery, and I. But he fought bravely.

He was trying to strangle me, when I got both feet up and hurled him backward. While he was still winded, I leaped on him and snatched his arm from under him and threw him over. So he lay face down, and I was on his back, and he could not rise. The singing rose to a long shriek, then sank into silence. The last gong stroke shuddered and died.

His face was in the dust; but I could tell his mind, as he felt this way and that to see if anything was left to do and understood that it was finished. In that moment my anger died. I forgot the pain, remembering only his courage and his despair. "Why should I take his blood upon me?" I thought. "He never harmed me, except to fulfill his moira." I shifted my weight a very little, taking good care because he was full of tricks, till he could just turn his head out of the dirt. But he did not look at me; only at the dark cleft below the rock. These were his people, and his life thread was twined with theirs. One could not save him.

I put my knee in his backbone. Keeping him pinned, for he was not a man to give an inch to, I hooked my arm round his head, and pulled it back till I felt the neckbone straining. Then I said softly in his ear—for it did not concern the people about us, who had given nothing to the sacrifice—"Shall it be now?" He whispered, "Yes." I said, "Discharge me of it, then, to the gods below." He said, "Be free of it," with some invocation after. It was in his own tongue, but I trusted him. I jerked his head back hard and fast, and heard the snap of the neckbone. When I looked, it seemed his eyes still had a spark of life; but when I turned his head sideways it was gone.

I got to my feet and heard from the people a deep sighing, as if they had all just finished the act of love. "So it begins," I said to myself; "and only a god can see the ending."

They had brought a bier and laid the King on it. There was a high scream from the throne. The Queen rushed down and threw herself on the corpse, rending her hair and clawing her face and bosom. She looked just like a woman who has lost her dear lord, the man who led her a maiden from her father's house; as if there were young children and no kin to help them. That was how she wept, so that I stared amazed. But now all the other women were crying and howling too, and I understood it was the custom.

They went off wailing, appeasing the new-made ghost. Left alone among staring strangers, I wanted to ask, "What now?" But the only man I knew was dead.

Presently came an old priestess and led me toward the sanctuary house. She told me they would mourn the King till sundown; then I should be blood cleansed and wed the Queen.

In a room with a bath of painted clay, the priestesses bathed me and dressed my wounds. They all spoke Greek, with the lilt of the Shore People, lisping and twittering. But even in their own speech they have Greek words. There is so much sea traffic at Eleusis, the tongues have got mixed there, as well as the blood. They put a long white linen robe on me, and combed my hair, and gave me meat and wine. Then there was nothing to do but listen to the wailing, and wait, and think.

What do the King Horse (page 104), Old Winter (page 244), and Kerkyon have in common?

Theseus, in "The Horse-God" (page 104), learned that the power of the sacrifice ritual lay in the consent of the victim. The power of Abraham's sacrifice ritual in the Bible lay in the fact that both he and Isaac consented. Does Kerkyon consent? Does Theseus? What do their attitudes tell about the value and the power of this ancient ritual?

From what you now know about rituals, what do you think the "power" of a ritual is? How do rituals (such as the one in this story) give people the sense that they are participating in, and even controlling, the cycles of nature?

The Gettysburg Address

ABRAHAM LINCOLN

Four score and seven years ago our fathers brought forth on this continent a new nation, conceived in liberty, and dedicated to the proposition that all men are created equal.

Now we are engaged in a great civil war, testing whether that nation, or any nation so conceived and so dedicated, can long endure. We are met on a great battlefield of that war. We have come to dedicate a portion of that field as a final resting place for those who here gave their lives that that nation might live. It is altogether fitting and proper that we should do this.

But, in a larger sense, we cannot dedicate — we cannot consecrate — we cannot hallow this ground. The brave men, living and dead, who struggled here, have consecrated it far above our poor power to add or detract. The world will little note nor long remember what we say here, but it can never forget what they did here. It is for us the living, rather, to be dedicated here to the unfinished work which they who fought here have thus far so nobly advanced. It is rather for us to be here dedicated to the great task remaining before us — that from these honored dead we take increased devotion to that cause for which they gave the last full measure of devotion; that we here highly resolve that these dead shall not have died in vain; that this nation, under God, shall have a new birth of freedom; and that government of the people, by the people, for the people, shall not perish from the earth.

What power does this ritual — a war-time eulogy — give the people?

Aztec Lamentation

1

I lift my voice in wailing, I am afflicted, as I remember that we must leave the beautiful flowers, the noble songs; let us enjoy ourselves for a while, let us sing, for we must depart forever, we are to be destroyed in our dwelling place.

2

Is it indeed known to our friends how it pains and angers me that never again can they be born, never again be young on this earth.

3

Yet a little while with them here, then nevermore shall I be with them, nevermore enjoy them, nevermore know them.

4

Where shall my soul dwell? Where is my home? Where shall be my house? I am miserable on earth.

5

We take, we unwind the jewels, the blue flowers are woven over the yellow ones, that we may give them to the children.

6

Let my soul be draped in various flowers; let it be intoxicated by them; for soon must I weeping go before the face of our Mother.

Translated by DANIEL G. BRINTON

How do these images suggest both a natural and a human season?

The Falling of the Leaves

Autumn is over the long leaves that love us,
And over the mice in the barley sheaves;
Yellow the leaves of the rowan above us,
And yellow the wet wild-strawberry leaves.

The hour of the waning of love has beset us,
And weary and worn are our sad souls now;
Let us part, ere the season of passion forget us,
With a kiss and a tear on thy drooping brow.

WILLIAM BUTLER YEATS

The first verse of this poem uses natural images, the second uses human images. How is this poet doing the same thing that the ancient myth-makers did in telling the stories of Persephone (page 234) and Adonis (page 241)?

Which season is "the season of passion"? Why?

After Apple-Picking

My long two-pointed ladder's sticking through a tree
Toward heaven still,
And there's a barrel that I didn't fill
Beside it, and there may be two or three
Apples I didn't pick upon some bough.
But I am done with apple-picking now.
Essence of winter sleep is on the night,
The scent of apples: I am drowsing off.
I cannot rub the strangeness from my sight
I got from looking through a pane of glass
I skimmed this morning from the drinking trough
And held against the world of hoary grass.
It melted, and I let it fall and break.
But I was well
Upon my way to sleep before it fell,
And I could tell
What form my dreaming was about to take.
Magnified apples appear and disappear,
Stem end and blossom end,
And every fleck of russet showing clear.
My instep arch not only keeps the ache,
It keeps the pressure of a ladder-round.
I feel the ladder sway as the boughs bend.
And I keep hearing from the cellar bin
The rumbling sound
Of load on load of apples coming in.
For I have had too much
Of apple-picking: I am overtired
Of the great harvest I myself desired.

There were ten thousand thousand fruit to touch,
Cherish in hand, lift down, and not let fall.
For all
That struck the earth,
No matter if not bruised or spiked with stubble,
Went surely to the cider-apple heap
As of no worth.
One can see what will trouble
This sleep of mine, whatever sleep it is.
Were he not gone,
The woodchuck could say whether it's like his
Long sleep, as I describe its coming on,
Or just some human sleep.

ROBERT FROST

This poet is equating a season with a particular time of his life. What is the
season? What is the time? What is the "human sleep"?

What previous selection in this unit does this line remind you of: "I feel
the ladder sway as the boughs bend." Do you think the two selections are
saying the same thing? What is it?

The Birthday Party

GINA BERRIAULT

The boy, wakened by the sound of his mother's heels as she went past his door, ran out into the hallway. She turned when he called to her. She had her coat on; her face was without make-up, and pale.

"Where you going?" he cried.

"Get back in bed," she called back. "You're old enough to be left alone."

"*You* get back!" he shouted.

She went on through the living room, her head down.

"It's very late," he pleaded. "I'm already in bed."

"When you wake up I'll be back already," she said. "Call Grandma if I'm not. If I'm not, then I'm never."

When the room was empty he heard, from where he stood in the hallway, the faint music from the radio. In the past few weeks, she went out often during the day or was not home when he returned from school, but she always came back before it was time for supper; she left him often in the evening, but the girl from the apartment downstairs always came in and did her homework at the desk and stayed with him. His mother wept often and brooded often, but she had never left him late at night and had never threatened not to come back. Though she had wandered the apartment all evening, saying no word to him, her jaws holding back the furor so forcibly she could not open them to eat or speak, he had not expected her to go out in the middle of the night.

He ran into her bedroom. It was untidy; a dresser drawer was out, her white negligee was on the floor, and the big, black-marble ashtray on the bed table was filled with cigarette butts. The bed's silk spread was wrinkled and there were small depressions where her fists had pounded. He crawled under the covers and lay down in the center of the bed, and the return of sleep was like her return.

The sun, and the lamp still lit, shocked him awake. Afraid that she had not returned, he leaped from the bed and ran out into the hallway, calling. She answered from his room and sat up in his bed when he went in. She was in her slip, her coat and dress on the chair.

"You said you weren't coming back!" he shouted. It sounded like an accusation that she had not kept her promise.

"That's all right," she said. "If I hadn't, you're seven years old, you're old enough to do without me. That's a sign of maturity," she said, her mouth dry—"to do without a person."

"You said you weren't coming back!" he shouted again. He stood in his pajamas in the doorway, terrorized by her troubles that had driven her out at midnight and detached her so from him that her return seemed imagined. The man she was going to marry—who was going to be a more fatherly father, she had said, than his own had ever been— had not come by to see her for many weeks, and it was to see him that she had gone out in the evening so many times, and it was probably to see him that she had gone out last night.

· "I always come back," she said. "Like the cat the man was always trying to get rid of in the song. He tied her to the railroad tracks and he threw her into the ocean with a rock, but she always came back the very next day." She reached to the chair, her fingers digging into her coat pockets. "Well, no more cigarettes." She shrugged. "All I did was drink coffee at the places that stay open all night. You would have enjoyed it. Saw two motorcycle cops eating hot apple pie. They had their helmets off and they looked human. And I slept in the car a little while, but my legs got cramped. You should see the stars out there at four in the morning."

She tossed off the blankets, hung her clothes over her arm, and walked past him in her bare feet to her own bedroom. He followed her, unwilling, now that she had returned, to let her go from his sight.

"Who's going to take me to Molly's party?"

"I'll take you," she said. "Grandma's going early, and it's out of her way to pick you up, anyway. But it's not until two."

"We've got to buy a present," he said, afraid that nothing would be attended to from now on, that everything would be neglected; using the party to urge her to look after him again, to distract him again, and engage him again.

She picked up her negligee from the floor and clasped it around her and roamed the room, looking for cigarettes. She gazed into the gilded, oval mirror above her dressing table, while her fingertips felt among the jars and bottles for cigarettes. "Oh, don't you fret, don't you cry," she said to him mockingly; she gazed at herself as if she were trying to accept as herself the woman with the swollen eyelids. "We'll be there on time and we'll bring a present too. You're an anxiety hound," she said. "Oh, the champion anxiety hound."

He began to prepare himself for the party, searching for his shoe-polish kit and finding it in his closet under a stack of games. He sat down on the floor and polished his best shoes. He was not fond of Molly, who would be nine, and he saw her seldom, but he prepared himself now as if he and Molly were the best of friends. In his pajamas he went into the bathroom and combed his hair, wetting it until it was black and drops ran down his face, and combing it over and over. He slipped on a shirt, put on his suit, and turned the shirt collar down over the collar of the jacket, the way his mother always did. At noon he called to her from her doorway, waking her.

In the jewelry store, where he had gone with her a few times to buy presents, they looked at a tray of bracelets. Around the walls were large, colored pictures of coats of arms; on the counter tops were silver trays and bowls and candlesticks. When she asked him if he preferred a silver chain with charms or a silver chain with one small pearl dangling from it in a silver claw, he did not balk at a choice, as he had done in the past when he had not cared and had known that even if he cared she would have made her own choice. He put his finger on the one with the pearl. Like himself in the past, she did not care, or else he had persuaded her with his decisiveness, for she nodded at the salesman, who smiled as if it were the most appropriate choice anyone would ever make and caught it up with graceful fingers.

He followed his mother down the few stone steps to the terrace, above which strings of red and blue triangular flags crossed from the upper windows of the gray stucco house to the balustrade. Under the flags, a throng of children wandered in twos and threes and clustered together over games, their voices rising high on the warm, still air. His mother had a little swing to her walk that implied that parties for children were what she liked best in life, and, walking this way, went into the midst of so many children that he lost her. At the moment that he saw her again, his grandmother clapped him over the ears, lifting his face to hers and kissing him on both cheeks. Above her head, as she bent to him, the flags burned their colors into the clear sky.

With her arm around his shoulders, his grandmother led him away to the corner of the lawn, where Molly's mother was trailing her bare arm above the long table, dropping colored candy, tiny as seeds, into the red crepe-paper basket at each place. He could hear the small sound of the seeds falling because the commotion of the children was far enough away.

"We filled them all last night," she said, "Tons. But today they look half filled. Up to the brim, that's the way," she said, motioning him to cup his hands and pouring candies into them. He began to help her, awkwardly, following her to drop a few more into baskets she had already filled. "Where's your mother?" she asked.

"She just stayed a minute, to kiss Molly," his grandmother said. "She's coming back later to pick him up."

"Is that you, Elsie?" somebody called to his grandmother from the kitchen. Because his hands were empty and Molly's mother seemed to have lost all sense of his presence, he followed his grandmother. She was small and quick in her coral dress, and her large, yellow beads made a faint jangling. In the white, sunlit kitchen, Molly's grandmother, in a smock stitched with a large red rose whose stem was as long as the smock, was sticking tiny pink candles into the high pink cake. Her hand, small and bony, covered with brown spots like freckles melted together, was trembling. She was his grandmother's best friend; they were so close they were like sisters.

"Tell me if I ought to use the white candles, if you think I ought to use the white candles," she begged.

"You can alternate," his grandmother suggested.

"Oh, that's strange, don't you think? Who does that?" the old lady demanded crossly. One pink candle fell into the thick frosting. "Oh, pick it out!" she cried to him. "Your fingers are littler!" But while he thought about the possibility of his clumsiness, she darted her hand in among the upright candles and picked it out herself. "All the same color!" she cried decisively. "Little girls like pink." But in a moment she was undecided again. "Elsie," she wailed, "is pink all right?"

The old woman's wailing over the candles alarmed him. He wondered if his mother was gone already, and he went out the back door of the kitchen, down a narrow passage overhung with vines, and out onto the terrace again. She was not there among the children; he leaned over the balustrade, and she was not with two other mothers standing and chatting in the small garden below, and again he felt the terror of the night before. He was afraid that she would not return for him, that her threat of the night would be carried out that day, and he wished that he had not gone off with his grandmother and that he had not reminded his mother of the party, and he imagined himself fighting her, if she had remembered the party herself—clinging to the bedpost and to the railing on the front steps and to her.

A little girl passed by, ringing a bell, and he was jostled along by the other children toward the birthday table. In the throng roving around the table he looked for his name on the triangular paper flag above each crepe-paper basket. There were so many names that, after a time, he got confused and found himself going around behind the same chairs, now with children seated in them. He read only at empty chairs and found his place. Under a high, red-paper canopy affixed to her chair back, Molly sat at the head of the table. At her elbow, the many presents were piled in a red-paper cart with blue wheels. The cake was carried in by Molly's mother, followed by his grandmother bearing a great, cut-glass bowl of pink ice cream. Molly's grandmother went along behind the children, pouring pink juice from a large, white-china pitcher into paper cups; another pitcher, of glass, frosted from the cold liquid, waited on a corner of the table.

Molly braced her hands against the edge of the table and blew at the candles. Seven stayed out, two flared up again.

"You're too excited," her mother cried. "You're gasping." Although her voice was amused and loud, he heard an edge of annoyance. Molly, after a calm, deep breath, blew again, and the two little flames became rising wisps of smoke.

Molly's grandmother sat down beside her to eat a bit of cake. He was next to her, around the corner of the table, and her bony knees knocked his. "Oh, I think this is the nicest party I've ever been to!" she cried, beating the edge of the table with her fingers as if rapping time to a tune. Her voice seemed to him deliberately quavery, appealing to the children. "Isn't it, dear? Isn't it?" she begged him, patting him on the knee with rapping fingers.

Molly, under her canopy, lifted the presents one by one up from the ribbons and rustling papers. Each time she swung to the side to take a present from the cart, or clapped her hands, her long hair bounced against her back. The children nearest her, himself among them, fingered the gifts piling up before her—a long bow and a leather quiver of arrows, a small doll with a bald head and three wigs, dyed red and yellow and black, each like a puff of cocoon silk; a lifelike poodle dog of dark gray wool; a white petticoat with blue ribbons entwined in it, for which she kissed her grandmother, whose restless hands rested for that moment on the wrapping papers she was folding. The transistor radio she turned on at once, and the tiny, crackling voices of the singers went on and on under the tissue paper and other presents. She held up the bracelet, shaking it high above her head, as if it were something musical, and dropped her hands to open another present. There was a gift from each one at the table and from other people who were not there—uncles and aunts who lived in other cities. There was such a profusion of gifts that it seemed to him the reason for the party was more than that the day was her birthday. The party, he felt, was to take care of any crying to come.

On the terrace a puppet tent had been set up, a rickety frame draped with red cloth. Up high in it, like a small window, was the stage. The children sat on the ground, and behind them sat the women in bamboo chairs. From the corner of his eye he saw his grandmother in her chair; he saw the coral dress and heard the beads jangle whenever she shifted her body or clapped. Last night his mother had told him to call his grandmother in the morning, and her presence now, a few feet away, at this time when the party was tapering off and some mothers were already returning and watching the puppet show, was like proof that his mother would not return. Up in the little stage the jerky puppets with cawing voices, the Indian chief with a feather headdress, an eagle, a bluebird, and a pioneer boy with a coonskin cap, shook their arms and wings and heads at one another and sometimes collapsed over the edge of the stage. The laughter around him startled him each time, because he was watching the steps from the street and each mother coming down.

When the curtains jerkily closed, a young man with a beard, wearing a tunic of coarse cotton embroidered in red, and a woman with long hair that hung down her back like a little girl's, came out from behind the stage. The man bowed; the woman picked up the sides of her wide, flowered skirt and curtsied like a good and proper child. Some of the mothers slipped sweaters over their children's shoulders and guided them across the terrace and up the steps, and some gathered in a cluster with Molly's mother while their children gathered around the puppeteers to see the puppets put away in the tapestry satchel, each one waving as it went down. From a chair he watched the women and children climb the steps, until only one mother was left, chatting with the three other women while her two daughters wandered the terrace with Molly. He was watching the red tent carried up by the couple, swaying between them, when he saw his mother coming down, nimbly sidestepping. He saw her change the expression of her face, smiling at the couple and expecting to smile at whomever she saw next. She waved to him, the only child among the empty chairs, a wave that implied she knew the party had been wonderful, and crossed before him to the women. She had a sweater on now, as did the other women whose circle she joined. He saw his grandmother kiss her on the cheek, grasping and shaking her elbow, and his relief was expressed for him a little by his grandmother's emphatic claiming of her.

"So, Molly?" his mother called to the girl. "How does it feel to be nine?"

"What?" called Molly.

"To be nine? How does it feel?"

"Oh, I feel the same, I guess," Molly called back, a slight wonder and vexation in her voice. She went on wandering with the other girls — some purpose to their wandering that only they knew — their heads bent over something in her hands. The light wind picked up the ends of their hair and the ends of their sashes.

Molly's mother laughed. "In a few years she'll begin to feel the difference," she said.

"When she begins to feel it," her grandmother said, "you won't need to throw any more parties. She won't let you. Isn't that so, Molly?" she called, but her voice was too frail to be heard far.

"She can't know if it's so," said her mother, again with that loud voice that was both amused and annoyed.

His mother motioned to him and began to move away from the others, and his grandmother joined her. He got up from the chair and was a step ahead of them. All over the terrace the seedlike candies lay scattered, and a few ribbons, here and there, were blown along an inch at a time.

"You act like you want to get away," his mother said behind him, raising her voice a little to make sure he heard, but keeping it too low to be heard by the women they were leaving. "I came down and saw him in that chair as if he were suffering punishment," she said to her mother. "This morning he couldn't wait to go. He was ready at six."

"It wasn't that early," he said, hurt by her ridicule.

"No, he wasn't ready at six. I was out till six," she said, and the sound of the anguish remaining in her throat from the night silenced the three of them.

"Is it over? With that man? Is it all over?" his grandmother asked her as they climbed.

He turned, because he no longer heard their heels on the stone steps, and saw that his mother was covering her face with her hand and with the other hand was clutching her purse to her breasts. The way her chest bowed in and the way her fingers spread, trembling, over her face made her appear as fragile as her mother.

"Ah, not here, Lovely. Not here," his grandmother pleaded, touching his mother's fingers. So much love went out to her daughter that her old body seemed depleted suddenly. "The children, they can see you," she warned. "They can see you, and they've had such a nice day. Ah, not here." With her arm around his mother's waist, she made her continue up the steps. Before he turned away, he saw the three girls gazing up at them curiously from under the strings of red and blue flags fluttering in the wind.

What does this line tell you about one of the reasons for our rituals: "The party, he felt, was to take care of any crying to come"?

Why would this story fit with the selections under "The End of Childhood"?

How is this a story of several human seasons?

What rituals usually take place at birthday parties? Can you imagine what they might stand for?

Immortal Autumn

I speak this poem now with grave and level voice
In praise of autumn of the far-horn-winding fall
I praise the flower-barren fields the clouds the tall
Unanswering branches where the wind makes sullen noise

I praise the fall it is the human season
                                now
No more the foreign sun does meddle at our earth
Enforce the green and bring the fallow land to birth
Nor winter yet weigh all with silence the pine bough

But now in autumn with the black and outcast crows
Share we the spacious world the whispering year is gone
There is more room to live now the once secret dawn
Comes late by daylight and the dark unguarded goes

Between the mutinous brave burning of the leaves
And winter's covering of our hearts with his deep snow
We are alone there are no evening birds we know
The naked moon the tame stars circle at our eaves

It is the human season on this sterile air
Do words outcarry breath the sound goes on and on
I hear a dead man's cry from autumn long since gone

I cry to you beyond upon this bitter air

ARCHIBALD MACLEISH

What qualities of autumn and what qualities of humans suggest to the author that autumn is the human season? Do you agree?

Bavarian Gentians

Not every man has gentians in his house
in Soft September, at slow, sad Michaelmas.

Bavarian gentians, big and dark, only dark
darkening the day-time, torch-like with the smoking blueness of Pluto's
    gloom,
ribbed and torch-like, with their blaze of darkness spread blue
down flattening into points, flattened under the sweep of white day
torch-flower of the blue-smoking darkness, Pluto's dark-blue daze,
black lamps from the halls of Dis, burning dark blue,
giving off darkness, blue darkness, as Demeter's pale lamps give off
    light,
lead me then, lead me the way.

Reach me a gentian, give me a torch!
let me guide myself with the blue, forked torch of this flower
down the darker and darker stairs, where blue is darkened on blueness,
even where Persephone goes, just now, from the frosted September
to the sightless realm where darkness is awake upon the dark
and Persephone herself is but a voice
or a darkness invisible enfolded in the deeper dark
of the arms Plutonic, and pierced with the passion of dense gloom,
among the splendor of torches of darkness, shedding darkness on the
    lost bride and her groom.

D. H. LAWRENCE

These gentians are plants that have blue flowers with dark centers. They
bloom late in the year (Michaelmas is September 29). What does their
blueness remind the poet of? Where does he ask the gentians to lead him?
Why does the poet think of Persephone at this time of year? What images
suggest a fascination with death—with Pluto's "dark-blue daze"?

There's a Certain Slant of Light

There's a certain slant of light,
On winter afternoons,
That oppresses, like the weight
Of cathedral tunes.

Heavenly hurt it gives us;
We can find no scar,
But internal difference
Where the meanings are.

None may teach it anything,
'Tis the seal, despair,—
An imperial affliction
Sent us of the air.

When it comes, the landscape listens,
Shadows hold their breath;
When it goes, 't is like the distance
On the look of death.

EMILY DICKINSON

What qualities of winter is the author using to describe her inner feelings?

Deck the Halls

Deck the halls with boughs of holly
Fa la la la la la la la la

'Tis the season to be jolly
Fa la la la la la la la la

Don we now our gay apparel
Fa la la la la la la la la

Troll the ancient yuletide carol
Fa la la la la la la la la

See the blazing Yule before us
Fa la la la la la la la la

Strike the harp and join the chorus
Fa la la la la la la la la

Follow me in merry measure
Fa la la la la la la la la

While I tell of Yuletide treasure
Fa la la la la la la la la

Fast away the old year passes
Fa la la la la la la la la

Hail the new, ye lads and lasses
Fa la la la la la la la la

Sing we joyous all together
Fa la la la la la la la la

Heedless of the wind and weather
Fa la la la la la la la la

Years-End

Now winter downs the dying of the year,
And night is all a settlement of snow;
From the soft street the rooms of houses show
A gathered light, a shapen atmosphere,
Like frozen-over lakes whose ice is thin
And still allows some stirring down within.

I've known the wind by water banks to shake
The late leaves down, which frozen where they fell
And held in ice as dancers in a spell
Fluttered all winter long into a lake;
Graved on the dark in gestures of descent,
They seemed their own most perfect monument.

There was perfection in the death of ferns
Which laid their fragile cheeks against the stone
A million years. Great mammoths overthrown
Composedly have made their long sojourns,
Like palaces of patience, in the gray
And changeless lands of ice. And at Pompeii

The little dog lay curled and did not rise
But slept the deeper as the ashes rose
And found the people incomplete, and froze
The random hands, the loose unready eyes
Of men expecting yet another sun
To do the shapely thing they had not done.

These sudden ends of time must give us pause.
We fray into the future, rarely wrought

Save in the tapestries of afterthought.
More time, more time. Barrages of applause
Come muffled from a buried radio.
The New-year bells are wrangling with the snow.

RICHARD WILBUR

How does the author see winter as the season of suspension between wish and nightmare? What comparisons does he use to emphasize the image of suspension in time?

How does this poem explain why people sing the song "Deck the Halls" in the middle of winter?

Orpheus

A Greek myth
Retold by PADRAIC COLUM

Many were the minstrels who, in the early days of the world, went amongst men, telling them stories of the gods, of their wars and their births, and of the beginning of things. Of all these minstrels none was so famous as Orpheus; none could tell truer things about the gods; he himself was half divine, and there were some who said that he was in truth Apollo's son.

But a great grief came to Orpheus, a grief that stopped his singing and his playing upon the lyre. His young wife, Eurydike, was taken from him. One day, walking in the garden, she was bitten on the heel by a serpent; straightway she went down to the World of the Dead.

Then everything in this world was dark and bitter for the minstrel of the gods; sleep would not come to him, and for him food had no taste. Then Orpheus said, "I will do that which no mortal has ever done before; I will do that which even the Immortals might shrink from doing; I will go down into the World of the Dead, and I will bring back to the living and to the light my bride, Eurydike."

Then Orpheus went on his way to the cavern which goes down, down to the World of the Dead—the Cavern Tainaron. The trees showed him the way. As he went on Orpheus played upon his lyre and sang; the trees heard his song and were moved by his grief, and with their arms and their heads they showed him the way to the deep, deep cavern named Tainaron.

Down, down, down by a winding path Orpheus went. He came at last to the great gate that opens upon the World of the Dead. And the silent guards who keep watch there for the Rulers of the Dead were astonished when they saw a living being coming towards them, and they would not let Orpheus approach the gate.

The minstrel took the lyre in his hands and played upon it. As he played, the silent watchers gathered around him, leaving the gate unguarded. And as he played the Rulers of the Dead came forth, Hades and Persephone, and listened to the words of the living man.

"The cause of my coming through the dark and fearful ways," sang Orpheus, "is to strive to gain a fairer fate for Eurydike, my bride. All that is above must come down to you at last, O Rulers of the most lasting World. But before her time has Eurydike been brought here. I have desired strength to endure her loss, but I cannot endure it. And I have come before you, Hades and Persephone, brought here by love."

When Orpheus said the name of love, Persephone, the queen of the dead, bowed her young head, and bearded Hades, the king, bowed his head also. Persephone remembered how Demeter, her mother, had sought her all through the world, and she remembered the touch of her mother's tears upon her face. And Hades remembered how his love for Persephone had led him to carry her away from the valley where she had been gathering flowers. He and Persephone stood aside, and Orpheus went through the gate and came amongst the dead.

In the throng of the newly-come dead Orpheus saw Eurydike. She looked upon her husband, but she had not the power to come near him. But slowly she came when Hades, the king, called her. Then with joy Orpheus took her hands.

It would be granted them — no mortal ever gained such privilege before — to leave, both together, the World of the Dead, and to abide for another space in the World of the Living. One condition there would be — that on their way up neither Orpheus nor Eurydike should look back.

They went through the gate and came out amongst the watchers that are around the portals. These showed them the path that went up to the World of the Living. That way they went, Orpheus and Eurydike, he going before her.

Up and through the darkened ways they went, Orpheus knowing that Eurydike was behind him, but never looking back upon her. As he went his heart was filled with things to tell her — how the trees were blossoming in the garden she had left; how the water was sparkling in the fountain; how the doors of the house stood open; how they, sitting together, would watch the sunlight on the laurel bushes. All these things were in his heart to tell her who came behind him, silent and unseen.

And now they were nearing the place where the cavern opened

on the world of the living. Orpheus looked up towards the light from the sky. Out of the opening of the cavern he went; he saw a white-winged bird fly by. He turned around and cried, "O Eurydike, look upon the world I have won you back to!"

He turned to say this to her. He saw her with her long dark hair and pale face. He held out his arms to clasp her. But in that instant she slipped back into the gloom of the cavern. And all he heard spoken was a single word, "Farewell!" Long, long had it taken Eurydike to climb so far, but in the moment of his turning around she had fallen back to her place amongst the dead. For Orpheus had looked back.

Back through the cavern Orpheus went again. Again he came before the watchers of the gate. But now he was not looked at nor listened to; hopeless, he had to return to the World of the Living.

This famous myth tells about an attempt to conquer the natural cycle of life and death. What human feeling prompted Orpheus's quest to conquer death? How does the myth show that the same feeling that prompted the quest also caused its failure?

In what ways is Orpheus's story like that of Demeter and Persephone (page 234)? Do the myths of Demeter, Adonis (page 241), and Orpheus all confront the same mystery? How?

How is Orpheus's battle like the battle waged between the May king and Winter (page 244)? How is it different?

How could you see a "seasonal" movement in the events of this tragic story: from spring (hope), to fall (death), to despair (winter)?

What images in this myth contrast the world "above" ground with the world "below"?

Which of the children's rhymes that open this unit could relate to the story of Orpheus and Eurydike?

A Turn with the Sun

JOHN KNOWLES

It was dusk; the warm air of the early spring afternoon was edged with an exhilarating chill, and in the half-light the dark green turf of the playing field acquired the smooth perfection of a thick rug, spreading up to the thin woods lightly brushed with color along one sideline and down to the river, with the stolid little bridge arching over it, along the other. Across the stream more playing fields, appearing smoother still in the distance, sloped gently up to the square gray shape of the gymnasium; and behind it the towers and turrets of the boy's school were etched against the darkening blue sky.

The lacrosse game was over, and the Red team, pleased by a three-to-two victory, but only mildly pleased since it was just an intramural game, formed a loose circle and cheered for themselves and their opponents: "Reds, Reds, Reds, Reds, Rah, Rah, Rah, Blues!" A few players tarried for some extra shots at the cage, which the second-string Blue goalie made half-hearted attempts to defend; but most of them straggled off toward the bridge, swinging their lacrosse sticks carelessly along beside them. Three boys played catch as they went; one of them missed a pass near the bridge and the ball plopped into the stream.

"Nuts!" he said. "I'm not going in after it."

"No, too cold," the others agreed.

As Lawrence stepped onto the gravel road which led over the bridge he experienced that thrill of feeling himself strong and athletic which the sound of his cleats on a hard surface always excited. His stride became more free swinging, authoritative.

"I scored," he said simply. "D'you see that, Bead? I scored my first goal."

"Yeah." Bead's scratchy voice had an overtone of cordiality. "Good going, boy. The winning point too."

They crunched along in silence up to the bridge, and then Lawrence was emboldened to issue an invitation. "You going to the flick tonight? I mean I guess it's Shelley Winters or someone. . . ."

Bead balanced his companion's possible new status for an indecisive instant and then elected to hedge. "Yeah, well I'll see you after dinner in the Butt Room for a smoke. I'm prob'ly going. Bruce," he added with careful casualness, "said something about it."

Bruce! Lawrence sensed once again that he was helplessly sliding back, into the foggy social bottomland where unacceptable first-year boys dwell. He had risen out of it just now: the goal he had scored, the sweaty ease of his body, the grump-grump of his shoes on the gravel had suggested something better. But here was Bead, like himself only seven months at the school, and yet going to the movies with Bruce. Lawrence marveled at the speed with which Bead was settling into the school, and he marveled again at his own failure, after seven months, to win a single close friend.

Not that Lawrence Stuart was a pariah; the hockey captain had never invaded his room, as he had Fruitcake Putsby's next door, and festooned his clothes through the hall; he had never found a mixture of sour cream and cereal in his bed at night; no one had ever poured ink into the tub while he was bathing. The victims of such violations were genuine outcasts. But the very fact of their persecutions had, Lawrence reflected, some kind of negative value. They were at least notable in their way. "There goes Fruitcake Putsby!" someone would shout, "Hi ya, Fruitie." They had a status all their own; and a few of them, by senior year, could succeed by some miraculous alchemy in becoming accepted and even respected by the whole school.

Lawrence was neither grotesque enough nor courageous enough for that. He merely inhabited the nether world of the unregarded, where no one bothered him or bothered about him. He had entered in fourth form year, when the class was already clearly stratified, knowing only one person in the school; he came from a small Virginia town which no one had ever heard of, his clothes were wrong, his vocabulary was wrong, and when he talked at all it was about the wrong things.

He had been assigned to an out-of-the-way house (instead of to one of the exuberant dormitories) with six other nebulous flotsam, and there on the edge of the school he had been waiting all year for something to happen to him, living alone in a little room tucked up under the eaves.

His failure to strike out in some, in any, direction puzzled him in

October, when he had been at Devon six weeks, angered him in December, made him contemptuous in February, and on this burgeoning April day when everything else stirred with life, took on the coloration of tragedy.

He crossed over the bridge with Bead, and his heart stopped for an instant as it always did on this bridge; in his imagination he again stood on the railing, with his image white and mysterious in the green-black water twenty-five feet below, and he leaped out and over, as he had done last September on his fourth day there, somersaulting twice while most of the school looked on in admiration at the new boy, and knifed cleanly into the icy water.

Last September, his fourth day at school. He hadn't been thinking of anything in particular there on the bridge; everyone was diving from it so he did too. When he plunged from the railing he had been just another of the unknown new boys, but when he broke the surface of the water in that remarkable dive, one that he had never attempted before and was never to repeat, he became for his schoolmates a boy to be considered. That is why Ging Powers, a senior from his own town who had seemed these first days to be decisively avoiding him, came over in the shower room afterward and dropped an invitation to dinner like a negligible piece of soap. "Come over to the Inn for dinner tonight. Got a couple of friends I want you to meet."

There is a trophy room in the Devon School gymnasium much visited by returning alumni; during June reunions they wander whispering past its softly lighted cases, in which gleam the cups and medals of athletic greatness. Proud banners hang from its paneled walls, inscribed with the records of triumphant, forgotten afternoons. It is like a small, peculiarly sacred chapel in a great cathedral.

At the far end, standing long and bright in the focal niche, the alumni would admire the James Harvey Fullerton Cup, Awarded Each Year to That Member of the Sixth Form Who, in the Opinion of His Fellows and Masters, Most Closely Exemplifies the Highest Traditions of Devon. There is no mention of athletics on the inscription, but it has come to rest in the gymnasium, in the place of honor, because the highest tradition of Devon is the thinking athlete. Thirty-four names have been engraved on its burnished surface since Mr. Fullerton, feeling disturbed by the activities of German submarines, decided to confirm the reality of his untroubled childhood by donating it, with a small endowment, to his old school, like some symbol of royalty.

Lawrence had approached it that afternoon, his fourth day at the school, and was struck by the beauty and sacredness of the place. This surely was the heart of Devon: the chapel was like an assembly hall, the library was a clearing house, the houses were dormitories, the classrooms, classrooms; only here did he sense that behind the visible were deeper meanings, that these trophies and banners were clues to the hidden core of the school. He left the gymnasium lost in thought.

He had felt he was still in the air as he walked from the gym back to his room that afternoon, still spinning down upon his own bright image in the murky water. He dressed hurriedly for the dinner at the Inn, for this was surely the beginning of his career at Devon. He explained how wonderfully everything was going in an ardent letter to Janine, and then walked, holding himself back from running by an intoxicating exercise of will power, and arrived at last at the Inn. Everything within him was released; it was as though his dive into the river had washed away his boyhood, and he stood clean and happy, wondering dreamily what he would be like now.

The hushed dining room was pervaded by the atmosphere of middle-aged gentility characteristic of Inns at boys' schools: the dull walnut woodwork, the pink and green wallpaper depicting Colonial scenes, the virginal fireplace. At the far end of the room Lawrence saw his dinner partners huddled conspiratorily at a corner table. He wheeled past other, empty tables, bright with white cloths and silver, realized dimly that there were murmuring groups dining here and there in the room; and then Ging, his thin frame unfolding from a chair, was muttering introductions. "This is Vinnie Ump," he seemed to say, and Lawrence recognized Vinnie James, vice-chairman of the senior council, a calm, blond Bostonian who was allowed to be as articulate as he chose because he was so unassertively sure of himself. "And this," said Ging, in a somewhat more stately cadence, "is Charles Morrell." Lawrence recognized him too, of course; this was Morrell, the fabled "Captain Marvel" of the football field, the baseball field, and the hockey rink. Lawrence had never seen him at close quarters before; he seemed more formidable than ever.

Vinnie James was talking, and after pausing for a neutral, birdlike nod to Lawrence, he continued. "So if you want to put up with being patronized by a lot of crashing bores, then you can go to Harvard, and be Punched all sophomore year."

Captain Marvel leaned his heavily handsome face out over the table, "I don't get you, Vinnie, what's this Punching?"

"That's how you get into the clubs at Harvard, Dim One," Vinnie's eyes flickered humorously at him for an instant. "They invite you to Punch parties all sophomore year, and when they stop inviting you then you know you're not going to be asked to join the club."

"Well," Ging looked with masked apprehension from one to the other, "they've got to take *some* guys, don't they? And Devon isn't such a bad background."

"It's not Groton," said Vinnie mercilessly, "of course."

"Groton!" Ging clutched his tastefully striped tie savagely. "I wouldn't be caught dead at that snobatorium. I could 'ev', if I'd wanted to I could 'ev' gone to Groton. But mother said wild horses couldn't drag a son of hers to that snobatorium."

Lawrence felt dizzy at the barefacedness of this lie. He knew that Mrs. Powers would cheerfully have violated most of the customs of civilization to get a son of hers into Groton. Devon had been a hasty compromise after Groton had proved out of the question.

"In any case," Vinnie remarked drily, "Marvel here won't have any trouble. Personable athletes are kidnaped by the most desirable clubs the moment they appear." Vinnie made no comment on Ging's chances.

Lawrence disliked and felt superior to Ging at once. The climber! He had never realized before what a fool Ging was, it made him feel older to realize it now. It was so clear when you could see him beside Captain Marvel, cool, unconcerned Marvel, who would easily rise to the top of every group he entered, leaving Ging clawing and snarling below.

Lawrence looked away irritably, regretting that it was Ging who had introduced him to the others. At the same time he felt himself more thoroughly aware than he had ever been of how the world went, of who fitted where, of what was grand and genuine and what was shoddy and fake. Devon had posed a question to him and demanded that he do something. This afternoon he had done a single, beautiful dive, it was just right and he knew it the moment he hit the water. And now he had come to understand Captain Marvel. The answer was athletics; not just winning a major D, but the personality of the athlete itself, the unconscious authority which his strength, his skill, his acclaim gave him. Lawrence stirred his tomato soup reflectively, and felt his diffuse ambitions coming into focus, experienced a vision of himself as the Majestic Athlete; he decided instinctively and immediately to accept it, there at dinner among the walnut and silver and the polite murmurings of the other diners. He gathered about himself the mantle of the Olympiad, and lost in its folds, he burst into speech.

"I have some cousins, two cousins, you know, Ging—George and Carter—they're in clubs at Harvard, I mean a club at Harvard, one club, both of 'em are in the same club. It's the . . . the . . ." Lawrence was suddenly stricken with the thought that George and Carter might very easily not be in the best Harvard club, or even the second best; but everyone, even Marvel, was listening with interest, "It's called," he felt his color rising at the inelegance of the name, "The Gas—or something."

"Oh yes," said Vinnie crisply, "that's a very good club, for New Yorkers mostly, they have some very good men."

"Oh," Lawrence breathed with fake innocence and real relief. This success swept him spinning on. "George and Carter, they go there for dinners, but they always have lunch in the—is it the Houses?" his wide, brightened blue eyes searched his listeners' faces avidly; Vinnie nodded a brief assent. "They said those clubs make you so ingrown, you just know all these fancy socialites and everything they wanted to know, you know, everybody, they didn't want to be exclusive or anything like that. It isn't like up here, I mean there isn't, aren't all these clubs and things. They said that I'd get raided and my bed peed and all but nothing like that seems to happen up here; but they *did* say that when I went on to Harvard, if I do go there, that after being here it'll be easier and I'll know people and not have to study, but I don't really study so hard here, 'course it's only been four days, but after what everybody said about prep school I thought I'd be studying all the time, but, well, take this afternoon"—that was good, *take this afternoon* smacked of maturity; he paused an instant for the two important seniors (Ging was a bystander now) to catch the overtone of authority in it—"we went swimming off the bridge, and that flip, I thought a two-and-a-half flip might be tough, but . . ." he paused again, hoping Ging might make himself useful as a witness to this feat; nothing happened so he finished a little out of breath, "it wasn't."

"Yeah," Captain Marvel said, "I saw you do it."

This swept down Lawrence's last controls. His best moment had been seen, and doubtless admired, by the most important athlete in school. He rushed ahead now, eager to impress him even more; no, by golly, he was through impressing people. Now he was ready to leap, in one magnificent bound, to the very peak of his ambitions, to become Captain Marvel's protégé, to learn what it meant to be unconcerned, powerful, and a man. So he stuttered gaily on, snatching at everything inside him that seemed presentable—home, his family, Janine, the play he had seen in New York; he assumed every grown-up attitude he could find. All of it he brought forth, as an offering of fealty.

The seniors followed this unwinding of a new boy carefully, looked where he pointed, gauging all his information and attitudes according to their own more precisely graded yardsticks, and took his measure.

"Devon is like some kind of country-club penitentiary, where the inmates don't take walks around the courtyard, they go to the private penitentiary golf course for eighteen holes. And the dean, is that who he is? that queer, stuttery old bird, you know, the one in chapel the first day, the one who looks like Hoover with an Oxford accent. . . ."

"Yes, that's the dean," said Vinnie, fingering his water glass, "Dean Eleazer Markham Bings-Smith."

"No!" exploded Lawrence, "is that his name! His honest name?" He regretted the *honest*, it should have been *actual*.

"Why does he talk that way, and *look* that way! Like my beagle, that's the way he looks, like the beagle I've got at home, my beagle looks just like that right after he's had a bath."

There was something like consternation passing around the table. Lawrence felt it and looked wonderingly from one to the other. Ging was watching an elderly couple making their way toward the door. The others examined their desserts.

"Was that the dean?" Lawrence asked in a shocked whisper. "Did he hear me?"

No one really answered, but Lawrence, alive in every nerve now, responded symbolically. He slipped like a boneless organism from his chair and sank beneath the table; there he performed the appropriate expiation; he banged his head, not too hard, against the table's underside.

There was a scraping of chairs, Lawrence saw napkins flutter onto the seats, and suddenly he realized the impossibility of his position: under a table in the Anthony Wayne Dining Room of the Devon Inn, making a fool of himself.

He could not recall afterward how he got to his feet, but he remembered very clearly what was said.

"I have an appointment," Vinnie was informing Ging, and then to Lawrence: "That was not the dean, that was Dr. Farnham, the registrar. I doubt whether he heard you. And if he did, I doubt whether he knows or cares *who* you are."

"Are you British?" demanded Captain Marvel with heavy distaste. "Is that why you talk so queer?"

Lawrence felt the exuberance within him turn over, leaving a sob pressing against his chest. He could not speak and would not cry, but drew a deep, shuddering breath.

Marvel and Vinnie strode out through the door, Ging followed, and Lawrence roamed out a few paces behind, out into the damp September night, down the deserted street to the quadrangle, where the dormitory lights streamed hospitably from cozy windows. Ging said "G'night" there as though he were saying "pass" during a dull bridge game, and Lawrence was left to wander down the lane to the cluttered old house, to the little room stuck up under the eaves where he lived.

In the next weeks, after the first storms had subsided, Lawrence tried again and again to analyze his failure. Whom had he offended, how, why? Why was everything he had ever wanted sparkling like a trophy in his hands one minute, and smashed to bits at his feet the next?

Defeat seemed to follow upon defeat after that. Having missed the peak of his ambition, he assumed that lesser heights could be attained automatically; he felt like a veteran of violent foreign wars whose scars entitled him to homage and precedence. Instead he was battered on every occasion: one day he offered to move into the empty half of a double room down the hall and the boy living there had simply ignored him, had pretended not to hear. Then he turned wildly delinquent; he threw his small steamer trunk, filled with shoes and books, down the long flight of stairs under which the housemaster lived. It slammed against Mr. Kuzak's door at the bottom, and the resultant methodical investigation and punishment made him briefly notable to his housemates, until they concluded that he was strange.

This was the final, the unbearable affront; they thought him strange, undisciplined, an inferior boy given to pettish tantrums. He would show them. If there was one thing he was sure he possessed, it was a capacity for self-discipline. If there was one thing he would not be, it was a clown, a butt. He knew there was a certain dignity in his bearing, even though it shaded into pomposity, and he would not violate that, he would not become a Fruitcake Putsby, even if people would like him better that way.

He decided, in the season when the last leaves were drifting down from the trees bordering the playing fields, and the sunlight cut obliquely across the town, that there remained this one quality on which he could rely: his capacity for self-discipline. He would turn his back upon the school, he would no longer be embroiled in Devon's cheap competition for importance. He would be intelligent; yes, he told himself, he would be *exceedingly* intelligent; and by God, if he only could, he would be the greatest athlete ever to electrify a crowd on the playing fields of Devon. The greatest, and the most inaccessible.

The earth was turning wintery; the season of Steam Heat arrived. It filled every inhabited room in the school, the steam hissed and clanged with power, and could not be shut off. Slowly the heat drained the spirit from them, dried their healthy faces, seared the freshest skin. The usual number of colds appeared, the usual amount of force faded from lectures and application from homework, the usual apathy slipped into the school through the radiators. Winter was here.

Lawrence moved from one steaming box to another, crossing the sharp, drily cold outdoors in between, and felt his own inner strength grow as it waned in those about him. He had learned to study very systematically, and as his responses in class were apt and laconic, several of his teachers became noticeably interested in winning his good opinion; they would make remarks about Kafka or Turgenev and then glance at him. He would smile knowingly back, and resolve to find out who these people might be.

His free time he spent watching athletes, religiously following the major sports, football games and football drill, enjoying every moment except when Captain Marvel made a really brilliant play, which made him feel uneasy and guilty. He watched soccer and track and tennis and squash, and as winter sports replaced them, he watched basketball, wrestling, boxing, hockey, and even fencing.

In the fall he had played a little intramural football at which he was generally inept and abstracted, but once in a while he would startle everyone, including himself, with a brilliantly skillful play. But there was too much freedom on a football field, too much room to maneuver, too many possibilities; so in the winter he turned to swimming, in which the lanes were rigidly predetermined, and he had only to swim up and down, up and down. Into this he poured all the intensity he possessed, and as a result made the junior varsity squad. He was uniformly cooperative with his teammates, and the coach thought him a promising boy.

His housemates now felt disposed to revise their opinion of him;

yes, Stuart was strange, but if he was going to turn out to be not only bright but also something of an athlete, they thought they had better accept him.

The proctor and the others made a few fumbling, gruff overtures. Lawrence sensed this at once and became more thoroughly disturbed than at any time since the dinner at the inn. He loathed them all, of course, and he felt cheated; now that his defenses were invulnerable they were calling off the assault, inviting him to talk terms, asking for a conference out in the open. The cold wind tore around the angles of the old house, and Lawrence camped in his steamy room, speaking politely to those who came to his door, doing his homework, and feeling confusedly vindicated. He had proved the strongest of all, for what was strength if not the capacity for self-denial? He had divorced himself from them so successfully that now he didn't care; *they* cared, so it seemed, now; they were seeking his friendship, therefore they were weak. Strength, Lawrence was sure, was the capacity for self-denial; life was conquered by the strong-willed, success was demonstrated by austerity; it was the bleak who would inherit the earth. Yes, that was right and he would not allow them to change the rules now that he had won; he decided to continue his triumphant game, even though he was playing it alone.

Only in his anger did he draw close to them; one dismal afternoon in February Billy Baldwin, the boy down the hall who had refused to room with him in September, came to his door:

"Hi, Varsity." This was the nickname Lawrence had been given by the other boys, who understood him better than he thought. "You going to Bermuda for spring vacation?" Since he was excluded from the gay round of parties which the boys from Boston and New York described as typical of their holidays, Lawrence had intimated that he was going to Bermuda with his family. This afternoon he was too depressed to lie.

"No," he parroted, "I'm not going to Bermuda for spring vacation."

Billy was a little put off, but continued with determined good humor. "Well then how about coming down, I mean if you aren't going home. . . ." Billy had no champagne vacation in the offing either, but he had grown up a little during the winter and forgiven his parents for making their home in Bridgeport, Connecticut. He had also changed his mind about Lawrence, whom he now thought pleasantly temperamental and handsome. "Why don't you, if you want, you could always. . . ."

"What?" interrupted Lawrence irritably. "Why don't I what?"

"All I was going to say," Billy continued on a stronger note, "what I was going to say if you didn't interrupt all the time. . . ." but then he couldn't say it.

"You were going to say nothing," Lawrence said disgustedly, turning back to his book, "as usual."

"Just one thing," Billy exclaimed sharply. "All I was going to say was why *don't* you go to Bermuda? If you're so rich."

"Rich enough," Lawrence's voice thickening with controlled anger, "richer than some people who live in little dump towns on the New Haven Railroad."

"Yeah!" Billy shouted. "Yeah, so rich your pop couldn't pay the last bursar's bill on time!"

"What!" screamed Lawrence, tearing the book from his lap and jumping up, "what'd you say?" His blood was pounding because it wasn't the truth, but it was close to it. He was standing now in the middle of his little garret, his shoulders slightly forward. His voice turned coarse, "Get out." Neither of them knew his voice had a savage depth like that. "Just get out of my room." Then in a single motion, he snatched the book from the floor and hurled it at Billy's head. Billy sprang back from the doorway, deeply frightened, not so much *of* him as *with* him. Both of them stood panting on either side of the doorway, and then Billy went back to his own room.

Lawrence pretended to be totally unconcerned about such flare-ups, which occurred several times in the late winter. He eventually allowed Billy to reestablish a civil relationship with him; *After all,* Lawrence reasoned, *he should be the one to make up, after the way he insulted me right in my own room. I never did like him,* he reflected with strengthening satisfaction, *no I never did.* Billy didn't matter to him; in September when he was so alone, Billy could have helped. But now; what good was Billy? He was no athlete, no star, he did not possess that unconcerned majesty, he was a person of no importance. And Billy, who was just finding out about kindness, looked regretfully elsewhere for friends.

Except for these explosions, Lawrence maintained his admirable outer imperviousness throughout the winter. He spent spring vacation in Virginia with his family. It was an uneventful two weeks except for a bitter little fight with Janine. "You're changed and I hate you," she cried at the end of it, and then indignantly, "who do you think you are, anyhow? I hate you!"

He returned in the middle of April to find Devon transformed. He had forgotten that the bleak lanes and roads were beautiful when the earth turned once again toward the sun. Tiny leaves of callow green sprouted from the gray branches of the skeletal trees, and the living scents of the earth hung in the air. Windows which had been stuck closed with winter were opened to allow the promising air to circulate; the steamy dryness of his little room drifted away; when he opened the single window and the door a tantalizing breeze whipped across his papers and notebooks, fluttered the college pennants on his wall, and danced on to the other rooms where his housemates stirred restlessly.

Then, unexpectedly, he began to slip in his studies. For two successive French classes he appeared unprepared, and when called on to discuss the lesson, he fumbled. The others snickered behind their notebooks. But the boy sitting next to him, with whom he had had a relationship consisting only of "Excuse me," and "Hard assignment, wasn't it?", nudged him in the ribs as they were going out after the second class and exclaimed robustly, "Boy, did *you* stink today!" Lawrence was about to coin some cutting rejoinder when the boy grinned broadly. "You were really lousy," he added, punching him again. Lawrence tried and failed to keep from grinning back, and then muttered that Well, it was spring wasn't it.

That afternoon he went as usual to watch the varsity lacrosse team practice. His own intramural team was having a game that day and could have used even his unsteady stick, but he had wrangled a medical excuse. Varsity lacrosse was almost as meaningful for him as varsity baseball, and he didn't have to watch Captain Marvel there. So he sat alone on the empty bleachers and followed the practice shots intently, watching the careless skill of the players, marveling at the grand unawareness with which they played. *This is the best part of the day*, he thought, *this is wonderful.* He pondered the assumptions on which these athletes operated, that they would not miss the ball, that if they did they would catch it next time, that their teammates accepted them regardless, that there was a basic peace among them taken for granted. Lawrence could take nothing for granted; *yes, this is the best part of the day*, he told himself, and as he watched the skillful, confident boys warming to the game he saw only himself, he watched the others but he was seeing himself, doing all the skillful, impossible things. He looked very pleased, *This is the best*, he thought, and despair flamed up in him.

He decided not to stay for the whole practice, and wandering back to the gym he met his own team coming out; Hey, Lawrence, get dressed, There's a game, Lawrence, C'mon, Stuart, Whathahelleryadoin? The one thing he had wanted to avoid that day was his own team. Lately he always seemed to be stumbling into the very situations he wanted fervently to avoid.

"Yeah," he called lamely to them, "but I got a . . ." *medical excuse?* An Olympian unable to take the field because of sniffles? It wouldn't do. "Yeah, okay, I was just . . . the varsity . . . I thought maybe if I watched them . . ." Shouting complicated explanations was impossible. "You know," he yelled even though they were moving away, not listening, "I thought I might learn something."

"Forget the varsity, Varsity," one of them called over his shoulder. "The second-string Red midfield wants you."

. . . This then was the afternoon when Lawrence scored his first goal. He felt an odd looseness playing that day, the hot rays of the sun seemed to draw the rigidity out of his body, leaving his muscles and sinews free to function as they would. Something about the way he held his stick was different, he found himself in the right place at the right time; his teammates sensed the change and passed the ball to him, and in the last minutes of the game he made a fast instinctive turn around a burly Blue defenseman and scored the winning goal with a quick, sure shot.

It was a minor triumph which calmed his spirit for approximately seven minutes, until the invitation to the movies was issued and turned aside, until he crossed over the little arching bridge, observed the water where his heroic reflection had shone, and stepped onto the turf on the other side, the varsity field. By the time they reached the gym it was Lawrence the unrecognized Olympian again, Lawrence the unknown and unloved.

After his shower he dressed and went, as he so often did, into the trophy room for a pacifying moment of dreaming. He knew the inscription and most of the names on the Fullerton Cup by heart, and in the space below 1951—Robert Graves Hartshorne, he would visualize 1952 —Charles Taylor Morrell, for unquestionably the cup would be Marvel's this year. And the list should go on and on, with one celebrated name after another (even perhaps 1954—Lawrence Bates Stuart); but here reality always intervened. The fact, the shocking fact was that the front plate of the cup was almost filled, after Marvel's name had been inscribed the list would reach the little silver relief statues around the base

—the old-fashioned football player looking slim and inadequate, the pompous baseball player with his squarely planted little cap, and the others—there would be no more room. Nor was there any space to start a second list, since all the remaining circumference of the cup was devoted to an etched allegorical representation of the flame of knowledge passing from hand to hand through the ages, until it found its way into a device at the top, a coat-of-arms of birds and Latin and moons which was the seal of Devon.

Always a little amazed at this finiteness of the cup, Lawrence backed thoughtfully away from it. Wasn't this the core of everything, didn't it sum up, absorb, glorify everything at Devon? And still, the cup would be full this year. One of these days it would be moved to a case along the walls with the other old trophies which had once reigned in the niche, it would be honorably, obscurely retired. In his imagination the heroic list stretched back over cup after cup, into the past, and forward, upon cups not yet conceived, into the future. It was odd, he thought, all these great names fading into the past, getting less important every year, until finally they must just go out, like the last burned out ember in a fire. It was sad of course, but well, there was something almost *monotonous* about it.

Lawrence squirmed. He had never thought about time's passage before. It made him feel better to realize it now, to see that the circle of the years changed things; it wasn't all up to him personally.

Puzzled, he gazed around this chilly and damp chamber which had seemed so cool and serene in February, untouched by the bone-chilling winds outside or the rasping steam in the other rooms of the school.

But now it was April, and Lawrence felt and saw April everywhere. This room isn't a chapel at all, he thought with a passing wave of indignation, it's a crypt.

Then, right there in the trophy room, he yawned, comfortably. And stretching his legs, to get a feeling of cramp out of them, he strode contentedly toward the door, through which the sunlight poured, and as he stepped into it he felt its warmth on his shoulders. It was going to be a good summer.

He never knew that he was right in this, because Lawrence drowned that night, by the purest accident, in the river which winds between the playing fields. Bead and Bruce tried to save him; the water was very cold and black and the night moonless. They eventually found him, doubled over among some rushes. He had not cried out when the cramp convulsed him, so they did not know where to begin searching and after they found him, it was a hard, clumsy job getting him to shore. They tried artificial respiration at first, and then becoming very frightened, started for help. But then Bruce thought again and came back to try to revive him while Bead ran to the gym, completely disrupting the movie in his frantic search for a master.

There was a conference two days later, attended by the headmaster, the dean, Mr. Kuzak from Lawrence's house, Bruce and Bead. The boys explained that it had been just a little lark; students always swam in the river in the spring, and although they usually waited until it was warmer, they had decided in the Butt Room Saturday night to have the first swim of the season while the rest of the school was at the movie. Bruce and Bead had planned it alone, but Lawrence had been there, very enthusiastic to go to the movie. Then when he heard they were going swimming, that had become the one thing he wanted to do.

"You know, sir," Bruce explained earnestly to the dean, "he was a good swimmer, and he wanted to go so much."

"Yeah," Bead confirmed this eagerly, "we didn't ask him to go, did we, Bruce?"

"No, he just asked if he could and we said yes."

Bead set his face maturely, "He wasn't a very good friend of ours, but he just wanted to go. So we said okay, but it wasn't like we planned it together. I didn't know him very well, did you, Bruce?"

"No, I didn't either."

Mr. Kuzak studied the backs of his hands, and the headmaster asked, "Who were his close friends?"

"I don't know," Bead answered.

"The fellows in his house, I guess," said Bruce. Everyone looked at Mr. Kuzak, who thought of several perfunctory ways of confirming this, but knowing it was not true, he was unable to say anything. It is easy to write, "Lawrence Stuart is beginning to find himself" on a report to the dean, when Stuart was alive and could be heard trudging up the stairs every day; undoubtedly he *would* have found himself. But now the boy was dead, Mr. Kuzak had seen his body, had telephoned his parents; he said nothing.

Irritated, the headmaster leaned out of his thronelike chair. "He *had* close friends?" he persisted.

Still Mr. Kuzak could not speak.

"Well," the dean broke the uneasy silence, his kind, mournful eyes studying the two boys, "Well how did he, was he—" his fingers searched the lines in his forehead, "he enjoyed it, did he?" The dean's face reddened, he indulged in his chronic cough for several seconds. "He seemed lively? I mean did he act . . . happy, before, before this cramp seized him?"

"Oh sure!" Bead exclaimed. "Yes, yes he did," Bruce said at the same time.

"When we first got there," Bruce continued, "he got up on the bridge. Bead and I just slipped into the water from the bank, it was awfully cold."

"I never was in such cold water," Bead agreed.

"But Stuart got up on the bridge and stood there a minute."

"Then he dove," said Bead.

"Dived," someone corrected abstractly.

"It was a real dive," Bruce added thoughtfully. "He did a beautiful dive."

It had been like the free curve of powerful wings. Lawrence had cut the water almost soundlessly, and then burst up again a moment later, breaking a foaming silver circle on the black surface. Then he twisted over on his back and sank out of sight.

"I believe he enjoyed the water," said Mr. Kuzak quietly.

"Yeah," Bead agreed, "he liked it a lot, I think. That was the one thing he did like. He was good in the water."

"I don't think he cared," Bruce remarked suddenly.

The headmaster straightened sharply. "What do you mean?" Bruce's thoughts doubled over this instinctive statement to censor it or deny it, but then because this was death and the first he had ever really encountered, he persisted. "I mean in the dive, he just seemed to trust everything, all of a sudden. He looked different, standing up there on the bridge."

"Happy?" asked the dean in a very low voice.

"Something like that. He wasn't scared, I know that."

The conference ended afterward, with everyone agreed that it had been a wholly accidental death. A photograph of Lawrence in his swimming suit, taken when he made the junior varsity team, was enlarged, framed, and hung on the wall of the gym among pictures of athletic teams. He stood very straight in the picture and his young eyes looked directly at the camera.

But the season moved on; that summer was the most beautiful and fruitful anyone could remember at Devon. Blossoms scented the air and hung over the river winding quietly through the playing fields. And the earth, turned full toward the sun, brought forth its annual harvest.

We have seen a number of characters who "die" and are reborn again in spring: Persephone (page 234), Adonis (page 241), the king of an ancient Greek community (page 248). Do you think Lawrence is reborn in any way? Why or why not?

In what rituals does Lawrence participate? What power does he gain from them? What does he lose? Why?

Show how the stages of Lawrence's development through the story follow a cycle of "inner seasons." What kind of person is he at the beginning of the story? At the end?

Lawrence's emotions and actions do not perfectly match the actual seasons of the year in the story, although they do occasionally correspond. Human life is much too complex to be divided into four neat consecutive stages. However, every one of Lawrence's moods can be described in seasonal imagery. Choose some lines from this story or from previous poems and stories in this unit and apply them to different stages of Lawrence's life.

The drawing that opens this unit is a whimsical image of nature caring for people—one way of expressing the deep interrelationship between us and nature. Write a story or a poem, or create an image, of what human life would be like if some particular element of nature did not exist. If there were no green world, would we create one? If, one day, the sun did not rise—how would people react?

Throughout this book, we have met characters who have been searching for themselves, trying to discover what it means to be human. What qualities seem to be common to all or most of them? What experiences do they share?

Through literature, we can share in the lives and experiences of characters we would otherwise never know. What do we gain from this sharing? What seem to you to be the most meaningful uses of the imagination?

In the beginning, people looked around them. They saw a sun that rose and set and rose again, a moon that waxed and waned and waxed again, a year that flourished and decayed and flourished again. They saw the whole world responding to and participating in cycles.

It probably was not long before people imaginatively began to express nature's cycles in human terms. They began to think of the world in metaphors. The sun became a god who, in daytime, drove a fiery chariot across the sky, put his horses in a dark stable at night, and began the journey again the next morning. Flowers became gods who were born, died, and were reborn again the next spring. It is easy to see how these metaphors were extended into stories — myths. The narratives of myths also followed the natural cycles. Some god or goddess, often a young person associated with crops, appears, has adventures, dies, and somehow returns to life again.

But it was not only stories that people patterned after the cycles of nature. Even before they began telling stories, they patterned their actions after nature. They created bodily movements and sounds to imitate nature, to participate symbolically in the cycles of the physical universe. A rain dance, for instance, was a ritual which created an imaginary thunderstorm, a human one. People clustered their rituals about the cyclical processes in nature — the movements of the sun and moon, seed-time and harvest, reproduction and decay. They also clustered rituals around every crucial period of their own life cycle: birth, initiation, marriage, death. Ritual was one of people's ways of synchronizing the human world with the natural one.

Rituals were not just recurrent acts related to nature. They were also social acts that expressed people's most deeply felt wishes and nightmares. A rain dance, or the ritualistic killing of a king, expressed a desire for fertility as well as a fear of

drought and barrenness. Most of the old rituals eventually fell into disuse, but even today, in our imaginative expressions, we still use the two patterns that distinguished rituals: the cyclical pattern and the opposition pattern, the cycle of birth, death, and rebirth, and the conflict of wish and nightmare.

In literature the rhythm of the seasons provides a store of opposing images that relate to emotions that swing back and forth in the human mind and heart. It is not by chance that a poet's expression of despair is set in winter and an expression of love in spring. The poet identifies "outer weather" with a corresponding "inner weather." Spring, the time of planting and growth, is related in the imagination to youth, hope, courtship, and love. Summer, a time of ripening, is related to the maturing of relations, to comradeship and community, to fertility and passion. Fall, the time of harvest, is related to reflection and declining vigor. Winter, when the earth seems sterile, is related to death and emptiness.

Rituals are pre-verbal actions; literature is the verbal form of our quest for identity, our never-ending effort to humanize the world, to complete the portrait of the person we want to become and of the society we want to live in. Today, just as people did long ago, we use our imagination to try to control the universe, rather than have it control us. We still want to create the truly human society, a society that combines the power of nature and the potential of human beings. These are our goals, and the discoveries we make as we seek to fulfill them are the many meanings of our life. The achievement of these goals demands the full and final uses of the imagination.

A Glossary of Terms

ARCHETYPE A character, an event, a story, or an image that recurs in different works of literature. One famous archetype is the flood story, manifested in an ancient Babylonian myth (page 157) and in a modern song (page 154). Another is the image of the Golden Age, manifested in an ancient Greek myth (page 14) and in a modern poem (page 22). The word archetype means "an original pattern, or model."

IMAGE A mental picture suggested by words. Images appeal primarily to our sense of sight, but they can also appeal to our senses of smell, taste, hearing, and touch. Images are sometimes categorized as divine (what we wish for) and demonic (what we fear).

LITERATURE All of our myths, songs, poems, stories. Taken all together, literature reveals our imaginative vision of who we are, how we should live, and what our lives mean. The earliest literature of any society is its myths.

METAMORPHOSIS In literature, a marvelous change or transformation from one form to another. Famous metamorphoses include the transformation of Pygmalion's statue into a woman (page 192), and of a frog into a prince (see the illustration on page 218). When the Roman writer Ovid collected the old Greek myths together, he called them *Metamorphoses*, which means in Greek "changes of form."

METAPHOR In literature, an identification between two things that are basically unlike. Metaphors reveal our imaginative desire to see the likenesses in life, rather than the differences. When William Wordsworth (page 21) describes "This sea that bares her bosom to the moon," he is using a metaphor identifying the sea as a woman and the moon as her lover. When William Shakespeare (page 227) addresses his friend as "Thou that art now the world's fresh ornament," he is using a metaphor identifying his friend with a jewel that adds beauty to the world.

MYTH A story which a particular people have regarded as sacred. Myths are frequently stories of divinities and of their relationships to people. Myths are our earliest attempts to create order out of chaos, to make the world understandable.

MYTHOLOGY All of the myths of a particular society collected together. The most fully developed mythologies often begin with creation, tell how death and evil came into the world, and conclude with the end of the world. A fully-developed mythology tells people everything they are most deeply concerned about: Who are they? How should they live? What is their destiny?

RITUAL A ceremony or important action that people perform at regular intervals. Rituals usually cluster around the cyclical processes in nature (seedtime and harvest) and around the crucial periods of a human lifetime (birth, coming-of-age, marriage, and death).

SYMBOL A thing, an event, an action, or a person that stands for something much broader than itself. Spring, for example, is often used as a symbol of youth and rebirth; winter is often used as a symbol of age and death.

Index of Authors and Titles

L 4
M 5